D1272274

THE FESTIVE TRADITION

THE FESTIVE TRADITION

Table Decoration and Desserts in America, 1650-1900

LOUISE CONWAY BELDEN

A WINTERTHUR BOOK

W·W·NORTON & COMPANY

New York *London*

Published simultaneously in Canada by George J. McLeod Limited, Toronto.
Printed in the United States of America.

The text of this book is composed in Caledonia, with display type set in Bulmer. Composition by Vail-Ballou. Manufacturing by Murray Printing. Book design by Jacque Chazaud.

First Edition

Library of Congress Cataloging in Publication Data

Belden, Louise Conway.
The festive tradition, table decoration & desserts in America, 1650–1900.

Bibliography: p.
Includes index.
1. Table setting and decoration—United States—History. 2. Desserts—History. 3. Cookery, American—History. I. Title.
TX879.B44 1983 642′.6 83-2343
ISBN 0-393-01618-8

W. W. Norton & Company, Inc. 500 Fifth Avenue, New York, N.Y. 10110
W. W. Norton & Company Ltd. 37 Great Russell Street, London WC1B 3NU

1 2 3 4 5 6 7 8 9 0

To G. C. B.,
unfailingly tolerant.
And to the Winterthur Guides,
who like to have things documented.

Contents

Preface *ix*
Acknowledgments *xi*

1 Setting the Gentleman's Table *3*
2 Centers Pyramidal and Bold *41*
3 Dressing Out the Sweetmeats *91*
4 Syllabubs, Fools, and Flummeries *135*
5 "Fancy Goods and Baked Eatables" *169*
6 Excellent Entertainment of Fruit and Wine *219*

Recipes *255*
Notes *295*
Glossary *311*
A Selected Bibliography *321*
Index *331*

Preface

A decade or so ago I began hunting answers to questions about early American table setting. At first I was interested only in the way people used their silver and glass and such endearing possessions as dishes shaped like cauliflowers. But a number of enthusiasts encouraged me to broaden my hunt. The most importunate individual was Charles Montgomery, then director of Winterthur Museum, who had been seduced by Helen McKearin's *Antiques* article, "Sweetmeats in Splendor."[1] He hoped to install a dessert table in the museum's new teaching wing. The more persistent of the group made themselves known through a stream of letters wanting to know if colonial spoons lay face down, if housewives put flowers on dining tables, and so on.

Driven by these petitioners and by Edgar Richardson, who succeeded Charles Montgomery as director of Winterthur and suggested a book, I took the hunt across the eastern third of the United States from Maine to Georgia and Boston to Chicago, and in and out of the British Isles, Holland, and France. I looked at domestic objects, explored two-hundred-year-old rooms, read household accounts and inventories, and studied cookbooks and copybooks, paintings, and engravings.

Above all, I searched letters and diaries. In these often domestic records travelers told of tables brilliant with sweetmeats, fruit, and elaborate centerpieces. French visitors who were escorted from routs to balls, young misses who glided from tea parties to dances, and statesmen who hurried to noon dinners and late suppers all described enormous desserts of jellies, creams, cakes, syllabubs, comfits, and sugar figures. Out of their descriptions came a picture of party tables of fascinating complexity and of The Dessert as a prime form of amusement produced by considerable labor.

The creation of a dessert is the subject of this book. The first two chapters look at the table and its "dressing out" from the setting for the dinner that preceded the dessert to the tea and coffee that followed; from the white linen cloth to the resplendent center to the tea tray. The middle chapters talk about the regale itself: the sweetmeats, cakes, jellies, and creams and their manufacture out of ivory, seeds, and other exotic ingredients; the vessels they were cooked and served in; and the tableware they were eaten from. The last chapter considers the fruit, cheese, tea, coffee, and wine that crowned the whole.

The subject is of great interest today to people who are setting the tables of historic houses and confronting the puzzle of sweetmeats, epergnes, and surtouts. It also is of interest to owners of antiques and to people who like to cook. The subject certainly holds charm for people with a sweet tooth and for those who agree with the mid-nineteenth-century cookbook author Eleanor Parkinson that "confectionary is the poetry of epicurism" and with the Victorian Mrs. Beeton who echoed her, vowing, "If there be any poetry at all in meals . . . there is poetry in the dessert."[2]

Acknowledgments

Many people have helped this book along its long road. There are the obliging staff members of museums, libraries, and historical societies who brought out manuscripts, books, and bits of their own vast knowledge. There are benefactors like Jeanette Eckman, Alice Gilborn, and Tyrell Collins-Conway who typed, edited, and suggested. There are members of the Winterthur publications office, among them John Morse, Louisa Turley Buonasisi, Susan Terdiman, Ian Quimby, Catherine Maxwell, Catherine Hutchins, Susan Greenberg, and Patricia Lisk, who put their editorial shoulders to the wheel. And, above all, there are such friends at Winterthur as Nancy Goyne Evans and Benno Forman who faithfully sent me plums from their own research. The deepest gratitude to all of them and to the many others on my lengthy list of helpers.

L. C. B.

THE FESTIVE TRADITION

1

Setting the Gentleman's Table

Feb. 7, 1795. Snow above the shoe deep, snowing all day. [For dinner] soup, veal, turkey, tongue, fish, veal's head (drest turtle fashion), jelly, creams, mince pies, puffs, chescakes, flumery, apples, nuts, raisins & almonds etc., 2 bottles porter, 4 table-beer.

Martha Blodget's Diary,
Prince George County, Virginia.[1]

To arrange a gay and intricate dessert table was hard work two hundred years ago, yet everything about it provided welcome pastimes for a woman of means in an age when she seldom went to public places of enjoyment but found recreation at home in musical evenings, table games, dancing, and reading aloud. Producing her own and criticizing her friends' dessert tables supplied her with never-failing pleasure in the century before there were restaurants, country clubs, or nightclubs, when for excitement she gave or attended dinner parties, evening tea parties, and balls.

It was to furnish a climax for the parties and balls that a hostess prepared a bright dessert table; it was for this high point of her entertaining that she did her best to create a spectacle that people would talk about. At the very least, using every device she could contrive, she aimed to make her table novel and eye-filling. She decked custards and cakes with blossoms, mounded sugared fruit in dishes shaped like vegetables or animals, and molded strawberry jelly, pistachio cream, or almond flummery into the shapes of quivering temples, birds, hens, or fish. She built pyramids of crystallized fruit; ranged glasses of jellies and syllabubs on piles of glass salvers; heaped silver and glass centerpieces with fruit and comfits; composed pastoral scenes with sugar or porcelain shepherds and sheep.

The creation of dessert displays offered such scope for imagination, ingenuity, and taste that it might almost be called one of the leisure arts. Practicing the art, a hostess could rise to heights of excellence or sink to mediocrity in the opinions of guests who judged her efforts not alone on the quantity and quality of the dessert but on its novelty, beauty, and wit. Traditions that prescribed profusion, balance, and order hedged her in. Whether within those bounds she felt herself original or imitative, ingenious or unimaginative, she knew that reputations were won or lost on the number of dishes, the location of an ice, or the shape of a jelly.

Like desserts and dessert tables, dinners and dinner tables challenged a woman's stamina and creativity. They had done so in America since well before the colonies were one hundred years old, when men of property in the foremost cities of England's American possessions provided abundantly for their guests. Thanks to colonial hospitality, British visitors, finding many of their transplanted countrymen using fine furnishings in the latest London fashions and eating food as familiar as plum pudding, felt almost at home. As they traveled up and down the Atlantic coast they saw Americans smothering their dinner tables with meats and their party tables with creams and jellies in the best English manner. Tureens, platters, vegetable dishes, cream bowls, and sauce boats elbowed each other from end to end of damask-covered tables. Display is good and the more the better was the maxim of American hosts, just as it was of British hosts.

The William Binghams of post-Revolutionary Philadelphia entertained well. Even a middling ball supper at Lansdowne, their country seat on the west side of the Schuylkill River, was something to write home about. Mrs. Benjamin Stoddert, wife of the country's first secretary of the navy, found it so. She sent a long letter to her sister describing one such affair in 1798. The refreshments began early in the evening, she wrote, with punch, lemonade, and ice cream offered by servants carrying trays. The food and drink reached their peak at eleven o'clock when the doors to the dining room were thrown open and a table was revealed, brilliant with fowl and game, gay desserts, and amusing decorations spread out in the light of many candles (Pl. 1:1). The enthralled Mrs. Stoddert told her sister:

> In the middle was an orange tree with ripe fruit, [its] root . . . covered with evergreens [and] some natural and some artificial flowers. Nothing scarcely appeared on the table without evergreens to decorate it. The girandole, which hangs down immediately over the table, was let down just to reach the top of the tree. You can't think how beautiful it looked. I imagine there were thirty at the table, besides a table full in another room, and I believe every soul said, "How pretty!" as soon as they were seated.[2]

Like all dinner party, tea party, and ball supper tables of the time, the Binghams' table was laden and waiting for the guests when they strolled through the open door. As Mrs. Stoddert approached it she saw a turkey, fowls, pheasants, and tongues, "the latter," she asserted, "the best that ever I tasted." The dessert, which also was on the table, consisted, she was sure, "of everything that one could conceive of except jelly, though I daresay there was jelly, too, but to my mortification I could not get any." Though jelly eluded her, she fared well on the other desserts, which with their attendant figurines inspired her to claim:

> I never ate better than at Mrs. Bingham's. Plenty of blancmange, and excellent. Near me were three different sorts of cake. I tasted all but could eat of only one. The others were indifferent. Besides a quantity to eat there was a vast deal for ornament and some of [the ornaments] I thought would have delighted my little girl for her baby-house.[3]

Eighteenth-Century Party Tables

The Binghams' ball supper table with its orange tree centerpiece and little ceramic figures surrounded by fowl and game dishes and a host of blancmanges, jellies, and cakes, all decorated with greenery, was set in the lavish, intricate style that had been followed for evening party tables throughout the eighteenth century. The Binghams, to be sure, were very rich, but there were many Anglo-Americans less so who laid tables as lavish. Not only at their evening parties but at their afternoon dinners they used fine white linen and serving dishes of porcelain, glass, and silver and at both kinds of party presented as many as two dozen dishes at once. For dinner parties the host or hostess saw to it that the table held two courses of meats and vegetables, each very like the other, these to be followed by a course of sweets and a finale of fruit. In the sweet course he or she made sure that fully as many dishes were offered as there had been in the second course. And the family's good reputation seemed to increase with the number of dishes.

Tradition of Crowded Tables

Crowded, elaborate tables had been a mark of status in England since the early fifteenth century when the king and the princes of the church had vied with each other to demonstrate their wealth and power. The aristocracy, as was usual, copied royalty and nobility. In turn, wealthy merchants and lesser folk aped the aristocracy. As a result, from generation to generation throughout the centuries, a great display of food and a rich setting for it had been a measure of man's position in society. In the seventeenth century when Englishmen left home to colonize, they still strove to load their dinner tables with food and to set them handsomely. Not everyone in the colonies, of course, dined as well as Judge Samuel Sewall did in 1701 when he gave his guests a dinner of boiled pork, beef, and fowls along with roast beef, turkey pie, and tarts; most of the colonists still made do with cornmeal, game, fish, squash, and pumpkin. But, rich or poor, a man's goal was a groaning board and fine vessels.[4]

Seventeenth-Century Rooms for Dining

The rich, at the end of the seventeenth century, were just beginning to add to their houses special rooms for dining. For the majority of people, either the main room, called the hall in medieval parlance, or the second room, newly termed the parlor after the French word *parler*, "to converse," or even the upstairs bedrooms, called chambers, served very well. Diners simply set a table where it was cool in summer and warm in winter, and kept their eating and drinking vessels in upstairs or downstairs cupboards, wherever convenience and the season suggested.

Seventeenth-Century Table Carpets

During the seventeenth century the table that people most often used for dinner in a downstairs room was an all-purpose one covered night and day with a heavy carpet. Table carpets came in many different materials. Some, like the red or green linsey woolsey ones owned by the Boston sea captain, George Corwin were of plain material; others were woven in patterns or embroidered; still others were of wool yarn knotted in Turkey or other countries of Asia Minor (Fig. 1:2; see also Pl. 6:5). Such knotted wool carpets were known inexactly as "turkey carpets" as today they are known loosely as "orien-

FIG. 1:2. Robert Feke, *Isaac Royall and Family*. Boston, 1741. Oil on canvas. (Harvard University Portrait Collection, gift of Dr. George Stevens Jones.)

FIG. 1:3. Jan van Steen, *The Merrymakers*. The Netherlands, ca. 1660. Oil on canvas. (Kassel Museum.)

tals." A few table carpets were of darmick, or darnix, a coarse linen from the Belgian city of Doornik, or Tournai. Although darnix lacked the richness and cachet of a Turkey carpet, it nevertheless was considered a substance of quality. Even Samuel Mavericke of Boston, who was wealthy enough in 1663 to have in his hall a court cupboard, six Russian leather chairs, and a gilded leather cushion, used four yards of it on his long table.[5]

Seventeenth-Century Tablecloths

From the time English settlers first arrived on the American continent they protected their table carpets with white linen at mealtime as was the custom in Europe and England (Fig. 1:3). As early as 1642, the widow Ann Uttinge of Dedham, Massachusetts, at the end of her life owned along with her Bible and bed linens a tablecloth and two napkins. If the gentlemen, merchants, and

FIG. 1:4. Abraham Bosse, *L'Hyver*. Paris, ca. 1665. From Nicole Villa, *Le XVIIe siècle vu par Abraham Bosse* (Paris: Les editions Roger DaCosta, 1967), pl. 78. (Winterthur Museum Library.)

artisans who emigrated to the New World did not bring fine napery with them, they soon acquired it from men like Captain Joseph Weld of Roxbury, Massachusetts, who kept holland linen by the yard and other linens ready made into tablecloths and napkins. A careful housewife pressed her family's table linen so that its folds stood up sharply (Fig. 1:4). In between meals she maintained the folds with the help of napkin presses of the kind Hezekiah Usher of Boston owned in 1697 and Captain William Holberton of the same city owned in 1716 (Fig. 1:5). The listing "table, table carpet, and cloth" frequently appears in seventeenth- and eighteenth-century house inventories. So often is this trio seen, in fact, that one suspects that the housewife brought out a cloth to lay a bite for the inventory taker, or that a not-so-careful housewife left the cloth on around the clock.[6]

FIG. 1:5. Press for flowers, copybooks, or napkins, England or America, 1750–1800. Mahogany; H. 30.4 cm., W. 30.4 cm., D. 17 cm. (Winterthur Museum, 66.746.)

Seventeenth-Century Napkins

Table napkins, like tablecloths, formed an important part of New England household equipment in the seventeenth century. There are people today who maintain that as forks came into use in that and the following century, napkins went out. It is possible that this was the case in England. In America, however, judging by inventories, napkins continued without ceasing as part of a well-furnished table. The word *napkin* in the seventeenth century referred to a small cloth whether it was used for wiping fingers and mouth at the table, encircling the throat as a kerchief, diapering the baby, or covering the table carpet during a small meal in place of a tablecloth. Napkins, like tablecloths, were made from linen of varying degrees of fineness and could be found in all degrees in early American houses. Joseph Gillam's Boston shop in 1681 could provide four different grades: coarse, dowlas, diaper, and holland. A few of the napkins listed with tablecloths in colonial inventories definitely were not for wiping fingers at the table. Those enriched with stiff needlework like the "laid wrought napkinnes" in the wealthy Boston households of John Baker and Antipas Boyce or those wrought with blue stripes or edged with fringe or lace were suitable only to embellish a small table, chest, or cupboard. If they covered the top of a large court, livery, or press cupboard, they served not only to ornament that imposing piece of furniture but to provide a safe resting place for the best eating and drinking vessels of the household. In some houses, like Jonathan Rainsford's in Boston, a rich napkin lay under a fringed or plain flat silk cushion that had been placed there to make an even safer resting place for the valued objects. The person who took inventory of Rainsford's belongings in 1671 recorded as a unit: "Courte Cubbard, Cushen & Cloth, & Earthen & Glass Furniture."[7]

Eighteenth- and Nineteenth-Century Table Coverings

In the eighteenth century a dining room came to form a part of every gentleman's house, but it was not used exclusively for dining. Desks for writing and chairs for reading made the room useful between meals—as if it were a second parlor. On the dining table householders continued to place heavy coverings, but this covering changed character over the years. Turkey carpets, once the royalty of covering, gradually were demoted to the floor and supplanted on the table top by thinner materials. Governor Tryon of New York and North Carolina used green broadcloth on his Jamaica mahogany dining table in 1773. New Yorker Thomas Duncan chose a painted cloth, probably of canvas, in 1757. Many people used baize, but one mid-century needlewoman of New York, clinging to the old tradition of a heavy covering, embroidered "Mary Oothout Her Table Cloath September the 9 1759" in blue, tan, and red wool crewels on woolen fabric (Fig. 1:6). When by the middle of the century dining rooms and dining tables had become standard equipment in the houses of the well-to-do, broadcloth or baize underlay the white linen and continued to do so throughout the nineteenth century. Many householders in that latter century covered the living room table with one heavy green cloth of bocking or baize and the dining table with another. It was the duty of the servant or housewife to shake both cloths and replace them after they had been used during a meal. In a number

FIG. 1:6. Table carpet embroidered Mary Oothout Her Table Cloath September the 9 1759. Long Island or New Jersey, 1759. Wool on wool; L. 259.5 cm., W. 74 cm. (Winterthur Museum, 66.74.)

FIG. 1:7. Detail of dessert on a bare table with floorcloth below. From Henry Sargent, *The Dinner Party*. Boston, 1814. Oil on canvas. (Courtesy, Museum of Fine Arts, Boston.)

of houses a green cloth would lie not only on the top of the dining table but also on the floor beneath, as one does in the Boston dining room pictured in *The Dinner Party* painted by Henry Sargent around 1814 (Fig. 1:7).[8]

Eighteenth-Century Tablecloths

Linen cloths of several degrees of quality furnished seventeenth-century houses in surprising numbers, as we have seen, but eighteenth-century houses acquired even larger and more diversified white linen supplies. Huckabuck and bird's-eye diapered varieties supplemented dowlas and holland. Fine damask, although twice as expensive as diapered linen, covered dining tables in many more houses. The linen advertised in colonial newspapers came most often from northern European principalities, less often from Ireland and Great Britain. To be sure, *Boston News-Letter* advertisements offered linens from Scotland in 1719 and striped hollands from Bristol in 1723, but advertisements for Irish and British linens were in the minority compared to those for linens from Danzig, Poland, and from Pomerania, Westphalia, Flanders, or Brabant. The term *holland* had little to do with Holland but was applied to any linen that the seller judged had a luster and whiteness that compared favorably to the special luster and superlative whiteness of linens that had been spread out to bleach on Holland's green fields near Haarlem. As they had in the seventeenth century, ladies kept their table linens sharply creased with the help of such devices as the "old Table Cloth Press" listed in John Moore's New York inventory of 1757.[9]

Eighteenth-Century Napkins

Americans of high and low degree continued to use napkins during the eighteenth century. Even in the inland village of Deerfield, Massachusetts, families of modest means owned at least two napkins for every cloth. The Reverend John Williams of that town kept eight for each one of his four linen tablecloths. John Moore and other New Yorkers at midcentury owned, in addition to plain linen napkins, linen napkins embellished with "worked stripes," possibly like the wrought blue stripes of the previous century. These may have served as sideboard cloths as they had in the last twenty years of the seventeenth century. Housewives folded plain linen table napkins four square, hid a roll inside, and laid one on a plate set at each diner's place. Although in a few upper-class American houses napkins were folded to resemble a Turk's cap, which was a distant cousin of the complicated forms of birds and animals to be seen in large European establishments, there seems to be no evidence that ordinary Englishmen or Americans spent much time on linen folding.[10]

Nineteenth-Century Linen and Table Coverings

When the nineteenth century was in full swing women abandoned the various table coverings of the previous centuries and at mealtime protected their dining tables with a plain piece of baize or with an old tablecloth spread out under the fine one. The century brought great variety in the patterning of fine linen. Americans, conscious of their new nationality, could buy "a beautiful assortment of table cloths with and without eagle patterns" from F. A. Vethake, a New York importer of 1804. From Bours, MacGregor, & Co. of that city they could buy cloths in sizes varying from four-by-eight feet to ten-by-fourteen feet in thistle, kings, queens, and clermont patterns, the last adorned with a basket of fruit in the center. They bought yard-square napkins to match and folded them squarely to lay on the place plates as in the eighteenth century. When a woman wanted clean tablecloths for the two courses and for the first dessert she spread one or two napkins on the top tablecloth. If she used napkins in this manner, she called them slips. Housewives who kept cloths folded in neat squares as their grandmothers had, found pressing hints in servants' guides and household instruction books like Catharine Beecher's, which told them to put the cloths in the press all night or under a plank made smooth and handy for the purpose. By the last quarter of the century, however, crisp folds were out of fashion. Instead, women smoothed the cloths onto the table "without perceptible folds or creases" and maintained them in pristine condition between meals by rolling them around tubes.[11]

Eighteenth- and Nineteenth-Century Sideboard, Tea Table, and Breakfast Cloths

Besides owning tablecloths and napkins, housewives of the eighteenth and nineteenth centuries owned cloths for special purposes: to protect the sideboards and serving tables that came into style after court, press, and livery cupboards went out and to cover kitchen tables, tea tables, and even oyster supper tables. Governor Tryon's household at Fort George, New York, before a fire destroyed his house in 1773, kept six fringed cloths for the breakfast table and four for the kitchen. Barrister Charles Carroll's Baltimore household had cloths of "stamped or painted silk or gauze" ordered from London in 1768 for "the table of china" in the parlor. Some ladies by mid eighteenth century indicated the use of their linen with embroidered letters such as *TT* for tea table.[12]

Cloths and napkins came in many sizes and degrees of fineness. Governor Tryon's house, for example, made use of eight large India huckabuck tablecloths and twelve huckabuck tea napkins, two large damask tablecloths and twelve damask tea napkins, three bird's-eye diaper tablecloths and twelve bird's-eye diaper tea napkins. Being of many sizes, table and tea cloths hung down from the tables in varying lengths, from a few inches to touching the floor. A housewife put cloths on a tea table or not, as she chose. She usually chose not to cover a table that had a fine molded edge.[13]

Table Mats

At mealtime, to protect the white tablecloth, housewives as early as the middle of the eighteenth century placed mats under serving dishes. The ladies referred to these objects variously as table, dish, or plate mats (Fig. 1:8). Furthermore, at tea time in unfashionable circles in the nineteenth century, housewives provided small mats to hold cups when tea drinkers who were in a hurry to cool their tea drank from the saucer. Both plate and cup mats were made of straw, willow, or cane and came from such far-off places as India, Guinea, Manila, Holland, and France. Before the middle of the eighteenth century mats were relatively rare in American houses, but Anthony and Cornelia Rutgers's New York inventory in 1760 listed "six small table matts," and Thomas Duncan of that time and city kept with his table linen "one Guinea Matt." In 1776 Philadelphians could buy India table mats from the merchant Joseph Stansbury; thirty-five years later they could find mats of great variety at the shop of N. Thomas, who sold dish and plate mats in sizes ranging from ten to sixteen inches in either figured or plain sets. By 1818 Philadelphia residents had a choice of common oilcloth mats or green baize oilcloth mats, both of which were to be found at the store of Isaac Macaulay. And everyone could use homemade willow mats. Lydia Child, author of *The Frugal Housewife*, first published in Boston in 1829 and subsequently through thirty-two editions by 1847, suggested that willow mats for the table and floor be made by children. The little woven or cloth cup mats were superseded by cup plates of earthenware or glass some time in the second quarter of the century in the houses of the respectable middle class, whose spokeswoman, Catharine Beecher, recommended them in 1842.[14]

FIG. 1:8. Detail of table mats. From James Gillray, *Dumourier Dining in State at St. James*, London, 1793, in *The Works of James Gillray*, n.p.

Doilies

Slips and mats seem overnice for the robust eighteenth century, but there were other table appurtenances that were even more so. Among them were doily napkins for use during the fruit and wine dessert. The term *doily* derived from D'Oyley, the name of a London draper who grew prosperous and famous at the end of the seventeenth century. D'Oyley stocked inexpensive woolen fabrics from which many articles of clothing and household usage were made, presumably including the small napkins hostesses offered their guests for wiping their fingers after their large napkins had been removed (Fig. 1:9). From early in the eighteenth century until well into the nineteenth doilies were used as napkins by the fastidious because, as the Bostonian who wrote *The Young Lady's Friend* in 1836 explained, "the juice of some fruits stains a white napkin." But in the late eighteenth century doilies came to be used also as protectors of the bare dessert table (Fig. 1:10). John B. Lyon of Newport, Rhode Island, in 1837 owned doilies by the dozen for this purpose. They were grouped in his inventory along with table mats and not with linen napkins, suggesting that when his table was set the doilies were used as protectors just as the Hill Carters had used them in 1833 at "Shirley," their plantation on the James River. Henry Barnard, a visiting Yale student, saw them that year on the Carters' breakfast table, which, he wrote to his family, was "bare save for doilies under the plates . . . each plate standing separate on its own little cloth."[15]

Dinner Table Procedure

The Carters lived in a style made possible by a yearly $10,000 income from a 900-acre plantation, and their guests found splendid hospitality at their table. Barnard told his family:

> You drink your porter out of silver goblets. The table at dinner is always furnished with the finest Virginia ham and saddle of mutton, turkey, then canvasback duck, beef, oysters, etc., etc., etc., [and] the finest celery. Then comes the sparkling champagne; after that the dessert, plum pudding, tarts, ice cream, peaches preserved in brandy, etc. Then the table is cleared and on come the figs, almonds, and raisins and the richest madeira, the best port, and softest malmsey wine I ever tasted.[16]

Barnard's description brings the Carters' dinners to life. We see a southern family in 1833 habitually serving at least two meats, two fowls, game, and fish, followed by a dessert of ice cream, pudding, pie, and preserved sweetmeats, also a dessert of fruit, nuts, and raisins, the meal accompanied by porter and four wines. Detailed as Barnard's letters are, they unfortunately stop short of

FIG. 1:9. Detail of fruit and wine dessert with doily. From W. H. Simmons, *The Chair*. London, 1841. Mezzotint after A. Crowquill. (Photo, The Old Print Shop, New York City.)

THE TABLE. 71

DESSERT FOR A PARTY OF EIGHTEEN.

ADAPTED TO FOLLOW THE PRECEDING TWO-COURSE DINNER.

1, 1, and centre, are ornamental Confectoinary.
The diamond shapes round the table are d'oyleys.

FIG. 1:10. Diagram for dessert for a party of eighteen showing placement of "d'oyleys." From James Williams, *The Footman's Guide*, 4th ed., p. 71. (Winterthur Museum Library.)

giving us a look at the table setting. They leave us wondering where the silver goblets were when the diners sat down; who poured the porter and from what vessel; who served the meats, fish, fowls, and vegetables, and—most important of all to those who look for answers to table-setting questions—where the knives, forks, spoons, salts, and serving utensils were placed.

These and many other questions about eighteenth- and nineteenth-century table procedure are not put to rest easily. No eighteenth-century American cookbooks exist to give us answers. None were written until Amelia Simmons produced her *American Cookery* in 1796. Earlier British cookbooks, which should be helpful, abound, but none gives all the answers. Those that are the most useful contain diagrams, but the diagrams tell only what meats and vegetables were available for the twelve months of the year and where they should be placed on the table. For example, John Farley's *London Art of Cookery*, which Philadelphians read before 1835, supplied such plans (Fig. 1:11).[17]

From Farley and other British cookbook writers we learn that the everyday dinner in an upper-class establishment began with a course of at least five meats and vegetables and proceeded to a second course of at least five similar dishes, varied occasionally by the addition of a sweet pudding or a tart, which today Americans call pie. A proper dinner party began with a course of as many as twenty-one dishes, moved on to a second similar course, and ended with a dessert of as many dishes as had been offered in the second course, the whole capped by a second dessert, this one of fruit. The diagrams tell us furthermore that whether a housewife chose a small plan of five dishes or a party plan of twenty-one dishes, she provided one or two soups, fish, and roasts in the first course. These were in addition to several meat pies and assorted dishes of game and fowl. She saw to it that they were all arranged in a prescribed, balanced plan. A roast, suitable for what the cookbooks called a "center," she placed in the exact center of the table. Or she put two or four roasts in the central *area* of the dinner table. Roasts, also suitable for "ends," she alternated with soups, pies, game, and fowl dishes at the top or the bottom of the table. Vegetables, stews, puddings, and such other "made dishes" as brown Scotch collops—those tasty meats now known across national boundaries as veal scallopini—she arranged as "sides" down the length of the table. Finally, she selected the most decorative dishes and made them serve importantly as "corners."

First Course

All of the dishes waited in their prescribed places on the table when the diners sat down. Early in the eighteenth century the soup and fish, which tradition said were meant to be eaten first, stood somewhere on the table as a center, side, or end. Late in the century they stood as ends near the hostess and host respectively, who served them promptly after grace was said. Not every diner wished to taste both soup and fish, but when everyone had had an opportunity to accept or refuse, the two dishes were taken away and "removes" of roasts or large fowl were brought on to fill the spots left vacant. The company then set to on the tableful of food. Whoever sat near the roast, game, and fowls was expected to carve and do a good job of it—seated. If wise, the carver had

Soup and Fish and Their Removes

Carving

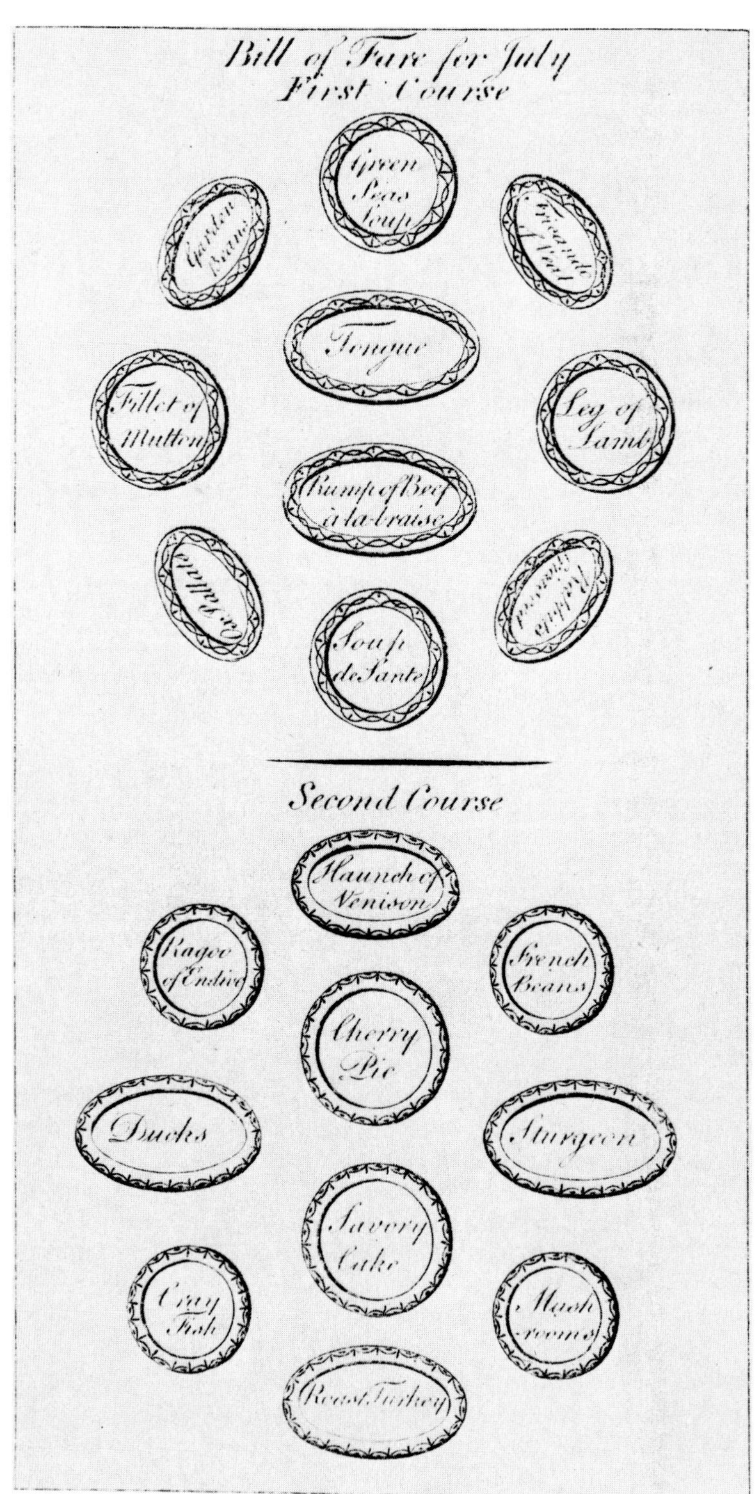

FIG. 1:11. Plan for the arrangement of serving dishes. From John Farley, *The London Art of Cookery*, preceding p. 1. (Winterthur Museum Library.)

studied books and sketches on carving and had practiced at home. Women rivaled men as carvers, and their friends often urged them to sit near a platter that called for skill. The carver of whatever sex, having demonstrated ability in dismembering a bird or dividing a roast, placed a slice of meat or a piece of fowl on a plate held by a servant who took it to whichever guest had expressed a wish for it. Another guest seated near the oyster loaves or fricassee of hare served these made dishes, and there followed a confusion of passing and of polite urging by host and hostess to "try a bit" of this or that. Guests indicated what they wished to drink to a servant who would bring it from the sideboard.

Second Course with Desserts

The first course finished, servants removed all dishes and the top tablecloth and brought on a second course. For the second course the would-be correct hostess provided at least the same number of dishes as for the first. They consisted of more but different meats and vegetables. In place of additional soup and fish, a sweet pudding and perhaps a cream, tart, or custard made an appearance. For everyday dinner this would suffice and the meal would end there. But for a dinner party the host and hostess provided two desserts—one of creams, cakes, preserved fruit, candies, and jellies and one of whole fresh fruits and nuts.

Eighteenth-Century Table Setting

The cookbooks' diagrams and recipes tell us a great deal about the food and the placement of serving dishes as well as about removes and the importance of carving. But, as already noted, none mentions the location of flatware, salts, and napkins. If we want to learn where those objects were placed on the approved eighteenth-century English and American table, we must hunt further. We go to paintings but look in vain; the few scenes of dinners portray only tables disturbed by diners who are well into a meal. We turn more successfully to English sketches and engraved social satires. Among them we find a small number picturing dinner tables ready for diners and not yet in mid-meal disarray (Figs. 1:12, 1:13). When we examine the tables we see a place setting familiar to modern Americans: a knife to the diner's right with sharp edge toward the plate, and a fork to the left, the tines most often turned up. Tablespoons for soup, with the back of the bowl showing its midrib, shell, or other decoration and the back of the upturned handle showing its initials or crest, if any, lie convenient to the right hand of the diner at the side of the knife. Dessert spoons, knives, and forks do not appear on the dinner table; their customary place is on the sideboard or serving table with the dessert plates. Teaspoons likewise are not in evidence but are on the tea tray to be used in the parlor following dinner. Bottles for oil and vinegar are ever present. A mound of butter sits in a glass butter tub or on a small plate with or without a glass cover. Small salt dishes occupy the outside corners of the table, sometimes with salt spoons lying face down across them, sometimes with no spoons. Serving spoons, either crossed or parallel to one another and facing in opposite directions, concave side down, flank the salt dishes (Fig. 1:14). The eighteenth-century table setting is seen to be orderly and logical.

FIG. 1:12. Detail of a place setting. From Thomas Rowlandson, *The Rainbow Tavern*. London, 1788. Line and stipple engraving. (Lewis Walpole Library.)

FIG. 1:14. Detail of tableware and cruets with dish mat. From James Gillray, *Temperance Enjoying a Frugal Meal*. London, 1792. Engraving. (Lewis Walpole Library.)

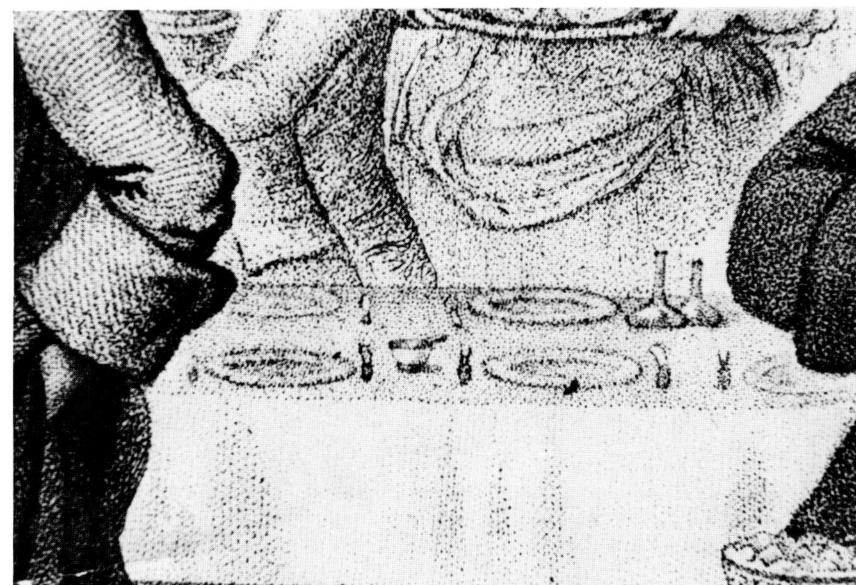

FIG. 1:13. Detail of place settings. From Henry W. Bunbury, *The Country Club*. London, 1788. Stipple engraving. (Lewis Walpole Library.)

Nineteenth-Century Table Setting

When it comes to finding answers to questions about nineteenth-century place setting we do not have to look far. Such books as Thomas Cosnett's *Footman's Directory and Butler's Remembrancer* of 1825 diagram complete tables for dinner and dessert, being specific not only about serving dishes but also about centerpieces and flatware (Fig. 1:15). And Robert Roberts's *The House Servant's Directory*, which in 1827 borrowed heavily from Cosnett, describes in satisfying detail how the table of an American statesman was set by his black house servant, who had learned in England the proper English way to set the table for breakfast, dinner, dessert, after-dinner tea and coffee, and supper. Roberts's book, the first servant's manual written and published in the United States, is invaluable for its documentation of early nineteenth-century American household practice. Roberts and his wife were English house servants before they came to the United States and found employment in Boston households. In 1825 they entered the employ of Christopher Gore, former Massachusetts governor and United States senator, and ran the staff of fourteen servants in the Gores' fine federal house in Waltham, near Boston.[18]

Roberts and Cosnett, while continuing many upper-class eighteenth-century customs, varied them slightly. Roberts used only one tablecloth and that he spread so that the bottom of the design was at the bottom of the table. He put carving tools flanking a place setting at each of the ends and halfway down each of the sides of the table, and placed serving spoons, concave side showing, in a circle around the center area of the table instead of flanking the salts. The concave side was face up possibly because around 1770 the style of spoon handle changed and instead of turning up at the end, turned down, leaving the upper surface instead of the back free for engraving. He made the circle of serving spoons by placing one spoon high between each place setting, parallel to the edge of the table.

Early Nineteenth-Century Sideboard Setting

Setting the sideboard was an important part of dinner setting, and Cosnett, Roberts, and their fellow butlers took it seriously, with Roberts reminding his readers that "ladies and gentlemen that have splendid and costly articles wish to have them seen and set out to best advantage." They arranged the second course and dessert flatware in crescents on the sideboard, "as that was most sublime," and because the silver gave glass "a brilliant display." The glasses they lined up in concentric crescents, the tallest glasses in the outer half circle. In the arrangement of the sideboard a housewife lacking butlers revealed her taste or lack of it.

FIG. 1:15. Dinner table set out for twelve persons. From Thomas Cosnett, *The Footman's Directory*, 5th ed., p. 118. (Winterthur Museum Library.)

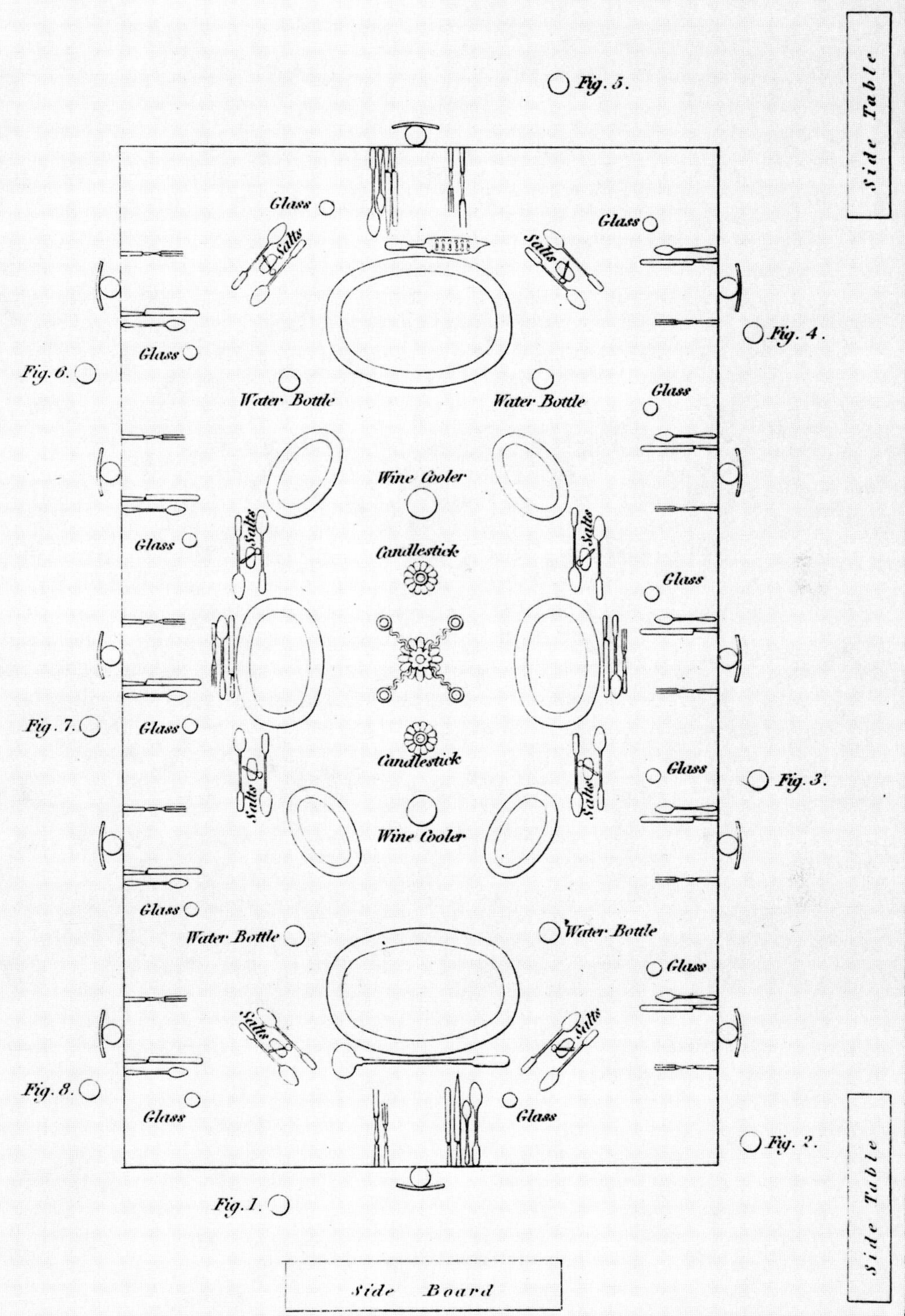

DINNER TABLE SET OUT FOR TWELVE PERSONS WITH EIGHT ATTENDANTS.

FIG. 1:16. Serving table. (Charleston Dining Room, ca. 1760, Winterthur Museum.)

Early Nineteenth-Century Side Table Setting

The side or serving table, which supplemented the sideboard as a repository of extra dishes and flatware, held balanced piles of second course dinner, pudding, and cheese plates (Fig. 1:16). It also held dessert plates if there was no room for them on the sideboard. Dinner knives and forks for the second course lay to the right of the center pile of three piles of dinner plates; any dessert knives and forks that had been crowded off the sideboard lay to the left. Roberts wanted the serving table, like the sideboard and the dinner table, to evince convenience, elegance, taste, and ingenuity. "Order and design, dishes well matched in size and color across the table, side dishes in a straight line and equidistant from each other" were his mottoes for the table setter. The same respect for neatness and balance moved him as had moved men of the eighteenth century. He differed from them only in holding the budding belief that a groaning table was no longer desirable but that a "middling and well-ordered meal had a more pleasing aspect than double as large a one when crowded and improperly put upon table."[19]

Mid Nineteenth-Century Middle-Class Table Setting

For learning about the practice of early nineteenth-century upper-class Americans of English background, Cosnett and Roberts are just what are needed. For learning about middle-class American ways, on the other hand, such works as the 1859 *Family and Householder's Guide*, supplemented by the ca. 1860 manuscript copybook of one L. Fiske (Figs. 1:17, 1:18), are useful. In the copybook, Mrs. Fiske sketched her wishes for her table, basing the sketch on a plan in the *Family Guide*. The sketch is worth reviewing for what it tells of the new table ways and of the persistence of old ones. In it Mrs. Fiske pursued the eighteenth-century segregation of the sexes at the dinner table, seating the gentlemen at the ends and the ladies along the sides. Also in the manner of the last years of the preceding century, she placed a castor in the center of the table. With seventeenth- and eighteenth-century regard for balance she put around it two mats for meat and two for pickles, two dishes for bread, two mats for gravy, and two mats for sauces. At each corner of the table she placed the old grouping of salt cellar, salt spoon, and crossed serving spoons. At each place she put a fork at the left and a tumbler high at the right, as was late eighteenth-century custom. The knife, however, she did not lay at the right but across the top. Carving knives and forks she put parallel to the table edge and above selected place settings, instead of flanking them.[20]

The displacement of the dinner knife from the right to the top of the place setting was one of many variations on old English practice that came to certain American houses in the nineteenth century. Keeping the knife at the right and putting a tablespoon or soup spoon between it and the plate was another. But most of the variations concerned the dessert ware. Some people placed the dessert knife and fork outside the dinner knife and fork at the beginning of the meal, with the dessert spoon by itself across the top; others brought the dessert knife, fork, and spoon to the table with the dessert as in the eighteenth century but placed them together on the table to the right of the finger cup and plate instead of on the table surrounding the dessert plate. Dessert ware was in some

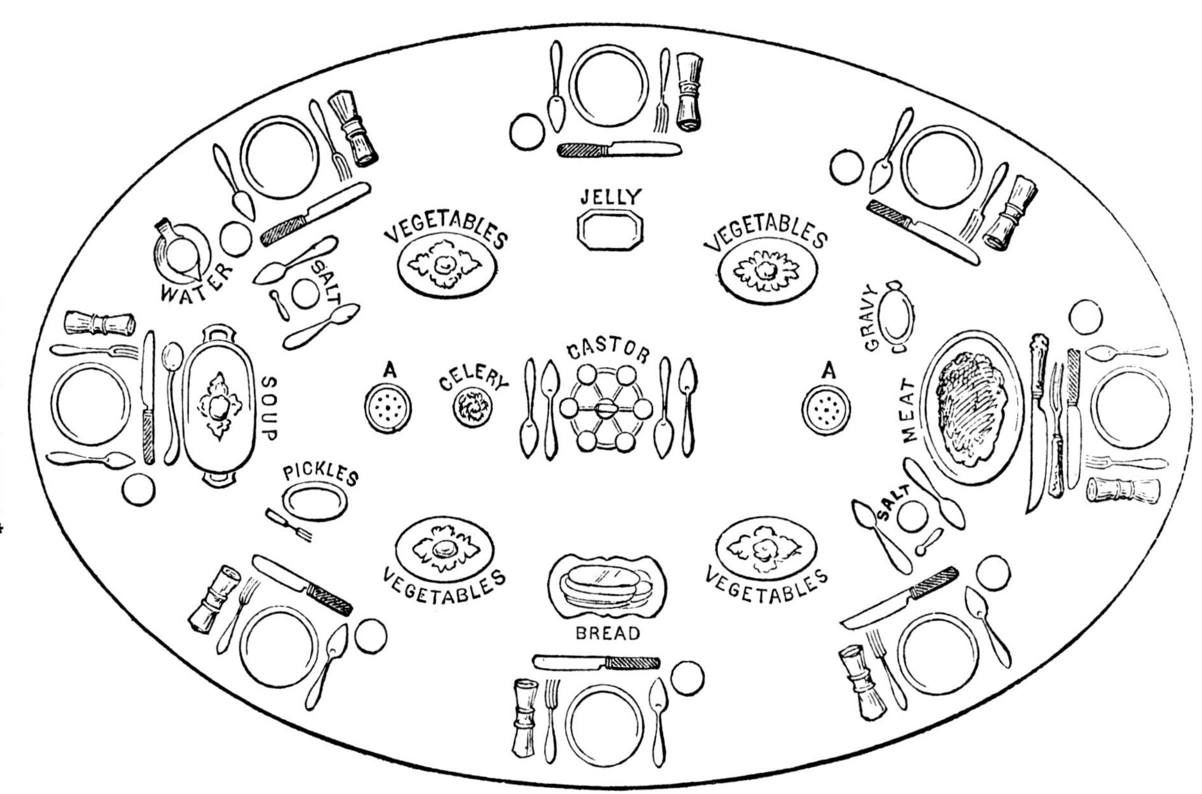

FIG. 1:17. *How to Set a Table*. From *The Family and Householder's Guide*, p. 29. (Winterthur Museum Library.)

FIG. 1:18. Diagram for a dinner table setting and seating. From L. Fiske, manuscript recipe book, probably Beverly, Mass., ca. 1860. (Winterthur Museum Library, DMMC.)

households brought to the table *on* the finger cup plate—the fork to the left, knife to the right, and spoon across the top of the finger cup—a practice that persists today with only the slight variation of spoon to the right, the knife having disappeared along with the fresh fruit dessert.[21]

Clearing the Table

So far in this first chapter, we have set the cloths, dishes, and flatware. It is now time to clear them off.

Removing the Cloth

As we have seen, with a cloth under it, a carpet or some baize and a cloth or two on top of it, and a dozen or so mats ranged up and down and across it, a dining table was thoroughly swaddled. It must have been a relief to diners who were to remain seated for a dessert to have all the mats stacked, cloths and baize rolled up, and the whole array of table protectors carried off. If a housewife wondered how the cloth or baize was to be removed gracefully before dessert, she found the answer in Londoner Thomas Cosnett's *Footman's Directory*. Cosnett directs two footmen:

> Let . . . the dirty things be taken out of the room by two of the waiters, while . . . the rest clear the table. . . . You, William, take off all the pieces of bread . . . while James . . . wipes off the crumbs and the other two put the finger and lip glasses on. When they are done with, put them into the trays appointed for them. When this is done, if the table cloth remains on the table, you must take off the napkins, or slips, of linen cloth. Then if you, William and James, go to the top of the table, one on each side, you will be able to roll the cloth or napkins down the table to the bottom.[22]

Who can say what scintillating conversation was interrupted by the liveried arms of William and James as they reached between a dinner party tête-à-tête?

Flatware, Plates, and Glass-Baskets

Clearing dinner tables and side tables laden from top to bottom and from front to back with dishes, plates, glasses, silverware, and miscellany was no small job. From at least the middle of the eighteenth century to facilitate clearing, well-to-do English-American households up and down the Atlantic seaboard used trays and baskets specifically designed for carrying both clean and used objects to and from the kitchen (Fig. 1:19). Glass-baskets held drinking vessels; deep, cylindrical plate baskets held plates; shallow, rectangular knife-and-fork baskets, with two compartments, held flatware. Usually made of wood or wicker, the baskets were sometimes tin-lined and sometimes, as in Lady Temple's Boston cupboard, japanned and gilded.[23]

FIG. 1:19. Knife trays and plate basket. From Henry Loveridge & Co., *Catalogue*, p. 11. (Winterthur Museum Library.)

Double Wicker Knifetray lined with Tin

No. 474

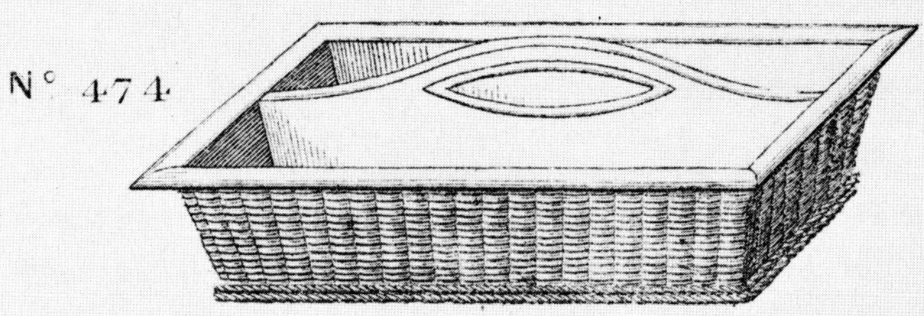

Single Wicker Knifetray lined with Tin

No. 475

Wicker Plate Basket lined with Tin

No. 476

No.
1
2
3

Knife Racks, Table Brushes, and Bells

In well-run households throughout the eighteenth and nineteenth centuries many small amenities made table service run smoothly. A small silver or ceramic knife rest held knives and forks at each place if diners wished to retain them while a clean plate was being supplied (Fig. 1:20). The rack was neater than the piece of bread they might otherwise use and certainly easier on the tablecloth than the common practice of balancing knives and forks on their heavy handles. Table brushes cleared a tablecloth of crumbs if the cloth stayed on from course to course. Table bells called servants.[24]

FIG. 1:20. Knife rest, Europe, 1720–60. Delft (tin-glazed earthenware); L. 9.2 cm., H. 4.1 cm. (Winterthur Museum, 62.597.)

Napkin Rings

Well before the middle of the nineteenth century, napkin rings found a place on middle-class tables. Most often they were of ivory or bone, but *The Workwoman's Guide* in 1840 gave directions as to how rings might be knitted in a checked pattern. In 1841 Miss Beecher advocated numbering ivory rings.[25]

Dish Covers

Festive meals in large houses could involve so many foods and objects that it might take several servants up to twenty minutes to carry the dishes to the table before the guests sat down. During this running to and fro, and while diners were doing away with the soup and fish, domed covers kept food, if not hot, at least warm. When diners were ready to begin serving each other, servants lifted the covers, flipping them up with a quick wrist movement to catch the condensation of steam. The British Mrs. Basil Hall said that she did not see dish covers when she visited New York City in 1826, but inventories show that the Jonathan Ashleys of Deerfield, Massachusetts, and such other families of wealth as the Elias Hasket Derbys of Salem, Massachusetts, did make use of them.[26]

***Early Nineteenth Century: Service* à la Russe**

Fashions in dining changed slowly during the nineteenth century. Crowded tables and an overabundance of food continued to burden the majority of hostesses and guests, yet increasing numbers of people began to feel that sumptuousness was outmoded. In 1837 Thomas Walker in *The Art of Dining* deplored householders' fear of a bare table and urged them to conquer it. The American author Catherine Sedgwick, traveling in Germany in 1839, met with a new style of dining that featured an uncluttered table. At a dinner in Frankfort, instead of being greeted with a tablecloth covered with meats and vegetables steaming out their savoriness, she was greeted with a tablecloth clear except for fruit, flowers, and confectionery arranged in the center. Dinner was brought on a dish or two at a time. She was enchanted, she wrote, because she was enveloped with "the most delicious atmosphere of fruit and flowers instead of being stupefied with the fumes of meat." Furthermore, she said, there was "no bustle of changing dishes, no thrusting in of servants' arms." Miss Sedgwick encountered this new method of service again in Milan, and, before her *Letters from Abroad* were published in 1841, she found that her fellow Americans had taken up the idea. She added a footnote to her *Letters:* "I am told that within the last few months [this] has become common in New York. So easily do we adopt foreign fashions."[27]

The new fashion that delighted Catherine Sedgwick in 1839 involved a number of changes. It meant that a center decoration was decorative and not merely expedient. It meant that a hostess allowed the tablecloth to be seen instead of requiring it to be hidden under countless dishes of food. It meant also that servants passed food to each diner instead of putting it on the table to get cold before he or she sat down. Finally, it meant that servants had the responsibility for carving, formerly considered the duty of the host, hostess, or skilled guest, and that they did the carving in the kitchen or on a side table.

Mid Nineteenth Century: Old Service Holdover

Called service *à la russe* because it was said to have been introduced by the Russian ambassador in France in 1810, the new fashion rapidly gained acceptance in certain cosmopolitan British and American households.[28] But it failed to move the majority. Philip Hone's, presumably, was one household that was not moved. Early in 1840 the New York mayor wrote in his diary: "My wife Mary and I dined at Judge Pendleton's. We had a stylish dinner and an agreeable party. I do not like the new fashion of the servants' handing round the dishes; it interrupts conversation and I would rather see my dinner that I may be 'free to choose.' " Mrs. Fiske, the De Witt Clintons of Albany, and readers of the monthly *American Agriculturalist* decidedly were among those who neither modified the number of dishes they put on the table nor provided for the passing of dishes. Nor were they among those who introduced off-table carving. At their dinners meats, vegetables, sauces, bread, pickles, and salads continued to greet diners when they came to the table, and crossed serving spoons and a center caster awaited them. On the usual white tablecloth, mid nineteenth-century diners in middle-class American houses maintained the eighteenth-century custom of carving and serving at the table, and table setting continued to be dominated by dishes crowded together and arranged in strict regularity. *The Family and Householder's Guide*, concerned with arrangement, put it bluntly to its readers in 1859: "Dishes should not look as if they had fallen down like hailstones."[29]

The Hill Carters of Virginia also were among the families who clung to tradition. Well into the nineteenth century they kept the afternoon dinner hour and retained the eighteenth-century custom of exposing all of the dinner in one or two courses. At their house, after a bowl of rum and water, gentlemen still led ladies in to dinner by the hand in the old manner while the first course waited on the white damask of two tablecloths. From their table the top cloth was removed with the first course and the bottom cloth with the second course, leaving the mahogany exposed for the fruit dessert. Henry Barnard in 1833 gives us almost the whole old-fashioned story:

> The master and mistress of the house are not expected to entertain visitors till an hour or two before dinner, which is usually at 3. If company has been invited to the dinner they will begin to come about 1—ladies in carriage and gentlemen horseback. After making their toilet, the company amuse themselves in the parlor. About a half hour before dinner, the gentlemen are invited out to take grog. When dinner is ready (and by the way Mrs. Carter has nothing to do with setting the table; an old family servant, who for 50 years has superintended the matter, does all that), Mr. Carter politely takes a lady by the hand and leads the way into the dining room, and is followed by the rest, each lady led by a gentleman.[30]

Henry Barnard leaves us to imagine the gentlemen pulling out the chairs for the ladies and settling them solicitously, Mr. Carter saying grace and encouraging the diners to fall to, then continues:

> Mrs. Carter is at one end of the table with a large dish of rich soup, and Mr. C. at the other with a saddle of fine mutton. Scattered around the table you may choose for yourself ham, beef, turkey, ducks, eggs with greens, etc., etc., vegetables, potatoes, beets, hominy. This last you will find always at dinner; it is made of their white corn and beans and is a very fine dish. After you have dined there circulates a bottle of sparkling champagne. After that, off passes the things and the upper table cloth, and upon that is placed the dessert consisting of fine plum pudding, tarts, etc., etc. After this comes ice cream, West India preserves, peaches preserved in brandy, etc. When you have eaten this, off goes the second table cloth and then upon the bare mahogany table is set the figs, raisins, and almonds, and before Mr. Carter is set two or three bottles of wine—madeira, port, and a sweet wine for the ladies. He fills his glass and pushes them on. After the glasses are all filled, the gentlemen pledge their services to the ladies and down goes the wine. After the first and second glass the ladies retire and the gentlemen begin to circulate the bottle pretty briskly. You are at liberty, however, to follow the ladies as soon as you please, who, after music and a little chit-chat, prepare for their ride home.[31]

This kind of one- or two-course meal followed by one or two desserts persisted in the face of the new uncrowded "Russian" service in the majority of English houses as well as in American houses, even though the new custom was well established in Europe. As an aid to mid nineteenth-century European travelers in the British Isles who were daunted by the everything-on-the-table-at-once English dinner, a German who had lived in England wrote *The Illustrated Guide to London* (London, 1851). In it he told his compatriots how to choose and acquire the courses they were used to:

> With an occasional "if you please" thrown in one quietly informs the servant which course one wants to eat and he in turn makes his way to the gentleman before whom the appropriate dish has been placed and asks him to serve the guest. The same procedure is followed with the vegetables, &c. One eats only one or two vegetables with the meat course and no more than two or three main dishes. It is permissable to take second helpings of any course but fish. This is regarded as even better manners than to keep asking for different foods.[32]

Late Nineteenth-Century Service à la Russe

Toward the end of the century a horde of cookbook authors followed Thomas Walker's effort to do away with crowded tables. *Cassell's Household Guide*, an English encyclopedia published in New York as well as in London and Paris, tried around 1870 to write the obituary for the old English dinner with its multiplicity of dishes that "served for ornament rather than for use, less than a third of which were tasted." "It was hard work for a family," the guide needlessly reminded the householder, "to have to eat their way out of the leavings of a dinner party." Following Cassell's guide and one or two other books, a few more enlightened housewives put the tradition of centuries behind them and cleared their tables, serving, at least when *en famille*, five to seven small courses *à la russe*. The dinner they offered was usually made up of a soup, a fish with boiled potatoes, a roast and a vegetable, an entrée, a salad and cheese, and a dessert. But the tradition of lavishness dying hard, they increased their offering to eleven or twelve courses of a dish or two each when they entertained. Mary Henderson of New York in 1880 pronounced the following bill of fare "long enough and good enough for any winter dinner party":

OYSTERS ON THE HALF-SHELL
AMBER SOUP [BEEF CONSOMMÉ]
SALMON; SAUCE HOLLANDAISE
SWEET-BREADS AND PEASE
LAMB-CHOPS; TOMATO-SAUCE
FILET OF BEEF, WITH MUSHROOMS
ROAST QUAILS; SARATOGA POTATOES
SALAD: LETTUCE
CHEESE; CELERY; WAFERS
CHARLOTTE-RUSSE, WITH FRENCH BOTTLED STRAWBERRIES AROUND IT
CHOCOLATE FRUIT ICE-CREAM
FRUIT
COFFEE[33]

Long enough it certainly is by late twentieth-century standards, but by standards of a hundred years ago it was modest. At that time even luncheon parties were lengthy, held for the age-old purpose of displaying status. Washington ladies of the 1870s went to many such affairs. A typical luncheon, given in 1872 by Mrs. John Creswell, wife of the senator from Maryland under President Grant, began with oysters on the shell, "or rather," as her guest Mrs. James G. Blaine remarked, "on shell china plates." Then came clear soup followed by sweetbreads and French peas, roman punch, chicken cutlets, birds, and chicken salad. These courses were surmounted by ices, jelly, charlottes, candied preserves, and cake and topped off with fruit, tea, and coffee, the whole lubricated by four kinds of wine. When Senator Blaine heard of it he proclaimed the lunch to be "too much altogether—for women folks." What he said when, soon after, Mrs. Blaine herself gave a luncheon still larger, which included among its nine courses turtle soup, roast chicken, fried potatoes, and asparagus, is well lost to history.[34]

Mrs. Beeton

For hostesses like Mmes. Creswell and Blaine on both sides of the Atlantic, Mrs. Beeton's *Book of Household Management* served to shore up flagging energy before a party. One dip into her store of inspirational homilies and they knew their hard work was not for naught. Reading her, they strengthened themselves with the thought that as hostesses they were a bulwark against savagery and were taking forward steps in civilization's march toward perfection. "The nation," Mrs. Beeton wrote, "which knows how to dine, has learnt the leading lesson of progress. It implied both the will and the skill to reduce to order and surround with idealisms and graces the more material conditions of human existence, and wherever that will and that skill exist, life cannot be wholly ignoble."[35] Fanny Farmer's *Boston Cook Book,* Irma Rombauer's *Joy of Cooking,* and Julia Child's *French Chef* have stood beside three generations of American hostesses, but none has used the inspiring, grandiloquent vocabulary, provided the know-how for running a household, nor had the long-staying popularity that Mrs. Beeton's books have had. Mrs. Beeton's fame began when, as a bride of twenty-one in 1859, she wrote about household management in twenty-four threepenny supplements to be sold with her husband's *Englishman's Domestic Magazine*. Mr. Beeton, finding the supplements much in demand, published them as the *Book of Household Management* in 1861. In its 1,100 pages the new volume contained everything that the young mistress of a household could want to know about food, etiquette, servants, children, illness, and more. As a consequence, the fat green book with its red spine had a *succès fou*. Excluding the war years and the seventies of the present century, scarcely twelve months have gone by since its publication without the appearance of a new edition or at least sections of the book under new titles. In 1963 Ward, Locke & Company of London and Melbourne, which had bought out Mr. Beeton following his wife's death at twenty-eight in 1867, printed *Mrs. Beeton's All About Cookery* and *The Beeton Home Books*. And in 1977 Farrar, Straus & Giroux of New York produced a facsimile of the 1861 household management original.[36]

Late Nineteenth-Century Pre-Dinner Half Hour

That "Mrs. Beeton's" has had over one hundred years of usefulness stems from its young middle-class author's feeling for the problems of the universal housewife, mother, and hostess. She knew the woman intimately. She felt for her as the hostess stood at bay during the half hour before a dinner party, in a panic lest the early arriving guests be bored and the tardy guests ruin both the dinner and the cook's disposition. It was the custom in the 1860s for a guest to arrive any time during the half hour before the specified dinner hour (usually five o'clock in the city)—but not one minute after. The gentlemen's surreptitious bowl of punch had been dropped during Victoria's reign, and a hostess could feel stranded. Mrs. Beeton recognized the "great ordeal through which the mistress . . . will either pass with flying colours or lose many of her laurels," and suggested some devices to make conversation flow: a new book, a curiosity of art, an article of vertu, a photograph or crest album, a piece of new music. These would, she assured her readers, aid in engaging the attention of the company. There were other conversation pieces that would serve as well. Some ladies of Chicago in 1876 chose as icebreakers for "that very stupid half hour" a new picture, a grotesque sculpture group, a rare plant, the latest news, a personage whom everyone wanted to meet, or a pretty girl.[37] With these devices the harried hostess tried hard to put her guests at ease but often without success. Not until World War I liberated her, and she introduced the cocktail to the drawing room was the pre-dinner half hour anything but trying.

Late Nineteenth-Century Dinner Procedure

To help a new hostess with her dinner giving, Mrs. Beeton went into details of the proper procedure. The Chicago ladies, like other well-bred Victorian Americans, agreed with her instructions. During the before-dinner ordeal the host and hostess assigned dinner partners with a casual remark to each gentleman. When dinner was announced, each gentleman offered an arm to his partner and walked with her into the dining room to sit down by couples where place cards indicated. The hostess "helped the soup" into soup plates piled in front of her while ladies removed their kid gloves and laid them across their laps underneath their partially unfolded napkins. Servants passed the filled soup plates to those who wanted soup. No soup taker asked for more lest he or she receive glances from diners anxious to taste the rapidly cooling dinner spread out before them. The rest of the dinner proceeded as it had in the eighteenth century with the business of choosing, serving, and passing. Mrs. Beeton and other arbiters did not ignore service *à la russe*, however. For those who chose that style they outlined the procedure in which servants carved, offered dishes at the side of each diner, and served every meat, fowl, and fish with a vegetable or two as separate courses.[38]

Many cookbook authors tried to rival the popular Mrs. Beeton. In the 1880s the Americans Mary Henderson, with *Practical Cooking and Dinner Giving*, and Juliet Corson, in *Practical American Cookery*, were two who published hints to the hostess and etiquette as well as recipes. Their most valuable contribution was a "compromise plan" for American dinners. Miss Corson, superintendent of the New York School of Cookery, wrote her plan with the "marked social changes attendant on the Civil War" in mind. Her section entitled "The American Dinner" outlined a form of service that combined the advantages of both the old English method and the method *à la russe*. The American way, she said, placed the "principal dishes" on the table around a center of flowers, relishes, confectionery, and small sweets "to add to its pleasant aspect" and brought the vegetables in hot to be passed at once by the servants.[39]

Late Nineteenth-Century Dinner Tables

The stage for playing out Victorian dinner dramas of either style was brilliant. Under gaslights a border of flowered service plates and a forest of stemmed glasses—set for as many wines—stretched the length of the table. On each service plate a yard-square napkin, folded neatly in a rectangle or cleverly in the shape of a water lily or bishop's miter, hid a roll or piece of bread cut one inch thick and three inches long. The napkin matched the tablecloth with its Greek, Moresque, Celtic filigree, or diaper patterns, which in 1880 were preferred to the arabesque or fruit patterns of fifty years earlier. Thick baize lay under the cloth. In the "best" houses, knives, forks, and spoons for all courses lay waiting on either side of the service plate, a salad fork to the left of the plate, then a dinner fork, and on the outside a fish fork. To the right of the plate lay the dinner knife, its sharp edge turned in; then a fish knife and a soup spoon. The teaspoon, as before, did not appear until after-dinner tea and coffee were served in the parlor or at the table. In simpler houses many variations, brought from Europe, were handed down from generation to generation. In some few, the soup spoon lay inside the knife. In others, the knife, as at Mrs. Fiske's, lay at right angles to the fork, above the plate. Its blade was apparently used for more than cutting even as late as 1885 when Miss Corson found it necessary to remind her readers tactfully that eating from a knife—a practice "fostered by the old-fashioned two-pronged steel fork which is not often seen now"—was not as "convenient as eating from a three- or four-pronged fork." In many houses people used the knife in a way that is today recognized as The Great American Shift. A German, writing in 1832, spoke of the method as a habit of people on the Continent, "who mostly lay down the knife when they have cut with it, then take in the right hand the fork in order to convey the food to their mouths." This was in contrast, he said, to the method of the English, who "convey the pieces they have cut with the right hand to the mouth with the left hand."[40]

Silverware

The multiplication of silverware in the late nineteenth century was awesome. Stamping machines turned out silver and silver-plated flatwares in enormous variety and quantity. Men made wealthy by these and other machines thronged to buy the new, cheaper table luxuries. People were object mad, and the array of utensils for a fashionable dinner demonstrated it. It wasn't enough to have a knife, fork, and spoon for each of three courses and dessert; a host must have carving knives and forks, serving spoons and forks, cheese knives or scoops, coffee spoons, fish slices and fish forks, entrée forks, cucumber forks, and ice-cream fork-spoons. Hostesses who were up-to-the-minute put each serving implement beside the dish it was to serve and no longer crossed it with its mate near the salt or at the corners of the table, as their grandmothers had. They placed a butter server on the butter dish so that it might be used by diners to transfer butter to individual butter plates, which were also newcomers to the dinner service. They no longer put butter on their dinner plate as their ancestors had.[41]

Everyone high or low used table, dish, or plate mats on the cloth. For supper, or tea, on a bare table some used them at each place and under each dish; some put mats only at children's places. Doilies lay under finger bowls and sometimes served to wipe fingers, as of old.[42]

China

If the eighteenth-century and early nineteenth-century hostess had a wide choice of dinnerwares, the Victorian hostess had an almost limitless one. She could select from the ironstone and granite wares that flooded the market to supplement creamware and porcelain. She could choose from French, India, Gold Band, and "printed" wares that replaced embossed, shell, and feather-edge creamware. "Porcelain opaque ware," which imitated white French china in shape, finish, and weight, existed for her everyday use. The fanciful shapes that proliferated for her party table challenged her daring, taste, and pocket-book. In a sturdy earthenware called majolica, pink shells large enough to serve as platters were fashionable and so were shell-pink, shell-like dessert, salad, and oyster sets of the kind Mrs. Blaine saw at Mrs. Creswell's luncheon party. As a party meal of the 1880s shifted from course to course, each course displaying a different bright set of plates accompanied by ruby, bohemian, amber, or silvered glass, the table blazed a testimony to its creator's artistry—varicolored and entertaining as a kaleidoscope.

2

Centers Pyramidal and Bold

The Pyramid for the Centre I would have of very rich Cut glass but not too large; the 4 for the corners may be omitted, unless they come very cheap.

Joseph Barrell, Boston, 1795[1]

A table set and ready for dinner three hundred years ago had no centerpiece but extended flat and unbroken without candles, decoration, or drinking vessels. Plates, platters, and bowls covered the surface with nothing to distract the attention of diners as they concentrated on choosing from among the foods spread out to view (Fig. 2:1).

Roasts or Vegetables as Centers

Early in the eighteenth century, instead of filling the center area with a pair or quartet of flat dishes holding ordinary meats and vegetables, a housewife who sought novelty chose a particularly handsome roast or decorative vegetable for the exact center (Fig. 2:2). With a try at drama she raised it above the rest of the dishes so that it would stand out in the manner of a fountain rising among the balanced and evenly spaced beds of a baroque garden. She had at her disposal several devices to give the dish height. One such device was the "fashionable ring to set a dish upon in the middle of the table," which the Thomas Joneses of Virginia ordered from London in 1728. It derived from such "wicker rings to set under dishes" as were listed in the 1677 inventory of Mary Norton, a modest Massachusetts housewife, and from the rings of "hard metal" that Governor Burnet's staff used in Boston in 1729. New Yorkers Susannah and Samuel Cornell owned a handsome pierced-silver example made by the New York silversmith Myer Myers around 1760 (Fig. 2:3). Dish rings similar to the Cornells' came in quantity from the benches of Irish silversmiths, but the Cornells' ring is the only known American example.[2]

Dish Rings

FIG. 2:1. E. Read, *A View of the Inside of Guildhall as It Appear'd on Lord Mayor's Day*, 1760. From *Gentleman's Magazine* 31 (December 1761): following p. 548. (Winterthur Museum Library.)

FIG. 2:2. Family dinner with a roast as centerpiece served in tortoiseshell earthenware of the kind associated with the potter Thomas Whieldon, England, 1740–60. (Winterthur Museum.)

FIG. 2:3. Dish or table ring by Myer Myers (1723–95). New York, 1760–80. Marked *Myers* in script. Inscribed SSC for Susannah and Samuel Cornell, New York and New Bern. Silver; H. 10 cm., D. (top) 19.7 cm., (base) 22.5 cm. (Mabel Brady Garvan Collection, Yale University Art Gallery.)

Standing Salts

If a household had no dish ring, standing salts of delft, pewter, or silver would do to raise a dish (Fig. 2:4). Both spool-shaped salts and salts with little arms could be put to use, although the original purpose of the arms that seventeenth-century Londoner Randle Holme called stays had been to hold the covers of sixteenth-century steeple salts. In seventeenth-century French and Dutch paintings salts can be seen supporting a plate or shallow dish of fresh or preserved fruit just as if they were the spool-shaped "stands for a dish" that Holme said were commonly used "to set another dish upon . . . to make the feast look full and noble as if there were two tables or one dish over another" (Figs. 2:5, 2:6).[3]

FIG. 2:4. Standing salt, Lambeth, 1640–60. Delft (tin-glazed earthenware); H. 11.4 cm., D. (base) 13.5 cm. (Winterthur Museum, 64.624.)

Salvers

A third device available to the housewife who wanted to give dignity to a center dish had come on the scene in the seventeenth century. This was the salver. Thomas Blount's often-quoted *Glossographia* called it "a new fashioned piece of wrought plate, broad and flat with a foot underneath, used in giving beer or other liquid thing to save or preserve the carpet or clothes from drops." Charles Carroll ordered one in 1768 from London, asking for "1 fashionable genteel large silver waiter or salver [and] one plain ditto about eight or nine inches in diameter or over." "This must be cup or pillar footed," he wrote, "as it is for the middle of a table . . . to support a dish." He also ordered "1 salver or something proper to raise a middle dish on table of either glass or china, rather china."[4]

FIG. 2:6. Jan Treck (1606–52?), *Still Life*. Amsterdam. Oil on canvas; H. 76.5 cm., W. 63.8 cm. (National Gallery, London.)

FIG. 2:5. Abraham Bosse, *Dinner of Kings*. Paris, 1633. Engraving; H. 115.5 cm., W. 138.4 cm. (Prints Division, New York Public Library.)

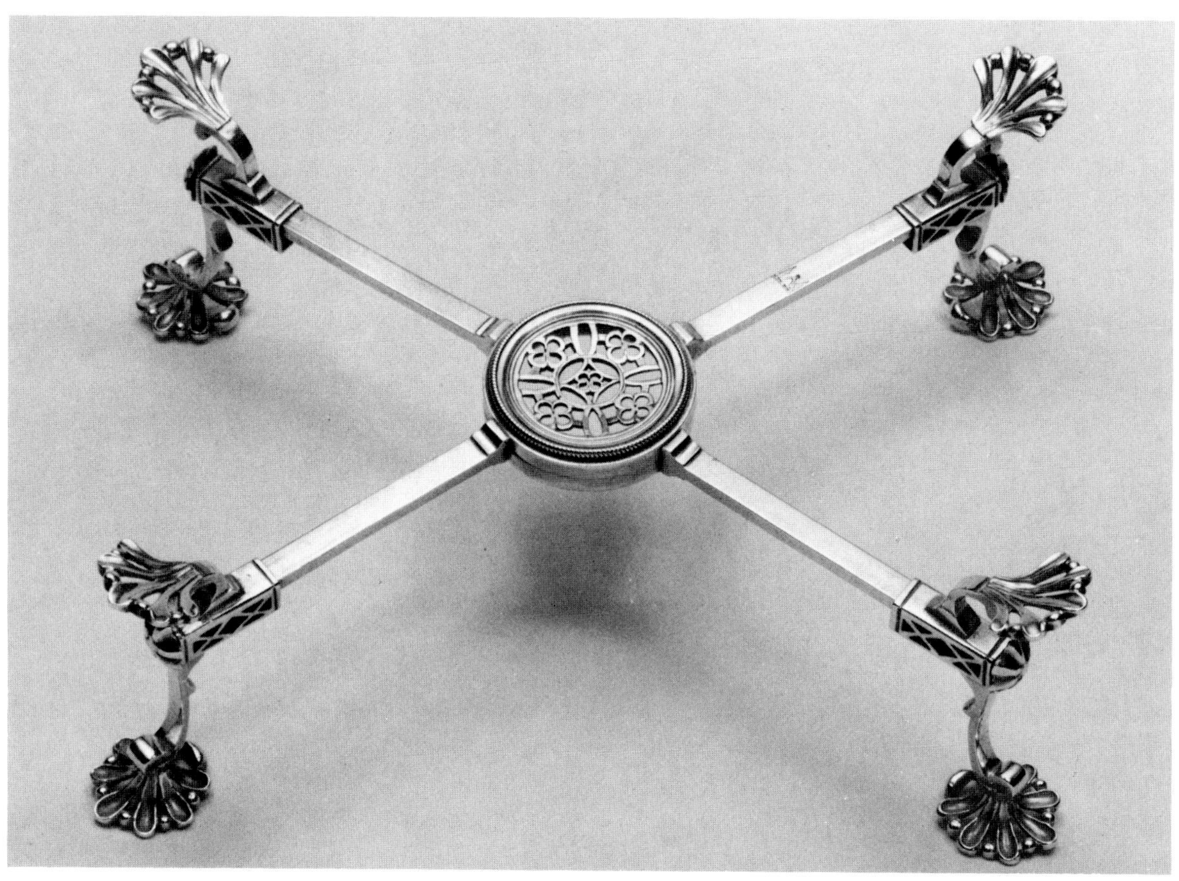

FIG. 2:7. Dish cross by Myer Myers (1723–95), New York. Silver; H. 7.8 cm., W. 27.5 cm. (Mabel Brady Garvan Collection, Yale University Art Gallery.)

Dish Crosses

Householders, if they chose, could raise a middle dish with a dish cross, or table cross, a contrivance that consisted of two small bars crossed and mounted horizontally on short legs and fitted with brackets that could be slid back and forth to hold dishes of any size (Fig. 2:7). The dish cross came in two forms. One form was designed simply to raise a dish above the table level. The other, which was supplied with a wick and a small font for oil, both raised a dish and kept it warm. Most American households had no dish cross. Those that did owned no more than one. Even the well-equipped closets of the Binghams and Cadwaladers of Philadelphia and the Edward Lloyds of Wye, Maryland, held only one dish cross, a fact suggesting that on an eighteenth-century table, where balance was required, the one acceptable place for the cross was the center. American silversmiths may have made dish crosses in quantity, but only one—again by Myer Myers—is definitely known to be American, although a half dozen bearing their makers' initial marks have been so attributed. If American-made crosses were scarce in the eighteenth century, American householders could order English examples from agents in London or from friends in Europe, as George Washington did in a letter to Lafayette in 1783; or they could buy the imports from such silversmiths as Edmond Milne of Philadelphia, who, in 1763, advertised "imported ex's with sliders and lamps for dish stands."[5]

Middleboards, or Frames

Whereas rings, salvers, and crosses gave height to middle dishes during the first and second courses of an eighteenth-century dinner, ornamented middleboards, or frames, and several other specially designed centers provided height for sweetmeats and fruits during dessert. Early in the century a multilevel middleboard of wood and osier, either square, hexagonal, or star-shaped, displayed baskets full of comfits and fruits. Painted, gilded, or covered with silver or gilt paper, the middleboard was the descendant of the voider, or flat wicker basket, that before the seventeenth century held the fruit, nuts, and sweetmeats called spicery (Fig. 2:8, Pl. 2:9). John Nott in his *Cooks and Confectioners Dictionary*, first published in 1723 (borrowing from François Massialot's 1692 *Nouvelle instruction pour les confitures*), described it as "a great board in the middle [of a table] in the Form of a Square . . . or Hexagon or any other figure you please, . . . usually made of osier-twigs, in the Form of a Basket, and . . . gilt, silver'd over, or painted like fine earthen Ware." Elizabeth Pitts of Boston in 1726 owned what may have been a middleboard. It was an object listed in her inventory as a "japann'd fruit table" valued high at thirty shillings.[6]

FIG. 2:8. Detail of pyramids of fruit on a wooden frame, or middleboard. From Nicholas de l'Armessin shop, *Habit de fruitière*. Paris, ca. 1700. Etching. (The Old Print Shop, New York City.)

Fruit Pyramids

The fruits displayed on a middleboard or frame usually rose in pyramids. If the pyramids were made of fresh berries or of such small symmetrical fruits as cherries or grapes, construction gave the hostess little trouble. She could pile the fruits neatly with or without a cement of icing (Figs. 2:10, 2:11). If the pyramids were of larger fruits she could put plates in graduated sizes between layers to maintain stability. Sweetmeat pyramids, on the other hand, posed greater problems. To make them symmetrical and cohesive she would use a tin cone. Following the confectioner François Massialot's suggestion, she held the cone point down and filled it with sugared fruits and nuts, cementing them one at a time with icing and interspersing them with flowers. When she upended the cone onto a plate or platter, the cone deposited a stable, symmetrical, toothsome, and decorative pile (Pl. 2:12). This she could make more "ingenious," as eighteenth-century cookbooks liked to say, by spinning a web of sugar

Sweetmeat Pyramids

FIG. 2:10. Dessert of fruit with delft (tin-glazed earthenware) tableware and tiles. (Queen Anne Dining Room, 1750–60, Winterthur Museum.)

FIG. 2:11. *A Dessert . . . for Twelve . . . .* From François Massialot, *Le Cuisinier royal et bourgeois*. (Vehling Collection, Cornell University Library.)

FIG. 2:13. *The Desert Thus.* From Charles Carter, *The Compleat Practical Cook*, p. 41. (Winterthur Museum Library.)

around it. Stationed at opposite corners of a middleboard in the manner John Nott recommended, or placed directly on the table in pairs, quartets, or trios as Charles Carter advocated in *The Compleat Practical Cook* (Fig. 2:13), pyramids in porcelain platters or shallow bowls proclaimed the superlative taste of both host and hostess. The pyramids did so in great numbers on the outdoor fête tables of Versailles and throughout the succeeding hundred and fifty years or lesser tables on both sides of the Atlantic (Fig. 2:14). As late as 1848, Catharine Beecher constructed one for the center of a table by buttering the outside of a stiff paper cone, frosting it, then sticking onto it with more frosting a great supply of macaroons, kisses, and "other ornamental articles" (Fig. 2:15). The frosting hardened so that she could remove the cone and display the pyramid on a platter. She put a bit of waxed candle with it, which, she said, made a fine effect. The candle, it is to be guessed, went inside the cone so that its light might flicker charmingly through the cracks.[7]

FIG. 2:14. Pyramids of dry sweetmeats. From Jean le Pautre, engraver, "La Quatrième Journée, 1676," in *Festes à Versailles*, volume of *Le Cabinet du Roi*, n.p. (Winterthur Museum Library.)

Rashly gilding the lily, hostesses added not only candles but gilt paper, green vines, artificial or fresh flowers, and leaves to their pyramids. Henry Busk's long poem *The Dessert* urged them to decorate a dish of apples with flowers and a center pyramid with gilt paper and vines:

> The dish by ruddy-cheeked Pomona crown'd
> Let Flora deck with lily-fingers round.
> Your center rise pyramidal and bold
> Where mimic gems may rival real gold.
> The loving myrtle and fraternal vine
> With leaves alternate, broad and slender, twine.[8]

Busk's high-flown language with its classical allusions doubtless raised a hostess's efforts to a lofty plane. Certainly, if she followed his ideas for fruit, flowers, sweetmeats, and leaves, her pyramids rose high and ornamental.

Pyramids of Salvers

Magnificent though fruit pyramids and sweetmeat pyramids might be, a third kind of pyramid rivaled them in dramatic effect. Late in the seventeenth century in England and about 1730 in America, daring individuals first mounted two to five footed glass salvers, graduated in size, one on top of the other. They put deep narrow jelly and syllabub glasses on each salver and crowned the whole with a pedestaled sweetmeat glass or a very small salver. Complete with a charge of "wet and dry sweetmeats in glass baskets or little plates, colour'd jellies, creams, &c., biscuits, crisp'd almonds, and little knicknacks, and bottles of flowers prettily intermix'd, the little top salver [with] a large preserved fruit in it," as the popular eighteenth-century cookbook author Hannah Glasse prescribed, these dessert centers took all prizes for resplendence (Pls. 2:20, 2:41, Figs. 2:17–19).[9]

Jelly and Syllabub Glasses

Indeed, one or more pyramids glinting in the afternoon sunlight on a dessert table following a dinner party or shimmering in the candlelight of a tea party or ball supper must have been considered devastating by American hostesses, judging by the many pyramids of glass salvers, jellies, and syllabub glasses listed in their household inventories between 1760 and 1820 and by the numerous advertisements for them in newspapers from Boston to Charleston throughout two thirds of the eighteenth century. As early as 1731 the *New England Journal* offered "whip syllabub and jelly glasses." In 1774 the *Boston News-Letter* had for sale "glass salvers or waiters chiefly from 9 to 13 inches . . . sold in pyramids or singly." The *News-Letter*, in addition to salver pyramids, offered "orange or top glasses" together with "common jellies and syllabubs . . . from 5 shillings to 8 shillings a dozen." Jellies and syllabubs could be either one- or

FIG. 2:15. Sweetmeat pyramids of seedcakes with other desserts in Chinese export porcelain. (Charleston Dining Room, 1770–80, Winterthur Museum.)

two-handled and either "bubbled, buttoned, common acorn, or bellbowl" of the kind Henry William Stiegel offered for sale in a 1772 *Pennsylvania Gazette*. Or they could be of cut glass like those advertised by the importers Mansell, Corbett & Company of Charleston in 1766 when they had received from London "cut salvers and pyramids containing 9 cut jelly, 4 sullibubs, 4 cut bottles with flowers, 8 cut sweet-meat cups with flower handles, and a cut and scallop'd top glass." Andrew Oliver's "pyramid of 5 glass salvers and sweet-meat glass," towering with its cargo of small vases of flowers and good things to eat, entertained proper Bostonians before the Revolution.[10]

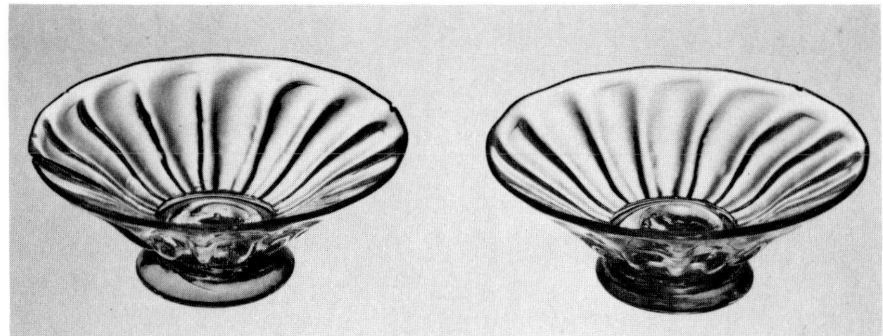

FIG. 2:17. Comfit dishes, England, 1730–80. Lead glass; H. 2.2 cm., D. 6.7 cm. (Winterthur Museum, 69.37.1, 2, ex coll. Milton H. Biow.)

FIG. 2:18. Flower bottles, England, 1730–80. Lead glass; H. 9.5 cm. (Winterthur Museum, 69.142.1–6.)

FIG. 2:19. Trade card of Maydwell and Windle's Cut-Glass Warehouse, London, 1765. (Heal Collection, Prints Department, British Museum.)

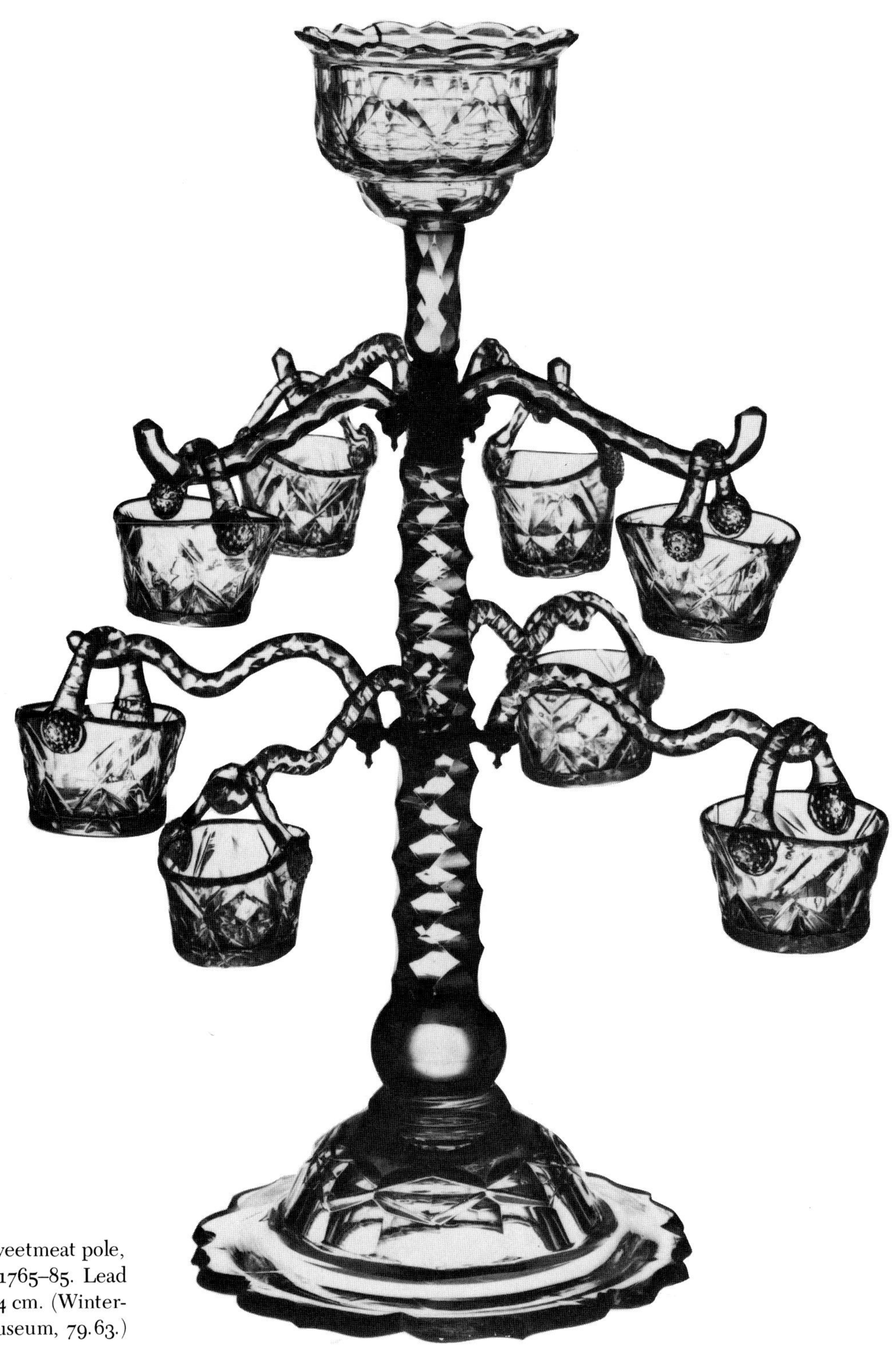

FIG. 2:21. Sweetmeat pole, England, 1765–85. Lead glass; H. 43.4 cm. (Winterthur Museum, 79.63.)

Sweetmeat Poles

Another cut glass centerpiece, this one in the form of a pole on a spreading foot, held out arms that bore little glass comfit baskets. Sometimes enriched with cut glass prisms that rose from the arms, it surpassed both the plain and the cut glass pyramids of salvers in grace if not in usefulness (Fig. 2:21). Beside such brilliant conceits of glass, cream-colored ceramic pyramids must have seemed insipid. Certainly they were completely useless. Nevertheless people made them for sale. Ebenezer Bridgham of Boston advertised them from 1772 to 1777 along with printed, gilt, and plain cream-colored salvers, fruit baskets, and pickle stands; and an English pottery manual, possibly from the Spode factory around 1816, pictured them in a step pyramid form fourteen inches tall, six and a half inches in diameter at the base, and topped by a "knob."[11]

Step Pyramids

Compotes

By 1800 rings, dish crosses, frames, and pyramids were going out of style, but people were still inclined to elevate dishes above the level of the table. Glassblowers, pewterers, silversmiths, and potters complied with fashion by putting pedestals on dishes, producing what contemporary inventories and bills termed footed salads, fruit bowls, compotiers, compotes, cream bowls, and sweetmeat dishes (Figs. 2:22, 2:24–26, Pl. 2:23). A hostess would place a single,

FIG. 2:22. Compotier and footed cake dish, attributed to Derby, England, ca. 1790–1811. Porcelain; H. (compotier) 17.8 cm., (dish) 6.3 cm. (Winterthur Museum, 65.2918.1, 2.)

footed dish holding preserved fruit, which she might call simply "sweetmeats" or fashionably refer to as *compote de fruits*, in the central spot of a dessert arrangement; or she would stand a pair, quartet, or octet of such dishes in formally balanced array across the central area, their shallow bowls filled, if not with preserved fruit, then with nuts, molded jellies, creams, or whole fresh fruits. She would buy compotiers with or without covers and stands singly or as part of dessert services like those the New York merchant James Brooks ordered from England, which were made up of twelve or twenty-four plates, six or twelve compotiers, one centerpiece, and three molds, which he termed shapes.[12]

FIG. 2:24. Footed dish by Crossman, West, and Leonard, Taunton, Mass., 1829–30. Britannia with traces of gilt, blue, and green paint; H. 10.8 cm., D. 17.4 cm. (Winterthur Museum, 64.130.)

FIG. 2:25. Detail of fruit in lobed footed bowls, France, ca. 1750. From a panel of brocaded silk. (Los Angeles County Museum of Art, Mr. and Mrs. Allen C. Balch Fund.)

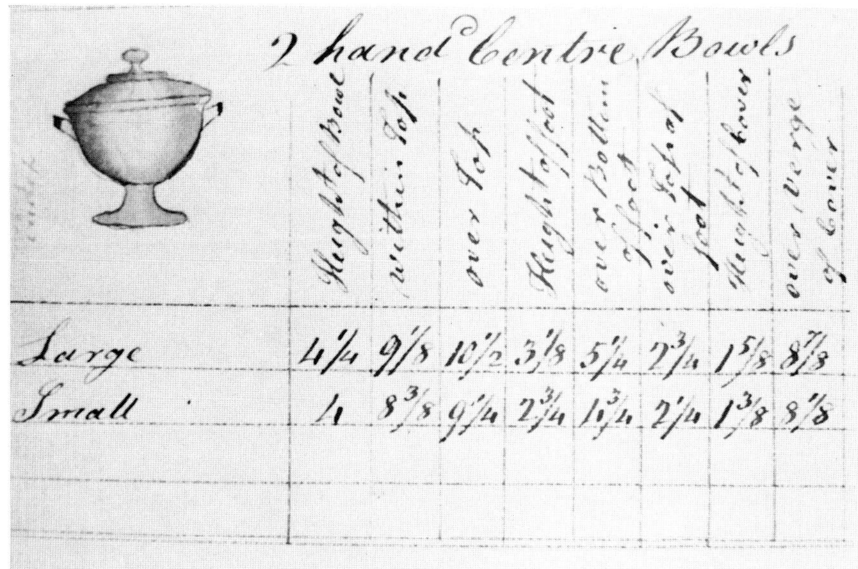

2 hand Centre Bowls

	Height of Bowl	within top	over top	Height of foot	over Bottom of foot	over top of foot	Height of cover	over verge of cover
Large	4 1/4	9 1/8	10 1/2	3 1/8	5 1/4	2 3/4	1 5/8	8 7/8
Small	4	8 3/8	9 1/4	2 3/4	4 3/4	2 1/4	1 3/8	8 1/8

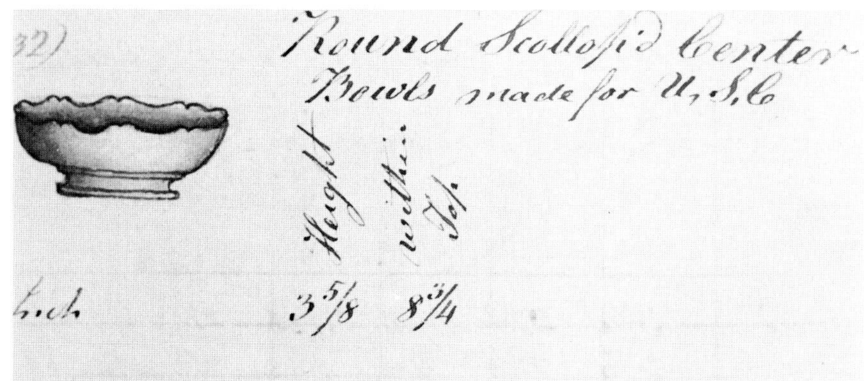

Round Scollop'd Center Bowls made for U.S.C

	Height	within top
inch	3 5/8	8 3/4

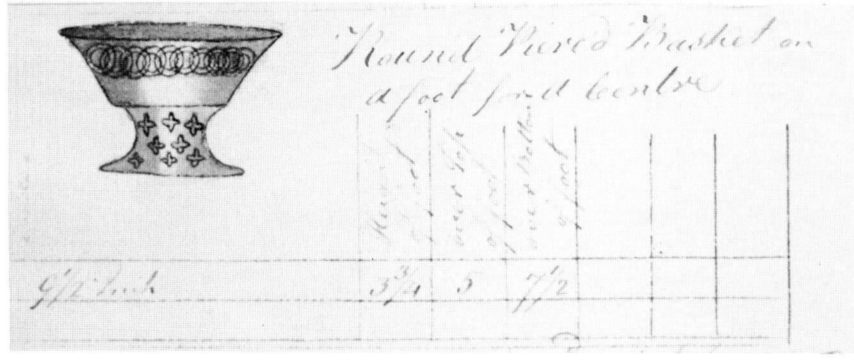

Round Pierced Basket on a foot for a centre

	Height	over top of foot	over Bottom of foot
inch	3 1/4	5	7 1/2

FIG. 2:26. Centers. From a manuscript potter's manual, attributed to the Spode factory, England, ca. 1815–21, pp. 43, 96, 115. (Winterthur Museum Library, DMMC.)

Plateaux

Several decorative and practical centers evolved from the wooden ornamental frame or middleboard of the eighteenth century. Made either of wood, earthenware, porcelain, plated silver, silver, or silver gilt, they were known by the French terms *plat de ménage*, or *plateau*, and *surtout de table*. The latter was known also by the English term *epergne*. The *plat de ménage* held bottles and casters for vinegars and seasonings as a useful household *plat*, or tray, should. The plateau, more decorative than useful, held only bisque porcelain figurines, candlesticks, candelabra, and/or small vases of flowers on its three-part mirrored surface (Fig. 2:27). It was greatly admired in America and extended down the center of many modish tables after the Revolution. Edward Lloyd ordered "an elegant and by no means paltry" six-foot-four-inch example suitable to his long Maryland table, with twenty-nine alabaster images to stand inside its silver gilt balustrade. The Binghams, equally grand, owned a plateau holding a couple of dozen gods and goddesses. With figures from classical mythology the fashion at federal dinner parties, even the mere quartet of marble Olympians on the *plateau de dessert* with silvered balustrade, which Thomas Jefferson bought in Paris in 1785 for Abigail Adams to use in London, was a reliable conversation piece.[13]

There was no doubt that the plateau was the most fashionable table decoration in the United States at the turn of the century. Like many of his rich friends, Joseph Barrell ordered one from abroad. He wrote to a fellow Bostonian living in London in the spring of 1795: "If you meet with a handsome Cover for a Table of Looking Glass, and a Pyramid of handsome Cut Glass for the middle of the Table, which were formerly some of the great folks, I wish you to buy them." Only two American plateaux are known today. Both were made by New York City silversmiths. One is a simple one-part ovoid galleried tray by Benjamin Halsted (1734–1806) made for Daniel Crommelin Verplanck (1761–1834) and his bride in 1789. The other is a tray in the empire style by John W. Forbes (w. 1802–35). Like the plateau at Mount Vernon in 1797 these simple plateaux may have held "alabaster figures taken from the ancient mythology but none of them such as to offend in the smallest degree against delicacy."[14]

The plateau that dignified President Washington's table during state dinners in New York was the focus of interest for many of his visitors. Theophilus Bradbury, congressman from Massachusetts, described it to his daughter in 1797 after he had attended a late-afternoon dinner for twenty presided over by the president and Mrs. Washington and served by four or five liveried servants:

> In the middle of the table was placed a piece of table furniture about six feet long and two feet wide, rounded at the ends . . . either of wood gilded or polished metal, raised only about an inch with a silver rim around it like that 'round a tea board; in the center was a pedestal of plaster of Paris with images upon it, and on each end figures, male and female of the same. It was very elegant and for ornament only.

FIG. 2:27. Plateau by Deniers et Matelin, France, 1817. Gilt bronze; H. (caryatid basket) 34.6 cm., W. 65.1 cm., L. 411.6 cm. (The White House.)

FIG. 2:28. *Surtout de table* holding fruit and sweetmeats for a dessert served in Spode porcelain. (Du Pont Dining Room, 1790–1810, Winterthur Museum.)

This six-foot gold and silver object sat on the table throughout the meal, Mr. Bradbury stated, with "an elegant variety of roast beef, veal, turkey, ducks, fowl, hams, etc.; puddings, jellies, oranges, apples, nuts, almonds, figs, raisins, and a variety of wines and punch . . . placed all around it."[15]

President Monroe's splendid three-part gilt bronze French plateau bordered by leafy swags and set with eight draped classical figures also aroused much comment. When William Greene visited Washington, D.C., in 1841 during the presidency of James K. Polk he went to a state dinner "in the most elaborate style of the palace" served at a thirty-foot table accommodating thirty people. There he saw the plateau and wrote to his daughter Kate, at home in Cincinnati:

> The gold Plateau and spoons which you have heard so much about both made their appearance and are simply *silver*, gold washed. The Plateau is a magnificent thing and is designed mainly to hold lights of which there were forty-two. It is twelve feet long.[16]

All plateaux were not of overpowering size and classical elegance. Many that were favored in England were made of wood. One such piece, painted apple green, displayed vignettes of children at play in blossoming meadows, its three parts bound in brass and standing on brass scroll feet. Another was of mahogany decorated with paper painted in scrolls bearing the date 1793 and the initials *MK.* A third, seen by Lord Colchester in 1796, was painted and ornamented with French white figures and vases of flowers.[17]

Surtouts, or Epergnes

Surtouts de table, or epergnes, rose higher above the table than *plats de ménage* and plateaux and were decidedly more useful than plateaux—at least as plateaux were used by Americans (Fig. 2:28). They held casters to be filled with salt, pepper, dry mustard, and sugar. Often they held bottles to be filled with oil and with mushroom, walnut, tomato, lemon, and cucumber catsups, or with other sauces and vinegars. Some also held baskets or bowls for such delicacies as cucumber pickles and nasturtium pickles, capers and anchovies, fruits and sweetmeats. Massialot, who pictures such a surtout, piles up the central bowl with flowers, oranges, or *limonier*, which may be translated as glacéed citrus fruits (Fig. 2:29). He does not call this surtout, or dormant, an epergne as the English and Americans would. The word *epergne* seems to be an English invention possibly derived from the French *épargne*, "saving,"

FIG. 2:29. Design for a dessert of forty-three sweetmeats and fruits for from twenty to twenty-five people. From François Massialot, *Nouvelle instruction*, new ed., facing p. 516. (Winterthur Museum Library.)

FIG. 2:30. Epergne by William Cripps, London, 1759–60. Silver; H. 40 cm., D. 66.7 cm., W. 66 cm. (Colonial Williamsburg.)

"economy." Eighteenth-century ladies wrote it "appurn" or "epurn." Today, because it is an English word and not a French word, it is properly pronounced "ayparn," "aypurn," or "eppurn," not "epairn."[18] Both graceful and useful, certain pierced rococo epergnes made in England around the middle of the eighteenth century epitomized the society that produced them—a society dedicated on one hand to being insouciant and charming and on the other to plumbing the secrets of nature, a society devoted not only to beauty but also to utility. The "neat polished silver epergne" offered by Stephen Deblois in the *Boston Gazette* in October 1757 and the epergne valued at fifty pounds listed with the silver of William Byrd III of Westover, Virginia, in 1769 were probably both of this serviceable yet infinitely appealing form designed to hold dry sweetmeats and fruit (Fig. 2:30).[19]

FIG. 2:32. Epergne, or *surtout de table*, England, ca. 1800. Owned by Sullivan Dorr, Providence, 1805. Silver on copper, flint glass. (Collection of Frank Mauran, a descendant.)

Late eighteenth-century epergnes, in contrast to the mid eighteenth-century rococo charmers, stood primly on American tables in the newly fashionable restrained and classical style (Fig. 2:31). Philip Schuyler of New York bought one in 1785 by the London silversmith William Pitts, and Sullivan Dorr of Providence ordered one in 1805 from Green, Ward, and Green, London goldsmiths and jewelers, who described it as a "best plated 4-branch Epergne with very richly chased white Silver border all round & 1 large and 4 small cut glass basons" (Fig. 2:32). When such epergnes were centered on a table symmetrically set with an array of four great platters of pineapples, grapes, apples, and plums; four shells of nectarines, figs, peaches, and walnuts; two wine coolers; two branched candlesticks; and four carafes, as suggested by James Williams's *Footman's Guide*, they appeared unquestionably splendid (Fig. 2:33).[20]

FIG. 2:31. Epergne, or *surtout de table*. Sheffield or Birmingham, ca. 1780. Owned by Roger and Elizabeth Thomas, Montgomery Co., Md., who were married in 1781. Silver on copper, flint glass; H. 43.2 cm., W. 41.6 cm. (Winterthur Museum, 70.402.)

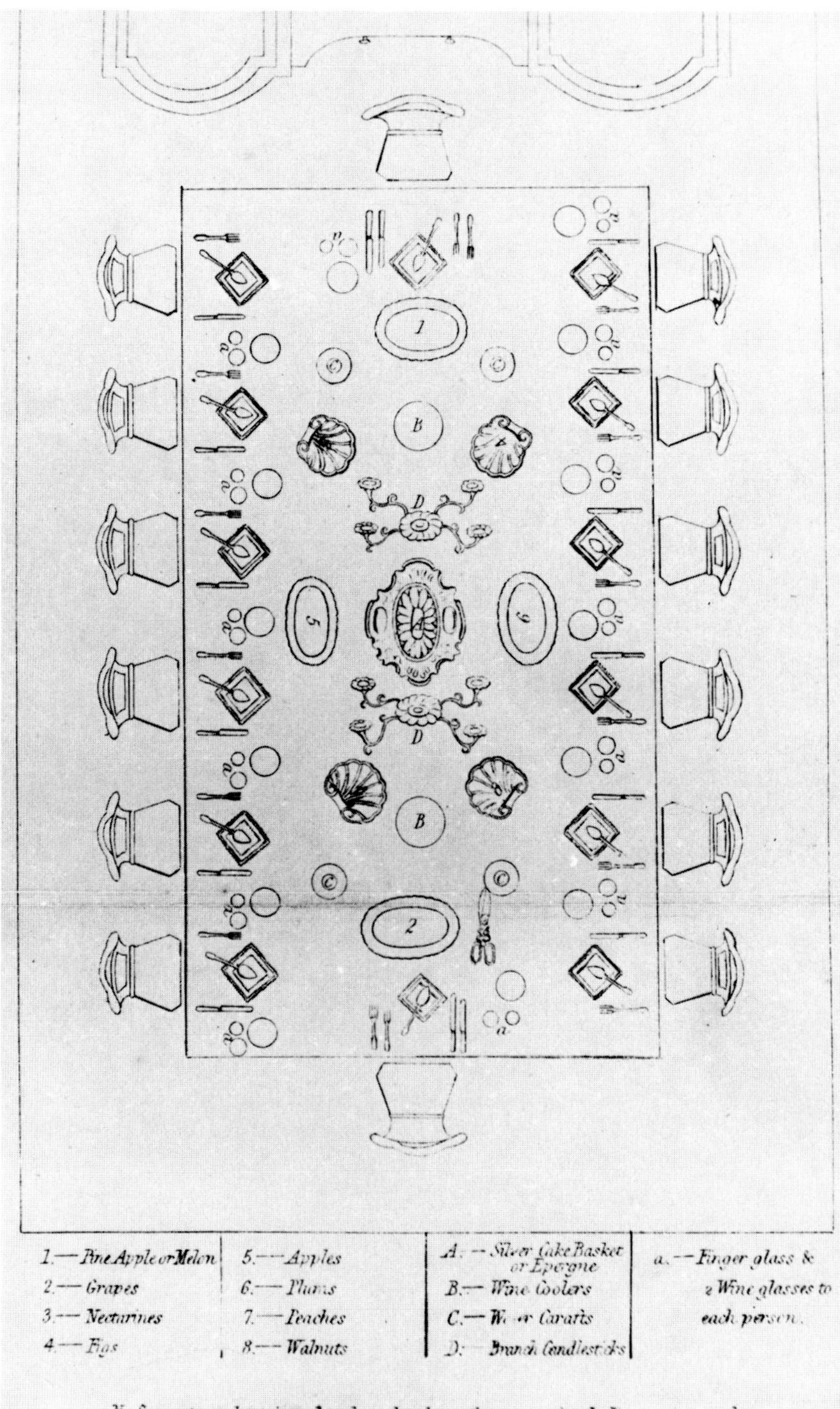

FIG. 2:33. *Dessert for Fourteen*. From James Williams, *The Footman's Guide*, 4th ed., pl. II, frontispiece.

Baskets and Casters

Hosts and hostesses who could not afford or did not choose to use large decorative centers of glass, china, or silver used a silver cake basket or a small caster stand. Williams advocated the basket; Mrs. Fiske used the caster. The cake basket held queen's biscuit, citron cakes, sugar cakes, seed cakes, rout drop cakes, jumbals, shrewsbury cakes, and such other cookies as macaroons, ginger nuts, and kisses. The caster or cruet stand held, as surtouts or epergnes did, two to five bottles filled with oil, vinegar, catsup, salt, sugar, dry mustard, soy, or similar necessities. It was such necessities that a French visitor saw Americans using at dinner for the purpose, as he put it, of "making sauce on their plates" (Fig. 2:34).[21]

FIG. 2:34. Caster stand by John David (1736–98), Philadelphia, 1760–70. Silver; H. 27.3 cm. (Winterthur Museum, 59.3362.)

Sugar and Pastry Scenes

For variety, a hostess with time and patience (or a willing cook) could spurn all manufactured centers and choose a rococo sugar and pastry scene. If she followed one of John Farley's recipes from *The London Art of Cookery*, she might be able to enliven a dessert with what Farley appropriately called "Desart Island." "Form a lump of paste into a rock three inches broad at the top" was his direction for dealing with a handful of piecrust dough. "Colour it," he ordered without wasting words, knowing he spoke to the woman who had gamboge, cochineal, syrup of violets, and spinach juice on her shelf. "Set it," he said, "in the middle of a deep China dish." He did not forget the desert castaway:

> Set a cast figure on [the rock] with a crown on its head and a knot of rock candy at its feet. Then make a roll of paste an inch thick and stick it on the inner edge of the dish, two parts round. Cut eight pieces of eringo roots about three inches long, and fix them upright to the roll of paste on the edge. Make gravel walks of shot comfits round the dish and set small figures on them. Roll out some paste and cut it open like Chinese rails. Bake it and fix it on either side of the gravel walks with gum, and form an entrance where the Chinese rails be, with two pieces of eringo root for pillars.[22]

One longs for a contemporary illustration of this late Georgian confection, but eighteenth-century illustrations of a table set with figures are rare. A French fantasy sketched for the stewards of great French establishments is as close as has been found (Fig. 2:35). The confectioner Joseph Gilliers, author of *Le Cannameliste français*, peoples it with little modeled figures, as Farley did his island. Made of caramel and gum sugar in the guise of Oriental gentlemen, they recline on caramel cushions or stroll among gilt-papered wooden scrolls, their miniature pastry parasols reflected in a many-sectioned mirrored plateau, or level. Surrounding the figures, Venetian goblets holding specimen pears, peaches, or pyramided berries alternate with two-handled cups of cream frothed high, while pierced baskets of fresh or artificial flowers flank three spun sugar fountains.[23]

The hostess who could not or would not make wood and gilt-paper scrolls and failed to own goblets from Venice could stand sugar shepherdesses near a sugar temple rising out of sugar meadow grass to produce a pastoral frivolity sure to charm the society of Voltaire's *siècle de petitesses*, that century of exquisite nothings when harlequins were heroes, women wore full-rigged ships in their hair, and the manner in which one offered snuff was all-important. Her confectionery table scene, however simple, would still be an echo of the great sugar allegories created by professional European confectioners, creations which themselves echoed the subtleties and *trionfi* that in the fifteenth century accompanied the banquet.

FIG. 2:35. Sketch giving two arrangements for a mirrored level. A different plan is shown on each side of the central fountain. From Joseph Gilliers, *Le Cannameliste français* (1768), pl. 5, p. 116. (Winterthur Museum Library.)

Professional Sugarwork

Eighteenth-century German confectioners specialized in making sugar allegories. Their complicated scenes, usually involving a classical temple and a throng of sugar, gum, and pastry gods, partly cast and partly modeled, provided conversation pieces at weddings and on state occasions. Early in June 1765 an ambitious emigré confectioner unveiled one of these massive displays in Philadelphia and advertised it in the hope of getting orders for his party decorations:

> To be seen, in Kensington, at Andrew Hook's, tavern keeper at the sign of Admiral Boscawen; (at 18 pence each person). A very fine and elaborate piece of Sugar-Work or Desart done by a German confectioner; and being such as never before was exhibited in this part of the world.
>
> This piece of art represents a gigantic temple on the top of which stands Fame with both their Britannic majesties' names in a laurel wreath; in the temple is the King of Prussia and the goddess Pallas; at the entries are placed Prussian guards as sentinels; without are trumpeters and kettle drummers on horseback, inviting as it were the four quarters of the globe, who make their appearance in triumphal cars drawn by lions, elephants, camels, and horses; together with many more magnificent representations, not enumerated in this advertisement.
>
> The above confectioner having for many years served the imperial, the royal Prussian, and other princely tables, and being now willing to make himself known in this part of the world, has thought it more expedient for that purpose to exhibit to the public this piece of his art, offering at the same time, if ordered, to make as well more indifferent as also much finer pieces, for gentlemen's tables, weddings, or other entertainments, at the most reasonable rates.[24]

Viewing this sugarwork was a popular pastime for Philadelphians. They flocked to see the grand temple for almost four months with interest that did not flag until October 1765 when the novelty of a double dozen of sugar men and animals began to wane, causing the entrance fee to be dropped from eighteen pence to sixpence. One wonders if the great work brought orders for dessert pieces that used such "figures suitable for Desart Tables [and] fountains, landscapes, scriptures in the Italian manner" as the confectioner Frederick Kreitner advertised in Charleston during the Revolution.[25]

Molds for Home Sugarwork

One wonders also if the sugar *tour de force* stimulated Philadelphia hostesses to greater creativity with their own small molds of wood or alabaster, molds that by the middle of the next century could be bought also of tin, copper, glass, pewter, lead, or sulphur (Figs. 2:36–38). With the molds ladies of either century could make both human and animal figures in two sections, the back and the front. *The Italian Confectioner* recommended that they fill the molds with "fine paste" of flour and butter and allow it to set. They could then easily remove the two sections from the molds by attaching a small handle made from a piece of moist pastry or by striking the molds with a mallet. After smoothing

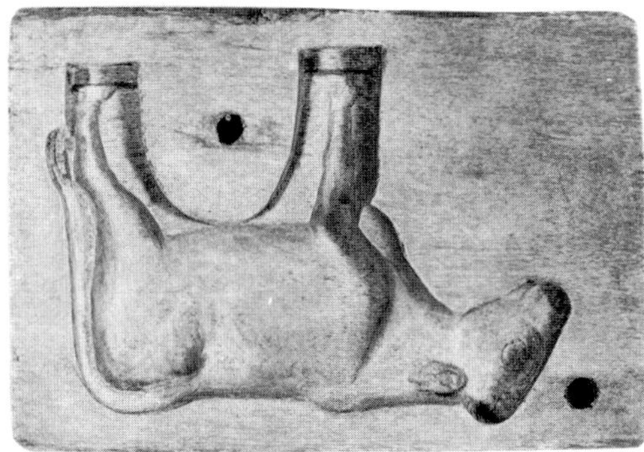

FIG. 2:36. Two-part gum sugar mold, attributed to America, 1800–1850. Cherry; L. 9.5 cm., W. 7.9 cm., D. 2.5 cm. (Winterthur Museum, 61.1397.)

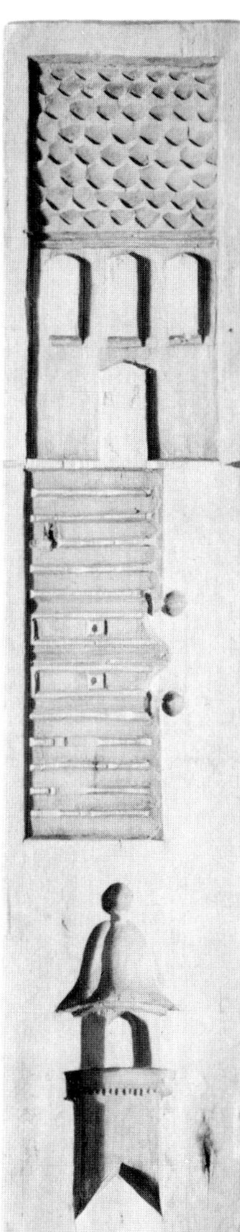

FIG. 2:37. Two-part gum sugar mold forming a four-sided building with steeple and a fence, attributed to Europe, 1800–1850. Linden; L. 30.2 cm., W. 6 cm. (Winterthur Museum, 61.1372.)

FIG. 2:38. Two-part gum sugar mold, attributed to America, 1800–1850. Cherry; L. 9.5 cm., W. 5.2 cm. (Winterthur Museum, 61.1711.)

the sections with a hair pencil they could fasten them together with gum tragacanth or stiff jelly. If they wanted to make figures of almond paste, they could pound almonds in a mortar with orange water or rosewater added to prevent oiling and then sugar, color, and mold the paste.[26]

There were other ways for ladies to mold decorative objects. *The French Cook* directed that when they were imitating fruit, flowers, animals, temples, pyramids, or other ornaments, they were to roll out almond paste as thin as possible on marble and put it in buttered molds. In the Richmond, Virginia, kitchen of Frances Parke Custis, mother of Martha Washington's first husband, servants dried a pound of almond paste over a chafing dish of coals, printed it with molds or modeled it by hand, then gilded it. When they prepared to mold three-dimensional objects, they soaked double molds of wood in water for two hours, dried the surfaces, then filled them with almond paste or with gum sugar. They allowed the resulting figures to get entirely hard before they gilded them and used them to "garnish marchpanes," that is, to decorate large cylindrical cakes covered with almond paste or to embellish thick almond-paste disks and rectangles.[27]

FIG. 2:39. Cherubs for a dessert: The Four Quarters of the Globe, Chelsea or Chelsea-Derby, 1770–75. Porcelain; H. (average) 5.7 cm., D. (base) 13.6 cm. (Winterthur Museum, 58.2622.1–4.)

FIG. 2:40. Detail of a plan for a dessert table using the dessert service Frederick the Great gave to Catherine II in 1771. From Gustav Berthold Volz, "Ein Geschent Friedrichs des Grossen an Katharina II," *Hohenzollern Jahrbuch* (October 22, 1908): 53.

Glass and Ceramic Figures

Early in the eighteenth century ladies on both sides of the Atlantic could supplement or even supplant their sugar- and almond-paste figures with fragile, nonedible sculptures. In 1702 a London glassblower produced "beasts, birds, fowls, images, figures of men and women . . . of all colours of glass," and the Meissen pottery near Dresden in the 1740s began to produce figures in porcelain to take the place of sugar and paste sculpture. The Chelsea pottery in England soon sold entire dessert scenes made up of a few of their own figures to be set against a large piece of German or French architectural porcelain. Figures representing Europe, Asia, Africa, and America were among the "many figures for a Desart" listed in the Chelsea pottery catalogue of 1756 (Fig. 2:39).[28] A sketch of a plan for a dessert service that Frederick the Great of Prussia gave Catherine II of Russia in 1771 suggests how these and other small figures could be used on an ovoid level alternating with small flower pots and vases, surrounded by pierced baskets and cream cups (Fig. 2:40).

Boston hostesses could buy china images from Stephen Deblois who offered in the *Gazette* of October 17, 1757, "a complete set of dessert scenes, with arbors, alcoves, hedging, china flower pots, and with grass and gravel." Elizabeth Hutchinson, one of the foremost of the hostesses in Boston in the 1760s, owned twelve "burnt china images." For Virginia hostesses, the *Virginia Gazette* of July 25, 1766, advertised harlequins, sailors, boys, flowers, birds, squirrels, lambs, dogs, and sheep (Pl. 2:41, Fig. 2:42). Interest in figurines continued unabated even after the Revolution, and little table decorations could still be found in many dining rooms at the turn of the century. Captain Solomon Ingraham's Norwich, Connecticut, rooms in 1806 held "six Chinese figures of Moors and Persians, figures of apples and bananas, and two large ones of a Chinese man and woman." Over twenty years later, Francis Child, Jr., a New York merchant, sold seventy cases of "East India China Toys." With such porcelain trinkets hostesses could create a table scene resembling Governor Tryon's when on gala occasions his table was set with Italian temples, vases, china images, baskets, and flowers. They could also imitate Mrs. Washington's table at the official mansion in New York where in 1791 Senator William Maclay of Pennsylvania saw it "garnished with small images and . . . flowers," which he took care to note were artificial. "A great dinner," he said, "all in the tastes of high life."[29]

Artificial Flowers for the Table

Small sprigs of artificial flowers like those on Martha Washington's dessert table delighted eighteenth-century hostesses. They bought French ones or made their own to put on plateaux, frames, or middleboards, between pyramids of fruit and sweetmeats, and on pyramids of glass salvers (see Figs. 2:16, 2:19, 2:35, 2:40, 2:41). Occasionally a hostess used fresh flowers if she had no artificial ones, although real flowers for the table, particularly in the early years of the rococo century, were considered countrified. To be sure, a hostess always used fresh flowers when she decorated perishable foods. She topped a molded orange jelly with a single flower or crowned it with a wreath. She garlanded the plate that held a glass bowl of floating island and floated blossoms on the soft custard between its islands of egg white and sugar. She capped with blossoms a dozen codlin apples that had been baked and coated with a sifting of fine sugar, plunged a sprig of borage into a molded lemon cream, and planted a sprig of myrtle in a dish of apple snow.[30]

Fresh Flowers on Foods

FIG. 2:42. Middleboard, figurines of Whieldon-type earthenware, and pyramids of fruit. (Charleston Dining Room, 1760–70, Winterthur Museum.)

FIG. 2:43. Holly in the vases of a garniture. (Bowers Parlor, 1795, Winterthur Museum.)

FIG. 2:45. Flowers in and figurines between the vases of a garniture. From the trade card of John Morris, china merchant of Lincoln's-Inn Fields, London, 1777–93. (Heal Collection, Prints Department, British Museum.)

FIG. 2:44. Detail showing punch table and mantel with greenery. From *Christmas Gambols*. London, 1780. Engraving. (Courtesy, Lewis Walpole Library.)

Fresh Flowers in the House

An eighteenth-century hostess used real flowers on food with only decoration in mind; she used flowers and growing plants throughout the house because she felt that an aura of good health came with them, as it did with herbs (Fig. 2:43). To hold the house flowers she kept such vessels as the "delft flower pots with handles" sold by John Welch of Boston in 1758 and the "flower pot of silver" that Nicholas Bayard of New York owned in 1765. The pots probably held fresh-cut flowers, as Randle Holme suggested they do when in 1688 he defined a flowerpot as "a jug with two ears, or a pot double-handled . . . much used to keep flowers fresh in chambers and windows having water put into them."[31] Eighteenth-century English engravings picture double-handled ceramic urns or narrow-mouthed jugs with little bunches of flowers stiffly protruding and show two-handled vases of several kinds filled with flowers, holly, or other leafy branches, standing on mantels as garniture (Figs. 2:44, 2:45). English engravings also picture slightly flaring cylinders that may have been called flowerpots. Certainly these containers resemble today's flowerpots. Filled with growing plants, they stand on windowsills or on dessert tables in the manner of the little flaring cylinders shown on the dessert plan for Frederick the Great's gift (see Fig. 2:40).

Flowerpots, whether juglike or cylindrical, were not the only flower containers that American householders used. As paintings and engravings attest, flower glasses, glass flower bottles, flower jars, and flower horns, or cornucopias, held blossoms on small tables, windowsills, mantels, and walls, and in the center area of dining tables. Probably delft or porcelain bowls of the large, broad, punch-bowl kind to be seen in English engravings holding flowers on English hearths held flowers at some time or other on American hearths as well.

Although American and English travelers had long been exposed to large vases of flowers on ultrafashionable European dining tables, large vases did not come to Anglo-Saxon tables until the nineteenth century. Lord Castelmaine, when he was the English ambassador to Rome, had seen them on Roman tables in 1688, and English readers of *Nouvelle instruction* knew that Massialot put flowers in the center bowl of a *surtout de table* (see Fig. 2:29). They also knew that large vases were to be seen on Louis XV's table (Fig. 2:46). But not until

FIG. 2:46. Detail of Louis XV's dining table set with flowers, May 15, 1744. From Pierre de Caraman, "Les Bonheurs et les dangers du Comte de Caraman," *L'Illustration*, no. 4787 (December 1, 1934): n.p. (Author's library.)

the end of the first quarter of the nineteenth century did the practice of using many flowers in a vase placed in the exact center of a dining table take hold in England and the United States. Even when a Spode potter designed a "Bowpot Centre" around 1816 it was intended not for the exact center but for a position in the *center area* along with other matching bowpot centers.[32] An American mother of the bride, writing to her son who was in London on business, tells us where flowers, flowerpots, and vases were used in a Philadelphia house in 1816:

> The morning of the 8th of June was clear and fine; not a cloud obscured the horizon throughout the day, and Lydia's friends seemed to vie with each other in sending her elegant presents of flowers. Some very elegant bunches came without any name, one or two sent by their friends, wishing to remain incog. In short they were so numerous that after decorating the parlour we put quantities in the cellar until evening for to ornament the supper table. . . . The company except bridesmaids and groomsmen were invited to come at 2 o'clock except a few who were invited to come at 7 in the evening. . . . The table was set in the room over the back parlour, and accommodated the company nicely. The dinner was abundant, well cooked and handsomely served up . . . and as thee could not be with us, . . . Lydia and Mary . . . placed thy likeness on the sideboard with a handsomely dressed flower pot on each side. . . . After retiring from the table the company enjoyed themselves according to their own pleasure either in walking the rooms, in groups conversing, or in any way that suited the fancy of the individual best. . . . We sat down to supper at half past 8—and here the bridesmaids and groomsmen had displayed their taste and fancy in disposing of the flowers which the generosity of their friends had supplyd. The choicest flowers were called to dress a vase opposite the bride, the bride cake was simply decorated with the white jassamine sprigs & lemon blossoms laid round it on the glass salver on which it stood. Aquilla had taken great interest in having a ring put in the bride cake which occasioned some pleasant excitement of who should be the fortunate finder.
>
> Having deviated from the bride to the table and cake I must now return to her and the groom who were seated immediately in front of the window, and to the distribution of flowers. An elegant wreath had been prepared, form'd by laurel (in bloom) and oak leaves with jassamine intertwined and ornamented with flowers of various hues. The wreath was suspended from the drapery of a white dimity curtain and hung immediately over their heads. It had a very fine effect. Vases of flowers were placed on different parts of the table, which when seen in contrast with the jellies, blanch mange, and pyramid ice cream formed a very handsome variety. Strawberries and cherrys were also in season with which the table was abundantly supply'd.[33]

FIG. 2:47. Detail of reception table. From James Rush, pencil sketches. Philadelphia, 1850. (Library Company of Philadelphia.)

FIG. 2:48. Sketch of reception table. From James Rush, pencil sketches. Philadelphia, 1850. (Library Company of Philadelphia.)

Flowers on the Table Center

Around 1835 the European fashion of center flower vases reached America. Thomas Walker saw what he called "a huge centrepiece of plate and flowers" in 1837, and Catherine Sedgwick in 1839 witnessed to the fact that there were center flowers in New York in the "quite novel" style of the dinner *à la russe* she saw in Frankfort, with its "china vase" holding a "magnificent pyramid of flowers."[34]

With the coming of the central bouquet, table centers of variety and originality went out of fashion. From 1840 to the end of the century, hostesses, when practicing the art of dessert table decoration, worked only with flowers or fruit in tall metal or glass containers and gave all sugarwork over to professional confectioners who made *pièces montées*, or "set pieces," for them to buy. The palette of the dessert artist in the home was cut in two.

A Victorian Table

A party plan offering festive fare for the entertainment of Philadelphia's best families made use of the nineteenth-century large flower vase and professional confectionery. The plan was conceived by Dr. and Mrs. James Rush for their new home, opened in 1850 after months of building. Dr. Rush and his wife, Phoebe Ann Ridgway, were noted for their parties and had designed their house with entertainment in mind. Sydney George Fisher, a frequent guest at Rush affairs, pronounced the new house to be full of "fine rooms splendidly furnished, . . . with extensive conservatories filled with bloom, perfume, and verdure."[35] Dr. Rush, who was an accomplished draftsman with a good inward eye, drew plans both for the outside of his dream house on Fourth Street beyond the Schuylkill and for the inside, readied for a grand reception. His drawings show in detail two adjoining rooms at the moment the doors are thrown open to surprise the guests (Figs. 2:47, 2:48). The great table, which Fisher said could accommodate sixty persons, stretches endlessly, shimmering in the light of thirty tall candles and thirty gas jets of two great chandeliers. The vast cloth hangs evenly halfway to the floor, its surface all but hidden under six many-branched candelabra, a tree, and six tall vases massed with flowers. Two thick cylinders of cake decorated with birds and elevated on salvers, two towering *pièces montées* of sugar and pastry (Fig. 2:49), six pyramids of fruit in footed bowls, and piles of fruit in countless baskets march down the center. On side tables, six joints of meat and roasts of fowl, an urn of coffee, more fruit, and more cake add to the immensity of the spread, while countless carafes, decanters, and wineglasses surrounded by a bulwark of plates bordering the table in piles of three await the guests. Decanters and wineglasses turned upside down stand not only on the side table but also on the main table.

Late Nineteenth-Century Party Tables

The Rushes' style of dessert setting, with its new tall vases, elevated dishes, and heavy candelabra, remained in fashion both for dinners and for evening parties right through the late Victorian and Edwardian years (Pl. 2:50). The white tablecloth, cylindrical cakes, decorative figures, pyramids of ice, and baskets of fruit—themselves all eighteenth-century holdovers—also remained. As the century progressed past the halfway mark, the elevated dishes grew more important and ubiquitous. Mrs. Beeton called them "tazzas, or dish with stem,

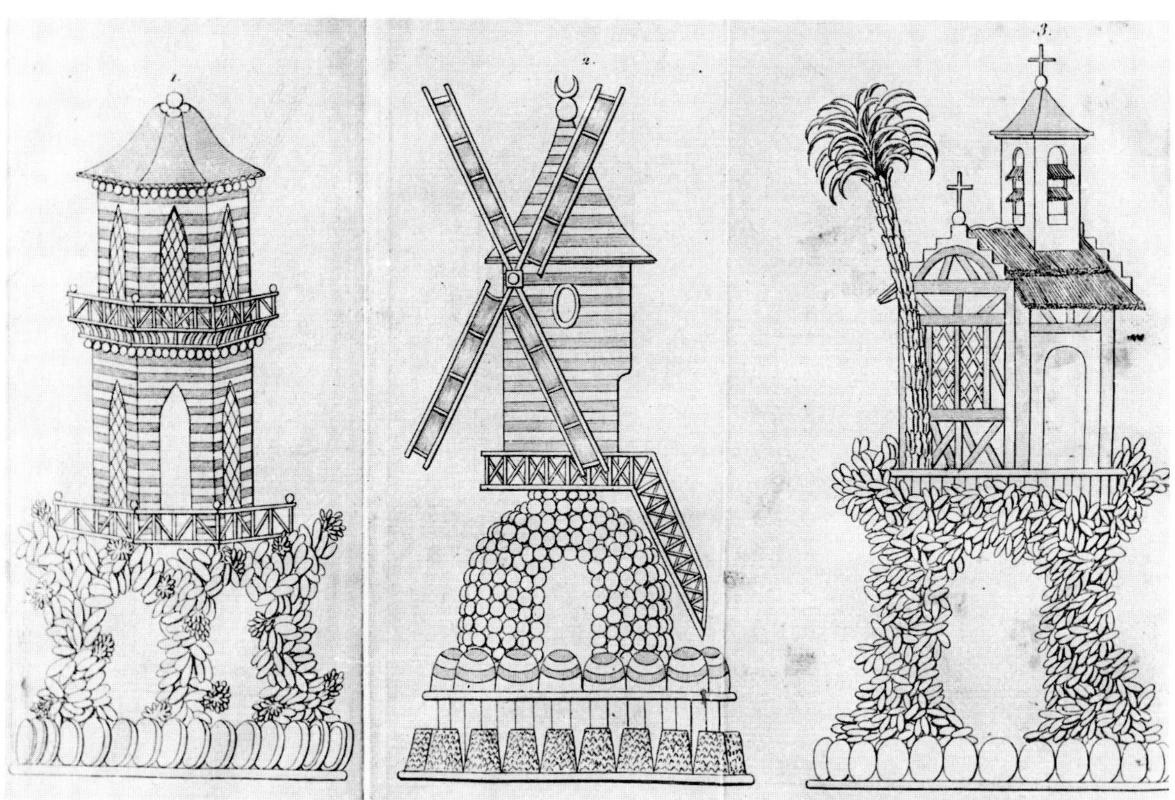

FIG. 2:49. *Pièces montées.* From M. A. Carême, *Le Patissier royal parisien,* 2 vols. (Paris: J. G. Dentu, 1815), 1:pl. 24, facing p. 429. (Vehling Collection, Cornell University Library.)

FIG. 2:51. Centerpiece, or tazza, by John Samuel Hunt, England, ca. 1860. Silver gilt, glass; H. 53 cm., W. (base) 31.7 cm. (Courtesy, Museum of Fine Arts, Boston.)

. . . now the favorite shape for dessert dishes," using, as was fashionable, the Italian word for cup because the stemmed dish resembled the sixteenth-century flat and shallow cup on pedestal (Fig. 2:51). "According to the general mode," she said, "they are placed down the center of the table, a tall and short dish alternately" (Fig. 2:52).[36]

Flower and Leaf Decorations

Flower and leaf decorations proliferated in the next two decades, with vine, laurel, holly, bay, or other broad-leafed evergreens embellishing dishes of nuts, mixed fresh fruit, dried fruit, or ices in cups. Leaves especially were the sine qua non of Victorian desserts. Every dish had a "tuft of green in this corner and that," with "just enough and no more," for in 1880 in the words of the editors who kept republishing Mrs. Beeton's book, "too many utterly spoil a dish, making it heavy and inartistic."[37]

FIG. 2:52. *The Dinner-Table.* From Isabella Beeton, *The Book of Household Management*, new ed., rev. and corr. [1880], p. 1239. (Winterthur Museum Library.)

FIG. 2:53. Centerpiece for fruit and flowers. From Isabella Beeton, *The Book of Household Management*, new ed., rev. and corr. [1880], pl. 10, p. 1140. (Winterthur Museum Library.)

Tall Centerpieces

Victorians were romantic about their decorations. They wanted things to look "pretty" and "artistic." But to achieve the effect they sought they combined idea after idea, forgetting to stop short of excess. One much-loved type of centerpiece made up of vases, baskets, bowls, and tazzas piled on top of each other had a fifty-year run during the latter part of the century—in that era of "quantity and breadth of choice," as Winslow Ames put it, when "abundance encouraged clutter" (Fig. 2:53). The centerpiece rose from a foliated base to a cluster of little berry baskets; mounted to a vase of flowers surrounded by dishes of leaf-decorated fruit and more vases; reached to a large tazza of fruit; and ended on high with another vase of flowers. Mrs. Beeton's editors in 1880 thought it a "remarkably handsome centre-piece, light and elegant yet useful withal, the style far surpassing the heavy, gaunt, sometimes positively uncouth middle ornaments that the souls of our ancestors delighted in."[38]

Heavy, gaunt, and uncouth they may have been to a Victorian, but the frames, pyramids, plateaux, and epergnes of the Georgians and their American cousins gave character to an otherwise undistinguished table setting and today move us to admiration. Although we know that they were all-year-round dinner appurtenances in the past, today we use them filled with sweetmeats and fruits at Christmastime to express holiday gaiety.

3

Dressing Out the Sweetmeats

I was at what I presume may be called a rout at Otis' on Saturday evening. There were at least three hundred persons present.

William Howard Gardiner,
Boston, 1817[1]

Letters and journals of the 1780s and 1790s brimmed with tales of a social whirl in the newly federated American states that reflected the gyrations of London's *haut monde*. Young Billy Tilghman of Maryland, visiting friends in Philadelphia in 1787, suffered in the best manner of a Regency buck through innumerable evening parties, circles, and *petit soupers*—his daily schedule fashionably crowded (his sister Molly reported to their cousin Polly) by morning calls and dinners. Abigail Adams, fêted as the wife of the secretary of state, called the winter of 1792 in Philadelphia "one continued scene of parties, balls, and entertainments equal to any European city."[2]

Presenting the Sweetmeats

At all of the evening affairs when gaiety had reached a fine pitch—usually about eleven o'clock—a table splendid with sweetmeats was revealed. Hidden until the crucial moment, it was exposed with a flourish. Diarists usually pictured the moment with exclamation points, writing, "The supper room was thrown open!" And whether the room was large and brilliant or small and dim, the throwing open was recognizable as a "pretty surprise" in the rococo mode of Versailles echoed at the parties of Philadelphia and New York.

The supper table might be set up in any room of the house save perhaps the kitchen, and the room lighted according to an old rule that called for at least one candle for every guest. At a Washington ball in 1819 tables were set up in three places—an upstairs hall and two bedrooms—with the principal table facing the guests as they mounted the stairs. The ball, given by Charles Bagot, ambassador from Great Britain, and his wife, niece of the Duke of Wellington, brought out the diplomatic set the year after Waterloo. The eminent Bostonian Harrison Gray Otis described the affair, which was put on in the height of fashion emulated by wealthy Americans. He wrote in detail to his wife, housebound in Boston:

> At 1/2 past eight I found the rooms well filled and the dancing begun. The ball was certainly brilliant and well conducted. The company I should judge not less than 250. All the foreign ministers were present, stiffened and sparkling in their laced costumes, and the heads of departments except Mr. A[dams] (who wore no lace). The ladies extremely well dressed in my judgment, and a general spirit of ease and affability pervaded the rooms. . . . About 1/2 past ten supper was announced. Mrs. B[agot] determined to command the rear guard, and allowed me to be her aid. She expressed a fear in going upstairs lest they should give way. On coming to the top of the stairs, the eye was met by a display of showy ornaments at the extremity of the entry placed on tables forming a sort of triple sideboard, the upper platform of which was decorated with plate and flowers, and the lower one [with] some very highly embellished dishes, the whole producing something like the effect of a handsome Roman Catholic altar. From this altar to the head of the stairs was laid one table protected from the wind and cold air by a curtain let down from the wall. Passing this table you discryed on each side into the two great chambers in which also tables were laid and covered with a most splendid variety of entremets, confectionary, porcelain and plate or plated ware. Probably some of both. The whole concern was extremely well conducted.[3]

On this occasion, the European ambassadors and American statesmen who viewed the highly embellished dishes wore rich coats, lace-trimmed shirts and neck cloths, brocaded vests, satin knee breeches, and white hose—the formal attire proper for evening, although long straight trousers were in style for daytime wear. As they paced the floor where dancing took place the guests enjoyed designs elaborately chalked to portray the British coat of arms and the United States seal. They appreciated the symbolism of the designs, which celebrated the new, equal footing of the two nations, secure in the knowledge that the chalk would prevent "those awkward and disagreeable incidents which a slippery floor inevitably occasions among the lively votaries of Terpsichore," as Mrs. Parkes put it.[4]

In contrast to the sophistication of the Bagots' ball with its second-floor supper rooms was the simplicity of a sedate evening tea party whose sweetmeats were passed on trays to guests in the parlor and dining room. Governor and Mrs. Clinton held it at the Governor's Mansion in Albany, New York, in 1827 and invited the British Basil Halls who were traveling in the eastern half of the

United States that year. Mrs. Hall wrote home about the party to amuse her sister in London:

> We were invited to tea and went at eight o'clock. On entering the first drawing room both Basil and I started back, for we saw none but gentlemen, not a single lady, and thought there must be some mistake in asking us there. But in a moment the Governor came forward and giving me his arm hurried me into the adjoining room at the top of which sat Mrs. Clinton who placed me on the seat next to herself. Round the room were placed as many chairs as could be crammed in, and a lady upon each—a most formidable circle. In the course of the evening the gentlemen did venture into the room and stood for a short time talking to one or other of the ladies, but there was seldom a chair vacant for any of the males to seat themselves upon, and altho' occasionally the ladies had courage to cross the room and change places with each other I never saw any lady standing during the whole evening, and the Mistress of the House alone seemed to enjoy the privilege of moving at her ease about the room. We had abundance of refreshments with several editions of tea and cake, then came two servants, one with a tray full of beautiful china plates of which he gave each lady one. Another man followed bearing a tray covered with-dishes of peaches and grapes which were in like manner handed round. Then followed another course of plates and in their rear a magnificent pyramid of ice, supported on each side by preserved pineapple and other sweetmeats. Then came wine, and again more plates and more ice. In short, Mrs. Clinton seemed to be of the opinion of a lady of whom I have been told by some of my friends at home, that the easiest way to entertain her guests was to keep them eating.[5]

An evening tea party like the Clintons' was a popular form of entertainment in eighteenth-century American society. Sophisticated circles might call it a rout and include cardplaying, but whether tea party or rout, guests always assembled in full dress to pay their respects to their hostess, to converse with acquaintances encountered in the throng, and to review the sweetmeats wherever they were offered (Fig. 3:1). Although most of the tea parties began earlier in the evening than eight o'clock, the hour at which the Basil Halls chose to enter the Clintons' drawing room, a Colonel Barclay's party began at six, which Mrs. Hall considered "primitive." Here, the "succession of trays, ice and coffee, then, creams and jellies, thirdly, preserves of various sorts, fourthly, hot whiskey punch, next, pickled oysters and collared port [pork], and to conclude, porter," caused Mrs. Hall to exclaim, "How stingy the Americans must think the refreshments provided at parties in England!"[6]

Tables of bright array brought glory not only to evening affairs but to daylight dinner parties. John Adams, writing from Philadelphia during the political deliberations of 1776, diverted his wife at home in Braintree, Massachusetts,

with accounts of dinners at town houses where hosts thought nothing of covering a table with sweetmeats of various sorts: curds, creams, jellies, twenty sorts of tarts, fools, trifles, floating islands, whipped syllabubs, Parmesan cheese, and pastries, accompanied by punch, wine, and beer. At the Governor's Mansion in Columbia, South Carolina, Mrs. Hall saw laid out on the table following the meat courses: eight pies, six glasses of syllabub and an equal number of jellies, and one or two floating islands, interspersed with dishes of ginger and other preserves.[7]

Sucket in Seventeenth-Century America

Among the sweetmeats of various sorts that John Adams enjoyed as the Revolution gained momentum were fruits preserved in heavy syrup and fruits candied until they were almost dry—in other words, the sucket, or succade, that Englishmen had long been fond of. The love of sucket had come across the ocean with the first settlers of the new England. Even when men were engaged in establishing the colonies and basic food preparation alone was back breaking, cupboards held a small store of the expensive sweets. As early as 1638 New England women offered them to the English traveler John Josselyn who reported with understandable hyperbole to potential colonists back in England: "Marmalade and preserved damsons is to be met with in every house." He went so far as to say, "The women are pitifully toothshaken, whether through the coldness of the climate or by the sweetmeats of which they have store, I am not able to affirm."[8]

Edward Johnson, another early visitor, knew as Josselyn did that fresh fruit, sweetmeats, and other fine foods were important to his fellow Englishmen. In 1645 when in London he published his *Wonder-Working Providence of Sion's Saviour in New England*, a book designed to recruit more settlers, he wrote of the orchards and gardens full of fruit in the colonies and of the good white wheat bread that even ordinary men could afford. He boasted too of an abundance of wine and sugar there and of the apple, pear, and quince tarts that second-generation colonial housewives could offer their families in place of the inferior pumpkin tarts and pies the first settlers had had to endure.[9]

It was true that within a generation of arrival, some colonists found that by applying themselves to the export of fish, lumber, wheat, and furs they could afford sweetmeats and other nonessentials once available only to the rich. Even before 1630 some of them were buying the loaf sugar, powdered sugar, nutmeg, cloves, cinnamon, mace, ginger, saffron, raisins, currants, and almonds

FIG. 3:1. Henry Sargent, *The Tea Party*. Boston, 1821–25.
Oil on canvas; H. 163.1 cm., W. 132.2 cm.
(Museum of Fine Arts, Boston.)

that came on ships from Holland and other European countries. By 1650, barrels of fruit and tender young ginger root, called green ginger, were added to their larders. In the years before 1680 Alexander Hamilton, a Boston barber, kept a supply of candied angelica, citron, green ginger, and sucket—possibly for sale.[10]

Eating sweetmeats had been a favorite pastime of the Elizabethans. Because Elizabeth I ("The Virgin Queen") had died in 1603, only four years before the founding of the colony named Virginia in her honor and only seventeen years before the landing of the Pilgrims at Plymouth, Massachusetts, certain of the colonists who had been her subjects could remember the spice banquets of raisins, figs, and currants she enjoyed and the passion for comfits of sugared seeds, nuts, and fruits that blackened her teeth. They had heard tales of the queen's progresses from manor to manor for which her courtiers expended their wealth on new houses and banquet pavilions, spicery, and sucket. During their lifetime, the kingdom's new prosperity made it possible not only for royalty, the nobility, and the aristocracy but also for city merchants to display on their tables such banquet fare as "gelliss of all colours . . . conserves of old fruits foreign and home-bred; suckets, codiniacs, marmalades, marchpane, sugarbread, gingerbread, florentines . . . and sundry outlandish confections altogether seasoned with sugar," as Harrison wrote in 1587 in his *Description of England.* Even men like William Brewster, who with his father had served King James's messengers in the tavern they managed on the Great North Road in Nottinghamshire following the queen's death, had tasted caudle, sack, and sugared wine.[11]

Spice Banquets

A sweetmeat banquet was a descendant of the "voide drink" (pronounced voidee) that in large fourteenth-century households was served at nightfall on a voider, or tray, when the great hall was being "voided" of travelers and of all who had no further business there. It was related to the voide of sugared seeds and nuts, dried fruits, and sugared roots that supplemented the voide drink when guests were present. A pleasant repast, it came to be repeated at other times of day, particularly when guests departed. It then was called a banquet, the term deriving from the French *banc,* the little bench on which the guests were invited to sit, corresponding to the Italian *banchetto,* the diminutive of *banco,* the board on which the repast was served. For two hundred years the word was used to refer to the amusing little repast of sweets provided on such special occasions as dinner parties, weddings, concerts, or masques.

In the sixteenth century, banquets grew so hectic in European court circles as to involve miniature catapults hurling comfits at sugar castles, and ladies pelting each other with sugarplums. During the next century, when European society delightedly adopted the frivolities of Versailles, the sweetmeat banquet acquired the order and grace of a minuet and with its new character came a new name. When Charles II and his courtiers returned to England from exile in Versailles-dominated Europe they brought with them the French term *dessert* to designate the entertainment of sweetmeats that was offered to guests after dinner had been cleared away, or "de-served." Little by little, when speaking of a repast of sweetmeats, the English adopted the new word, and the old word came to signify only a large and particularly festive feast of all kinds of foods, as it does today.[12]

Cookbooks in Seventeenth-Century America

The sweetmeats of the repast in the seventeenth century, whether served as "banquet" or as "dessert," comprised the spicery and sugar plate (similar to our fruit drops) and the sucket and marmalade that Harrison called sundries "altogether seasoned with sugar." It included especially the "conserves of old fruits foreign and home-bred" that Harrison spoke of. For homebred conserves American housewives went to their kitchens to follow the recipes printed in cookbooks or handed down by their mothers and grandmothers. But very few English colonial women were fortunate enough to own a printed cookbook. Of the small number of cookbooks published in English in the seventeenth century, only some half dozen are known to have reached New England before the first century of colonization was over. Among them was *The English Housewife* by Gervase Markham who defined the virtues essential to a complete woman as skill in nursing, in cooking, in distillation, in making perfumes, in processing wool, hemp, and flax, in making dairy products, and in doing "all other things needed in a household," including the making of sucket. So complete was Markham's do-it-yourself book that it continued in favor for several generations and was reprinted eleven times before 1684. If a woman did not have a copy of Markham she might own *The Compleat Cook,* first published in London in 1655 and later bound with *The Queen's Closet Opened* by an unknown "W. M." These two useful cookbooks appeared in many editions before the century was over, providing their readers with instructions in the virtuous arts, as they were called by Henrietta Maria, wife of Charles I. In the event the colonial housewife owned neither book she could send back home for an edition of Robert May's *The Accomplish't Cook,* first published in 1660, which claimed to give better methods than had hitherto been published in any language for dressing meat, fowl, and fish and for making pastes, sauces, and the banquet fare that May termed "all manner of kickshaws . . . with à la mode curiosities."[13]

Handwritten Recipe Books

Newcomers to America who failed to bring printed cookbooks to bolster their skills and keep them *au courant* brought handwritten copies of the recipes they and their mothers had used in England. Elizabeth Meade, a new American in 1697, came with such a manuscript recipe book. In it she kept proven methods for treating meats and vegetables and for making pastry, cakes, and sweetmeats. Her pastry recipes produced high cylinders for holding great stews of beef or lamb seasoned with lemons, raisins, and spices; turned out small meat pasties, or patties; and made cold paste, puff paste, or sugar paste to hold cheesecakes, custards, and raspberry, currant, and apricot sweetmeats. Her wet sweetmeat recipes made florentines, tansy pudding, jellies, and creams. One of the longest and most important of the recipes refined sugar and made preserves that she called sweetmeats.[14]

FIG. 3:2. Skillet, England, 1680–1720. PRAIES GOD FOR ALL raised on handle. Bell metal; L. (handle) 23.5 cm., H. 10.8 cm. (Winterthur Museum, 60.50.)

Kitchenware for Making Seventeenth-Century Sweetmeats

Another recipe copybook written in England for use in the new land was put together by Gulielma Penn, wife of Pennsylvania's founder. She intended it for young William to use when he joined his father at Pennsbury on the Delaware in 1703. Side by side with directions for meat puddings, fish stews, and bird pies, the book held Penn family formulas for tarts, custards, creams, and jellies and for such suckets as red marmalade of quinces, candied pippins, violet cakes, cherries preserved in jelly, and preserved plums.[15]

Both the Meade and Penn copybooks are fine documents of seventeenth-century English domestic practice at the time of colonizing. Gulielma Penn's is particularly illuminating as to the way vessels were used for making sweetmeats. She specified chafing dishes, porringers, pots, posnets, skillets, pans, and kettles with a precision that is invaluable to the twentieth-century historian who has looked at the earthenware, wood, tin, and pewter equipment of a three-hundred-year-old kitchen and wondered. In dictating her recipes to a scribe, she suggested the utensil proper for each procedure, implying what equipment was essential for a well-furnished kitchen.

Skillets

She put a skillet to several different uses: for boiling green pippins, cherries, or apricots with sugar until they became a paste; for boiling gooseberry juice, cherries, and sugar to make "Preserved Cherries in Jelly"; for cooking up apples, sugar, and orange peel for a "marmolet"; for boiling a hedgehog pudding tied up in cloth; for cooking almond paste, cream, and eggs to make almond butter; and, finally, for simmering a hasty pudding of bread, milk, eggs, and spices with mace and rosewater until "it will hold proportion of a skillet" (Fig. 3:2).

Pots, Posnets, and Pans

Gulielma put pots and pans to various uses in making other sweet dishes (Fig. 3:3). One pot held water under a covered bread pudding while it was being baked; another held gooseberries while they were stewing. A pewter pot served for simmering violets to make a syrup, and a posnet for simmering hartshorn and powdered ivory over embers all night in making gelatine. A preserving pan cooked cherries and sugar for a sweetmeat to fill tarts; a buttered pan baked apple pudding, and a buttered dish a pudding of eggs, bread, butter, and sugar. Tin pans baked gingerbread, and sheets of tin baked large wafers of almond paste. Patty pans baked orange tarts in puff paste, and pie plates baked meringue puffs.

FIG. 3:3. Kettle, England or Holland, dated 1657. Bell metal; H. 30.2 cm., D. 32.4 cm. (Winterthur Museum, 61.320, gift of Charles F. Montgomery.)

Pewter

Madam Penn did not hesitate to heat pewter dishes but directed that a pewter plate of mass cakes be put into an oven hot enough for biscuits. She used other pewter objects in mixing and measuring: a pewter dish for combining sugar, almonds, and rosewater in making macaroons; a porringer for measuring the proper amount of rosewater in flavoring lemon cream and of ale yeast in making French bread; a deep basin for mixing sliced almonds with double-refined sugar in making the wafers, or "bread," like outsize macaroons, called *massepain* by the French, *marzipan* by the Germans, and *marchpane* by the English.

Earthenware

Earthenware figured prominently in Gulielma's recipe book. She advised placing an earthenware pot half full of fresh beef broth or mutton broth directly on the coals or using it to make a meatball pudding "in the Allmon fashion," by which she meant Allemand, or German, method. She filled a large earthen pan with leavened batter containing currants and raisins. A deep earthen basin was her alternative for the deep pewter basin she used in mixing almond paste and sugar. Glazed earthen pots held pickled cucumbers, preserved plums, green pippins, or green walnuts. An earthen pipkin boiled raisins with hartshorn, mace, licorice, and "opening roses" in making hartshorn jelly; an earthen colander strained moisture from cherries (Fig. 3:4).

FIG. 3:4. Colander, Pennsylvania, 1800–1850. Redware; H. 14 cm., D. (of top) 30.5 cm. (Winterthur Museum, 60.109.)

Woodenware

Wooden utensils had various incidental uses in the Penn family recipes. A maple maser served as a pattern for a round almond cake spiced with musk, caraway seeds, rosewater, and ambergris. A wooden bowl held a quart of thick cream while it was beaten for snow cream. A rolling pin beat gingerbread paste until light, in preparation for baking. New, unwashed trenchers served as cutting boards when almonds were sliced for cakes.

Silverware and Glassware

Silver and glass dishes also played a part in Gulielma's directions. A silver porringer held shredded lemon peel chips steeping in lemon juice when lemon cream was being made. A silver basin served in sugaring apricots or plums when dry sweetmeats were in process. A glass held almond butter flavored with ambergris, or served as a cutter to stamp out mass cakes before baking.

Sieves

Among the other utensils that Gulielma specified, sieves were conspicuous. She called them variously searce, sieve, strainer, and riddle. A fine lawn sieve strained sugar that had been boiled with egg white in refining. A hair sieve strained curds to make cheesecake. A coarse strainer blended cream, eggs, almond paste, pistachios, and sugar in making a custard; a strainer of cotton cloth separated lemon chips from juice, egg whites from yolks, and rosewater from rose leaves in making lemon cream. A riddle held oranges, angelica, or other fruits to drip dry in the process of candying.

Mortars

Gulielma used a stone mortar when she beat almonds to a paste with rosewater; an alabaster mortar when she beat sugar, egg white, ambergris, musk, and aniseed together for Italian biscuit; a fine marble mortar when she beat sugar and egg whites for an hour with a fine wooden pestle in making pastry puffs. Among the miscellaneous objects she made use of was a chafing dish to hold a plate in drying almond paste for seedcakes and in melting sweet butter with rosewater in making almond mass cakes (Fig. 3:5). A brass ladle dipped out oatcake batter, and a feather or a tuft of silk iced a cake with a frosting of sugar beaten in a mortar with rosewater. The feather also covered flowers with water when they were being candied. Gulielma expected William's household to be equipped with a set of enclosed wooden shelves called a stove, which allowed air to circulate around trays of sugared fruit and flowers in order to dry them—a piece of European confectionery equipment akin to the pie cupboard or tin safe used by German-Americans of the nineteenth century.

Chafing Dishes and Ladles

Confectioner's Stove

All of the utensils Gulielma mentioned were represented in American households during the late seventeenth and early eighteenth centuries. The typical supply of Thomas Swift of Dorchester, Massachusetts, included ten platters and various basins, fruit dishes, potengers, quart bowls, and brass kettles. It also held an iron pot, a posnet, skillet, and brass mortar. The house was equipped with "other utensils" as well, according to Swift's inventory. These "other" without doubt referred to the wooden and horn dishes that inventory takers often failed to list because such dishes were of little value. Today they persist only in small numbers to teach us about the stock-in-trade of colonial kitchens.[16]

FIG. 3:5. Chafing dish, or brazier, by John Potwine, Boston, ca. 1730. Silver; H. 8.8 cm., D. 15.4 cm. (Winterthur Museum, 65.1347, ex coll. Francis Hill Bigelow.)

Preserves, or Wet Sweetmeats

Production of sweetmeats consisting of preserves, cakes, pastries, whips, and jellies, both molded and jamlike, fulfilled an important function in the domestic routine of the English housewife in America. Far from England, and moving as she did in a society dependent for its polite diversions on mutual hospitality offered at home, she needed a large repertoire of dessert dishes and a great deal of patience in preparing them. Her main concern in producing this variety of desserts, or what her grandmother termed banqueting stuff, was the processing of preserves, or wet sweetmeats (Fig. 3:6). Recipes for preparing the fruits and for refining the sugar that went into the preserves filled many pages in her copybooks and cookbooks. Because sugar was costly, sugared fruit was something of a status symbol, and the housewife was willing to spend long hours over the hot hearth in preparing it. That the arduous process required not only time but skill elevated it above other kitchen work to the realm of fashionable accomplishment. It was the unusual housewife who did not take pride in her work, guard against cloudiness in jellies, and strive for sweetmeats of transparency and bright color. Most engaged in preserving with considerable complacency, aiming to maintain their reputations and to economize during summer plenty for winter dearth. For some women, seeing shelves of glasses, earthen jars, and stoneware crocks of sucket ready to be put into tarts, pies, and creams for a future festive occasion was highly rewarding. In 1784 Nancy Shippen, a young lady of Philadelphia, proudly recorded in her journal: "I spent the day at home very busy making sweet-meats for the winter."[17]

FIG. 3:6. Wet and dry sweetmeats in the making. (New England Kitchen, 1790–1850, Winterthur Museum.)

Sugar

Making sweetmeats, although satisfying in its results, was tedious. It required hours of peeling, coring, or seeding fruit and equally long hours of stirring and cooking over an open fire. It took great effort to regulate the fire's temperature by adding or subtracting logs of wood, to lift off heavy kettles at the right moment, and to stir, ladle, and seal the finished product. The tasks were demanding even with a servant or a relative at hand to pick over and wash fruit; wash glasses and jars; refine, pound, and sift sugar; watch the fire and lift the kettle. One of the most time-consuming tasks concerned sugar. Sugar could be bought in some cities in several grades from coarse to fine. But if fine were not available, or too expensive, coarse had to be refined at home. The coarsest sugar on the market was raw brown muscovado left after molasses was drained off in the first process of sugar manufacture. It was sold in casks or barrels. Higher in refinement were single- and double-refined loaf sugar, their purity obtained at sugar refineries by several successive boilings and days of evaporation in earthenware cones sealed with fine white porous clay and stored upside down (Fig. 3:7). Double-refined sugar—referred to variously as sugar candy, candy sugar, or sugar royal—when crushed as fine as flour, produced powder or powdered sugar. As might be expected, the price of sugar increased according to the labor expended on refining. In 1629 the Reverend Samuel Skelton purchased powder sugar from the Massachusetts Bay storehouse for twenty pence a pound. In 1704 Henry Lloyd, merchant trader, sold muscovado in barrels and hogsheads for fourpence halfpenny per pound. In 1767 Mrs. Schuyler paid eighteen pence a pound for clayed sugar in cones. Sugar cones, or loaves, varied greatly in weight and size. Mrs. Schuyler's weighed from three to ten and a half pounds. The best sugar of the mid eighteenth century was thought to come from Lisbon, sugar of lesser quality from Cuba and Jamaica and by mid-nineteenth century also from Puerto Rico and from Santa Cruz on Tenerife in the Canary Islands. A French visitor to Rhode Island in 1780 remarked of Americans: "The kind of sugar they use marks generally poverty or richness."[18]

Refining Sugar at Home

If a woman decided that she must refine sugar at home she turned again to her cookbooks. Recipes usually specified boiling four quarts of water and two egg whites with twelve pounds of sugar. The mixture was to be beaten to a froth in a copper pan and allowed to boil up four or five times. At a certain moment a little cold water was to be added to prevent it from boiling over. The solution was then allowed to settle, skimmed with a brass sugar skimmer, strained through a bag of linen or flannel or through a hair sieve into a deep jar, and allowed to crystallize into candy sugar on strings. It might then vie in purity with clayed loaf sugar and could be rolled into granules or crushed to powder. As late as 1880 Mrs. Beeton's *Household Management* gave recipes for clarifying sugar and reminded housekeepers to pay attention in the evening after work to the breaking of "lump sugar," to pounding it well, and to sifting it through a fine sieve.[19]

FIG. 3:7. Sugar cones draining. From Charles C. Gillespie, ed., *A Diderot Pictorial Encyclopedia of Trades and Industry*, 1:pl. 41.

Breaking Sugar

A sugar loaf, although pure and desirable, was formidably hard. To reduce it to usable pieces eighteenth-century families wielded sugar cleavers, hatchets, mallets, choppers, or hammers, and, finally, nippers (Figs. 3:8, 3:9). For turning the pieces or the crystallized strings into grains and powder they used either a rolling pin and board, a mortar and pestle, or a grater. For storing it they used tin canisters, wooden chests, wooden boxes, or large earthen jars. Charles Carroll ordered "sugar boxes and mallets" for his wife in 1768. Susanna Whatman's mid-eighteenth-century manuscript housekeeping book outlined for the benefit of her servants her wishes concerning sugar breaking and storing:

> Plenty of sugar should always be kept ready broke in the deep sugar drawers in the closet storeroom. There is one for spice, one for moist sugar, and two for lump sugar. The pieces should be as square as possible, and rather small. The sugar that is powdered to fill the silver castor should be kept in a basin in one of the drawers to prevent any insects getting into it, and be powdered *fine* in the mortar and kept ready for use.[20]

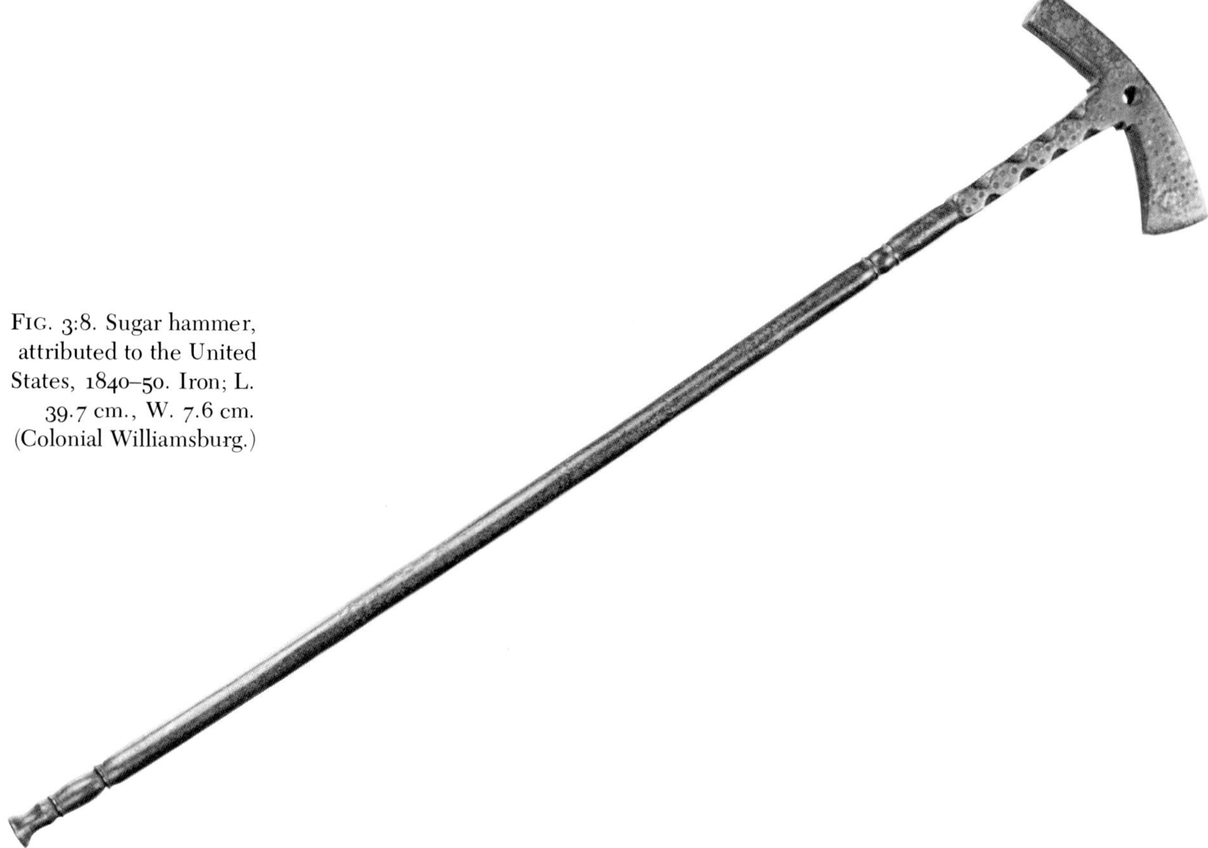

FIG. 3:8. Sugar hammer, attributed to the United States, 1840–50. Iron; L. 39.7 cm., W. 7.6 cm. (Colonial Williamsburg.)

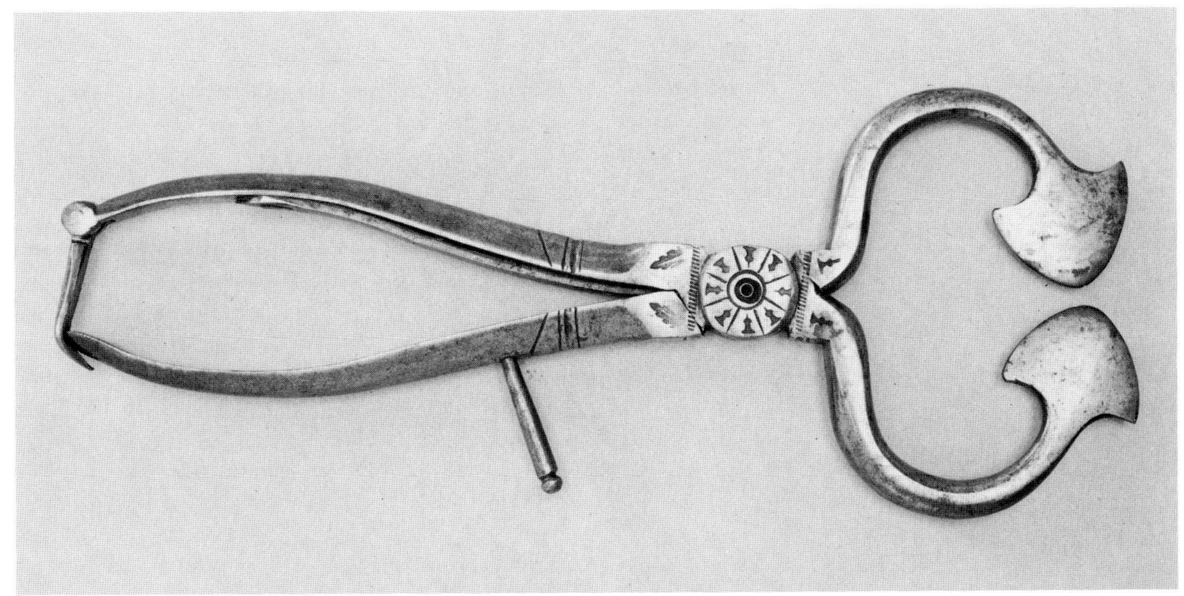

FIG. 3:9. Sugar nippers, England, 1750–1800. Marked B-SMITH. Steel; L. 24 cm., W. 8.7 cm. (Winterthur Museum, 59.145, gift of Mrs. John T. Tenneson.)

Making Sweetmeats

Little of the hard work involved in the preparation of sugar, in making and maintaining a fire, and in sealing sweetmeats shows through such deceptively simple formulas as appear in E. Smith's *The Compleat Housewife*, first published in London in 1737 and republished in Williamsburg, Virginia, in 1742. Its recipe for the making of whole raspberry preserves, for instance, directs the housewife first to cook equal weights of fruit and double-refined beaten and sifted sugar in a preserving pan "until some syrup appears," then to move it to a quick fire until the sugar melts. Finally, she is to boil it a couple of times, skim it, and put it in glasses. This seemingly speedy method produced an exceedingly good sweetmeat, especially if the mixture retained the fruit's bright color. Such a waterless method for making what we call jam was also included in 1796 in Amelia Simmons's *American Cookery*, the first cookbook written by and published by an American, and is the method used today by women who scorn powdered or liquid pectin.[21]

Sweetmeat Jars

In the cellars, closets, cupboards, and pantries of provident householders, as inventories record, brown earthenware pots, stone pots, and "bottles," filled with sweetmeats, stood ready to provide a dessert. The cost of the jars and pots added to the expense. Sarah Ann Bailey in 1822, soon after her marriage to Henry Latimer of Wilmington, Delaware, paid one dollar for a dozen pint glass jars, and the customers of James Brooks, a New York china merchant, in 1835 paid five pence each for brown earthenware sweetmeat pots (Fig. 3:10).[22]

Sealing Sweetmeat Jars

Until 1858 when the mason jar with sealing top was patented, and even after, the task of sealing sweetmeats so that they would not mold was a problem not always successfully resolved. Cookbooks did not agree on the best method. During the eighteenth century *The Accomplish'd Female Instructor* advised using leather closely tied for holding fruit cooked in sugar syrup "until it would rope." *Madam Johnson's Present*, a textbook for young ladies who attended Madam Johnson's cooking school in London, recommended covering pots with both a sheep's bladder *and* a piece of leather. Toward the end of the century, some ladies thought brandy-soaked paper a good substitute for the bladder, and others preferred white paper dipped in hot clarified sugar. In the early nineteenth century *The Young Woman's Companion* advocated brandy paper under leather dipped in rosin "to prevent the air getting in at the cork." It urged that mutton fat in addition to bladder and paper be used to seal jars of apples preserved in distilled vinegar. Mrs. Beeton in 1861 covered plum jam with oiled paper and with tissue paper brushed on both sides with the white of an egg, but she used either a wet bladder or a cork and wax for rhubarb jam. Her editors were still using a bladder on occasion in 1880. Mrs. Fiske around 1860 sprinkled jars of blackberries with brandy before laying over them a piece of brandy-soaked paper. She found that sweetmeats maintained over a fire for three or four hours before covering would sometimes keep six months or more without recooking. Sometimes! In spite of careful covering, housewives expected halfway through the winter to find it necessary to skim off mold and boil again.[23]

Imported Sweetmeats

Not all sweetmeats were made at home. Fine ones came from Paris and the West Indies and were sold by grocers or itinerant traders. Boston merchant Henry Lloyd in 1703 imported sweetmeats, raisins, currants, and allspice and sold them along with earthenware, hardware, and other domestic necessities up and down the Atlantic coast to such customers as the Boston silversmiths Peter Oliver, Anthony Blount, and Thomas Savage, merchant Jacob Wendell, and clockmaker Simon Willard. The sweetmeats Lloyd sold included green ginger and tamarinds, a West Indian fruit preserved in heavy syrup and marketed in tumblers and jars. Governor Burnet in 1729 owned a fair supply of West Indian sweetmeats made up of candied citron, ginger, angelica, and pineapple. Similar expensive fruits probably made up the "desert of West Indian sweetmeats" served to Abigail Adams at an inn in Wrentham, Massachusetts, sixty years later.[24]

FIG. 3:10. Sweetmeat jar or "bottle," England, 1800–1860. Flint glass; H. 16 cm., D. 9.5 cm. (Winterthur Museum, 57.18.5.)

Dishes for Wet Sweetmeats

Wet sweetmeats came to the seventeenth-century table in stylish shallow porcelain or earthenware bowls and in glassware (Fig. 3:11). Admired as a material for dessert dishes since the reign of Henry VIII when a "service all of glass" covered the royal table, glass was appropriate because it allowed the rich color of preserves to show through. By the late eighteenth century, purchasers of glass dessert dishes could choose covered cylinders on plates, shallow scalloped bowls, compotes, and many other forms. New Yorker Victor du Pont paid ten dollars in 1802 for "glass urns for a dessert," and Captain Ingraham of Norwich, Connecticut, owned a glass sweetmeat dish and plate (Figs. 3:12–14).[25]

FIG. 3:11. Gerard Wigmana (1673–1741), *Indische Familie*. Holland, 1697. Oil on canvas. (Dokkum Museum.)

FIG. 3:12. Covered sweetmeat dish and stand, England, possibly Newcastle, 1750–75. Lead glass; H. (dish) 7.3 cm., D. 11.7 cm. (Winterthur Museum, 69.141.1.)

FIG. 3:13. Confection bowl with its cover and stand. From a manuscript glass catalogue, Gardiner's Island, N.Y., 1800–1825. (Winterthur Museum Library.)

FIG. 3:14. One of a pair of sweetmeat urns, England, 1780–1800. Lead glass; H. 18.4 cm., D. (top) 13.7 cm. (Winterthur Museum, 63.939.)

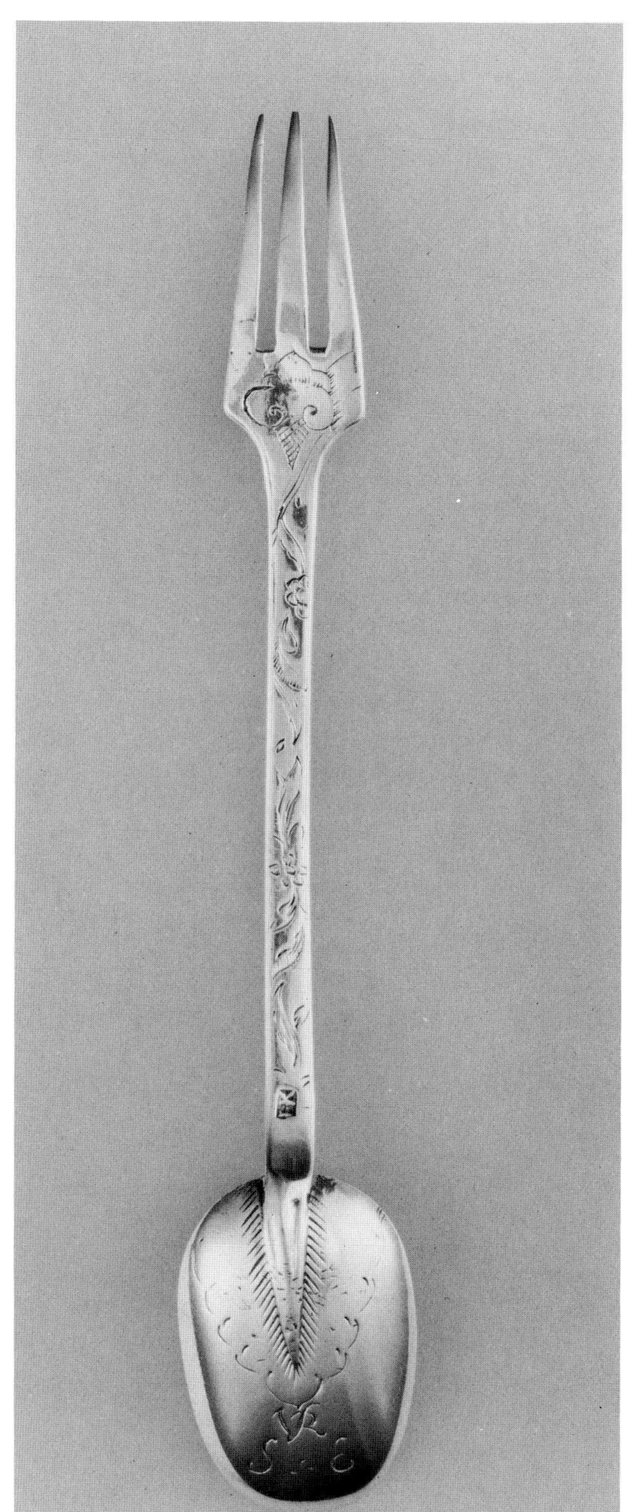

FIG. 3:15. Sucket fork by Jesse Kip, New York, 1682–1722. Marked IK in rectangle on back of handle. Inscribed on back of bowl VR/SE presumably for members of the van Rensselaer family. Silver; L. 13.5 cm. (Winterthur Museum, 63.52.)

Sweetmeat Forks

For eating wet sweetmeats a well-to-do colonial host provided a sucket fork or two (Fig. 3:15). James Claypoole of Philadelphia in 1688 owned a "forked spoon for sweetmeats," and in 1722 his fellow citizen Jonathan Dickinson owned "six silver sweetmeat forks." William Rouse of Boston made a pair of sucket forks before 1689, and Johannes Nys, Philadelphia and Wilmington, made a pair to commemorate the wedding of Hugh and Martha Huddy in 1701. Aside from long flesh forks for handling meat in the kitchen, sucket forks were the only forks used in middle-class seventeenth-century English and Anglo-American houses. Aristocratic Italians and Frenchmen had felt at ease with dinner forks since the early Renaissance, but most Englishmen even as late as the middle of the eighteenth century regarded them as effeminate, suitable only for women eating sucket. European artists of the fifteenth and early sixteenth centuries picture forks in the hands of languid ladies who loll at long tables set with plates and platters, while men wield only pointed knives. Some of the forks depicted have long thin handles and four curved short tines somewhat like those of a pitchfork, making them useful for eating every food, but particularly for picking up preserved oranges, tamarinds, ginger, and other wet sweetmeats. Some of the forks shown by the painters are short and straight, presumably like the silver-and-gilt spoon with sucket fork at the end, used by courtiers of Henry VIII. But even though Europeans used them, not until the late seventeenth century were forks in England more than playthings of the very rich.[26]

Sucket forks had a short life in the colonies. As the eighteenth century began, they went out of style in most households of English background. Although passé for many people, they still came from the New York workshops of the silversmiths Jesse Kip, Adrian Bancker, and Bartholomew LeRoux for the tables of the van Rensselaers, Roosevelts, and other families of Dutch background. And as late as 1743 the *South Carolina Gazette* advertised "silver spoon-handled forks imported from London."[27]

Dessert Knives and Forks

Gradually, sets of silver knives and forks for sweetmeats and gilt sweetmeat knives, forks, and spoons, in smaller editions of dinner flatware, supplanted sucket forks (Fig. 3:16). People could buy the new forms by the dozen by the middle of the eighteenth century and sets of dessert knives and forks appeared regularly thereafter on well-furnished tables, their handles suitably gay for sweetmeat eating (Fig. 3:17). Governor Burnet's table was set with a dozen each of silver spoons and dessert knives and forks before 1729. "One dozen of green ivory handle [dessert] knives tip'd and ferill'd with silver" cost John Cadwalader four pounds four shillings in 1769 when he bought them of Henry Shepherd of London (Fig. 3:18). Dessert knives came to other Philadelphians through such retailers as William Dawson who advertised in 1793 "imported ivory and fancy handled table and dessert knives and forks." Victor du Pont bought from Stephen Richard, in 1801, eighteen silver dessert forks and spoons engraved with a cipher and crest (Fig. 3:19). Bostonian Lady Temple's case of two dozen dessert knives and forks in 1809 were "black, silver mounted" to

FIG. 3:16. Table fork and dessert fork by William F. Ladd, New York, 1820–30. Marked Wm. F. Ladd. Inscribed EPC in script on handle backs. Silver, king's pattern; L. 21.3 cm. (Winterthur Museum, 62.240.1724, 1725, gift of Mr. and Mrs. Alfred E. Bissell, ex coll. Stanley B. Ineson.)

FIG. 3:17. Dessert knife, fork, and spoon from an eighteen-piece set, England and China, 1750–70. Porcelain with sepia and gold decoration, steel, and silver; L. (fork) 19.8 cm., (knife) 24.9 cm., (spoon) 21.1 cm. (Winterthur Museum, 63.763.1–16.)

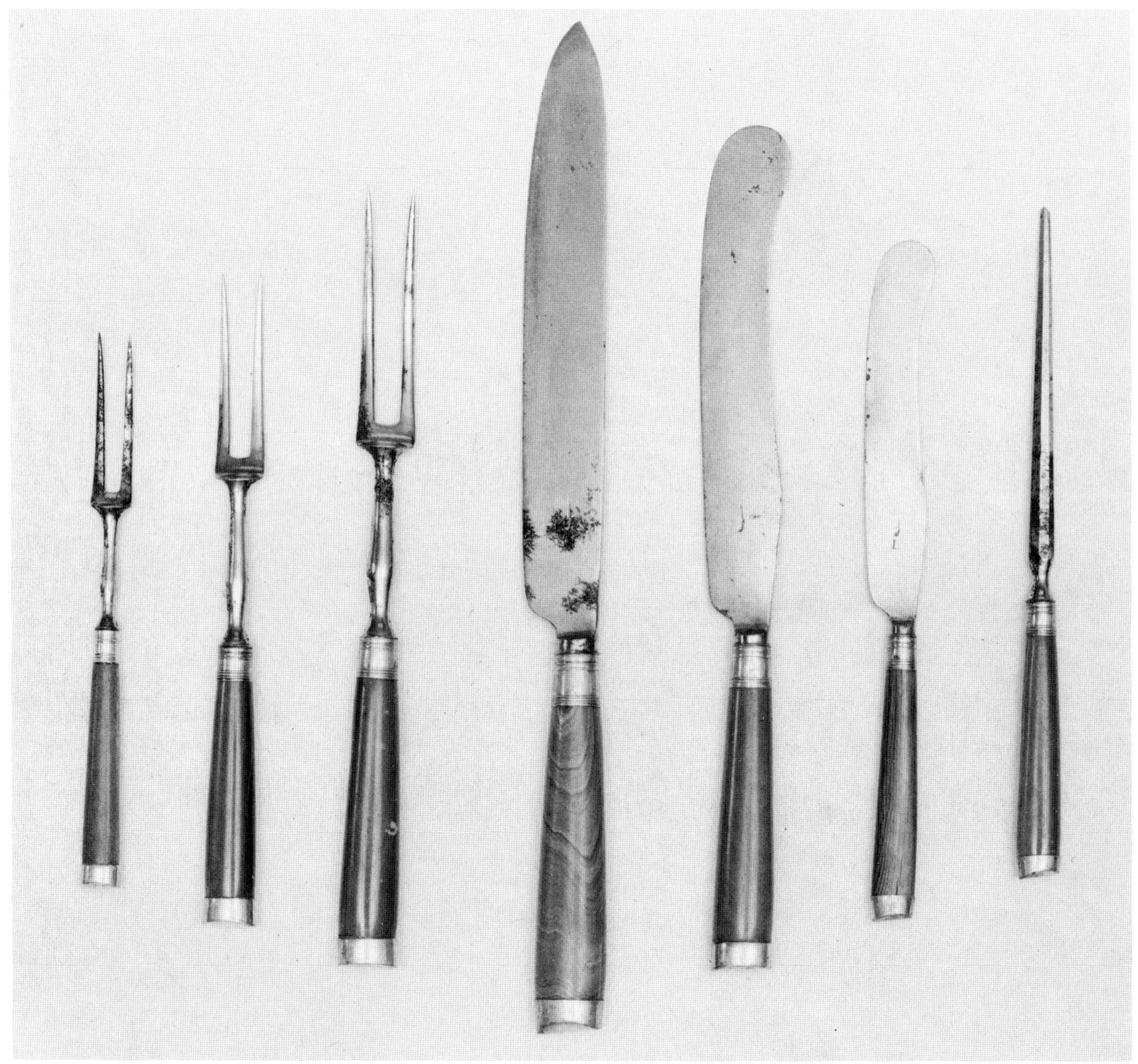

FIG. 3:18. Table, dessert, and carving knives and forks from a forty-nine-piece set, London, dated 1809. Knife blades impressed with the dagger of the London Cutlers' Company and cutlers' "L." Steel, silver and green stained ivory; L. (carving knife) 25.4 cm., and (carving fork) 27.7 cm. (Winterthur Museum, 54.79.1–49.)

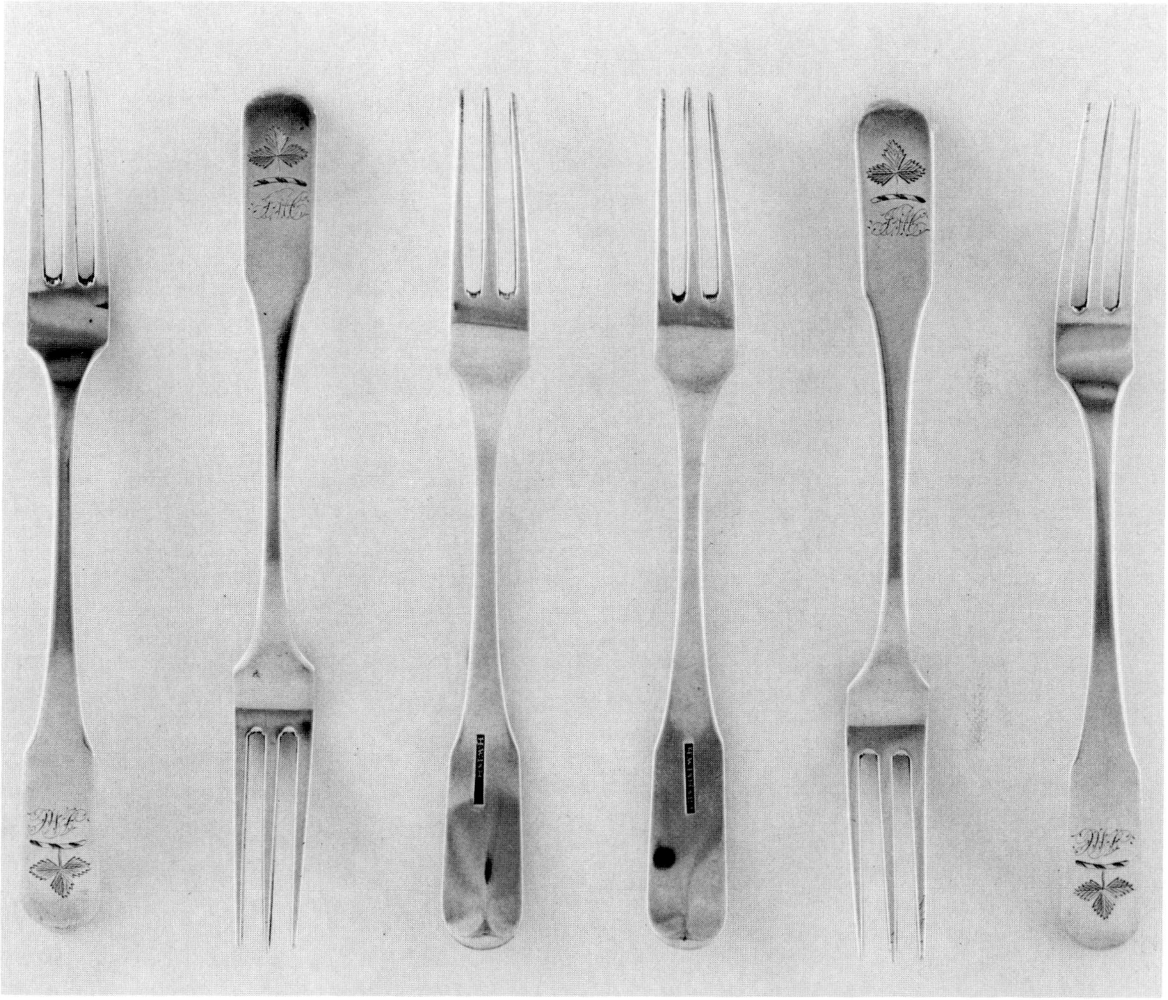

FIG. 3:19. Dessert forks by Hugh Wishart, New York, ca. 1800. Marked WISHART in rectangle on handle backs; inscribed IMC for original owner on handle fronts. Silver; L. 17.2 cm. (Winterthur Museum, 62.240.517.1–6, gift of Mr. and Mrs. Alfred E. Bissell, ex coll. Stanley B. Ineson.)

match her two dozen table knives and forks, and the dessert forks and knives that Abigail Robinson of Newport, Rhode Island, left in her will of 1835 were handled with "pearl."[28]

Confects, Comfits, or Sugarplums

In addition to homemade and imported wet sweetmeats of syrupy character to be eaten with special forks and spoons, housewives made or bought dry sweetmeats, or confects (Fig. 3:20). The word *confect* derived from the Latin word *confectus* meaning "prepared or made with." Originally it encompassed anything made with sugar, but in the eighteenth century it usually referred only to *dry* sugared things. The term was early corrupted to "comfit" and nicknamed sugarplum. Under the comfortable nickname, confects or comfits came from colonial kitchens in the form of candied fruit and fruit peels; sugared seeds, nuts, and flowers; fruit pastes and clear fruit drops—all of them sparkling, dry, and storable until needed to adorn a dessert.

Fruit Paste

The home confectioner frequently prepared large quantities of fruit pastes because they required little effort during long cooking. Since the fifteenth century, the thick chewy sweets had variously been called marmalade, fruit cheese, cheesecake, and fruit leather. Three centuries of cooks, among them Gulielma Penn in the late 1600s, Elizabeth Hutchinson, a Boston housewife of the middle 1700s, and the editors of the first number of *Godey's Lady's Book* in 1830, used similar recipes when they made the perennially favorite quince paste, or quince cheese. Madam Penn's recipe for "Red past[e] and Jelly of Quinces" produced both paste and jam. It called for cutting a pound of the hard fruit into quarters and mixing it with a pound of sugar and a pint of water and cooking it until it was bright red and soft. The fruit and the juice were then separated and an additional half pound of sugar chunks that had been dipped in water and boiled were added to the fruit. This sugar and fruit mixture was boiled together until the liquid was almost gone, and the resulting mass was laid on plates for drying. Meanwhile, the juice was boiled to a jelly (with a quarter pound of sugar added to each pint) and put into glasses, thus making two sweetmeats out of one batch of fruit. Elizabeth Hutchinson pressed sugared and cooked quinces through a sieve and solidified the paste in quince molds for slicing, whereas *Godey's* followers molded the paste in a large basin, pan, or deep dish and sliced it like cheese.[29]

Fruit Drops, Fruit Cakes, or Sugar-Plate

Fruit drops, known in the seventeenth century as sugar-plate and in eighteenth-century recipes as "clear fruit cakes," were more difficult to make than fruit paste was; the syrup needed straining through linen or cotton flannel jelly bags and boiling to the stage called *à la plume*, or the cracking stage. The cracking stage was called *à la plume* because the sugar syrup feathered when it was tested by dripping and blowing. Once properly boiled, the fruit syrup was poured onto "cake glasses" or plates to dry. The results might be the Pippin Cakes Transparent that Mrs. John Custis of Queen's Creek, Virginia, near Williamsburg, liked to make; or orange cakes, lemon cakes, and clear cakes of gooseberries such as *The Compleat Housewife* recommended—all of them the sugar-plate of the years before the eighteenth century. Before 1800 the noun *cake* meant, in respect to food, anything that was cylindrical and flattish, no matter what the size or substance.[30]

FIG. 3:20. Georg Flegel (1563–1638), *Grosses Schauessen*. Frankfort, 1622. Oil on canvas; H. 78 cm., W. 67 cm. (Bayerische Staatsgemäldesammlungen.)

Candied Fruit Peels, or Chips

Candying, a process of boiling a fruit or root in sugar until saturation was reached, produced other dry sweetmeats. One of the favorites that found a place in every cookbook bridges the years between Elizabethan sucket and today's candied orange peel. The recipe was called Orange Chips and involved soaking orange peels for two days, boiling them until tender, cutting them into "what lengths you like," letting them stand in an equal amount of sugar made into syrup, and heating them twice daily "until they are candied." Lemon peel, citron, angelica, and pineapple were candied in the same way and, with shorter cooking time, so were peaches, apricots, nectarines, apples, and pears. When the candied fruits were dried in sifted sugar and packed away between layers of paper in wooden boxes or placed in tin or glass canisters, as cookbook authors specified, they could be kept many months, on hand for making sweetmeat pyramids or for serving in pretty dishes (Figs. 3:21, 3:22).[31]

FIG. 3:21. Leon vander Hamen, *Still Life with Candy*. Spain, probably Madrid, 1596–1632. Oil on canvas; H. 39.7 cm., W. 72 cm. (Courtesy, Museum of Fine Arts, Boston, Maria Theresa Burnham Hopkins Fund.)

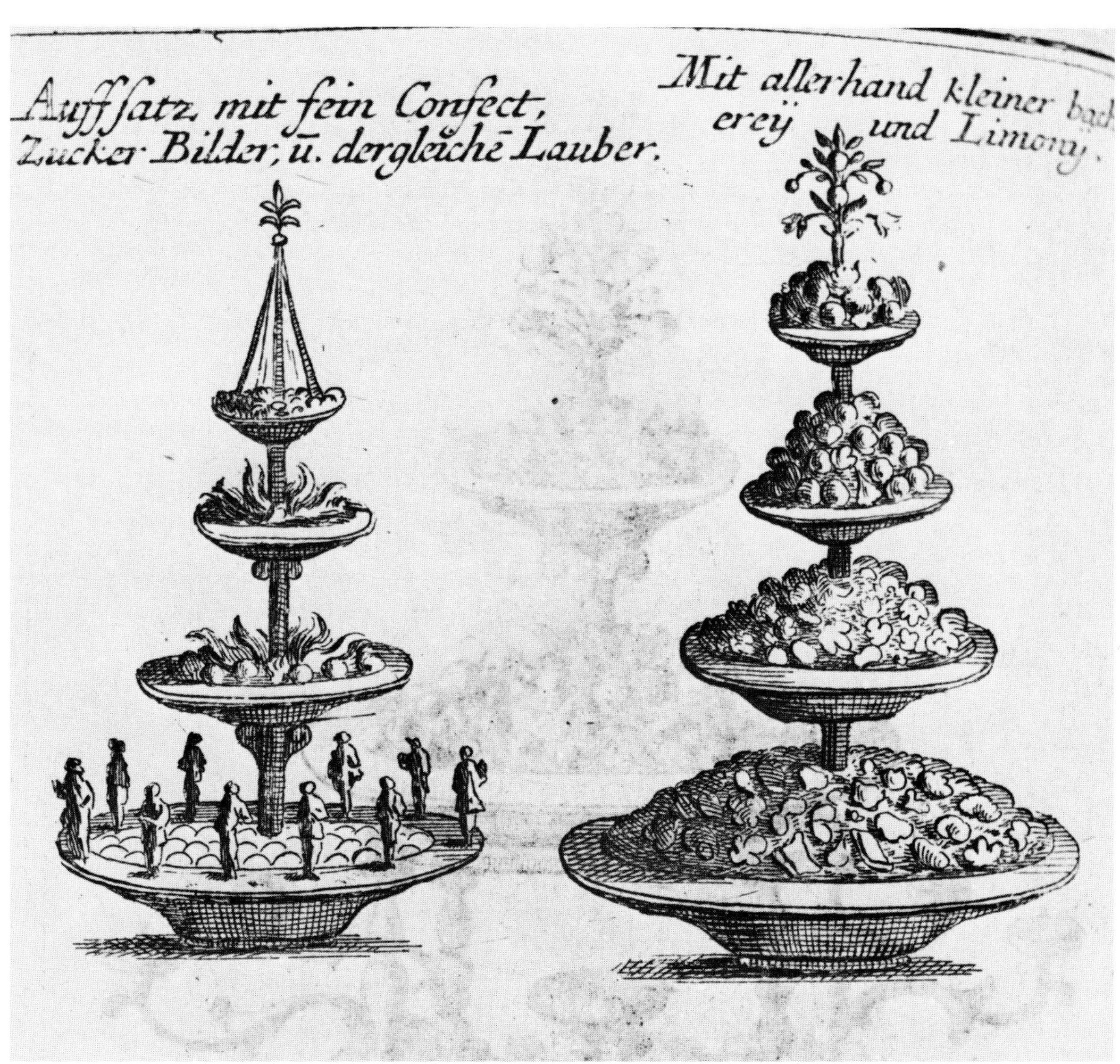

FIG. 3:22. *Surtouts with Comfits, Sugar Figures, Sugar Leaves, and with All Kinds of Little Pastries and Limony.* From Conrad Hagger, *Neues Saltzburgisches Koch-buch*, p. 224. (Vehling Collection, Cornell University Library.)

Sugared Nuts

Almonds, walnuts, and hazelnuts were easily confected and therefore a staple comfit. Ladies covered the nuts with brown or white sugar or with sugar tinted pink. In his *Cooks and Confectioners Dictionary*, John Nott included a recipe popular with the subjects of Queen Anne for almonds rolled in powdered sugar and egg white flavored with orange juice and orange blossoms and laid on paper for baking in a mild oven until dry. When done by a professional confectioner they must have resembled our jordan almonds.[32]

Sugared Flowers

No recipes for sugared flowers appear in the manuscript cookbooks of Elizabeth Mead, Elizabeth Coultas of Philadelphia, or Mrs. Fiske; flower sugaring was an avocation of the less harried among colonial housewives whose households like the Penns' and Custises' included servants. The Penn and Custis methods of candying roses, although practiced some seventy years apart, were simple and similar in all essentials save one: Madam Penn wet rose leaves with gum arabic dissolved in water before strewing them with sugar; Mrs. Custis simply wet them with rosewater before sugaring.

Gum Flowers and Fruits

Sugared nuts and flowers were considered moderately decorative for a dessert table, but artificial fruits and flowers made of sugar and gum arabic ranked higher. Antipas Boyce of Boston in 1669 had on hand "5 p[ape]rs. gum flowers" that he could use for decorating pyramids of salvers, cakes, or molds of jelly. His flowers were undoubtedly professionally made, but similar gum flowers and fruits could be made at home by following published instructions. Some instructions required the housewife confectioner to squeeze a paste of sugar and gum tragacanth between wooden or alabaster molds; some to mold it with the fingers. For making artificial fruits Francis Bacon's 1628 edition of *Sylva Sylvarum; or, A Naturall Historie* suggested molds of earthenware or wood, modeled, cast, or carved "when the fruit [used as model] is young." The *Accomplish'd Female Instructor* in 1704 recommended an alabaster mold of three parts and suggested giving the artificial fruit a few finishing touches of color, copying the leaves and stems realistically from fresh fruit. The surprise would be very great, the reader was assured, when guests expected real fruit and found it artificial. Ladies could take lessons in this deceit from such teachers as Hedewick Sorgen of Charleston who taught the "curious art of making pears, plums, currants, cherries which will keep a number of years as natural as if they were taken off the trees." However or wherever they were made, sculptured fruit and gum flowers were sure to please in the age of Queen Anne, which preferred clever artifice to lowly nature.[33]

Comfits of Sugared Seeds

Comfits of sugared aromatic seeds may not have been as highly prized in the eighteenth century as they were in Queen Elizabeth's day, but they remained a moderately favorite dry sweetmeat. To make them, all that a housewife needed were such seeds as anise, benné, cardamom, poppy, and caraway; some sugar boiled in a little water; a spoon; and a basin in which to stir and shake the seeds. To two ounces of coriander seed Nathan Bailey's *Dictionarium Domesticum* directed her to add three pounds of "fine, hot sugar"—in syrup, of course. The resulting comfits would be as white as snow, it declared.[34] If colored comfits were preferred, the sugar could be made red with cochineal or syrup of mulberries, green with spinach, or yellow with saffron. Thanks to pictures in Diderot's encyclopedia we can comprehend the making of comfits of sugared seeds and sugar gum flowers (Fig. 3:23). For certain comfits shop workers "burned," or pralinated, sugar until it was a deep red, dipped fruit and nuts into it, and spread them on brass screens to drip dry (a). For other comfits a worker added perfumed sugar syrup to almonds, anise, coriander, pistachio, and other nuts and seeds and shook them in a pan suspended by rope and pulley over hot coals in order to cover and polish them. He repeated the process until they had received eight to ten successive ladlesful of syrup, which built them to a diameter of a half inch or so (b, *left*). Another worker shook nuts and seeds covered with syrup in a pan without benefit of rope and pulley (b, *rear*), while still another made expensive beaded comfits with a pearled finish by coating seeds with boiled syrup dripped from a cone (b, *right*).

Gum Sugar Figures

Also thanks to Diderot we can understand the making of sugar figures. Sugar sculpture, Diderot explains, involved crushing gum tragacanth in a mortar (c, *right*), adding sugar and coloring it, rolling it out into a sheet on a marble slab, and cutting it into flower petals with a knife or pressing it into molds to form cups or other familiar objects (c, *left*). In his illustrations we can see flower petals made of colored sugar and gum tragacanth waiting, sorted in a box according to color, for workers to cement them together with icing to create nosegays or flowerets. It was this kind of expensive confectionery that Hezekiah Usher II paid a penny apiece for in Boston in 1751 when he bought "6 Gro. gum flowers."[35]

Comfit Dishes and Spice Plates

These sugar seductions, decorative if not mouth-watering to us today, earned attractive serving dishes. Queen Elizabeth gave comfits a lidded gilt coffer and a silver box in the shape of a tortoise whence she could pluck them with a silver spoon to eat or to array on spice plates or spice trays. A few of her subjects—among them Priscilla's John Alden—provided roundels for serving them. Roundels were thin, six-inch plates of sycamore or beech. During Elizabeth's reign they were decorated with designs of flowers and vines and inscribed with verses to be sung in roundelays, or rounds, by banqueters, once the plates were emptied of their spicery. Edward Winslow, Mayflower immigrant and governor of the Plymouth Colony in 1633, 1636, and 1644, owned a set of twelve, one of which is preserved today in the Plymouth Society museum (Fig. 3:24). Pasted on the center of the roundel is an engraving by Crispin van der Paas the Elder (ca. 1560–1643), which with its encircling verse suggests that each of the eleven other engravings depicted a farm chore appropriate to a month of the year. A few of Alden's and Winslow's contemporaries kept "red trenchers" and "painted trenchers" that may have been roundels. The presence of these decorated plates in seventeenth-century New England adds to the evidence that the Puritan-dominated colony was not entirely dour and unfrivolous but harbored colorful remnants of Merrie England.[36] Descendants of the first New Englanders in the early eighteenth century could have enjoyed

FIG. 3:23. Comfit manufacture and gum sugar sculpture. From *Encyclopédie*, ed. Denis Diderot, *Recueil des planches sur les sciences, les arts libéraux et les arts méchaniques*, 2: pt. 2 (1763), s.v. "Confiseur," pls. 1, 3, 4. (Winterthur Museum Library.)

fig. 4.
fig. 3.
fig. 1.
fig. 2.

FIG. 3:24. Banquet plate, or roundel, England, 1600–1650. From the set owned by Edward Winslow of the Plimouth Plantation. Engraving by Crispin van der Paas the Elder, Holland (1564–1643). Wood and paper; D. 15.2 cm. (Courtesy, Pilgrim Society, Pilgrim Hall Museum, Plymouth, Mass.)

FIG. 3:25. "Merryman" dessert plates, London, dated 1717. White, blue, and green delft (tin-glazed earthenware); D. 21.1 cm. (Winterthur Museum, 61.1337.1–6.)

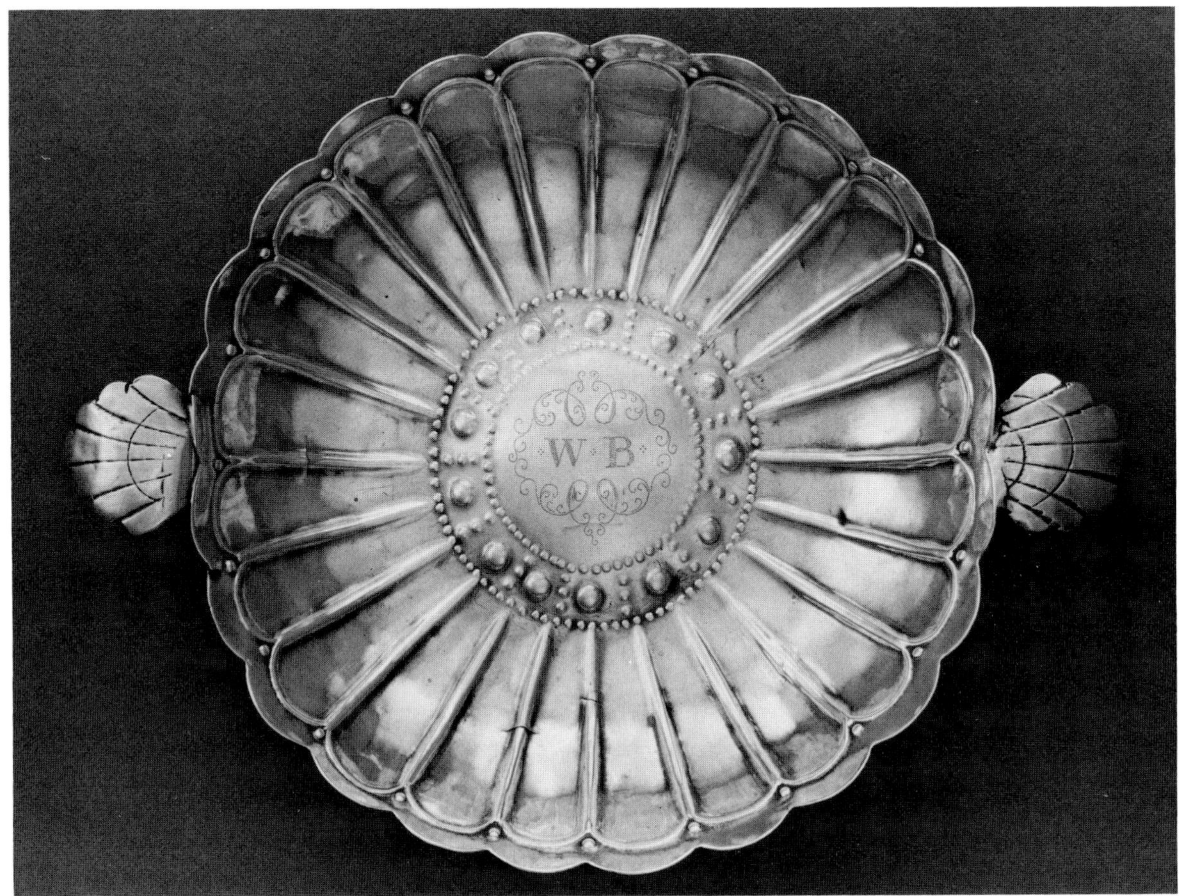

certain plates that seem to derive from roundels with their entertaining verses. The plates came in sets of six in English delftware with a line from an amusing verse on each plate (Fig. 3:25).

In Charles I's reign, comfits were served in shallow, eared silver bowls (Fig. 3:26). In the reigns of the Georges, they were served in porcelain cockleshells and little glass baskets or in glass and ceramic fancies in the shape of fruits, vegetables, leaves, and hearts (Figs. 3:27, 3:28). Most of such fetching containers today are correctly called sweetmeat dishes, but a few are surely the "enamelled pickle shells" advertised in the *Pennsylvania Evening Post* in 1776, the "glass pickle plates" in Sir William Johnson's closet in Johnson Hall, near Johnstown, New York, and the Cadwaladers' "pickle boat with leaves," which held not comfits but the cucumber, mushroom, cauliflower, nasturtium, and barberry pickles beloved of English colonials. Some of the small leaf-shape or quatrefoil dishes that persist today look fanciful enough to be sweetmeat or pickle dishes but are actually stands that sat under sauceboats, small tureens, or cream pots.[37]

Pickle Dishes

FIG. 3:26. Sweetmeat dish, attributed to New England, possibly John Mansfield, Boston, 1630–50. Marked IM in rectangle twice at lip. Inscribed W. B. in pricked lettering. Bradford arms possibly added later on bottom. Silver; H. 2.5 cm., D. 14.3 cm. (Yale University Art Gallery, gift of Josephine Setze for the John Marshall Phillips Collection.)

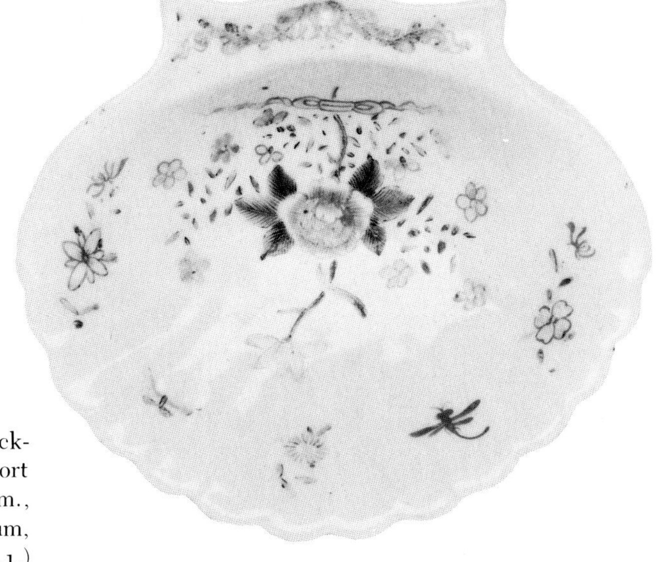

FIG. 3:27. Scallop-shell comfit or pickle dish, China, 1790–1810. Export porcelain; H. 3.8 cm., W. 12.1 cm., L. 10.5 cm. (Winterthur Museum, 60.504.1.)

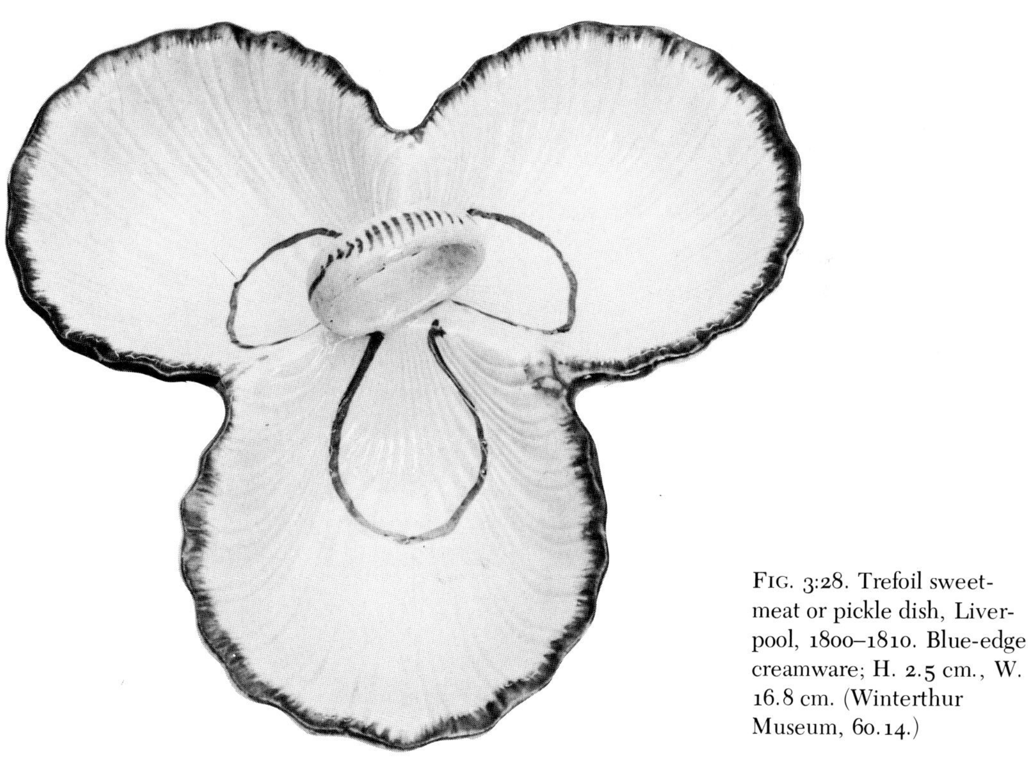

FIG. 3:28. Trefoil sweetmeat or pickle dish, Liverpool, 1800–1810. Blue-edge creamware; H. 2.5 cm., W. 16.8 cm. (Winterthur Museum, 60.14.)

FIG. 3:29. Sweetmeat basket, England, 1750–1800.
Lead glass; H. 9.5 cm., D. 13 cm.
(Winterthur Museum, 69.36, ex coll. Milton H. Biow.)

FIG. 3:30. Sweetmeat basket, United States, 1820–40. Pressed glass; H. 7 cm., D. (lip) 7.6 cm., (base) 5.1 cm. (Winterthur Museum, 59.3248.)

FIG. 3:31. Confectionery basket (stand missing), Leeds or Staffordshire, 1780–1820. Green-edge earthenware; H. 10.6 cm., W. 27.9 cm. (Winterthur Museum, 66.1080.)

Sweetmeat Baskets

Throughout two centuries ladies when arranging desserts made use of little confectionery baskets that could be bought in silver, glass, china, earthenware, wicker, and wax (Figs. 3:29, 3:30). The Leeds pottery catalogue of 1814 offered a pierced confectionery basket and stand made of creamware (Fig. 3:31). The Cadwalader ladies used little baskets of glass "for sugar plums." Other hostesses used edible baskets that they either made at home or bought from a confectioner. Fashioned of white wax and spermaceti lard inside a mold, or of caramel sugar spun over a mold, the baskets made ornamental party favors of a bright white or light golden color. Wicker sweetmeat baskets called *bonbonnières* came from Amsterdam in 1806, ordered by the Baltimore merchant F. F. Wessels along with table mats, fruit baskets, tumbler baskets, and knife baskets. The wicker *bonbonnières* were in the tradition of the small taffeta-covered wicker baskets adorned with ribbons advocated by John Nott more than eighty years earlier, which Nott said were to be placed on the table for each guest and filled with all kinds of sweetmeats, biscuits, marchpanes, orange and lemon faggots, and dried fruits, with the "most delicious comfits on top." Bewitchingly telescoping the centuries, the small Georgian confectionery baskets remind us that some fashions are long lived and that the familiar little crepe paper baskets filled with candies and nuts we see at children's birthday parties today come of a venerable line.[38]

4

Syllabubs, Fools, and Flummeries

Six dishes of glasses of syllabub and as many of jelly besides one or two "floating islands," as they denominate what we call whipped cream, and odd corners filled up by ginger and other preserves.

Mrs. Basil Hall,
Columbia, South Carolina, 1828[1]

Creams

Spicery may have been the mainstay of an Elizabethan banquet and sucket the star of a seventeenth-century banquet, but for the rococo eighteenth-century dessert creams got top billing. Whipped, plain, or frozen, they appeared in platoons on the tables of fashionable hostesses who doted on their prettiness and delicious flavors. Creams came in pistachio, lemon, raspberry, and many other flavors and colors, providing a pastel foil to the rich hues of plum and cherry sweetmeats. When piled high and studded with blossoms, comfits, or bits of jelly, they enhanced even the most beautiful table and made it as amusing and gay as the porcelain shepherdesses that surrounded them.

As a rule, men referred to creams contemptuously as "the little end of nothing whittled down" and fumed over all desserts with William Kitchiner, whose *Cook's Oracle* was reprinted for Americans:

> It is your second courses—ridiculous variety of Wines, Liqueurs, Ices, Desserts, &c which are served up to feed the Eye—that overcome the stomach and paralyze Digestion and seduce "children of a large Growth" to sacrifice the health and comfort of several days for the Baby-pleasure of tickling their tongue for a few minutes with Trifles and Custards.[2]

Syllabub

But a good syllabub was countenanced by many early Georgian males at any time of day or night. William Byrd of Virginia and Benjamin Lynde of Boston each liked one for supper, and, on occasion, also for breakfast. In a few foamy swallows these busy men could take on both nourishment and a bracer.[3]

Milking a cow into a bowl of cider, beer, or ale was one quick way of making a frothy syllabub. The milk might curdle but the drinkers did not mind; they were fond of curds and often ate a dishful plain or flavored with lemon, orange, or almond, much as we eat yogurt today. If a cow were unavailable or uncooperative in supplying the main ingredient, a teakettle of warm milk or cream was called upon. Poured from a height well above the bowl, its milky stream, though less fresh and elemental, raised a fine foam.

Syllabubs of this liquid frothy variety came to the drinker in large two-handled vessels (Fig. 4:1) or in small glass two-handled cups. Wealthy men owned big cups of silver, some fitted with covers like Governor Tryon's fluted pair or like the bowl Charles Carroll ordered from London in 1767, which he specified should have "a circular loose top of scalloped carved plate . . . to put on when used for syllabub and take off when occasion for punch."[4]

FIG. 4:1. Two-handled cup by Jurian Jeurisen Blanck, Jr., New York, 1666–99. Marked I:B with four conjoined circles below, in square, once on lid, twice below rim to the left of each handle. Inscribed I^C^B for Jacobus and Eve Philipse van Cortlandt. Philipse coat of arms. Silver; H. (with cover) 14.2 cm., D. (at base) 9 cm. (Winterthur Museum, 59.2298.)

FIG. 4:2. Posset pot, Lambeth, 1660–80. Delft (tin-glazed earthenware); H. 23.5 cm., D. (at top) 15.2 cm. (Winterthur Museum, 58.1533.)

Caudles and Possets

Drunk for nourishment from a bowl or cup, liquid syllabub did not belong on the dessert table but served the same life-giving purpose as similar but not so frivolous caudles and possets. All three drinks had in common a wine or a malted beverage, but each had its own thickening. Syllabub, made of sack or other wine, had whipped cream for its base. Posset, which was made of ale or beer, sack or other wine, had eggs, bread, naples biscuit, almond paste, or some kind of porridge—most often oatmeal. Caudle, which was made of sack or other wine, had eggs. A posset went down best when the winter wind blew cold and the drink was heated over the fire or with a hot poker so that as it passed from hand to hand it warmed both gullet and cold fingers. In its rounds it was inclined to separate and the thickener to rise to the top. It was then a convenience to have in hand a posset pot made with a tubular spout that rose from near the bottom "to let out the posset ale" (Fig. 4:2). A drinker who took a pull at the spout advantageously bypassed much of the bread or oatmeal. He also assured himself a good swallow of alcohol and kept foam from his face.[5]

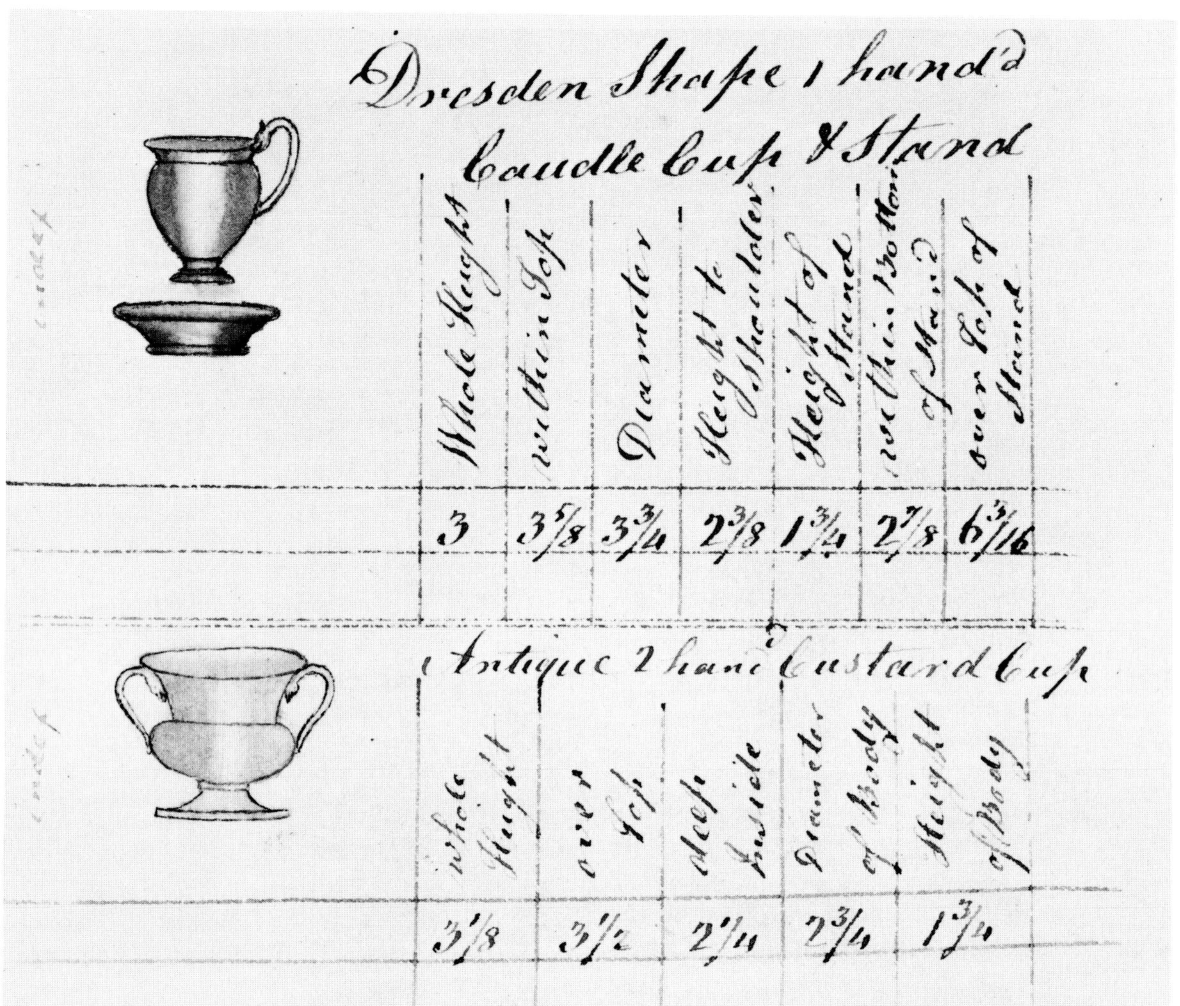

Dresden Shape 1 hand'd Caudle Cup & Stand

Whole Height	within Top	Diameter	Height to Shoulder	Height of Stand	within Bottom of Stand	over Top of Stand
3	3 5/8	3 3/4	2 3/8	1 3/4	2 7/8	6 3/16

Antique 2 hand'd Custard Cup

Whole Height	over Top	deep inside	Diameter of Body	Height of Body
3 1/8	3 1/2	2 1/4	2 3/4	1 3/4

FIG. 4:3. Patterns for caudle and custard cups. From a manuscript potter's manual, attributed to the Spode factory, England, ca. 1815–21, p. 50. Watercolor and ink. (Winterthur Museum Library, DMMC.)

Caudle, like posset, was served warm or hot. Neither a beverage as some syllabubs were, nor a dessert dish as whipped syllabub came to be, it nevertheless was a festive food/drink for such occasions as weddings and baptisms. It also suited the occasion for lyings-in to revive and sustain the new mother, celebrate the baby's arrival, congratulate the parents, and entertain visiting friends and relatives. As a ceremonial drink, caudle could command such fine vessels as the covered silver caudle cups that the women of John Freack's family used before 1675 in their Boston parlor, the porcelain bowls, or "burnt china caudle dishes," that belonged to William Burnet, and the porcelain caudle cups and saucers of Governor Tryon. It merited the ceramic bell-shaped caudle cups with one handle that came into style with a matching saucer after the revolutionary war (Fig. 4:3).[6]

Whipped Syllabub

Of the three nourishing drinks only syllabub became a decorative dessert. The seventeenth-century variety made with the help of a cow or a teapot was turned in the eighteenth century into a whipped refreshment that was partly to be eaten, partly drunk. To produce the new whipped syllabub, an eighteenth-century hostess beat cream to a fine froth with a whisk, rod, large chocolate mill, or "ventilator for syllabubs," as cookbooks variously suggested. The nineteenth-century hostess beat cream with a cylindrical device fitted with a plunger. Whatever instrument a hostess used, the procedure involved agitating the cream for a half hour or more to coax it, with additions of white or red wine, lemon juice, and sugar, into spoon-eating consistency. It meant skimming off the froth as it rose and laying it on a hair sieve that rested over a bowl to catch the drippings; pouring the remaining unwhippable liquid into cups or footed, spreading, syllabub glasses (Fig. 4:4); and then heaping the whipped cream as

FIG. 4:4. Syllabub glass, England, 1760–70, collection of Arthur Churchill. From G. Bernard Hughes, *English, Scottish, and Irish Table Glass*, p. 307. (Winterthur Museum Library.)

high as possible on top of the liquid. The whip was downed with a tablespoon after which the liquid was drunk. It was a point of pride to have a tall mound of whip on top of the liquid. One Englishwoman, in an effort to achieve the tallest mounds her guests had ever seen, tied paper collars around her glasses to support their pillars of cream. At the last second, before revealing the dessert table to the guests, her servants removed the collars. Whipped syllabubs of whatever height were unquestionably beguiling in the eyes of eighteenth-century female party-goers who thought no dessert complete without their fairy colors. Their pale lemon below and rich cream above, or rose below and pale pink above—tints that depended on the wine that was used—showed well through glass and complemented the currently fashionable enameled table porcelains.[7]

Solid or Everlasting Syllabub

Early in the eighteenth century a nameless syllabubmaker discovered that she could make a good syllabub without sieve and drippings bowl. She simply whisked the heaviest cream she could find with wine, lemon, and sugar until it would hold its shape, filled her glasses or cups, and let them stand overnight in a cool place. The resulting solid or everlasting syllabub stayed firm for three days or so without separating into liquid and froth and could be entirely eaten with a teaspoon. Like the frothy half-liquid syllabubs, it took a place on a pyramid of salvers side by side with glasses of jellies and piles of comfits, surviving masculine scorn and figuring prominently in recipe books for a century and a half.[8]

Trifle

Trifle—or "triffle," as it was pronounced as late as the late nineteenth century in a try at the French word *trufle*—stood out among the most delicious and beautiful of desserts, a delectable combination of four favorite eighteenth-century sweetmeats: syllabub, cake, custard, and jelly. It too survived male antagonism, although its name, which derived from the Italian *truffa*, "cheat" or "swindle," proclaims what Englishmen thought about it as food. A seventeenth-century hostess made one version of it by heating cream and allowing it to stand until it formed a crust like that on Devonshire cream. She made another version by solidifying cream with rennet until it grew to resemble cheese. To both trifles she added sugar and such spices as cinnamon and mace. The eighteenth-century hostess, on the other hand, preferred a fashionable whipped variety. For big occasions, abandoning all caution, she layered sherry-soaked almond cakes or naples biscuit with jam or jelly and soft custard and mounded a whipped syllabub on top, creating in an extravagant display of colors, flavors, and textures what the *Family Receipt-Book* called A Grand Trifle. When it was garlanded with almond cakes, flowers, and more jelly and served in "elegant cut-glass trifle dishes" that were "sufficiently large and elevated to convey an idea of grandeur," as Mrs. Raffald put it in 1769, it could not fail to stun the most critical party guest.[9]

Floating Island

Countless other creams and whips with fanciful names rivaled the Grand Trifle, and some of them, like floating island, almost equalled it. With its islands of airy pink egg white floating on a sea of sweetened cream, New Yorker Mary

Eubbs's version came close. But Mrs. Glasse's came closer. Its thin slices of French bread and currant jelly on liquid cream bore castles of whipped cream in a soup tureen or deep glass dish rimmed with sweetmeats, jellies, or jams and lighted by a ring of candles standing around it (Fig. 4:5). Either would have beautified the center of the Quaker Mr. Clifford's Philadelphia table when as a bride from England Ann Warder saw a floating island there in 1786. John Adams's favorite whortleberry fool, a concoction of soft custard, heavy cream, and mashed fruit, which the cookbook author Eliza Leslie called "a plain dessert with a foolish name," would approach it in handsomeness if Mrs. Adams served it in a blue and white bowl and matching dishes of the kind Mrs. Hutchinson owned. The *Accomplish'd Female Instructor*'s cream fool made of eggs, wine, and mashed raspberries or other fruit piled onto "carved manchets" of fine white bread, with sugar sifted over, was decorative enough to be in the running. Even Thomas Jefferson's simple sweetmeat cream could compete. It was made, he told his granddaughters, "for a dessert or evening party" by putting spoonsful of jam or jelly in a glass and covering them with "whip."[10]

Fools

Sweetmeat Cream

FIG. 4:5. Trifle dish, England, 1790–1820. Part of a dessert service with a tradition of ownership in the Dabney family of Maryland and Virginia. Lead glass; H. 15.8 cm., D. (at rim) 24.1 cm. (Winterthur Museum, 61.478.)

Dishes for Creams

Creams were served not only in soup tureens, deep glass dishes, small blue and white dishes, or glasses, but also in such special containers as large footed cream cups and cream bowls, or cream pots (Figs. 4:6, 4:7). They were also served in small cream buckets and in the small covered pots called *pots à crème* by nineteenth-century francophiles (Fig. 4:8). *Pots à crème* might be clustered on a dish or platter as they were on Mrs. Randolph's Virginia table, with a teaspoon placed neatly between each one (Pl. 4:9). Creams might be served also in melon- and leaf-shaped dishes like those in the box of English china Benjamin Franklin sent his wife in 1758, or in other fruit- and vegetable-shaped dishes in the colorful, playful manner valued by rococo-century hostesses.[11]

FIG. 4:7. Cream bowl with three claws, from a 130-piece service, France, 1820–40. Owned by Governor Mahlon Dickerson of New Jersey (1770–1853), U.S. senator and secretary of the navy under Presidents Jackson and van Buren. Porcelain; H. 21.6 cm., D. 15.3 cm. (From the original in the New Jersey Historical Society, courtesy, New Jersey Historical Society.)

3 heads on each

Round French Cream Bowl on 3 Claws

Height of Body	Diameter of Body	Height to Shoulder	within Neck	over Top	Height of foot	over Top of foot	over Bottom of foot	Height of Plinth	Diameter of plinth	Height of Cover	Width of Cover
3 1/2	5 3/4	2 3/8	4 7/8	6 5/8	1 3/4	3	4 1/4	1 1/8	5 3/4	1 5/16	6

FIG. 4:6. Round French cream bowl on three claws. From a manuscript potter's manual, attributed to the Spode factory, England, ca. 1815–21, p. 31. Rose purple watercolor and ink. (Winterthur Museum Library, DMMC.)

FIG. 4:8. Cream or custard cups, China, 1785–95. Gilt initials SS for Samuel Shaw, officer on Washington's staff and first unofficial ambassador to China from the United States. Porcelain; H. (with cover) 7.6 cm., D. (at lip) 6.1 cm. (Winterthur Museum, 63.721.1.)

Custards

Baked custards and soft custards sat on every American family dessert table. Before the eighteenth century, baked custards accompanied the second of the two main courses, but by the time the eighteenth century was under way, they had joined pastries and puddings as after-dinner desserts. Housewives baked them in deep china dishes, baking dishes, and "bakers" and for individual service in cream cups, china teacups, or china custard cups with or without covers. In some federal houses custard cups came to the table by the dozen, clustered as Mary Randolph's small cream pots were.

Molded Creams

Creams that were set with rennet or a jelling agent so that they could be molded decoratively became indispensable to the eighteenth- and nineteenth-century hostess. One of her favorites was steeple cream composed of almonds pounded in a mortar and mixed with sweetened cream and hartshorn, ivory dust, gum arabic, gum tragacanth, or some other jelling agent. She let it jell in large molds, flummery prints, or conical galley pots, or else in individual tall ale glasses or narrow-bottomed drinking glasses. When she turned it out into a shallow bowl, crowned it with blossoms, and surrounded it with whipped cream or preserved sweetmeats, it all but took the palm away from trifle.[12]

Ice Cream

Frozen cream, at least since the fifteenth century, had graced the tables of England's great houses, and in the eighteenth century, Englishmen of position and wealth ate it even in the North American colonies. About 1770 when Lord Botetourt, governor of Virginia, entertained guests at the palace in Williamsburg, ice cream that had been frozen in his three pewter ice molds was put before them. Guests of Governor Thomas Bladen of Maryland received no less, so that when William Black had dined in the Annapolis mansion he could write with delight about "the fine ice cream [that] with the strawberries and milk eat most deliciously." The Washingtons' visitors enjoyed desserts made in a "cream

FIG. 4:10. Food for the gods. From Emy, *L'Art de bien faire les glaces d'office*, frontispiece. (Winterthur Museum Library.)

machine for ice" bought for one pound thirteen shillings and fourpence in 1784, and Mrs. Washington, after the general became president, served ice cream and lemonade to the ladies who attended her levees. As the new republic grew, frozen desserts became less than state treats. When Philadelphia had an early hot spell in March of 1787 Mrs. Adams ate ices merely to cool herself, and during New York's hot weather Brannon's Tea Garden near Brooklyn sold ice cream to any of its customers who could escape the big city.[13]

Ice-Cream Dishes

Hostesses served ice cream in several ways. They piled it high in individual glasses or china cream cups (Figs. 4:10, 4:11), spooned it into an ice pail that was sometimes called a glacier, or *glacière*, or pressed it into a mold and turned it out onto a plate (Figs. 4:12, 4:13). Mrs. Randolph liked the English custom of serving it piled in individual handled glasses, not turned out into the kinds of tall molds preferred by ladies in Albany in the 1820s. Professor and Mrs. Ticknor of Boston liked to put it into their china ice pails that matched their Sèvres dessert service, the most beautiful, Mrs. Hall asserted, she had ever

FIG. 4:11. Cream cup and saucer, China, 1780–1800. Part of a dessert service owned by Samuel Shaw and subsequently by Josiah Quincy. The service bears the order of the Society of the Cincinnati of which Shaw was a founding member. Porcelain; H. (cup) 6.7 cm., D. 8.9 cm., H. (saucer) 3.3 cm., D. 14 cm. (Winterthur Museum, 53.166.1.)

FIG. 4:12. Dessert pail, or glacier, Spode, ca. 1805. Porcelain; H. 32.5 cm., D. 26 cm. (Winterthur Museum, 61.639.20.)

seen. Ice pails were designed to hold crushed ice around and on top of a container of ice cream or fruit ice to keep it cold on handsomely set tables during dessert. The term *ice pail* is subject to confusion. The English, notably the potters who put together a manual around 1817, used it to mean either a glacier or a wine cooler (Figs. 4:14, 4:15). But the Leeds pottery in its 1814 catalogue chose the term *ice cellar* and labeled wine coolers ice pails. Thus when the term *ice pail* was used in Philadelphia in 1776 it could have meant either wine cooler or glacier.[14]

FIG. 4:13. Ice-cream mold, Europe, 1875–1900. Pewter; H. 25.4 cm., D. (at base) 14.6 cm. (Winterthur Museum, 65.38.)

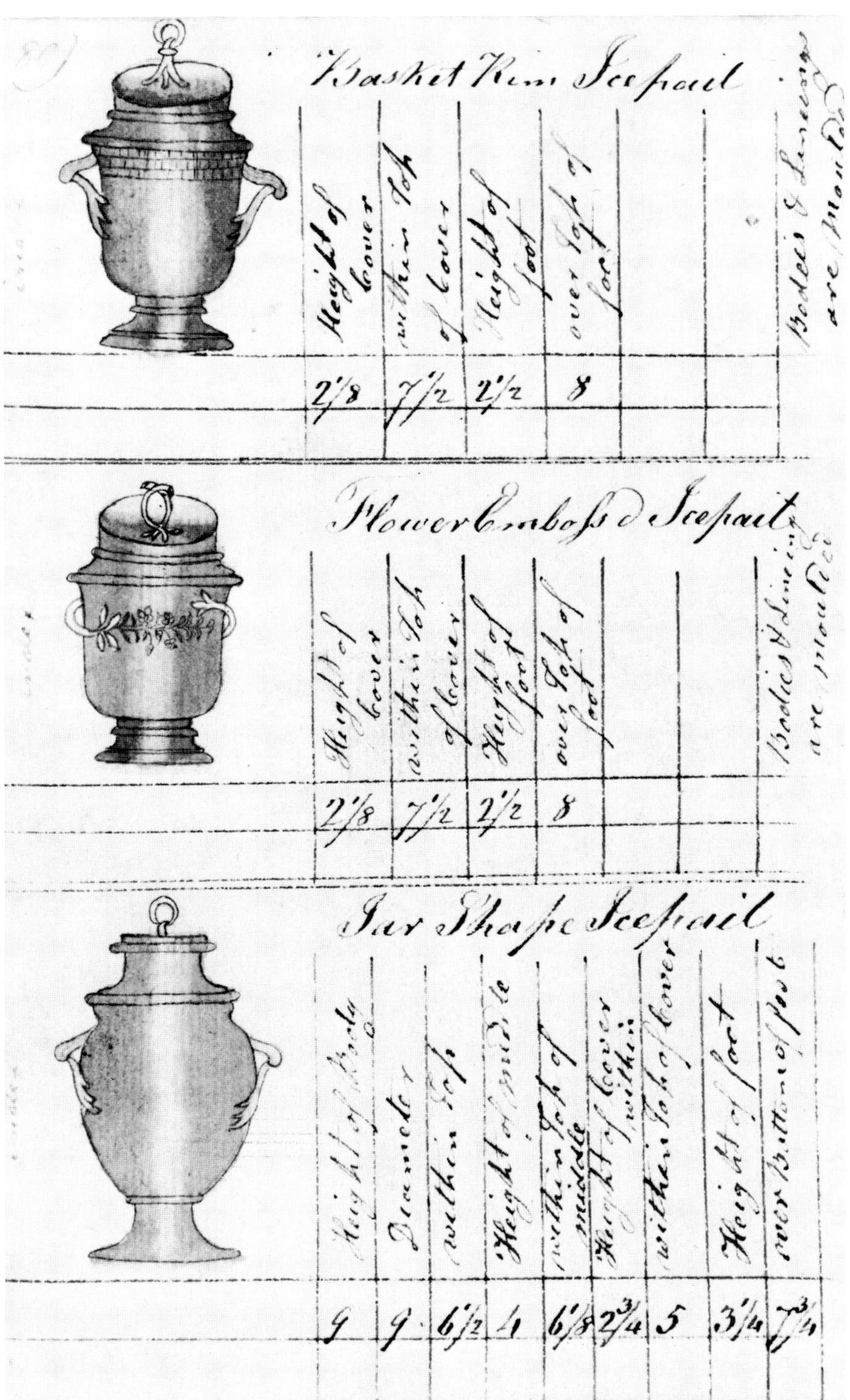

Basket Rim Icepail

Height of cover	within top of cover	Height of foot	over top of foot			Bodies & Linings are moulded
2⅛	7½	2½	8			

Flower Emboss'd Icepail

Height of cover	within top of cover	Height of foot	over top of foot			Bodies & Linings are moulded
2⅛	7½	2½	8			

Jar Shape Icepail

Height of Body	Diameter	within top	Height of middle	within top of middle	Height of cover within	within top of cover	Height of foot	over Bottom of foot
9	9	6½	4	6⅛	2¾	5	3¼	7¾

FIG. 4:14. Ice pails. From a manuscript potter's manual, attributed to the Spode factory, England, ca. 1815–21, p. 80. (Winterthur Museum Library, DMMC.)

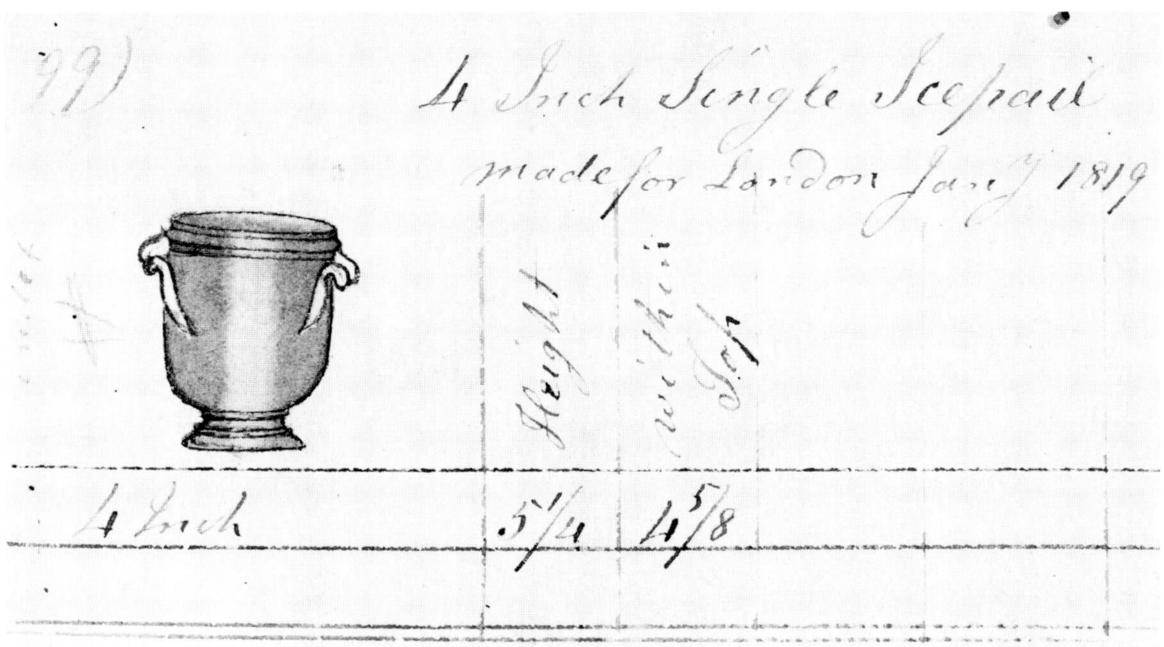

FIG. 4:15. Four-inch single ice pail. From a manuscript potter's manual, attributed to the Spode factory, England, ca. 1815–21, p. 27. (Winterthur Museum Library, DMMC.)

Ice-Cream Molds

Tin or pewter molds produced frozen desserts in many forms. Tall geometrical outlines or the shapes of fruits were among the most popular. It would be interesting to know the shapes of the six pewter ice molds and twenty block tin molds in which, with the help of three ice buckets and ice shovels, Edward Lloyd's kitchen staff froze decorative creams during Maryland's hot days of the 1780s. If the shapes were of fruit, the staff could attach stems and leaves of real greenery to the frozen creams before sending them to the table. M. Emy, who wrote *L'Art de bien faire les glaces d'office*, would have them crown a pineapple-shaped ice with a tuft of real pineapple leaves after removing a few of the leaves "so that it is less tufted than normal." We know the shape of Theodorick Bland's mold; he wrote from Virginia to ask his brother-in-law St. George Tucker to have a pewter mold made for him in an "obtuse cone with a top fitted to it." And we know that the Albany ladies' molds were shaped to look like "a great pillar" or like the "pyramid of ice rivalling those of Egypt" that amazed and amused Mrs. Hall when she dined at Governor Clinton's Albany mansion in 1827. Broad-based pillar molds and tall narrow pillar molds later in the Victorian century rose in turrets, battlements, and buttresses that reflected the Gothic revival architecture of the time (Fig. 4:16). Their concave and convex surfaces

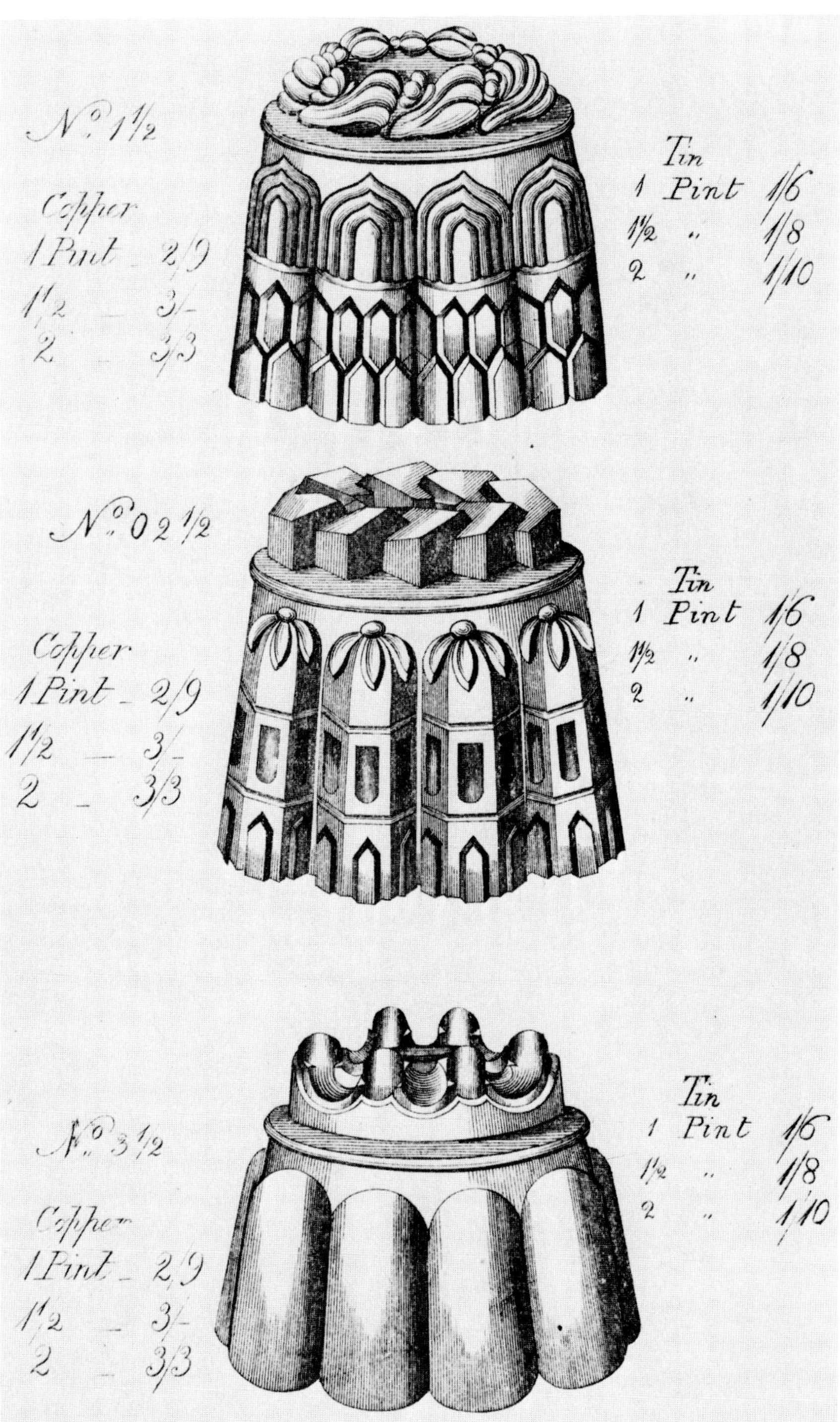

FIG. 4:16. Jelly and blancmange molds. From Henry Loveridge & Co., *Catalogue*, p. 381. (Winterthur Museum Library.)

suggested the concave surfaces of mansard roofs and the convex curves of towers. The smooth melon shapes of eighteenth-century molds gave place to arabesques and gothic crockets. Almonds and pieces of citron that formerly clung to the surface of hedgehog and other puddings gave way to bosses of red raspberries and mushrooms. Impressive architectural molds remained the fashion through the nineteenth century, but in addition, toward 1880, cozy domestic shapes not unlike those used for jellies and creams in the eighteenth century became the rage. One could see at handsome dinners in large cities such jelly shapes as a hen surrounded by her chicks, a hen sitting on the side of a spun-glass nest looking sideways at her eggs, or even a "perfect imitation of asparagus with a cream-dressing, the asparagus being made of the pistache cream, and the dressing simply a whipped cream." Mary Henderson thought all such shapes "very beautiful."[15]

Making Ice Cream in the Eighteenth Century

To make ice cream, or cream ices as they were often called, and to mold them in fashionable fruit shapes, the eighteenth-century housewife first needed to freeze a mixture of cream, flavoring, and sugar, then put it in molds and pack it in ice to refreeze it. Elizabeth Raffald, popular London cookbook author, used an eight-step recipe that involved paring apricots and beating them in a mortar, mixing them with sugar and scalding cream, working them through a sieve, breaking ice and packing it around a pailful of the apricots and cream, stirring the partially frozen mixture, repacking it for more freezing, unpacking and molding it, and finally refreezing it. A freezer consisting of a wooden tub and pewter or tin cylinder was used by professionals (Fig. 4:17), but some people were satisfied with a teakettle that they could twist around in the ice by the handle. A pewter cylinder was held by most people to be preferable to a tin one because, as Mrs. Randolph maintained, it was more resistant to wear and not given to rusting. Not until the middle of the nineteenth century could consumers indulge themselves either in a "patent freezer" that Williams & Co. advertised in O'Brien's Philadelphia directory in 1845 or in a "new and popular" machine with a crank and dasher of the kind to be found in 1857 in Peterson's Manufactory and Wareroom in New York City.[16]

M. Emy gives credit to Alexander the Great for discovering ice cream by accident once when he was near a glacier on his travels. Emy gives thanks to Sir Francis Bacon (1561–1626) for our knowledge of the physics of freezing ice cream and ices and of the effect of salt or saltpeter on the process. Bacon discovered that less salt was needed when the weather was dry, cold, or hot; more when the weather was cloudy, snowy, or rainy. Emy himself had found that the richer the mixture (called by the French *fromage* or *sorbet*) the greater the need for ice. He advocated turning the ice pail, in French *sorbétière*, ten or fifteen minutes, opening and scraping down the frozen sherbet, then closing the *sorbétière* and turning it ten or fifteen minutes more. Like other French confectioners, he recommended eggs, sugar, cream, and flavoring for a rich *fromage*. Most Americans omitted eggs, but Jane Janvier, housewife of Philadelphia, agreed with Emy. Her recipe, written down some time between 1817

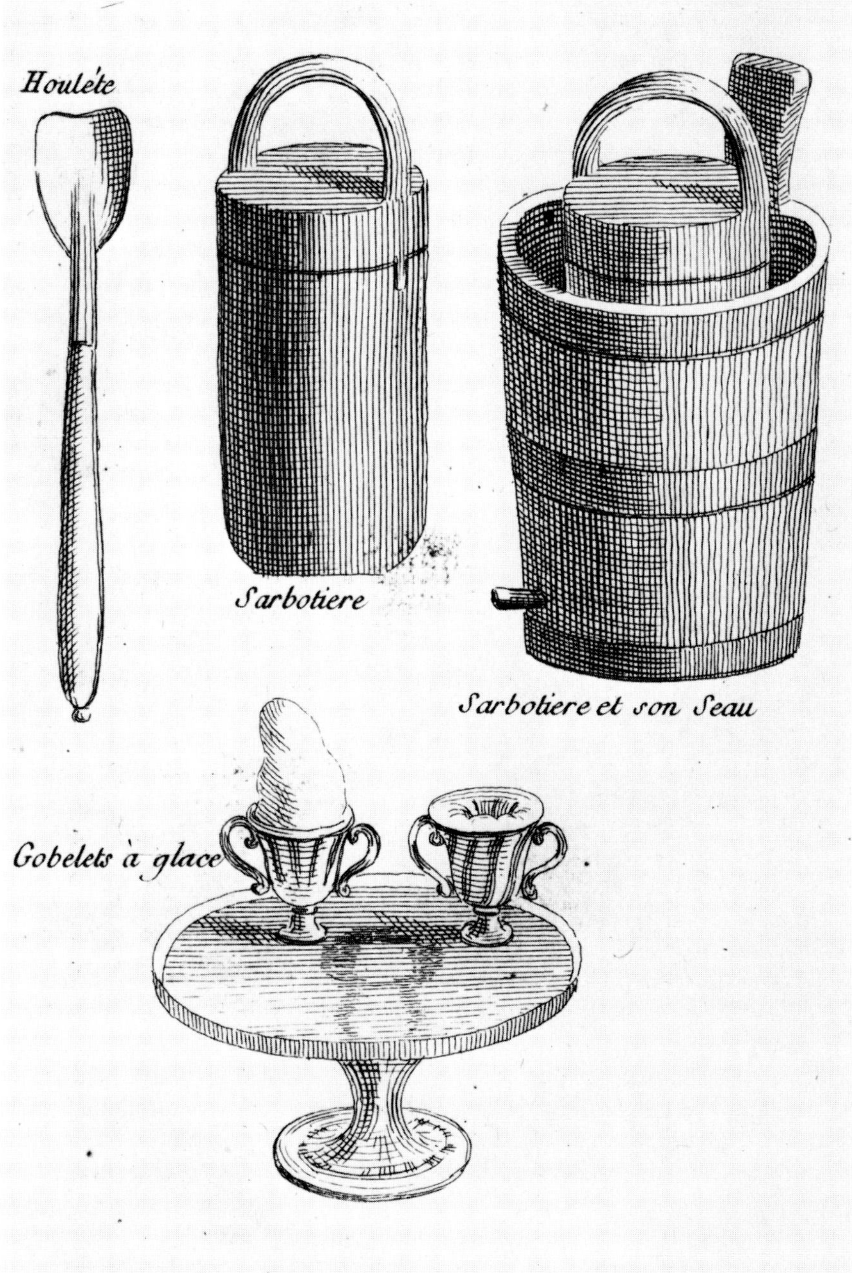

FIG. 4:17. *Sorbétière* and pail with spaddle and ice-cream cups. From Emy, *L'Art de bien faire les glaces d'office*, pl. 1, p. 72. (Winterthur Museum Library.)

and 1837 in a manuscript copybook, was not of the kind that established the reputation of Philadelphia pure cream ice cream but was of the French variety. She wrote of ice cream in a firm hand, "It is very poor without any eggs."[17]

Ice and Icehouses

To make sure that they could enjoy ice cream in summer, householders cut blocks of ice from lakes and rivers after the first deep freeze of winter and stored them underground. Governor Botetourt had an icehouse built at Williamsburg under the mount at the bottom of the topiary garden behind the palace, where it may be seen to this day. The Binghams of Philadelphia built an icehouse at their country seat at Black Point, New Jersey, and Victor du Pont had one dug at Goodstay, his house in Bergen, New Jersey. Mr. du Pont's icehouse expenses in 1802 amounted to forty-one dollars for payment to several workmen for digging a hole and twenty-eight and a half dollars for mason's work. Each eighteenth-century householder obtained ice locally, and it was not until the first quarter of the nineteenth century that ice was harvested in great quantities and sold commercially far from its source. Successful entrepreneurs like some in Wiscasset, Maine, shipped ice as far away as India and South America and made a profit despite the fact that sometimes 40 percent of the ice melted in transit.[18]

Vanilla

Although vanilla is today far and away the most popular ice-cream flavor, in 1800 people considered it an exotic bean with a "peculiar and delicious flavor, agreeable to some palates and disagreeable to others," useful largely as a medicine and as a perfume for chocolate. In the first American edition of his *Cyclopaedia*, Abraham Rees explained: "The fruit is only used in England as an ingredient in chocolate . . . but the Spanish physicians use it in medicine, and esteem it grateful to the stomach and brain, good for expelling wind, for provoking urine, resisting poison, and curing the bite of venomous animals." About this time, some venturesome confectioners—Thomas Jefferson among them—flavored ice cream with vanilla, and by 1828 when Miss Leslie published her *Seventy-five Receipts for Pastry, Cakes, and Sweetmeats*, a vanilla bean split into small pieces vied with lemons and almonds as the source of favorite flavors. By the time Miss Leslie's *New Receipts for Cooking* appeared in midcentury, "vanilla syrup," or "tincture of vanilla," either made at home or bought at the druggist's, had found its way into blancmanges, custards, plain creams, and frozen creams, where it has remained firmly at the top of the flavor list. But if cooks before 1800 largely ignored vanilla as a flavor for ice cream, they made good use of dozens of other flavors. All of the ordinary fruits and the not-so-ordinary currant and damson went into their mixtures, as did chocolate, pistachio, coffee, burnt almond, and (Howard Johnson take note) brownbread and Parmesan cheese.[19]

Molded Jellies

In 1820 Baron Axel Leonhard Klinkowström, a Swedish army lieutenant on fleet assignment to the United States, paused long enough in New York City to partake of domestic pleasures. A personable bachelor, Lieutenant Klinkowström was greatly sought after by hostesses and had ample opportunity to observe American social customs. At the New York Assembly he was introduced to the

FIG. 4:18. Jellies on a serving table. (Georgia Dining Room, 1830–40, Winterthur Museum.)

American pattern of evening entertainments, which, he noted, meant much dancing of quadrilles and anglaises but infrequent waltzing, promenading through the rooms with a lady, card playing, and enjoying refreshments. At the homes of local political dignitaries and of the bankers Thomas Morris and Augustus Lawrence, he dined and attended balls that he considered "rather brilliant with respect to costumes, expensive porcelain, and glass, and the quantity of silver used." Being entertained at the Park Place party of the Lawrences and the magnificent party in the Morrises' spacious and beautiful house gave him opportunity to survey the "splendid and tasteful clothes, fine man-

FIG. 4:19. Jelly, blanc-mange, or flummery molds, England, 1820–40. Glazed earthenware; L. (mold with grapes) 12.7 cm., W. 8.9 cm., D. 4.4 cm., L. (mold with fruit basket) 17.2 cm., W. 14 cm., D. 6.7 cm. (Talbot County [Maryland] Historical Society.)

ners, and graceful dancing" of the ladies of New York society and to eat suppers that featured oysters and were followed by a profusion of ices and confections.[20]

The confections served the baron undoubtedly included the molded jellies, creams, blancmanges, and flummeries that ladies commonly provided for their parties (Fig. 4:18). The ladies offered these creations not so much to satisfy their guests' appetites as to decorate the table and stimulate conversation. In fact, the more originality a hostess displayed in her molded dishes, the greater the number of favorable comments made by her guests, who were not beyond counting the variety of her offerings and openly rating her choice and execution

FIG. 4:20. Jelly and blancmange molds, America or England, 1830–50. Heavy tin; H. (largest fluted mold) 7.6 cm., L. 19.7 cm., W. 14 cm. (Talbot County [Maryland] Historical Society.)

of corner dishes. "Corners" were meant to be eye-catching. In pink, red, green, yellow, or purple, their color and complexity determined a table's success. Critical opinion was influenced by the number of times a particular style of corner dish appeared at parties, but even with a small repertoire or limited funds, a hostess, if inventive in varying the details, could score high. In 1824 Mary Eubbs used a recipe called Green Melon in Jelly to produce a tall, round, transparent colorless shape that revealed a green jelly fruit in its depths. Other hostesses used molds to make recipes called Hens and Chickens, Eggs and Bacon, Cribbage Cards, Hedge Hog, and Gilded Fish. They could buy countless molds for these jellied conversation pieces in many American shops. One shop alone advertised in the *Virginia Gazette* for July 25, 1766, tin blancmange molds for harlequins, eggs, stars, hedgehogs, fish, half moons, steeples, swans, obelisks, hens and chickens, packs of cards, and sunflowers. These and the blancmange molds in Lady Temple's Boston cupboards, the queensware molds of Edward Lloyd's Maryland kitchen, and the copper, earthenware, and whiteware molds of other households produced eye-catchers for many ball suppers and dessert entertainments (Figs. 4:19, 4:20). If the guests did more looking than eating, partially tasted jellies could be melted down into small molds or glasses to be used the following day.[21]

Jelly Glasses

Jellies, blancmanges, and flummeries did not always appear on the table in large molds but often in individual glasses, as steeple cream did. Individual jelly glasses by the dozens crowded the cupboard shelves of well-furnished houses (Fig. 4:21). In the late eighteenth century they came as part of great dinner sets like the 218-piece service of engraved table glass that the Stevens Glass Concern of Bristol, England, sold to Messrs. T. & T. Powell of Baltimore in 1797. The set included "two dozen round-foot jellies fluted and engraved, and one dozen round-foot syllabubs." It is not always easy to distinguish between jelly and syllabub glasses, but it is helpful to remember that early in the eighteenth century "jellies" were smaller and less flaring than "syllabubs." It is less helpful to realize that both could be bought with one or two handles or none.[22]

Decorations for Jellies

Picturesque shapes seemed not enough to ensure amusing jellies and creams; they must be embellished with all sorts of knickknacks such as sprigs of flowers and herbs, liberal scatterings of colored comfits and nonpareils, beaten tinted egg whites, and cream "frothed high." Sarah Harrison's recipe in her *House-Keeper's Pocket-Book* for the very popular snow required a branch of rosemary and some birch twigs to flavor and beat its foundation of sweetened cream. "It will look better and taste better," Mrs. Harrison said, "if you lay at the bottom of the dish you serve it in a little plate of silver made full of holes, and those stuck with long stalks of borage with the flowers on." Richard Briggs, author of *The New Art of Cookery*, suggested serving orange jelly garnished with pieces of other jellies and with sweetmeats, flowers, or anything the reader fancied. Elizabeth Raffald's fancy for Solomon's Temple in Flummery ran to red, white, and chocolate coloring, with four towers topped with sprigs. And, the fancies of cookbook writers for gay desserts scarcely changing with the years, blanc-

FIG. 4:21. Jelly or cream glass, England, 1750–60. Flint glass; H. 10.8 cm., D. (at rim) 7.3 cm. (Winterthur Museum, 60.187.)

mange "stuck all over with almonds cut lengthways" and garnished with green leaves or flowers was still modish in 1834. Furthermore, a blancmange garnished with preserves, bright jelly, or a compote of fruit was still the vogue in 1880.[23]

Coloring Jellies

Female guests judged flummery not only for its shape and decoration but for its coloring. To produce a lively hue the hostess employed techniques her grandmother had used and her children would use after her. Mrs. Rundell, whose *New System of Domestic Cookery* ran to thirty-five editions in London and the United States between 1807 and 1841, recorded in her *American Domestic Cookery* the following method to make

A Beautiful Red
to Stain Jellies, Ices, or Cakes

> Boil fifteen grains of cochineal in the finest powder with a dram and a half of cream of tartar in half a pint of water, very slowly, half an hour. Add in boiling a bit of alum the size of a pea. Or use beetroot sliced and some liquor poured over.

Mrs. Rundell made it sound easy to produce all the colors of the rainbow. She directed:

> For white, use almonds finely powdered with a little water, or use cream. For yellow, yolks of eggs or a bit of saffron steeped in the liquor and squeezed. For green, pound spinage leaves or beet leaves, express the juice, and boil in a teacup in a saucepan of water to take off the rawness.[24]

Cochineal, which Mrs. Rundell suggested for red, was a powder made of the dried bodies of the cochineal bug, *Coccus cacti*, which produced a great range of reds from pink to maroon when mixed with wine or with cream of tartar. As early as the sixteenth century it was imported by England from India, and in the seventeenth and eighteenth centuries American colonial grocers and pharmacists could either order it through their London agents or buy it at home from a merchant-importer. Edward Lloyd's inventory listed his supply as "2 papers vermillion" kept in a hair trunk with some hartshorn shavings.[25] A housekeeper might use alkanet, a plant of the anchusa family, instead of cochineal to make red; gamboge, or the heart of a lily, instead of saffron to make yellow; and parsley instead of spinach to make green. Although an up-to-date hostess colored flummery and blancmange shapes as realistically as possible, using chocolate brown to make the color called "sad" for hedgehogs, and red for strawberries and raspberries, she allowed her fancy free rein when she colored lemon-flavored jellies.

Making Clear Jelly

To make clear jelly required patience and a willingness to expend many egg whites as clarifiers. E. Smith directed that six whites of eggs beaten to a froth be boiled with the ingredients for hartshorn jelly and the whole run through a thick flannel jelly bag "till 'tis very clear." This required suspending the bag from a jelly stand like Mrs. Edward Lloyd's mahogany example or from a broomstick lying across two chairs in the homey make-do that housewives use today. In either case the bag hung untouched until it dripped no more. Assiduous housewives like Elizabeth Coultas of mid eighteenth-century Philadelphia made a hartshorn jelly that they strained not once, but twice.[26]

Two generations before Mrs. Lloyd and Mrs. Coultas were creating desserts, contemporaries of Gulielma Penn did not bother to clarify jelly, apparently satisfied with mere solidity. They sifted sugar over the finished product—a step guaranteed to lessen whatever translucence it might have had. If we tried making Gulielma's hartshorn jelly today, even though we substituted commercial gelatine for the rasped deer horns and elephant tusks she prescribed for the jelling agent, the dessert's sugary texture and its fragrance derived from mace, saffron, licorice, raisins, and rose petals might provide quick transportation back to the seventeenth century—especially if we ate the jelly with a round-bowled pewter spoon.

Jelling Agents

Hartshorn

Isinglass

Eighteenth-century housewives used ivory less often for a jelling agent than their grandmothers had, relying more on hartshorn, isinglass, calves' feet, and "burnt gums," or gums arabic and tragacanth. Hartshorn was the horn of a hart, or male deer, shed in the spring, which Great Britain imported from Germany in the eighteenth century. Like ivory and the hooves and horns of a cow, it turned to a gelatinous mass when boiled several hours in water. Isinglass ran hartshorn a close second in popularity as a jelling agent. It was obtained by boiling in water the air bladders of some fresh-water fish, especially the sturgeon, whose name in Old Dutch was *huisenblas*. The resulting mass was dried in thin sheets much as it is today for the use of confectioners. Because of their resemblance to sheets of isinglass, the mica obtained from quartz, and the sheets of gelatine made from hides and hoofs, came to be called isinglass. In the mid eighteenth century Russia was the prime producer of true isinglass and through the Hudson Bay Company supplied Great Britain, whence it was dispensed to the colonies. John Norton and Sons sent twenty pounds of it from London to Williamsburg at the order of James Minzies for the Earl of Dunmore in 1733; Edward Lloyd had a seven-pound supply valued at thirty-five shillings, which he stored along with pepper, raisins, and ginger. Using a word newly fashionable around 1820, Jane Janvier labeled a recipe Gelatine Jelly. To make it she let two ounces of isinglass soak in two quarts of water until the isinglass was soft. She then added the juice of a lemon, three lemon peels cut into strands "as fine as hair," four egg whites, a pound and a half of sugar, and a pint of wine. Putting the mixture over the fire, she let it come to a boil and immediately strained it into a three-quart mold. She undoubtedly used isinglass to jell blancmanges and flummeries as well as jellies, as her friends did. Catherine Flint thought an ounce of it in a quart of thin cream sufficient for her Blanche Mange.[27]

FIG. 4:22. James Gillray, *Heroes Recruiting at Kelsey's; or, Guard-Day at St. James's.* London, 1797. Mezzotint and line engraving. (Prints Department, British Museum.)

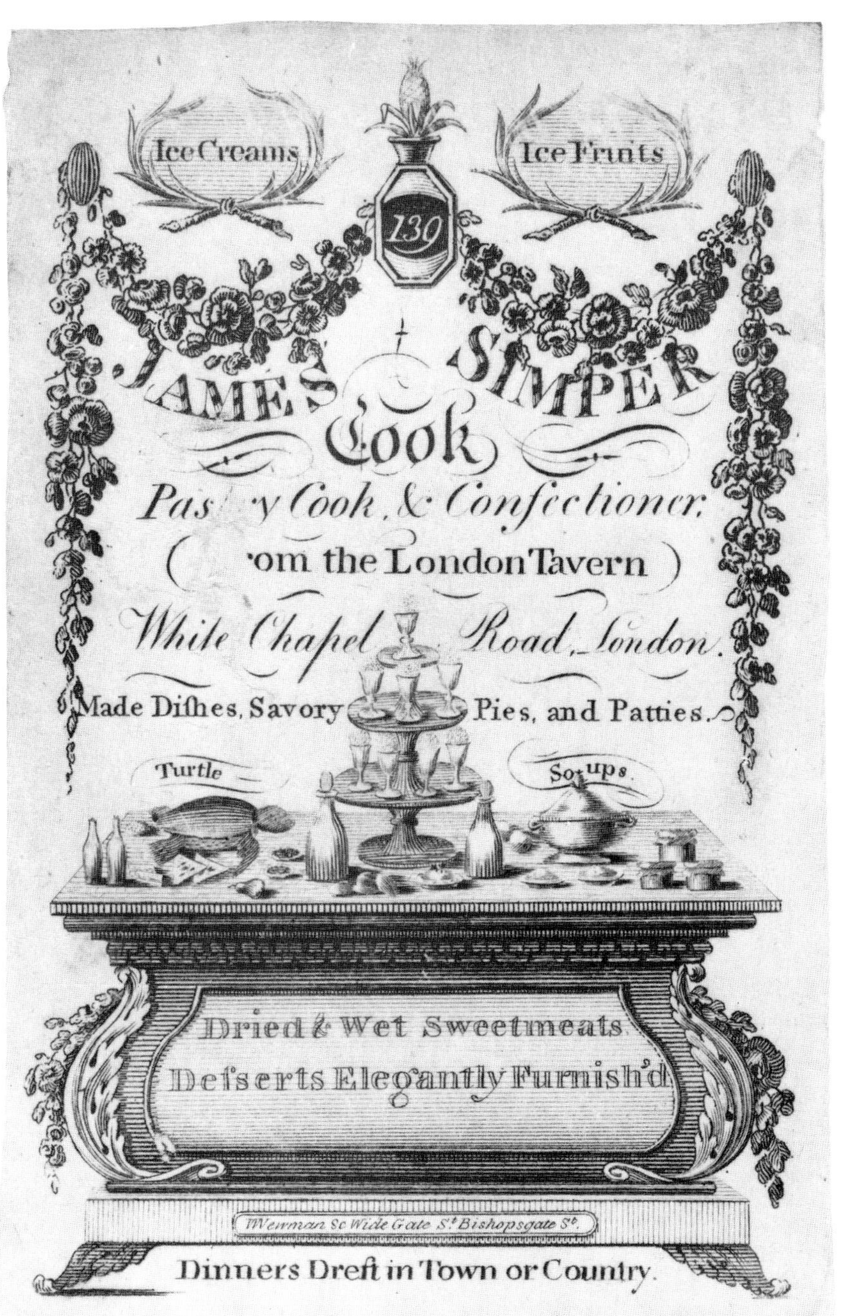

FIG. 4:23. Pastry cook and confectioner's trade card, England, ca. 1765. (Heal Collection, Prints Department, British Museum.)

Calves' Feet

Calves' feet produced a moderately satisfactory jelling agent. It was not entirely tasteless, as it should have been, but it was certainly cheaper than hartshorn and isinglass. Because it took a long time to prepare, many housewives bought it ready-made from a bakeshop or confectioner, although some people scorned this practice, claiming that store-bought jelly was not as delicate as homemade, "being almost invariably prepared with neat's feet, vulgarly called cows heels." Elizabeth Coultas's recipe for calves' foot jelly typified the recipes for it that American women wrote in their recipe books and read in their cookbooks. It required four calves' feet boiled in a gallon of water until the liquid was reduced by half. The liquid then was to be strained and cooled until it solidified. The fat was to be removed and the clearest part of the jelly cut away from the dross. To the clearer part, wine, lemons, sugar, and egg whites were to be added. The mixture then was to be beaten a half hour, strained, run through a jelly bag, and finally cooled in a mold until solid.[28]

In spite of the work involved, housewives turned out many jellies, molded

FIG. 4:24. The sugar-baker or confectioner. From J. L. Bailer, rev., *Neues Orbis Pictus für die Jügend . . . nach der Früdern Aulage des Comenius . . .*, p. 492. (Collection of F. H. Sommer.)

creams, and flummeries for the sake of the color they added to the climactic party table. Jellies especially they thought worth the trouble when they saw them raised high on footed salvers at the corners or in the center of the table, gleaming in the candlelight and casting bright spangles of amber, rose, and purple on the tablecloth.

Confectioners

Dressing out a table with sweetmeats involved a great deal of time and effort, as we have reiterated, but about the beginning of the eighteenth century ladies could avoid some of the work by patronizing specialists. They could buy not only calves' foot jelly but also dessert aids of many kinds from men and women who called themselves "grocer and distiller," "grocer and confectioner," or "pastry cook and confectioner" (Figs. 4:22–26). As early as 1710, Bostonians bought preserves and glazed fruits from Zabdiel Boylston, Dock Square apothecary, who sold wet sweetmeats and pomecitron along with painters' colors, raisins, tea, lancets, pills, and snuff. Philadelphians during the summer of 1769 called on men like the distiller and confectioner Peter Lorent who sold maca-

FIG. 4:25. Confectionery shop. From *The Young Tradesman; or, Book of English Trades*, 12th ed., p. 30.

roons, candied fruits, dried fruits, rock candy, capillary and orgeat syrup, sugar confects, and sugarplums of all sorts both wholesale and retail. If people wanted boxed sweetmeats, tamarinds, geneva macaroons, or sweet wafers, grocers and confectioners were in business in all of the biggest cities to supply them. Some of the dessert requirements people sought were made by the confectioners themselves; others the confectioners imported from the West Indies or from London where English merchants gathered them in from many countries: ginger paste from India; spices via Holland from the Near East; essence of lemons and lemons (at two for a penny retail in 1751 in London) from Sardinia and the fragrant orchards around Menton, San Remo, and Nice on the Mediterranean; lemon confects from Madeira; and *confitures belles et bonnes* from Paris. It is possible that American confectioners bought West India sweetmeats from Henry Lloyd who sold tamarinds in glasses as he ferried between Boston and Long Island in 1709. It is sure that a canny purchaser would not buy sweetmeats

FIG. 4:26. George J. Gatine (ca. 1773–1831), *L'Embarras du choix*. From a collection of some 118 colored etchings entitled *Le Bon Genre*, Paris, 1801–7, no. 44. (The Old Print Shop, New York City.)

unless, as the *Universal Dictionary* suggested, they were tender, "green and new, . . . clear and transparent, . . . well sugared above, plump, easy to cut, and . . . [not] punctured."[29]

Confectioners' Cakes

Like sweetmeats brought from far-off places, cakes bought at a confectioner's shop lent a certain chic to dessert tables. Ladies far from city confectioners might make a virtue out of necessity and serve homemade cakes with affected pride, but most city housewives simplified matters by going at some time or other to professionals. Philadelphia matrons in 1747 applied to Benjamin Betterton for a variety of cakes, including pound cake. South Carolina housewives, by sending word in advance to Joseph Calvert, baker from London, could pick up queen cakes, chelsea cakes, gingerbread, shrewsbury cakes, and whigs, or wigs, at his shop along with their morning hot rolls and bread. Marylanders could buy naples biscuits, crackers, seedcakes, and pound cakes with or without fruits and could order jellies and raspberry, strawberry, damson, and quince preserves at Jane Magg's Pastry Business in Baltimore. By 1833, when Henry Ridgely saw "almost Olympic" piles of his wife's favorite coconut cake that lately had joined the front ranks of popular cakes along with the old favorites pound, almond, fruit, and sponge cakes, "bought cakes" were quite acceptable. They received the ultimate accolade when the famous gastronome Alexis Soyer proclaimed: "Those who can afford it are quite right to patronize a first-grade confectioner and thus save themselves the trouble."[30]

Confectioners' Waters and Syrups

To supplement their own distillations of fruits, herbs, and flowers that they used in making desserts, women went to pharmacists and apothecaries for orange-flower water, rosewater, and oils of almond, lemon, and orange. New York women of the 1740s bought from the distiller Joseph Greswold at the Sign of the Lyon and Still in Pearl Street aniseed water, orange water, clove water, cinnamon water, and sundry other liquors. Confectioners and apothecaries in general did a good business in spite of the fact that some householders like Charles Carroll preferred to bypass them and obtain syrups and essences from abroad. Carroll in 1769 sent all the way to Barbados for "2 quarts best simple distilled orange flower water such as is generally used in cookery, in pint bottles well corked and waxed; and 2 quarts citron water in pint bottles."[31]

Confectioners' Ice Cream

Ice cream at the end of the century could be bought in Philadelphia and New York from French émigré confectioners who popularized it by opening ice-cream houses where it could be had by the quart or by the glass to be eaten on the spot. At Joseph Corré's at Eighth and Market, Philadelphians could buy ice cream "at the modest price of eleven pence per glass," which was not in the least a modest sum for 1795. M. Bosse ran two houses—one in Philadelphia and one in Germantown—to serve ice cream and sell it in quarts along with syrups, French cordials, cakes, clarets, and jellies. One M. Collot, who was thought by the French traveler Moreau de St. Méry to be the Creole son of the former president of the High Council of Cap François, San Domingo, sold ice creams and iced cheeses "in all the perfection of the true Italian mode," which M. de St. Méry declared "would bear comparison with that of the cellar of the Palais Royal in Paris." In January 1803 Victor du Pont patronized French confectioners who had settled in New York, paying M. Dusauttoir thirty dollars for dessert supplies; six months later he settled up with M. Contoit for decorative molds of ice cream at three dollars apiece. His brother Eleuthère, newly arrived from France in 1801, traveled between New York, Philadelphia, Wilmington, and Washington that year, buying from various confectioners en route an occasional ice, also "segars, nuts, cochlearia, lemonade, *sirop de fleur d'orange, essence de giroflée,* and sherry rum," and, like a thoughtful father, remembering to take home "bonbons pour mes petits" and "oranges, confitures, pruneaux, et joujoux pour Alfred." Eating confectioners' ice cream became a prime entertainment. During the nineteenth century Gray's Ferry in Philadelphia, Colombia Gardens in New York, and other pleasure spots founded in the United States on the order of London's Vauxhall and Ranelagh Gardens attracted by means of their ices even genteel young ladies like Eliza Boune who, visiting in New York in 1803, wrote to her friend Octavia Southgate: "In the cool of the evening we walk down to the Battery and go into the garden, sit half an hour, eat ice cream, drink lemonade, hear fine music, see a variety of people, and return home happy and refreshed."[32]

Confectioners' Desserts

A desire for decorations of professional flair and finish raised confectioners high in the esteem of ambitious hostesses. Ladies of 1773 in Charleston, South Carolina, felt themselves fortunate to be able to patronize Frederick Kreitner for his sugar "fountains, landscapes, scriptures, and Ovidic pieces in the Italian manner," which he offered together with macaroni, ratafias, wedding cakes, tea cakes, sugarplums, preserved pineapples, oranges, strawberries, ginger, lemons, and almonds. Like the Charlestonians, Philadelphia hostesses in the 1790s considered themselves privileged to have confectioners always at the ready. They had merely to go to Joseph Delacroix for "plateaux or dessert-boards elegantly decorated, and plates adorned with sundry sugar things." As for Cincinnati hostesses, they could apply for sweet things to the grocer-confectioner, the confectioner-baker, five grocer-bakers, fifteen bakers, or two confectioners who all listed themselves among the 10,283 inhabitants of the city in the directory for 1819.[33]

Erastus Corning's accounts with Joseph Brian and other confectioners and grocers exemplify the accounts of well-to-do nineteenth-century householders who ordered three or four times a month from professionals. Turnovers, pies, jellies, blancmanges, puffs, cakes, and almond drops, also pyramids of meringues, together with French candies, birds, mottoes, and molds of ice cream were the Corning family's customary wants. One February, the confectioners McCafferty and Holmes billed the Cornings for seventy pounds of New Year's cakes at one shilling fourpence the pound and for fifty pounds of crackers at a shilling a pound. Their grocer, E. R. Satterlee, at the end of December had sold them some thirty-seven gallons of madeira, canary, brandy, and champagne, and seventy pounds of New Year's cookies. Thus did Corning, railroad builder and mayor, handsomely welcome the arrival of the year 1817.[34]

5

"Fancy Goods and Baked Eatables"

1 Doz. tin molds . . . 2 large Cake pans, 6 small Cake pans, 44 Ditto, 9 large Ditto, 4 mince pie pans, 11 small pie pans, 16 Ditto, 14 flummery prints, 9 Past[e] Prints . . . 4 patty Pans . . . 2 Blue edge pud^{g} Dishes, 1 Queens ware ditto, 1 Ditto cracked.

Inventory of Madam Elizabeth Wentworth, Portsmouth, N.H., 1802[1]

Little Cakes

In pairs or quartets across eighteenth-century dessert tables, pierced-silver cake baskets and fanciful cake plates balanced each other among the sweetmeat dishes, waiting for party-goers. The baskets and plates were heaped with the marchpane and seedcakes that had been favorites in the sixteenth century, and with the macaroons, naples biscuits, almond puffs, and meringues that were enjoyed in the seventeenth century. Stylish queen cakes, jumbles, and savoy cakes, new to the baker's repertoire, crowned the heaps, and someplace in among them was traditional gingerbread. Even when families dined or took tea alone, both old-fashioned and new-fashioned cakes were de rigueur (Figs. 5:1, 5:2).

Margareta Schuyler of pre-Revolutionary Albany always provided a bountiful array. She and her family lived when the town was a small, tree-shaded gathering of a half dozen streets on the banks of the Hudson. Like their neighbors, the Schuylers kept a garden behind their house and a cow in the town's common pasture. Like them too they grew a field of corn sufficient to feed two or three slaves and a few horses, pigs, and poultry. At their house tea especially was a sumptuous affair made memorable to their niece Anne Grant by a great variety of cakes served along with cold pastry, sweetmeats, preserved fruits, and cracked nuts. The Schuylers and their neighbors, Mrs. Grant said when she wrote her memoirs, could spread their tables in true banquet tradition because they grew an abundance of fruit, which cost them nothing, and bought

FIG. 5:1. Cakes for a tea party on a table set with Chinese export porcelain and with silver by Joseph Richardson, Jr. (1752–1831). (Baltimore Drawing Room, 1812, Winterthur Museum.)

FIG. 5:2. Juan Zurbaran, *Still Life*. Spain, mid seventeenth century. Oil on canvas. (Courtesy of the Cincinnati Art Museum, gift of Jacob Heiman.)

sugar on easy terms in return for exports to the West Indies. The women of these households baked the sweetmeats themselves. In Mrs. Grant's opinion, the amateur lady bakers excelled in producing pastry and confectionery, and she thought astonishing the quantities of sweets and fruits they provided for their families whose lives were otherwise plain and frugal.[2]

Imported Ingredients

American families were indebted for the ingredients of their cakes to the enterprise of traveling merchants, ship captains, and grocers. They could supply their cupboards with dried fruits from abroad by dealing with merchant seamen like Henry Lloyd who sailed the waters between Boston and Queen's Village, Long Island, early in the century. They could buy licorice and nutmegs from men like Captain Francis Browne who carried spices along with wheat and rye to towns between New Haven and Boston. Lloyd and Browne and other men in the coastal trade bought their supplies from merchants whose ships plied the Caribbean and crossed the Atlantic in search of sugar, dried and sugared fruits, lemons, oranges, spices, wine, and nuts. The housewives who made use of their goods were well aware of the importance of the trade that kept American ships plowing the oceans. Through advertisements they learned the names of the far-flung sources of their dessert fare. Philadelphians reading the *American Daily Advertiser* for February 5, 1795, came upon an announcement of the arrival from Spain of a ship laden with provisions that made up the ingredients for the favorite plum cake. Like many other advertisements it read with the cadence of poetry:

> The Brig Fair Hebe, John McKeever master . . .
> Has for sale just imported in said brig from Malaga
> Old Mountain Wine
> Raisins of the Sun in Kegs,
> Figs in ditto, Prunes in ditto
> Muscatel and Bloom Raisins in boxes and jars,
> Grapes in ditto
> Oranges and Lemons in boxes,
> Shell'd Almonds in Casks.[3]

Some of the romance of buying from a cargo newly arrived in port was lost to the inland Schuylers because their dessert ingredients came through a middleman, Margareta's grandson, Philip Cuyler. The family's purchasing account, written in Cuyler's neat hand between 1765 and 1770, tells of the replenishing of their shelves from his store with three or four grocery items one to seven times a month. A fair percentage of the purchases consisted of the dried fruit, nuts, spices, wine, and sugar they used in baking cakes. Raisins, shipped from abroad in great baskets and kegs, they took home from Cuyler's supply in small baskets for a shilling a pound in 1769. Nutmegs they acquired at three-month intervals, one or two at a time, and, about twice a year, whole cinnamon, cloves, and mace. A pound and a quarter of the ground ginger they bought in 1766 lasted for two years, doubling in value during that time.[4]

Cake Molds

Much of the spice Mrs. Schuyler and other housewives purchased went into soft, or cakelike, gingerbread and into the hard traditional gingerbread that they rolled flat and either pressed with a decorative mold or cut with a tin cutter into a variety of shapes (Figs. 5:3; see also 5:8). Molding or shaping gingerbread and other small cakes derived from the Near Eastern practice of stamping decoration on holy bread, a custom that spread throughout Europe and Great Britain during the Crusades. For centuries thereafter, molds were used by Westerners only at Easter and Christmas, but by the seventeenth

FIG. 5:3. Gingerbread board, attributed to John Conger, carver and baker, New York, 1827–38. Impressed J. Y. WATKINS (New York tinsmith and owner of a kitchen furnishings warehouse, 1830–45). Mahogany; L. 18.2 cm., W. 10.5 cm., D. 2.5 cm. (Winterthur Museum, 61.1704.)

century housewives used them all year round, especially when they made gingerbread and the almond cakes called variously marchpane, *massepain*, or marzipan. When they came to the American colonies, women brought molds that had been in their families for generations and continued to use them year after year. As soon as the molds were worn out, their owners went to craftsmen for new ones, as the Isaac Paynes and Julius Warrens did. The Paynes bought a cake board for a shilling from Nathaniel Dominy of Easthampton, New York, in 1807, and the Warrens paid Robert Scadin, carpenter of Cooperstown, New York, seventy-five cents in 1831 for a gingerbread board and a mold in the shape of a letter *G*. The Warrens' mold for a letter cookie, or banquet letter, doubtless had Dutch ancestry. Even today in Holland women bake "banketletters" on St. Nicholas Day for members of their families.[5]

Colonists of whatever nationality enjoyed using decorative molds, prints, or boards, and carvers seemed to enjoy supplying them in countless designs and sizes. One amusing example stands out from among the many bearing vignettes of home and farm life that were popular throughout the nineteenth century. It portrays a man at a carpet- and cloth-covered table, seated in a high-backed Chippendale chair, his round face and Napoleonic pose suggesting an autocrat at the breakfast table or the chairman of the board (Fig. 5:4).

FIG. 5:4. Gingerbread or cake (cookie) board, England or Europe, 1775–1820. Cherry; L. 10.2 cm., W. 5.4 cm., D. 2.2 cm. (Winterthur Museum, 61.1390.)

Fig. 5:5. Nicholas de l'Armessin shop, *Habit de Paticier*. Paris, ca. 1690. Line engraving. (Prints Division, New York Public Library.)

469

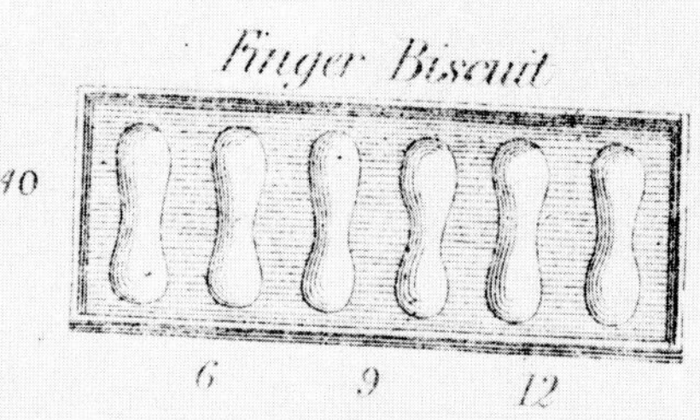

FIG. 5:6. Cake pans. From Henry Loveridge & Co., *Catalogue*, p. 469. (Winterthur Museum Library.)

Marchpane, or Marzipan

Marchpane of almond paste, like gingerbread, added pleasure to Christmas festivities and to country fairs. Cut into rectangles or molded in a "marsepyn pan" like the one Cornelis Steenwyck of New York owned in 1686, then baked and on occasion covered with a thin sheet of gold foil, it was piled neatly on plates and salvers to decorate a dessert table (Fig. 5:5). After the middle of the eighteenth century it was seldom seen on party tables in rectangular form but often in the shape of fruits, as marzipan is today. It also appeared as the icing of a cake as it still does in England.

Queen Cakes

More expensive to make than gingerbread, rich white queen cakes were nonetheless favorites of the Schuylers and their contemporaries all year round. Early in the eighteenth century the popular cakes were baked in tin or paper "coffins" four or five inches long and an inch and a half broad, or in cards folded like little dripping pans. Later in the century they were cooked for variety in small heart- or diamond-shaped tins (Figs. 5:6, 5:7). A housewife like Jane Janvier of Philadelphia used a family recipe for a queen cake that could be baked in one large tin and iced or merely sifted over with a little sugar. If on a festive day she applied a frosting, it was hard, smooth, and white.[6]

FIG. 5:7. Queen cake pans, United States or England, 1850–75. Tin; H. 2.5 cm., W. 7.6 cm. (Talbot County [Maryland] Historical Society.)

Cookies

Recipes for small sugar cakes and seedcakes were just as plentiful in family notebooks and cookbooks as recipes for queen cakes. New Yorkers early learned to call them *koekjes*, as their Dutch neighbors did. In New York City where *koekjes*, or cookies, were a New Year's Day specialty, John Morrison Duncan, a sojourner from England in 1818, was confronted with the old Dutch tradition that required every visitor to eat a cookie or to carry it away in his pocket. This tradition once had expected every family to provide a cookie of Brobdingnagian dimensions for its minister. Cookies were of some importance to young and old whether of English or Dutch background, and few houses were without the cookie-making apparatus that included a plain rolling pin called a molding pin to roll out dough on a plain board called a molding board; a wineglass, tumbler, or flour-dredging box to cut the dough into disks; and tin cake cutters in the shape of animals, stars, crescents, and leaves like the ones Benjamin Miles of Cooperstown, New York, made in 1821 (Fig. 5:8).[7]

FIG. 5:8. Cake cutters and patty pans, United States or England, 1850–75. Tin; H. 1.9 cm., L. 10.2 cm. (average). (Talbot County [Maryland] Historical Society.)

Wafers

The generous spread Anne Grant remembered in Albany included wafers, which were more delicate than cakes or cookies. According to Mrs. Raffald, they were proper for tea or for putting upon a salver to eat with jellies. To make them, a housewife beat equal parts of cream, sugar, flour, and orange water together for half an hour, then poured a spoonful onto a very hot wafer iron and baked it for a mere minute until it was light brown (Fig. 5:9). While the wafer was still hot she rolled it around a wooden roller, the handle of a rolling pin, or a wooden spoon handle and let it cool until it was crisp. The resulting fragile cylinder, cone, or horn she left plain or filled with whipped cream or custard (Fig. 5:10).[8]

FIG. 5:9. Wafer iron, Pennsylvania, 1757. Inscribed LI and AI 1757. Cast and wrought iron; L. (with handle) 81.3 cm., W. 21.6 cm. (Winterthur Museum, 65.2856.)

PL. 1:1. Dessert table set with *surtout de table*, orange trees, and Chinese export porcelain. (Du Pont Dining Room, 1790–1810, Winterthur Museum.)

PL. 2:9. Copy of a frame, or middleboard, with fruit pyramids for a dessert, here served in salt-glaze stoneware. (Charleston Dining Room, 1750–70, Winterthur Museum.)

PL. 2:20. Dessert of jellies and syllabubs in glass and fruits in salt-glaze stoneware. (Charleston Dining Room, 1750–60, Winterthur Museum.)

Pl. 2:50. Dessert table, 1870–80, Rockwood, Wilmington, Del. (Photo, Winterthur.)

Pl. 2:12. Dry sweetmeat pyramid on a dessert table set with a green Wedgwood dessert service. (Georgia Dining Room, 1830–40, Winterthur Museum.)

Pl. 2:23. Fruit dessert in French porcelain dessert service by Dagoty et Honoré of Paris ordered in 1817 by President Monroe. (Georgia Dining Room, 1820–30, Winterthur Museum.)

Pl. 2:41. Figurines with the kind of green glaze associated with Thomas Whieldon (England, 1740–60) surrounding pyramids of dry sweetmeats on a dessert table. (Charleston Dining Room, 1760–70, Winterthur Museum.)

PL. 4:9. Dessert of chocolate cream in Chinese export porcelain. (Billiard Room, 1790–1815, Winterthur Museum.)

PL. 6:17. Punch party setting in delft. (Marlboro Room, 1730–50, Winterthur Museum.)

Pl. 6:11. Family dessert with mixed fruits and dry and wet sweetmeats. Chinese export porcelain, *famille rose*. (Vauxhall Room, 1750–80, Winterthur Museum.)

Pl. 6:14. Dessert of fruit, queen cakes, and madeira. Neale & Co. creamware with lavender shell edge, Liverpool, ca. 1778–86. (Vauxhall Terrace, 1800–50, Winterthur Museum.)

Pl. 6:5. Fruit dessert in delft. (Delaware Room, 1650–1725, Winterthur Museum.)

PL. 5:22. Apple pie in redware. (Kershner Kitchen, 1750–1800, Winterthur Museum.)

PL. 6:1. Dessert of fruit and wine, Chinese export porcelain. (Du Pont Dining Room, 1790–1810, Winterthur Museum.)

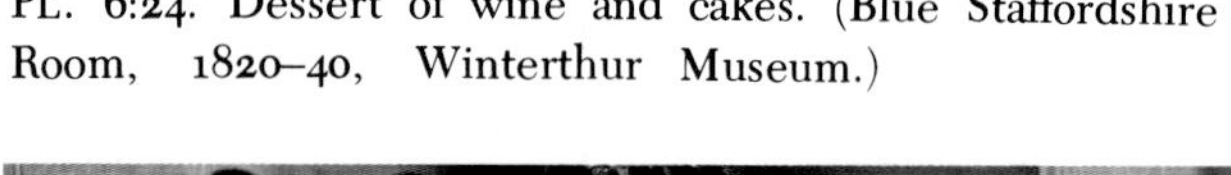

PL. 6:24. Dessert of wine and cakes. (Blue Staffordshire Room, 1820–40, Winterthur Museum.)

FIG. 5:10. A. Baugin, *Dessert of Wafers*. Paris, ca. 1630. Oil on canvas. (Collection of Georges Jairac, Paris. Courtesy of Pierre Tisné, Publishers, Paris.)

Naples Biscuits

Cookbooks and recipe books of the eighteenth century almost without fail included instructions for making naples biscuits—rectangular cookies baked in individual tin or paper coffins as queen cakes were or in large tin pans divided into narrow rectangles. Jonathan Dickinson of Pennsylvania owned three naples biscuit pans, and George Washington at Mount Vernon owned four. Just as naples biscuit formed the thickening for many possets, so, in the manner of modern graham crackers and vanilla wafers, it formed an ingredient of many puddings.[9]

Savoy Cakes

Certain other eighteenth-century small plain cakes persisted into the nineteenth century as savoy, or sponge, cakes and, like naples biscuits, were baked in little rectangular pans or finger shapes. An 1820 recipe for savoy cakes, or biscuits, published in *The Italian Confectioner*, directed that the three-and-a-half-inch-long cakes be iced with powdered sugar and placed back to back. Before the century was over they came to be called finger biscuits, or lady fingers (see Fig. 5:6).[10]

Round Loaf Cakes

Cylindrical, turk's cap, and melon-shaped "loaf" cakes were the standards of party fare (Fig. 5:11). Placed whole on a platter or pedestaled salver, these solid cakes often served as imposing centerpieces for desserts. Well into the nineteenth century the majority of cakes were regularly made with a little ale yeast

FIG. 5:11. Turk's cap cake mold, attributed to Pennsylvania, 1800–1850. Lead-glazed redware; H. 13.3 cm., D. 22.2 cm. (Winterthur Museum, 78.56, ex coll. Mr. and Mrs. William E. Phelps.)

FIG. 5:12. Raphaelle Peale, *Still Life with Raisin Cake*. Philadelphia, ca. 1813. Oil on canvas. (Collection of Mr. and Mrs. Donald S. Stralen.)

to give them lightness in the absence of baking powder. Saleratus, or baking soda, as a leavening agent began to substitute for the yeast around 1800. Pound and savoy cakes were among many cakes that did not call for either yeast or saleratus but depended solely on well-beaten eggs for leavening. Nearly all cakes, like most small cakes, or cookies, contained caraway, cardamom, or other seeds, and raisins, currants, and citron (Fig. 5:12). It was not until the nineteenth century that cakes were made in layers. Sugar was sometimes sifted on the upper surface, or a double coating of egg white and sugar was laid on the top and sides and dried in a warm oven to produce an enamel-like finish that housewives were proud to achieve. One unknown culinary artist made a note for a friend:

Icing

> Take of the best white sugar 1 lb. Pour over it cold water just to dissolve the lumps. Then take the white of three eggs and beat them a little but not to a stiff froth. Beat in a bowl in boiling water. . . . Spread it with a knife. It is white and glistens beautifully and is so smooth and hard you may write on it with a pencil.[11]

Cake Decoration

On gala occasions a cake's glossy surface was enlivened with three-dimensional sugar cherubs, castles, temples, swans, pineapples, or other images molded of gum arabic or gum tragacanth mixed with sugar and coloring. The gross of gum flowers that Hezekiah Usher II owned in 1751 may have decorated the cakes of Newport at midcentury. At one Virginia party in 1846 a large cake, edged with a sugar fence, held doves on a quiver of arrows. At another party a cake on a great glass plate was set about with alabaster figures, jellies, and custards.[12]

Twelfth Night Cakes

Twelfth Night cakes were always surmounted by a decoration of some sort. The great cakes were made for parties held to commemorate the arrival of the Wise Men in Bethlehem twelve days after Christmas. By tradition, plum cake covered with hard white icing and crowned with a sugar-and-gum figure or figures was baked with a bean in it. Any male guest who ate the piece of cake containing the bean was hailed as king; any female who did was elected to make the cake the following year. The king could command obedience from fellow revelers until midnight. Sometimes the cook added mirth-provoking mottoes, or cossets, to the cake. At other times the cossets were passed around to the guests (Figs. 5:13, 5:14).[13]

FIG. 5:14. Twelfth Night cake. (Du Pont Dining Room, 1790–1810, Winterthur Museum.)

FIG. 5:13. Joseph Cruikshank, *Twelfth Night*. Published by Laurie & Whittle, London, May 12, 1794. Line engraving. (Lewis Walpole Library.)

Not all eigheenth-century Americans were aware of Twelfth Night celebrations. Abigail Adams, for one, first encountered them when she lived in France in 1785. Like other New Englanders in their Puritan stronghold she had been brought up in ignorance of such "popishness," whereas southerners with a cavalier ancestry thoroughly enjoyed them. The Landon Carters and their Virginia neighbors counted Twelfth Night among the year's festivities and on January 7, 1770, went to Captain William Beale's "to eat a Twelfth Cake." In Quaker Pennsylvania in 1784 the much-traveled Binghams, never losing an opportunity for colorful entertaining, held a "magnificent Twelfth Night party."[14]

Cake Making

Any cake involved a great deal of work. According to the instructions of a recipe book begun in England in 1768 by a member of the Lamson family who crossed the Atlantic in 1791, the refined sugar a cake required presented one of the most vexing tasks in all of baking: hard, irregular sugar lumps had to be beaten fine or rubbed to a powder and sifted through a very fine hair or lawn sieve. Flavoring presented another hurdle. With commercially dried lemon peels often unavailable, Mrs. Lamson had to pare or grate fresh lemons, or rub them on hard sugar chunks. Finding imported almond paste expensive, she had to blanch almonds and beat them to a paste with rosewater. She had to grate nutmeg and pound cinnamon, cloves, and allspice in a mortar, or grind them in a mill. She had to dry flour by the fire, and sift it, as well as wash butter with rosewater, work it by hand, and beat it until creamy before rubbing it into the flour and sugar. She had to crack and chop nuts, pick over and wash raisins and currants and stem and seed them, and then beat the cake mixture for an hour with her bare hands while heating the oven to bake it two hours. Each dry ingredient she had to weigh by the drachm, ounce, or pound, and each wet ingredient she had to measure by the gill or pint, spoonful or cupful (Fig. 5:15).[15]

Nineteenth-Century Inventions

Mrs. Lamson was born one hundred years too soon. By 1850, laborsaving devices were burgeoning, and women could take it easy with such aids as eggbeaters, cylindrical whips with plunger, and powder-sugar mills. By 1856 they could buy even a syringe for cake decorating. They no longer had to bend over the hearth but could stand up to a Patent Cooking Stove with open roasting fire, hot-water boiler, baking oven, and hot plate. They no longer saw their work dimly by oil lamp or candle; gaslight put a glow on it. Flavorings came in bottles, and vanilla was unreservedly at their disposal with its now "delicious flavour" and "stimulating and exciting properties." They could keep perishables in such refrigerators as Jefferson had at Monticello and Samuel Ward of Newport had in 1840, or in the kind sold in New York in 1857 made with pulverized charcoal packing. They could still buy saleratus in lumps, pound it fine, and put it into corked bottles before using it in cake batter. In some towns they could buy soda or cream of tartar to lighten their creations. They could make cake in layers to save baking time and could be assured of a good chance of producing a successful cake because of a new solicitude among cookbook authors for exact measurements of ingredients.[16]

FIG. 5:15. Ingredients and red and yellow earthenwares used in making seedcake and batter pudding. (New England Kitchen, 1750–1800, Winterthur Museum.)

Measurements

Measurements had begun to concern cookbook authors in the 1820s. *The Cook's Oracle* in 1822 equated a middling-size teaspoon to about a drachm and four such teaspoons to a middling-size tablespoon, or half an ounce. The *Encyclopedia of Domestic Economy* in 1845 was careful to give amounts in "lbs. and oz." although it still prescribed "spoonfuls" and "tea-spoonfuls." Sara Josepha Hale in 1852 took a large step away from the take-a-pinch kind of recipe by printing a table of weights and measures in which four "large" tablespoonfuls were equalled to half a gill, a common-sized wineglass to a gill, and a common-sized tumbler to a half pint. Her equivalents broke down, however, when in a recipe she remarked: "Four table-spoonfuls will generally fill a common-sized wine glass," forgetting that she had equalled them to half a gill or half a wine-glass.[17]

Although adopting a standard of measurements was as slow a process in the nineteenth century as adopting the metric system is today, cake making continued to flourish and even to take on new and interesting character. Frosting, to be sure, stayed hard and smooth well into the twentieth century, but chocolate entered the top-flavors list. Light loaves christened Feather Cake and Delicate Cake threatened the reign of heavy plum cake, now called fruitcake. Layer cakes like boston cream, jelly, mountain, and orange gave variety to a housewife's repertoire.

FIG. 5:16. Cakepot, United States, 1800–1850. Stoneware; H. 16.9 cm., D. 27 cm. (Winterthur Museum, 59.1925.)

Cake Boxes

To expend time and energy on a beautiful cake and have it disappear at one meal can be as discouraging for the cook as it is gratifying. Many housewives wisely made large cakes that improved with age and could not be eaten up at one sitting. To keep the cakes moist and edible they stored them in covered cylindrical pots and pans and boxes (Fig. 5:16). Edward Lloyd's kitchen in 1796 was supplied with a pot of stoneware; Robert Scadin, the Cooperstown carpenter, made a wooden cake box for fifty cents in 1830; and Elizabeth Lea, author of *Domestic Cookery,* assured the housewife: "You can keep a pound cake a great while in a stone pan that has a lid to fit tight."[18]

Wedding Cakes

Great cakes reigned over eighteenth-century wedding receptions and christenings. Imposing solid cylinders customarily made from a queen cake or pound cake recipe, they were flavored with rosewater and brandy and baked in a deep, round tin pan. When crowned with sugar cherubs, a temple, tree, figure of Britannia, or whatever caught the fancy of the hostess, such a cake was impressive enough even to steal the show from bride or newborn baby. William Wirt, the distinguished Virginian, was delighted by a wedding cake surmounted by a tree nearly four feet high that was "more elegant than anything" he had ever seen. In his memoir of the year 1806 he wrote:

> It was past eleven when the sanctum sanctorum of the supper room was thrown open; and it was nearly twelve when it came my turn to see the show, and a very superb one it was, I assure you. At the ends of the tables were two lofty pyramids of jellies, syllabubs, ice creams, &c., the which pyramids were connected with the tree in the centre cake by pure white paper chains, very prettily cut, hanging in light and delicate festoons, and ornamented with paper bow-knots. Between the centre cake (the one holding the tree) and each pyramid was another large cake *made for use*. Then there was a profusion of meats, cheese cakes, fruits, etc., etc. But there were two unnatural things at the table: a small silver globe on each side of the tree, which might have passed . . . [for] a fruit, whose name I don't recollect, between the size of a shaddock [like a small grapefruit] and an orange, covered with silver leaf which was rather too outlandish for my palate.[19]

Such a cake centered with a tree festooned with paper chains and bowknots connecting it to pyramids of salvers laden with jellies, creams, and syllabubs started a wedding supper off splendidly. How much less dazzling were the cakes that came at the end of the Victorian century with their professional sugarwork connubial couple and their highly colored sugar tennis raquets, cricket bats, rowboats, and footballs! But from wedding cakes of whatever decoration and century, a slice was sure to find its way under the pillow of a young hopeful like Wilhelmina Ridgely of Dover, Delaware, whose friend Mathilda Dorsey of Baltimore sent her a taste to dream on the same year Mr. Wirt saw the cake tree and the paper chains.[20]

Patriotic Cakes

No state function of the new American republic was complete without cake. Martha Washington served it with ice cream and lemonade to the ladies who attended her levees, and each Fourth of July President Washington treated all the gentlemen of the city, the governors, officers, and companies, with two hundred pounds or more of it along with punch and wine. The day, Abigail Adams said, was reported to have cost him $500.[21]

As the center of attention at an eighteenth- or nineteenth-century party, many a great cake offered a sugary compliment to an especial guest or man of the hour. From Franklin to Kossuth a national hero might wake up any morning to find that a cake recipe had been named after him. Washington, Madison, Harrison, Taylor, and Lafayette all had that honor. Their names were printed in copybooks and cookbooks with the same nationalistic fervor that put Patriotic Cake, Election Cake, Federal Cake, and Columbia Cake there. To eat cake became almost a patriotic duty and endangered female complexion and health, moving social arbiters like Mrs. Hale to warn young ladies that they were not to partake of cake as a full meal but to remember that "social butterflies who attend evening parties several times in a week can hardly take too small a quantity of the sweet and rich preparations." "Many a young lady," Mrs. Hale admonished, "loses her appetite, bloom, and health by indulgence in these tempting but pernicious delicacies; and dyspeptic complaints frequently are aggravated, if not originated, by the absurd fashion of making our evening social circles places of eating and drinking rather than social and mental enjoyments."[22]

Pastry

Pie did not tempt the young ladies on their rounds; it never was served at an evening dessert party. It did, however, become one of America's family desserts when during the eighteenth century many households, largely servantless, eliminated meats and vegetables from the second course to simplify matters and concentrated the pies, custards, puddings, and other sweet things there. Old-fashioned housekeepers like Abigail Adams at the end of the century still served a sweet pudding with the meats, but expediency triumphed in most households. The Marquis de Chastellux in 1782 observed the new custom at a dinner that he said was served "in the American, or if you will in the English fashion, consisting of two courses, one comprehending the entrées, the roast meat and the warm side dishes, the other the sweet pastry and confections." "When this is removed," he noted, "the cloth is taken off and the apples, nuts, and chestnuts are served." Mrs. Basil Hall found the system widespread in 1827. "They have no meat along with the sweet things," she wrote from New

FIG. 5:17. Early eighteenth-century Dutch kitchen. From van de Aanhaugzel, *Volmaakte Hollandsche Keuken-Meid*, frontispiece. (Vehling Collection, Cornell University Library.)

Fig. 5:18. Nineteenth-century American kitchen. From Esther Allen Howland, *The New England Economical Housekeeper*, frontispiece. (Heritage Foundation Library, Old Deerfield Village, Mass.)

York, "but a most profuse supply of puddings, pies, jellies, sweetmeats, and ice."[23] Although English and European travelers saw a shift of sweet things away from the company of meats in some American households, the break was not as complete as they thought; on many tables sweetmeats continued to accompany the meat course and do so even today in such guises as pickled peaches, jam, applesauce, cranberry sauce, conserves, and sherbet.

Making Pastry

A housewife of the 1700s and early 1800s learned the art of pastry making when she was young and practiced it constantly because the customary dinner required "paste" not only for fruit pies, tarts, puddings, and custards but for meat pies as well. She considered pastry making her duty—even privilege—although in cookbook illustrations she is seen working in kitchens almost as inconvenient as those of the 1600s (Figs. 5:17, 5:18). She roasted and boiled over open fires, baked in brick ovens, and used tongs to mend the fire and bellows to fan it. She wielded a molding pin to roll out pastry on the table, with a lard bucket and saleratus box close at hand. Cast-iron covered pots on legs, like Edward Lloyd's dutch ovens, stood ready to be put on the hearth and piled high with hot coals for baking a savoy or pound cake. A tin reflecting oven like the Lloyds' three waited to broil birds or small game, or to brown a tart.[24]

Proper Philadelphia women regulated their mornings around pastry making. Frances Trollope, whose acid comments on life in the United States in the 1830s kindled the ire of many Americans, observed them at their task and wrote: "Her carriage is ordered at eleven; till that hour she is employed in the pastry room, her snow-white apron protecting her mouse-colored silk."[25] Here in this neat vignette lives a descendant of the seventeenth-century "accomplished gentlewoman" trusting to no touch but her own in the making of the banqueting stuff that her grandmother's and great-grandmother's cookbooks termed a lady's delight.

Pastry-room employment involved making three basic pastes. If a housewife wished, she could go to school to learn the processes. In the early part of the eighteenth century, following the reign of Queen Anne, whose penchant for childbearing and embroidery had directed women's attentions more than ever to the homely arts, young New Yorkers went to Martha Gazley, a recent arrival from Great Britain, who advertised in the *New York Gazette* in 1731 that she taught pastry making. South Carolinians attended a pastry shop in Charleston where, according to his 1746 advertisement in the *South Carolina Gazette*, Peter Pekin taught at reasonable rates. Their tutelage began with deep pies.

Deep Pies

They learned to make a crust and roll it one inch thick with their molding, rolling, or paste pin, keeping it sturdy enough to support a savory combination of meat, spices, lemon, and butter and to seal in the juices while the pie baked. They learned to cut a hole in the top crust when the pie was within a half hour of being done and pour in a lear, or sauce, of vinegar and melted butter, then seal it once again with a small pastry cap over the hole as their ancestors had done (Fig. 5:19). Although the custom of opening a deep pie for last-hour flavoring declined in the nineteenth century, Mrs. Fiske in the 1860s still poured

58 The *great* S.

HERE's great H, and I

With the Chriſtmas Pye ;

Who will eat the Plumbs out ?

I, H, and I.

h, i.

FIG. 5:19. Standing pie. From *A Little Pretty Pocket-Book*, p. 58. (Winterthur Museum Library.)

molasses and allspice through a hole in the two-inch crust of the deep apple pie she called "Common Pan Pie," after baking it for eight hours in an oven hot enough to cook beans. To keep the crust from darkening while she baked it a full hour longer, she covered it with a cabbage leaf.[26]

Standing Pies

The student pastry cook learned that this kind of raised crust, or standing paste, was strong, cheap, and meant not to be eaten. With its contents it could be baked either standing alone on a flat pie pan or in a deep pan or "mold," to be turned out on a platter for serving. Inedible crust continues in use today in Europe and in some American establishments in pâtés, but it disappeared early from the tables of frugal American households.

Puff Pastry

Diligent readers of Amelia Simmon's *American Cookery* learned as many as six different varieties of pastry. The most useful paste they learned was puff paste, needed for small turnovers and for large or small shallow pies, interchangeably called tarts. "Puffs" frequently made a supper for Judge Benjamin Lynde as he traveled his circuit around New England. In 1741 he "supped on apple puff at Wardell's," and at other places on "puff apple pie and cheese" with such accompaniments as a bottle of ale, an ear of corn, or a "sugar brandy dram."[27]

FIG. 5:20. Puff pan, attributed to United States, possibly New England, 1850–1900. Yellow are with tan, brown, and green glaze; L. 48.9 cm., W. 24.2 cm., D. 5.7 cm. (Winterthur Museum, 65.2338.)

Pie Pans

The pies, tarts, and puffs of a mid eighteenth-century repertoire required a sizable stock of pans of various shapes, sizes, and materials, with or without covers (Figs. 5:20, 5:21, Pl. 5:22). For baking high pies and deep pies, William Wright of New York in 1757 kept in his kitchen two small copper pie pans with handles, two large pie pans, and two brass pie pans, one without cover. The upkeep on Wright's copper pie pans was undeniably a nuisance and expense; the interior had to be tinned from time to time to keep the copper with its inevitable verdigris from contact with the pie. Eleuthère Irénée du Pont in 1802 paid John Ranger of New York eleven shillings for tinning a large copper stew pan and a pie pan. Fortunately, pie pans of earthenware, iron, and tin were available in place of copper.[28]

FIG. 5:21. Examples of puff pans. From Henry Loveridge & Co., *Catalogue*, p. 468. (Winterthur Museum Library.)

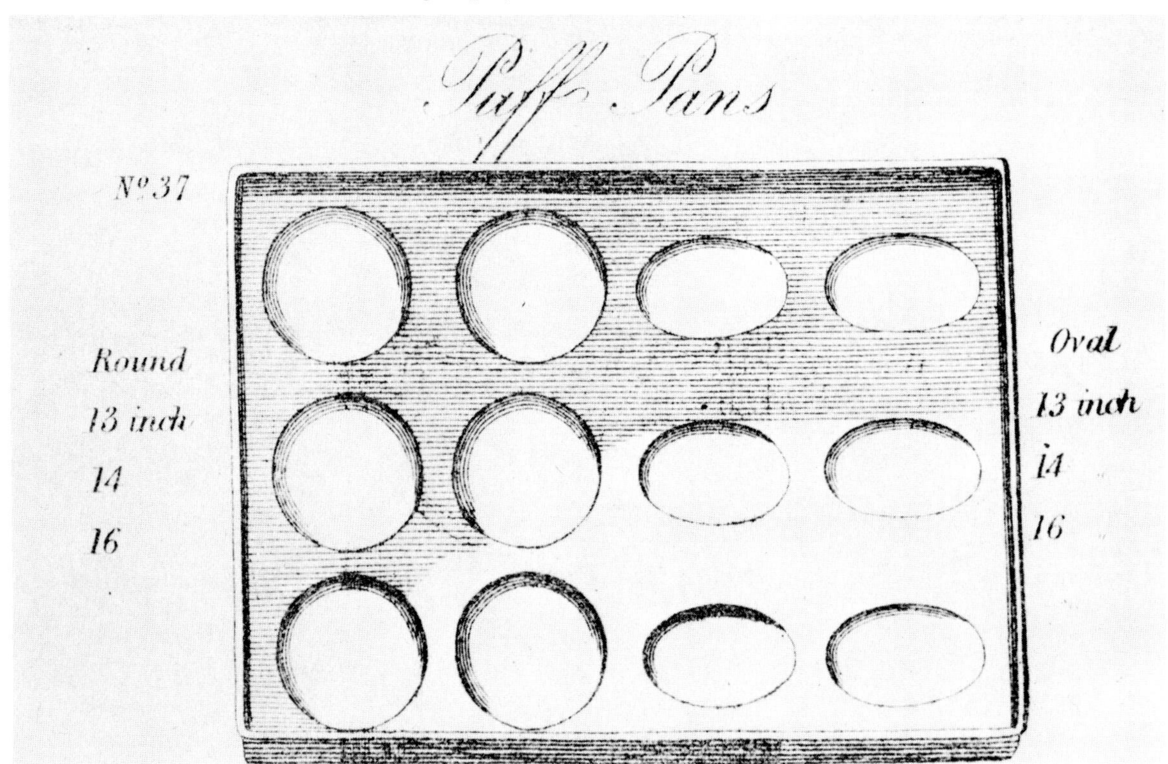

FIG. 5:23. Pie dish, England, 1750–1800. Yellowware, brown slip; D. 34.9 cm. (Winterthur Museum, 58.1066.)

Pie Plates, or Pie Dishes

For shallow pies, a householder kept among his kitchenware a few earthenware, round-bottomed, rimless vessels. These were called pie plates or pie dishes to distinguish them from deep cylindrical pie pans. Made of heavy red or yellow clay that was glazed and decorated with stripes or simple designs trailed on in a contrasting clay slip, they sat on the shelves of families of both English and German background. One potter decorated such a dish with the word "Pie" in large letters. Many pie dishes displayed serrated edges to resemble the edge of piecrust, which was customarily crimped for strength and finish (Fig. 5:23). Pie plates like the two in Joseph and Anne Dowding's Boston kitchen in 1716, and the two earthen pie plates in the 1749 kitchen of Samuel Allen of Deerfield, Massachusetts, undoubtedly were of this shallow kind, and held fruit and berry pies more often than meat pies.[29]

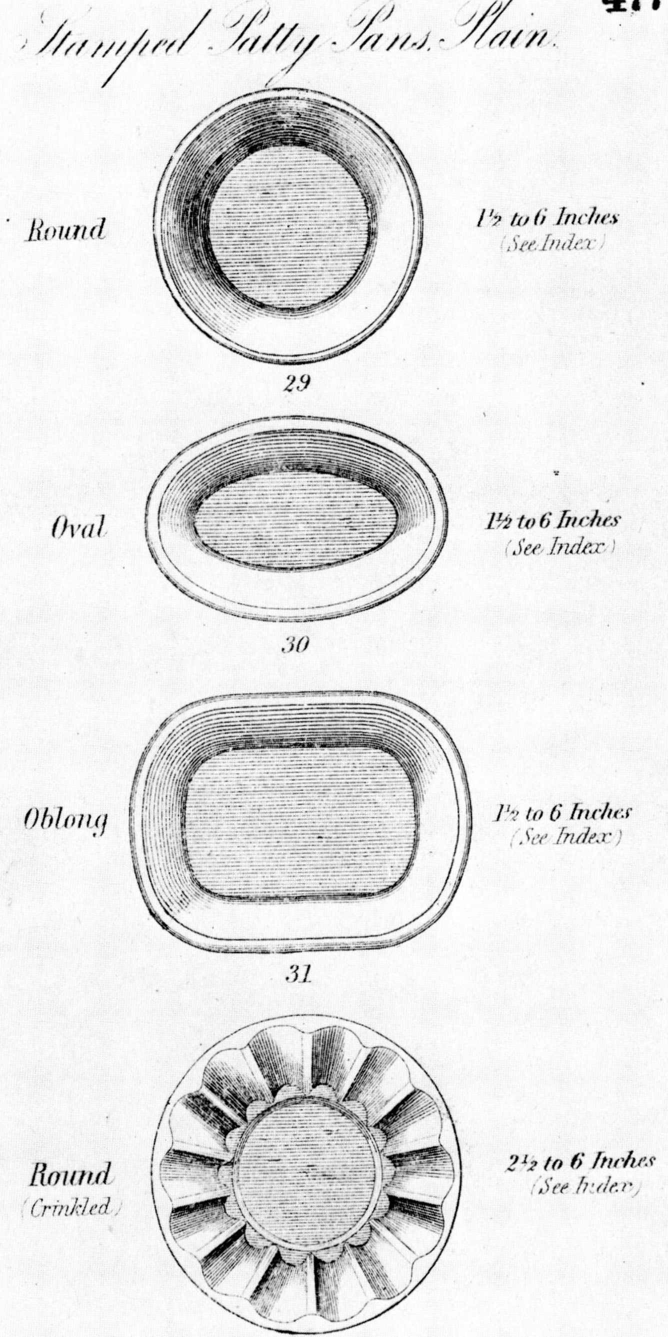

FIG. 5:24. Stamped plain patty pans. From Henry Loveridge & Co., *Catalogue*, p. 477. (Winterthur Museum Library.)

FIG. 5:25. Patty pans, China, 1790–1810. Export porcelain; D. 11.6 cm. and 11.7 cm., H. 4 cm. and 3.8 cm. (Winterthur Museum, 61.865, 61.835.2.)

Pastry Plates, Pasty Plates, Patty Pans, and Tart Pans

Pastry plates, pasty plates, patty pans, and tart pans also held shallow fruit pies. Either round bottomed or flat bottomed and made of tin, brass, or brown stoneware, they came in sizes from one-and-a-half to twelve inches in diameter. Weekly, they entered the ovens of colonial householders (Fig. 5:24). Surprisingly, so did glass patty pans and china patty pans (Figs. 5:25, 5:26). Both glass and china patties were owned or advertised by many people, including New York's Francis Thurman in 1758 and Thomas Duncan in 1757, Boston's Elizabeth Hutchinson in 1765, and North Carolina's Governor Tryon before 1788. John Adams, a Boston merchant-importer, in 1773 sold patty pans of porcelain, which he called India china (Fig. 5:27). From his shop a Boston housewife could furnish not only her kitchen with porcelain patty pans but her table with English stoneware. She could also find there earthenware "turtle-shell" plates and dishes of the kind Margareta Schuyler bought from her grocer-importer grandson in Albany.[30]

FIG. 5:26. Pattern and dimensions for round patty pans. From a manuscript potter's manual, attributed to the Spode factory, England, ca. 1815–21, p. 111. (Winterthur Museum Library, DMMC.)

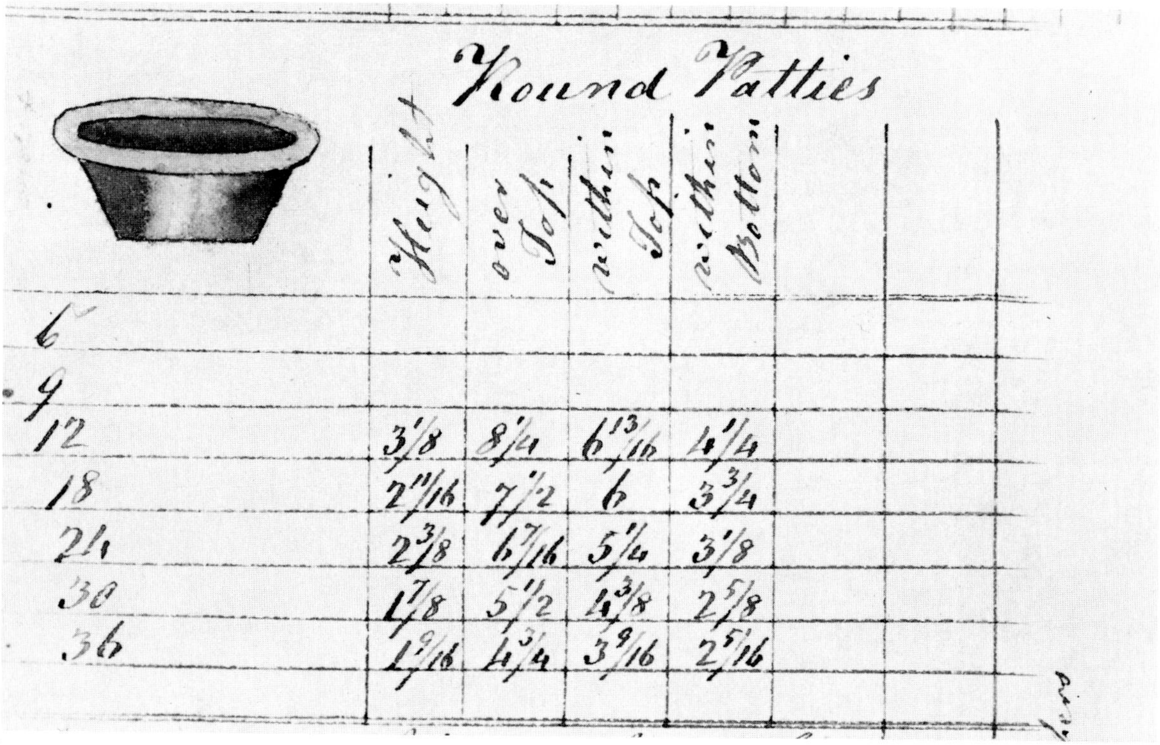

Round Patties

	Height	over Top	within Top	within Bottom
6				
9				
12	3 1/8	8 1/4	6 13/16	4 1/4
18	2 11/16	7 1/2	6	3 3/4
24	2 3/8	6 7/16	5 1/4	3 1/8
30	1 7/8	5 1/2	4 3/8	2 5/8
36	1 9/16	4 3/4	3 9/16	2 5/16

John Adams,

(At his Shop opposite the Old-South Meeting-Houſe,
BOSTON)
Hath received from *London* and *Liverpool*,

A Great Variety of the beſt India China, conſiſting of Cups and Saucers, Tea Pots, Cream Pots, Sugar Diſhes, Coffee Cups and Saucers, large and ſmall Bowls, Plates, Pudding Diſhes, Sauce Boats, Patty Pans, Quart and Pint Mugs.

A fine Aſſortment of Double and Single Flint Glaſs, plain fluted and enamel'd cream-coloured Ware, plain white, blue & white, and enamel'd Stone Ware, with all Kinds of Ware uſually imported, ſuch as black, brown, tortoiſe-ſhell, agate, coll flower, blue and white Delph, &c. It being a large Aſſortment, too many Articles for an Advertiſement. All which he will ſell as cheap as can be bought in the Province, by Wholeſale or Retail.

ALSO,

The beſt Iſle Shoal Dumb Fiſh per Quintal, Double and ſingle refined Loaf Sugar, Brown Sugars, Coffee, Chocolate, Raiſins, Oatmeal, Flour, Rice, beſt Poland and this Country Starch, Durham Muſtard in ¼ and ½ Pound Bottles, Cotton and Wool Cards per Dozen or leſs, fine large Capers, Pepper, Pimento, Ground Ginger, beſt French Indigo, Pipes by the Box or leſs, Snuff, Sweet Oyl, Mace, Cinnamon, Cloves and Nutmegs, choice Weymouth Cheeſe,—Allum, Brimſtone, Copperas, Salt-Petre, Redwood and Logwood, Split Peas, Hemp, Rape and Canary Seed, &c.

FIG. 5:27. Advertisement for porcelain patty pans, pudding dishes, and sauce boats. From John Adams advertisement, *Boston Gazette*, June 7, 1773. (Winterthur Museum Library.)

If the patty pans a pastry cook chose to use were of tin, she made both a coffin and a lid of pastry for the bottom and top in order, as she said, "to remove the pies more easily." If the patty pans were of glass, she made no bottom crust in order to eliminate the need for great heat, which endangered the fragile pans.[31]

In place of patty pans, the pastry cook could use saucers when she baked tarts. She could also use soup plates and deep, broad-rimmed, block-tin dishes the size and shape of large soup plates if she had no china tart pans (Figs. 5:28, 5:29). Whatever dish she used for a two-crust pie, she turned it over on a platter to remove the pie, turned the pie right side up, and strewed sugar on it before serving.[32]

FIG. 5:28. Plate for pudding, pie, or soup, United States, 1830–40. Lead glass; H. 2.2 cm., D. 9.5 cm. (Winterthur Museum, 64.898.)

FIG. 5:29. Stamped tin table and soup plates. From Henry Loveridge & Co., *Catalogue*, p. 468. (Winterthur Museum Library.)

Pastry Decoration

To decorate pies and tarts, a housewife added pieces of pastry cut to her own design or copied from cookbooks. She then sifted sugar over them or iced them with a mixture of sugar, rosewater, and egg white applied with a feather. Richard Briggs's *New Art of Cookery* told her that the little decorative pieces of pastry could be cut to resemble flowers, tulips, birds, "or any shape you fancy" (Figs. 5:30, 5:31). Her fancy often ran to leaves, crescents, wheels, or diamond shapes cut with the help of flat tin patterns traced around with her edging iron, variously referred to as a jagging iron, dough spur, paste spur, or "runner with twichers," as Randle Holme called it (Fig. 5:32).[33] To simplify her pastry decorating she could invest in cylindrical earthen or metal pie molds that impressed or raised designs on the walls of standing pies. She had to choose wisely because not every mold produced decorations. The decorative molding and cutting of pastry for pies and tarts in the eighteenth and nineteenth centuries, while less intricate than pastry sculpturing of the fifteenth and sixteenth centuries, stemmed from the same human urge to manipulate whatever is plastic.[34]

FIG. 5:30. Pattern for cut pastry. From Robert May, *The Accomplisht Cook*, p. 220. (Vehling Collection, Cornell University Library.)

FIG. 5:31. Pie decorated with a pastry bowknot and border. Pieter Claesz, *A Table Still Life*. The Netherlands, ca. 1625. Oil on wood panel; H. 48.2 cm., W. 67.3 cm. (Collection of the Lyman Allen Museum.)

FIG. 5:32. Pastry wheel, attributed to America, 1780–1830. Iron; L. 20 cm. (Winterthur Museum, 63.66.)

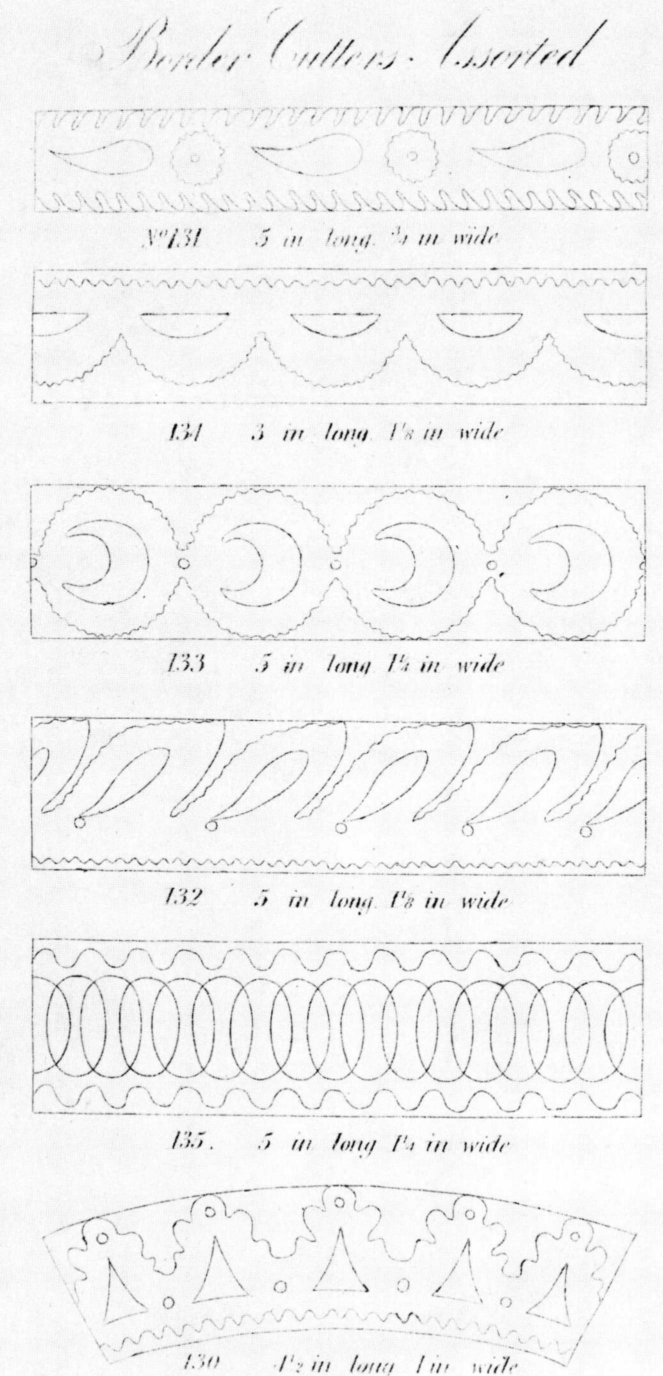

FIG. 5:33. Assorted border cutters. From Henry Loveridge & Co., *Catalogue*, p. 476. (Winterthur Museum Library.)

Pastry cooks could make the decorating of the crust of high pies easy by using various types of tin border cutters (Fig. 5:33). With these cutters or patterns they traced out with a sharp knife or edging iron all kinds of beguiling rabbits, deer, boars, dogs, and lambs to apply to the top and sides. Briggs recommended ornamenting a Christmas pie in bold style, as small pieces of pastry did not withstand the long continued heat required for baking such a large dish. Eliza Leslie suggested that cooks notch a beefsteak pie handsomely with a knife and decorate it with a pastry tulip and leaves.[35]

Pudding

Pudding, like pie, was a latecomer to the dessert scene. Until well into the nineteenth century it was a mainstay of the first course of English and American dinners, its currant-studded substantiality lessening appetites for more expensive meats and vegetables. To an Englishman, dinner without pudding was not dinner. A boiled batter pudding linked itself so securely to the British way of life that even in a cookbook for German young ladies it appeared as "Englisches Puding." Keeping pudding from getting cold at dinner played a central part in many domestic arguments and appeared often in literature as a prominent protagonist. In a sketch published in 1787 in the first issue of the *Columbian Magazine*, an irritated wife typifies the put-upon cook of all ages who hates to have her artistry lose its bloom before it is tasted. About to sit down to the table with her family, the hapless female complains of her bookish husband:

> If I call him to dinner . . . tho I assure him that the pudding will grow cold, . . . I can't budge him one minute before his own time.
>
> . . . We might as well not bought our flowered tablecover, which no one can see for the plagy books, and if a body does but scold a little about it, away they are all cramm'd in the closet where the children keep their playthings.
>
> . . . The pretty flowered paper in the hall is all cover'd over with nothing but maps and drafts and charts. . . . One mout as well talk to the china image over the fireplace.[36]

"Pudding first" was out of fashion in 1787 when this rare and revealing sketch of an eighteenth-century middle-class American family at home surrounded by its possessions was written, but it lingered on in a few other households. As late as 1817 Henry Bradshaw Fearon, an English dinner guest at the home of John and Abigail Adams in Braintree, Massachusetts, found the ex-president still wedded to it. Fearon saw him served a pudding made of Indian corn, molasses, and butter for the first course, which preceded a course of veal, mutton, potatoes, cabbages, carrots, Indian beans, and madeira wine.[37]

Indian pudding, which figured so largely in early American diet, was simply European meal pudding made with "Indian" cornmeal instead of with the usual European rye or barley. Whether of meal, batter, or bread, a pudding could be cooked by three different methods: boiling in a bladder, cloth bag, or deep

Boiled Pudding

dish; cooking and stirring over a fire; and baking. Boiling in a bag was accomplished with much the same technique in the eighteenth and nineteenth centuries as it had been in Chaucer's day. A cook poured batter into a sheep's bladder, into a cloth bag, or into a mold with a cloth around it. She then gathered the cloth or bladder loosely to allow room for the pudding to swell and tied it securely with a string. Lowering it into a deep pot of boiling water, she left it to simmer for from one to six hours. Just before serving, she dipped the bag into cold water for easy removal of the pudding.

Preparing bag puddings was a risky operation; too much meal, bread, or flour and too close tying of the bag made them heavy. Some individuals rightly considered them an indigestible peril. Nonetheless, bag puddings filled many pages in the recipe books and cookbooks of American housewives. Not until the middle of the nineteenth century did they yield first place in the hearts of our forebears in favor of lighter puddings made of sago, cornstarch, tapioca, and rice. That is not to say that boiled puddings disappeared from Victorian tables. On the contrary, even in America they were clung to in several variations. Plum pudding was the best loved and was served especially at Christmastime. Victorians sometimes made it not with currants and raisins but with "more elegant" conserves and preserved ginger.[38]

Baked Pudding

Elizabeth Coultas's well-used copybook and the copybooks of other pre-Revolutionary American housewives suggest that baked puddings enjoyed a popularity second only to bag puddings in households of English background (Figs. 5:34, 5:35).[39] Sweet baked puddings consisted of eggs, sugar, and milk mixed with thickenings of meal, bread, broken biscuits, or flour, just as bag puddings did, but they went into the oven in pans or dishes instead of into the kettle in cloth bags or bladders. Sunderland pudding, a white-flour batter pudding, was a favorite. Indian pudding, rice pudding, and a bread-and-apple mixture called marlborough pudding were seldom omitted from Anglo-American recipe books. Whether served hot or cold they were to be covered with a sweet sauce of melted butter, wine, and sugar poured or dipped with ladles from a sauceboat or from the small tureens of a dessert service (Fig. 5:36). Although some sauceboats were designed with a lip presumably for pouring, sketches of eighteenth-century meals show them equipped with ladles resting on the pouring lip for dipping out the sauce. With mouth watering, one reads of the "sweet sauce" of melted butter and sugar prescribed by Amelia Simmons for cream almond pudding, apple pudding dumpling, flour pudding, and sunderland pudding, and of the custard Eliza Leslie directed the housewife to send up in a sauceboat.[40]

Not all puddings were sweet. Many consisted simply of batter or meal, rice, potatoes, carrots, squash, pumpkin, or other vegetables and are recognizable today in yorkshire pudding, corn pudding, spoon bread, sweet potato pudding, and spinach soufflé. One variety, forever connected with frontier simplicity and fortitude, thanks to Joel Barlow's panegyric, was hasty pudding, a rye- or cornmeal mush, neither baked nor put into a bag, but boiled over the open fire to speed up dinner getting.

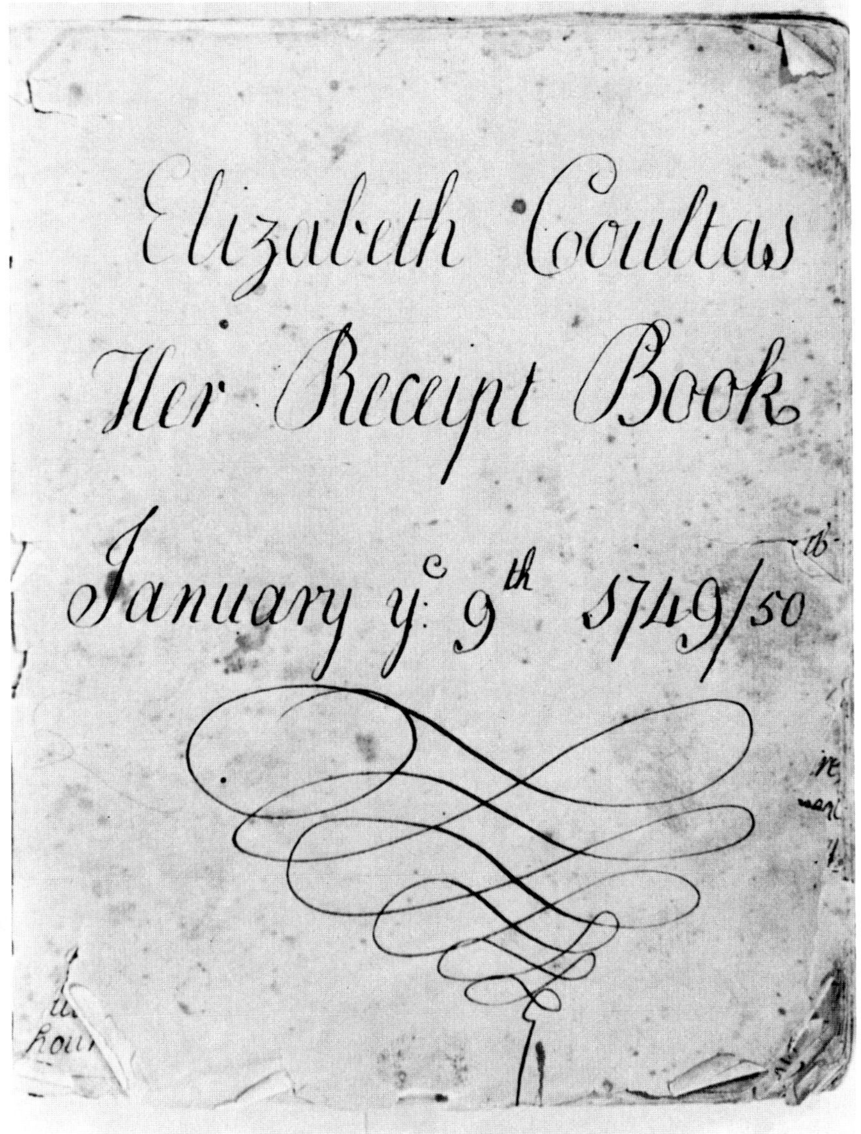

FIG. 5:34. Elizabeth Coultas, cover of manuscript recipe book, England and Philadelphia (?), dated 1749/50. (Winterthur Museum Library, DMMC.)

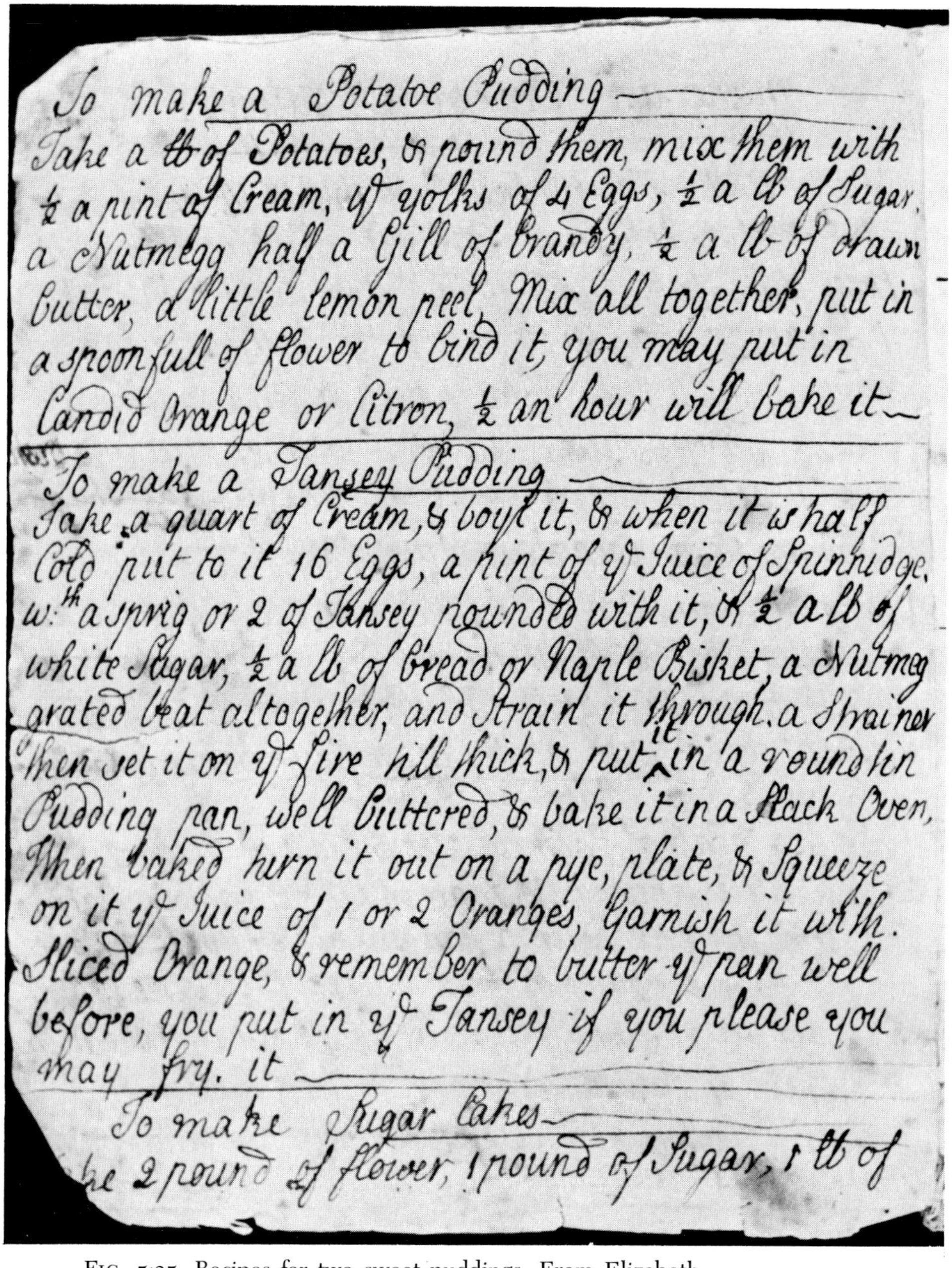

To make a Potatoe Pudding

Take a lb of Potatoes, & pound them, mix them with ½ a pint of Cream, ye yolks of 4 Eggs, ½ a lb of Sugar, a Nutmegg half a Gill of brandy, ½ a lb of drawn butter, a little lemon peel, Mix all together, put in a spoonfull of flower to bind it, you may put in Candid Orange or Citron, ½ an hour will bake it—

To make a Tansey Pudding

Take a quart of Cream, & boyl it, & when it is half Cold put to it 16 Eggs, a pint of ye Juice of Spinnidge, wth a sprig or 2 of Tansey pounded with it, & ½ a lb of white Sugar, ½ a lb of bread or Naple Bisket, a Nutmeg grated beat altogether, and Strain it through a Strainer then set it on ye fire till thick, & put it in a round tin Pudding pan, well Buttered, & bake it in a Slack Oven, When baked turn it out on a pye, plate, & Squeeze on it ye Juice of 1 or 2 Oranges, Garnish it with Sliced Orange, & remember to butter ye pan well before, you put in ye Tansey if you please you may fry it

To make Sugar Cakes

[Ta]ke 2 pound of flower, 1 pound of Sugar, 1 lb of

FIG. 5:35. Recipes for two sweet puddings. From Elizabeth Coultas, manuscript recipe book, England and Philadelphia (?), dated 1749/50. (Winterthur Museum Library, DMMC.)

FIG. 5:36. (*a*) Sauce tureen, Stoke-on-Trent, Henley, Staffordshire, 1810–20. Impressed ADAMS with eagle and WARRANTED STAFFORDSHIRE. Blue-edge pearlware; H. 17.6 cm., W. (with cover), 14.6 cm. (Winterthur Museum, 64.1943.) (*b*) Sauceboat, attributed to Chelsea, 1740–50. Soft paste porcelain, polychrome; L. 20 cm., W. 10.8 cm., D. 8.9 cm. (Winterthur Museum, 61.927.)

Pudding in Pastry

No eighteenth-century housewife need have felt that daily puddings were monotonous; they came in many guises. Richard Briggs published recipes for eighty-two boiled, baked, and hasty varieties. Among them were many puddings to be encased in pastry laid in paper or tin coffins. Elizabeth Coultas and Jane Janvier of Philadelphia, Mrs. Fiske of Massachusetts, and countless others thus entombed their custard, orange, coconut, and lemon puddings. Even in the late 1820s Eliza Leslie prescribed coffins for puddings. But coffins were shortly to be doomed in homes of the fashionable. In 1859, in her *New Cookery Book*, Miss Leslie announced that lemon puddings were no longer made with an undercrust. People in the know, she said, put either a handsome border of puff paste around the edge of the pudding dish, a pattern of leaves and flowers on the top, or a thick band of paste cut into small squares about an inch wide on the rim, the squares placed alternately up and down, *cheveux de frise* fashion. The new pudding with its battlemented border, she affirmed, "is a genuine baked lemon pudding such as is well known at Philadelphia dinner parties . . . and must have no flour or bread, only butter, sugar, and eggs (with the proper flavoring). . . . When baked," Miss Leslie confided, "it cuts down smooth and shining, like a nice custard."[41]

Vessels for Baked Pudding

Miss Leslie said her lemon pudding was to be baked in a white broad-brimmed dish. Other American puddings were baked in earthen pudding pans, white and brown Liverpool pudding pans, tin pans, and copper pans. Earthenware dishes, called bakers, and individual dishes called nappies by pottery dealers then and now, were available in sizes from five to sixteen inches in diameter. They came with covers to be used when a recipe called for a "covered dish," or they came without covers for use when a pudding was baked "under paste" (Fig. 5:37).

FIG. 5:37. Baker, England, 1800–1825. Redware; H. 14.6 cm., D. 17.8 cm. (Winterthur Museum, 58.120.21.)

Serving Dishes

Large porcelain dishes that the Anthony Rutgers of New York called china pudding dishes in 1760 were widely used for serving the pudding. Small porcelain pudding dishes were used for individual helpings. John Reed of Philadelphia, who had set up bachelor quarters in 1799, invested in a scalloped, fluted example in 1811 (Fig. 5:38). A versatile vessel, it could have held blanched cream or Indian custard pudding with equal ease. It undoubtedly was related to the dish in Oudry's well-known painting *The White Duck* shown holding a citron-studded pudding (Fig. 5:39). Such a bowl may have been used half a century later by those who followed a recipe in Lucy Emerson's *New England Cookery* for a pudding that she directed was to be boiled in a china basin tied in a cloth and served with melted butter and fine sugar sprinkled over.[42]

FIG. 5:39. Jean-Baptiste Oudry, *The White Duck*. Paris, 1753. Oil on canvas. (Tate Gallery.)

FIG. 5:38. Pudding dish, Pennsylvania, 1790–1850. Mottled redware; D. 22.2 cm., H. 10 cm. (Winterthur Museum, 59.2189.)

J.B. Oudry
1753

FIG. 5:40. Pudding dish and pudding knife by Shepherd and Boyd, Albany, N.Y., 1814. Silver; D. 27.3 cm., L. (of knife) 25.4 cm. (Collection of Mrs. Robert P. Browne.)

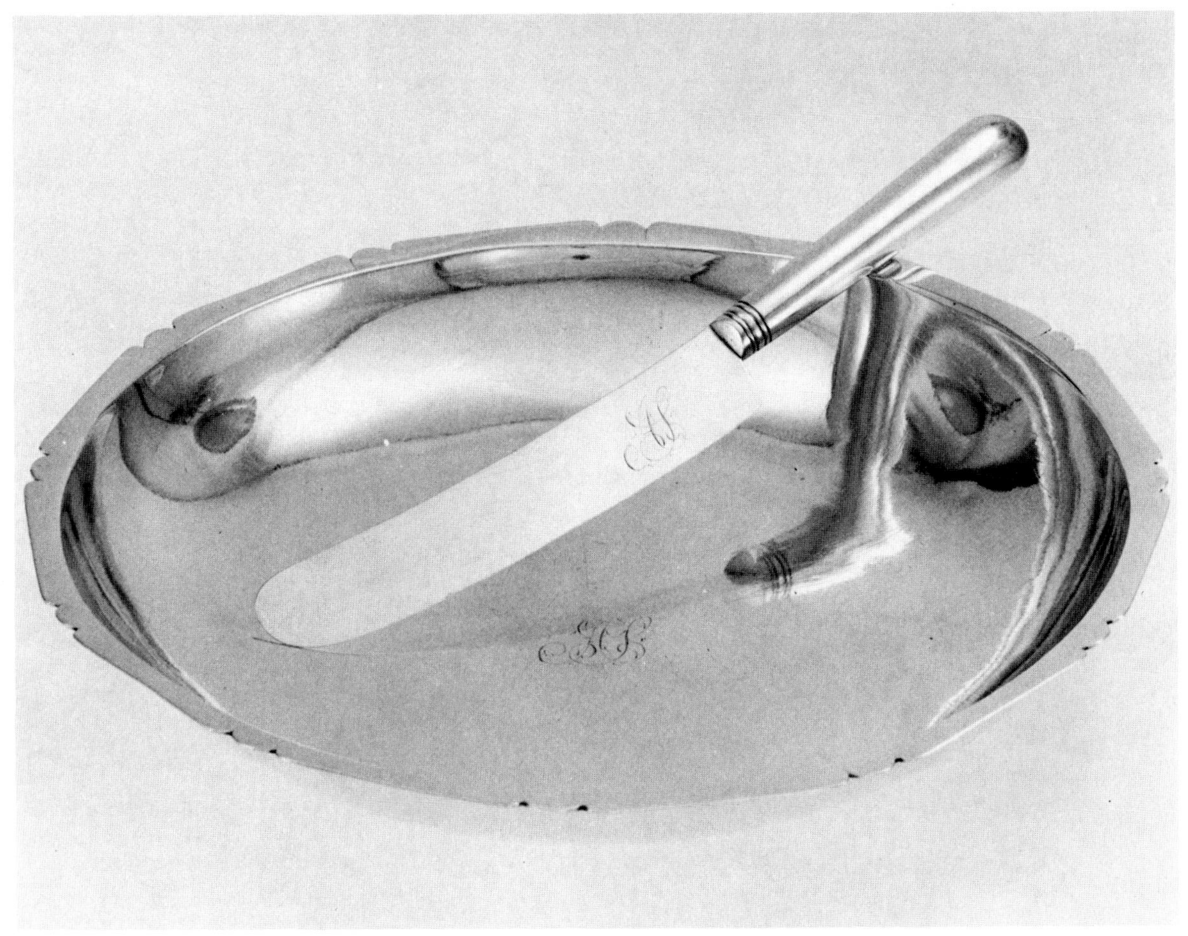

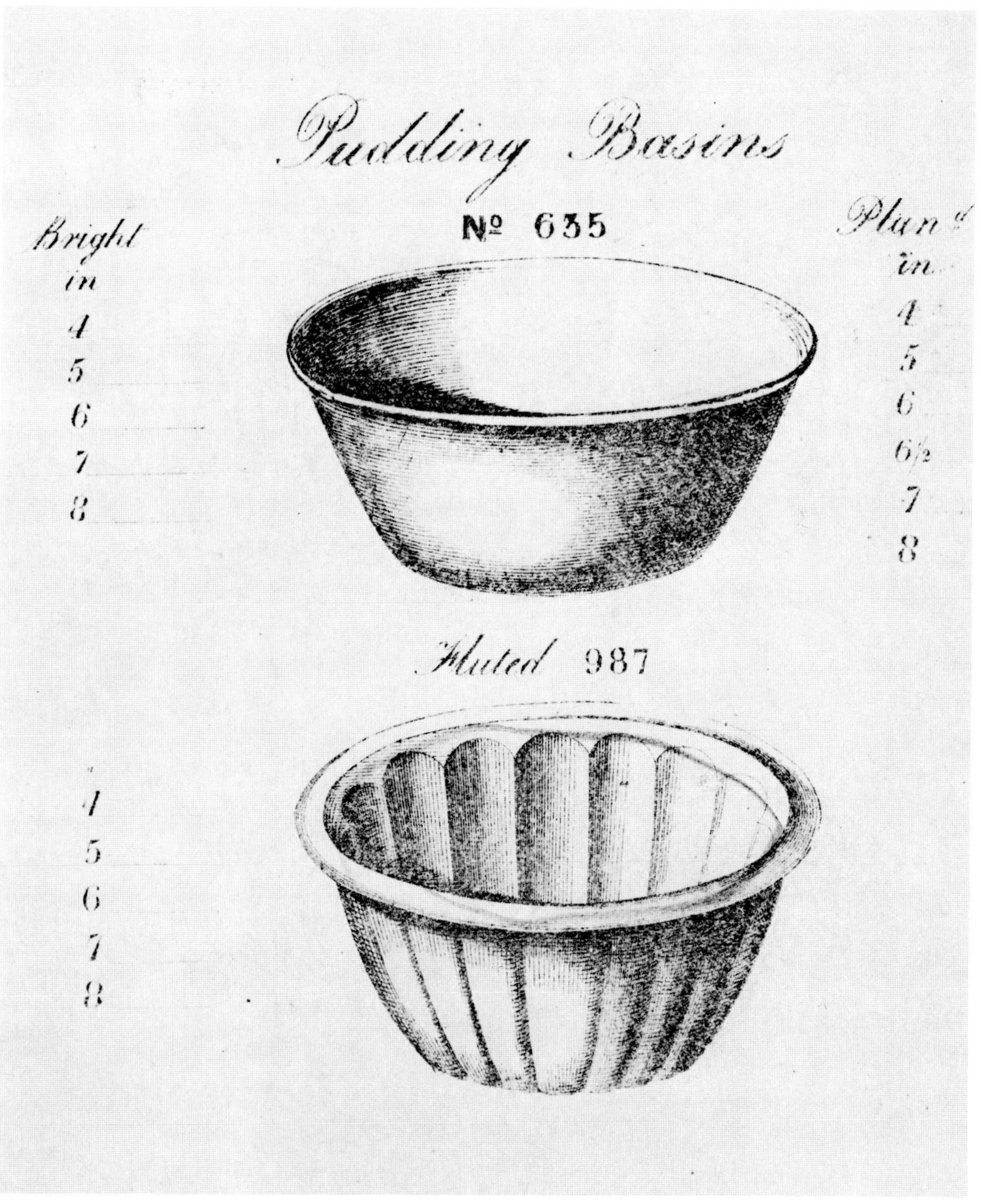

FIG. 5:41. Pudding basins. From Henry Loveridge & Co., *Catalogue*, p. 370. (Winterthur Museum Library.)

Well-to-do Americans could serve their puddings not only in porcelain but in silver. The Philadelphia Cadwaladers owned a large chased silver pudding dish, and Anne Stevenson, daughter of John and Magdalena Douw Stevenson of Albany, acquired an initialed silver example with a silver pudding knife made by Shepherd and Boyd in 1814 when she became the second wife of Pierre van Cortlandt II (Fig. 5:40). Less affluent families used tin pudding dishes that were commonly offered for sale in newspapers of the 1770s (Fig. 5:41), or they used the cream-colored, green- or blue-edged creamware and pearlware pudding dishes that gained favor at the end of the eighteenth century. Not until the 1830s did housewives gradually replace dishes of edgeware with dishes that pottery merchants listed as Grecian, green sprig, white ironstone, alpine moss, lavender water lily, granite, and mocha "puddings."[43]

Of whatever design and material, pudding and the pudding dish were once fixtures in every household. Like apple pie they either played a role among the meats and vegetables or sat solidly on family dessert tables, indelicately elbowing out the whips and preserves.

6

Excellent Entertainment of Fruit and Wine

Phil invited B. to take batchelor's dinner. . . . bought a pair of fowls, a pair of ducks . . . made a large bowl of punch . . . fixed us at a game of whist. . . . In a couple of hours dinner was laid . . . good old Madeira, Claret, and Champagne in abundance.

Charles Buck, New York, 1791[1]

Fruit ended a festive meal in style. Steep-sided cones or broad-based pyramids of cherries, strawberries, raspberries, and currants rose alternately with uniform piles of apples, pears, peaches, and plums, their bright color reflecting from the polished mahogany of a dinner table and offering a final compliment to guests.

Both Europeans and Americans were fond of fruit and ate it with great enjoyment. They gave it the place of honor as the finale of a dessert and took time, even after a long dinner, to savor it. "Fruits were the diet first allowed man," Sara Hale observed in 1839, "and it seems the Eden taste still lingers in our race." European travelers who were served American fruits in American houses and hotels never failed to be impressed by them. In New York Dr. Alexander Hamilton, after a "fine dessert of fruit and sweetmeats," extolled the white grapes. In Philadelphia Mrs. Warder exclaimed over the abundance of pineapples, strawberries, and cherries and especially over the watermelons "like sweetened snow." From Boston to New Orleans Mrs. Hall praised the strawberries and cream that appeared at dinners "in great perfection," and in Maryland Mr. Wirt applauded "the large delicious" peaches and pears.[2]

Although Europeans still reverently peel a specimen fruit to crown their dinner, most Americans have all but given up the tradition. Perhaps at holiday time an American hostess may end a meal by serving fruit, nuts, and raisins.

But only on the menus of the largest hotels and steamships is fruit called The Dessert, and only in a few well-to-do households is fruit imported every month. For most of us fresh fruit does not complete our dinner parties nor even appear on family tables save as a decoration or as an escape from calories.

Fruits at Parties

People of the eighteenth century, on the other hand, seem to have eaten fresh fruit not only with enjoyment, but even with abandon. Although they did not eat it for breakfast, tea, or supper, they overdid it at dinner and at parties. One can read of their heedlessness in writings of the century. Peter Kalm in 1748 called New Yorkers reckless in the way they ate quantities of melons, watermelons, peaches, and "other juicy fruits," thereby prolonging their bouts of summer fever. "The Trifler," writing in the *Columbian Magazine* of 1787, felt it necessary to caution women against overindulgence in "the blooming peach, luscious pear, and refreshing apple" and to warn them against eating "the sour, half-grown plum and hard, green blackberry."[3] If fruit was eaten with abandon it was also eaten with gusto. People could scarcely eat it any other way when standing about at evening parties. Demolishing peaches, plums, and apples leisurely at the dinner table with the help of knife and fork, plate, finger doily, and finger cup was one thing; biting into those juicy and noisy fruits when standing at a party, dressed in brocade, satin, and lace, was another.

It was fortunate for the guests at a ball given in New York by the French minister in 1782 that it was mid July, when only cherries, strawberries, and raspberries were ripe. Accounts of this ball give us a picture of fruit as esteemed party refreshment. The ball was a large one, held to honor the birthday of the dauphin of France in a style that Americans considered truly fashionable. The seven hundred guests who came were invited for "half an hour after seven o'clock in the afternoon," and their host, the Chevalier de Lauzun, received them in a dancing room splendid with numerous lights and dresses of "brilliancy and variety," as Dr. Benjamin Rush of Philadelphia described it. Two private refreshment apartments were provided nearby where servants passed "all kinds of cool and agreeable drinks with sweet cake, fruit and the like." At twelve o'clock the company was called to a supper that was laid out on tables set up under three large marquees erected on the lawn. The supper was "a cold collation, simple, frugal, and elegant, and handsomely set off with a dessert consisting of cakes and all the fruits of the season."[4]

Elizabethan Fruit Banquets

This eveningful of fruit had a two-hundred-year history of fruit eating behind it. Fruit banquests had made their appearance in England when orchards increased in Queen Elizabeth's reign, and they had become as popular as spicery banquets. Men of modest income served them because they were less expensive than spicery; men of wealth served them in addition to spicery simply because they were enjoyable. Shakespeare's Justice Shallow in *Henry IV, Part 2*, offered both banquets when he invited Falstaff after supper one evening to go to an arbor to eat "a last year's pippin . . . with a dish of caraways and so forth."[5]

Fruit and the Colonists

English colonists who came during the post-Elizabethan years to the eastern shore of North America found a variety of fruit growing wild. Plums, cherries, mulberries, and raspberries were there for the picking in the fields and woods of Virginia, as Captain John Smith wrote home to the Virginia Company. Persimmons, too, grew plentifully. New to Captain Smith, they seemed to him to be a kind of medlar that when ripe was "as delicious as an apricock." The small pink-orange fruit remained a novelty to visiting Europeans for a hundred and fifty years, inspiring them to express their interest whenever they found the persimmon among the sweetmeats of a dessert or made into wine.[6]

Colonists who followed the Jamestown settlers not only promptly made use of the native fruits they discovered but industriously planted fruits they had known in England, so that by 1681 the botanist John Rea saw people in Virginia harvesting twenty varieties each of cherries and apples, forty-four of plums, thirty-five of peach, and three of mulberries, besides grapes and figs. In the Massachusetts Bay Colony, as well as in Virginia, orchards flourished from the first half century of settling to provide householders with banquet fare. Even such a sober Puritan as Bostonian Samuel Sewall made a festive occasion out of fruit eating. One Saturday afternoon in June 1685 he took his wife with him on his horse to a nearby town to indulge in fruit with friends. "Carried my wife to Dorchester to eat cherries and raspberries," he wrote in his diary. And probably because the expedition smacked of Elizabethan revelry and was therefore unbecoming a would-be good church member, he rationalized the motive for the trip and added, "Chiefly to ride and take the air." He enjoyed fruit as refreshment forty years later when he helped his friend Colonel Fitch celebrate his daughter's marriage with "oranges and pears, good bride-cake, wine, and beer."[7]

The numbers of orchards and vineyards increased rapidly throughout the colonies in the eighteenth century. Settlers grafted from each other's trees or patiently grew their own trees from seeds. Nurturing fruit trees from seedlings is no small accomplishment, but there was at least one man who claimed to have done it. In 1742 William Stephens of Georgia transplanted nearly four hundred grape vines, two hundred mulberry trees, and a number of apple, pear, nectarine, and plum trees, "all raised," he wrote in his journal, "from stones of the best kinds . . . after eating the fruit."[8]

Pineapples

When travelers tell of the fruit they enjoyed in America they often mention pineapples. Mrs. Warder had them in Philadelphia in 1786, and Henry Tudor saw "pines" in 1831 along with the melons, grapes, nectarines, peaches, apples, and other fruits that always closed the hospitable entertainment of the hotels he stayed in. Although these travelers took pineapples for granted, their grandparents had thought them exotic. People of that earlier generation had coveted pineapples because they were rare and expensive. The fruits had been known to Europeans ever since the fifteenth century when Spanish and Portuguese sailors found them growing in the West Indies, Central America, and South America. Although small, the fruits were considered delectable and made a sensation in sixteenth-century European courts. Owning pineapples became a craze. Gardeners tried to grow them in hothouses and merchants imported them. By the early seventeenth century Dutch nurserymen were successful in raising them, and in 1657 England's Oliver Cromwell received a gift of several. Charles II in 1660 had his royal portrait painted receiving one from his gardener John Rose and in 1668 offered some to the French minister Colbert. There is no proof that Rose grew pineapples, but it is certain that in 1721 Sir Matthew Decker's gardener, Henry Tellende, did. Right through the eighteenth century hostesses craved the decorative curiosity for their dessert tables, and some went so far as to rent a few for a party.[9]

Americans, like their English cousins, had admired pineapples throughout the seventeenth century, but the fruit was still unusual enough in Massachusetts in 1734 to move Judge Benjamin Lynde to record in his diary that his wife's brother had sent her "a fine pineapple" through the kindness of one Captain White. In the next half century pineapples came to the eastern shore of America, either fresh or preserved as a sweetmeat, in ships that had touched in the semitropics. American gardeners began to grow them, and by 1794 Henry Wansey in his travels could say that Mr. Ashton Harvey of Salem and Mr. Joseph Barrell of Boston raised them in their excellent hothouses. Furthermore, in New York, for twenty pence, Mr. Wansey could buy good ones grown in the Bahama Islands.[10]

Somewhere and sometime within the last four centuries the pineapple began to serve as a sign of hospitality. It is said that a small pineapple was fastened onto dwellings in certain South and Central American Indian villages as a sign of friendship, but the place of its first use as a symbol by Europeans is elusive. Carved pineapples sprout from eighteenth-century European and American fenceposts and furniture; pineapple designs enliven ceramics, textiles, and wallpaper; special pineapple stands exist in glass, porcelain, and earthenware (Pl. 6:1, Fig. 6:2). But nothing has been discovered that tells of the origin of the fruit as a symbol. We know that the pinecone, which the pineapple resembles, gave the fruit its name and itself was once called a pine-apple. We find that the cone appears in ancient art, particularly in the Middle East, as a symbol of fertility. We see the cone on the tip of the thyrsus of Dionysus and as a distinctive motif in Norman and Renaissance ornament. Conventionalized as it is in this early art we sometimes mistake it for the pomegranate, Ceres' symbol of regeneration. We even take it for the artichoke or the magnolia. But when we see it used before the late fifteenth century we know enough not to mistake it for the pineapple because the pineapple had not yet left the New World.[11]

Fruit Dishes or Bowls

With fruit of all kinds so highly regarded, it is understandable that dishes were especially designed for it. In the seventeenth century people owned what inventory takers called "fruit dishes." Thomas Swift of Dorchester had several, and James Claypoole of Philadelphia had one. Like the bowl that covers the breast of engraver Martin Engelbrecht's *Porcelain Maker* and is labeled "Frücht

FIG. 6:2. C. Watson, *Ball Supper*. England, ca. 1805. Colored engraving after sepia wash by Maria Cosway, London, 1803; H. 22.9 cm., W. 28 cm. (Collection of the author.)

oder Confect Schälen," and "Coupe à Confitures et Fruits," the fruit dishes might have been shallow and lobed (Fig. 6:3). Also like the *frücht schälen*, "fruit bowls," they could have been made of porcelain, or burnt china, although they were more probably of English delft (Fig. 6:4, Pl. 6:5). In the eighteenth

Fruit Baskets

century people owned fruit baskets that they put on the table in sets (Fig. 6:6). Governor Burnet's two were of glass. Many of his contemporaries' were of English salt-glaze stoneware (Fig. 6:7). The Cadwaladers of Philadelphia and the John Browns of Providence had them of porcelain made in China in forms especially designed for export to the West (Figs. 6:8, 6:9). In the nineteenth century fruit baskets came as part of large dessert services. President Monroe's were of French porcelain, part of a dessert set that included thirty-six flat and eighty-four deep plates. Other people owned fruit baskets of silver like the pair Robert Oliver of Baltimore had in 1835.[12]

FIG. 6:3. Detail of lobed fruit and sweetmeat bowl. From Martin Engelbrecht, *The Porcelain Maker*. Augsburg, Germany, 1684–1756. Engraving; H. 37.8 cm., W. 2.1 cm. (Winterthur Museum, 55.135.7.)

FIG. 6:4. Lobed bowl, England, probably London, 1640–60. Arms of the Drapers' Company. Delft (tin-glazed earthenware); H. 5.7 cm., D. 64.9 cm. (Winterthur Museum, 64.620, ex. coll. Charles J. Lomax.)

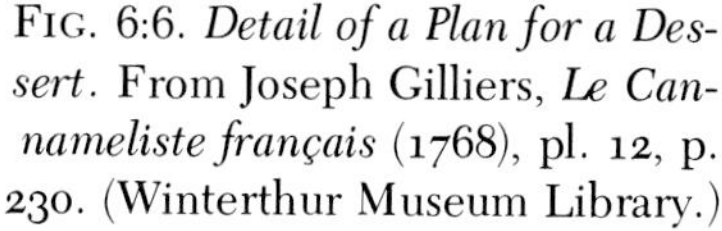

FIG. 6:6. *Detail of a Plan for a Dessert*. From Joseph Gilliers, *Le Cannameliste français* (1768), pl. 12, p. 230. (Winterthur Museum Library.)

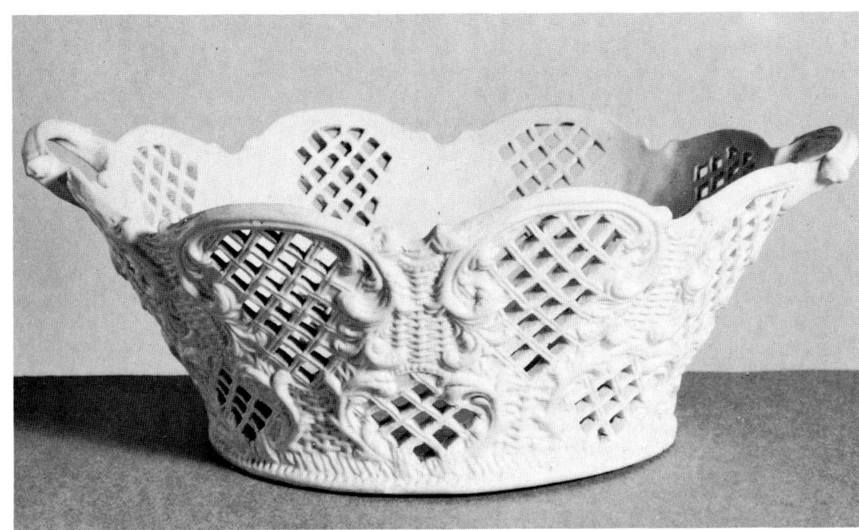

FIG. 6:7. Fruit basket, Staffordshire, 1760–80. Salt-glaze stoneware; H. 9.4 cm., W. 25.5 cm. (Winterthur Museum, 58.859.)

FIG. 6:8. Dessert dishes from a blue, gold, and sepia dinner service, China, 1790–1810. Export porcelain. (Winterthur Museum, 61.655.)

FIG. 6:9. Raphaelle Peale, *Still Life with Peaches*. Philadelphia, 1821. Oil on canvas; H. 34 cm., W. 48.9 cm. (Courtesy of the Brooklyn Museum, Caroline H. Polhemus Fund.)

Sets of Fruit Bowls, Baskets, and Plates

At the end of the eighteenth century china fruit bowls in sets were popular. Eleuthère Irénée du Pont bought a set of four in 1806. Fruit plates and fruit dishes of porcelain and earthenware came by the dozen or double dozen as part of large dessert services. The service of Pennsylvania's Governor Mifflin, which was big enough to cover three large tables and to furnish twenty-four guests with three clean plates apiece during dessert, contained twelve fruit baskets and stands.[13]

Fruit on Boards and Trays

Not all those who served fruit at their tables owned special fruit dishes, plates, bowls, and baskets. Many people used whatever they had of all-purpose containers and did as Massialot, the French confectioner, suggested when he remarked in his *Nouvelle instruction:* "One may dress one's fruit whether raw or cooked, in bowls, baskets, or footed cups. . . . In default of bowls and baskets one can still dress the fruit in a very proper manner in ordinary vessels or on little boards." Whatever Americans had of platters, plates, and bowls, whether made of ordinary wood, wicker, pewter, or earthenware, served very well to dress fruit. Even John Baker's "baskets, alias voyders" and Antipas Boyce's "round wicker voyder" could set off admirably the pippins, plums, and peaches of a New England autumn.[14]

Mixing Fruits

Whether dressed on porcelain or on wicker, fruit pyramids trimmed with bits of greenery, rising in balanced pairs, quartets, or sextets around a large center pyramid, made a handsome table. They had done so at least since Louis XIV's stewards ranged them on Versaille's fête tables (Fig. 6:10). One kind of fruit to a pyramid or basket was the rule during most of the eighteenth century. As late as 1790 the rule held in such cookbooks as Charlotte Mason's *Lady's Assistant,* which Lady Temple used in Boston. But some Americans advocated putting two or three different kinds of fruit together (Pl. 6:11). Mrs. Hall, seeing the practice in Boston for the first time, thought it worth copying in England and told her sister, "It not only has a prettier effect, but prevents the necessity of pulling about the dishes over the table."[15]

Mrs. Beeton, too, apparently thought a mixture was better; she stood a pineapple on a tumbler in the footed dish she called a tazza, surrounded it with pears, plums, and apples on a thick layer of wet moss, and over the fruits draped a bunch or two of grapes "in a negligé sort of manner." Other women pyramided fruit in layers with evergreen leaves peeking out between each layer. They especially liked to layer cherries, raspberries, and strawberries in footed dishes, with cherries on the bottom, strawberries on the top, and leaves in between them.[16]

Cheese and Dessert

It was at the beginning of the nineteenth century, some sixty years before Mrs. Beeton created her pineapple pyramid with grapes *négligés,* that cheese began to enter the dessert picture. Always a staple of English diet, cheese had for centuries been eaten regularly for supper by Britons and Americans of every estate and, by country people, also at the main meal of the day. In the last quarter of the eighteenth century it began to insinuate itself into the stylish dinner party. Although cookbook authors of the eighteenth century omitted it

FIG. 6:10. Detail of a party table in the courtyard at Versailles. From Jean le Pautre, engraver, "La Quatrième Journée, 1676," in *Festes à Versailles*, volume of *Le Cabinet du Roi*, n.p. (Winterthur Museum Library.)

from their menus and diagrams, hostesses frequently provided it with the second course. Small wheels of cheese came to the table in their own cradlelike coasters or stands of wood, earthenware, or silver (Fig. 6:12). The cheese, resting on its rim, allowed people to cut a wedge without difficulty. As early as the 1790s cheese scoops made of silver and mahogany helped them to dig a mouthful from a deep hard cheese or even from a cheese like the "excellent cream cheese" that Mrs. Norris of Jane Austen's *Mansfield Park* saw on the table at an 1811 dinner.[17]

FIG. 6:12. Cheese cradle by Frederick Marquand, ca. 1830, marked F. MARQUAND in rectangle. Silver; H. 8.2 cm., L. 30.2 cm., W. 7.2 cm. (The Metropolitan Museum of Art, gift of Mr. and Mrs. Samuel Schwartz, 1976.)

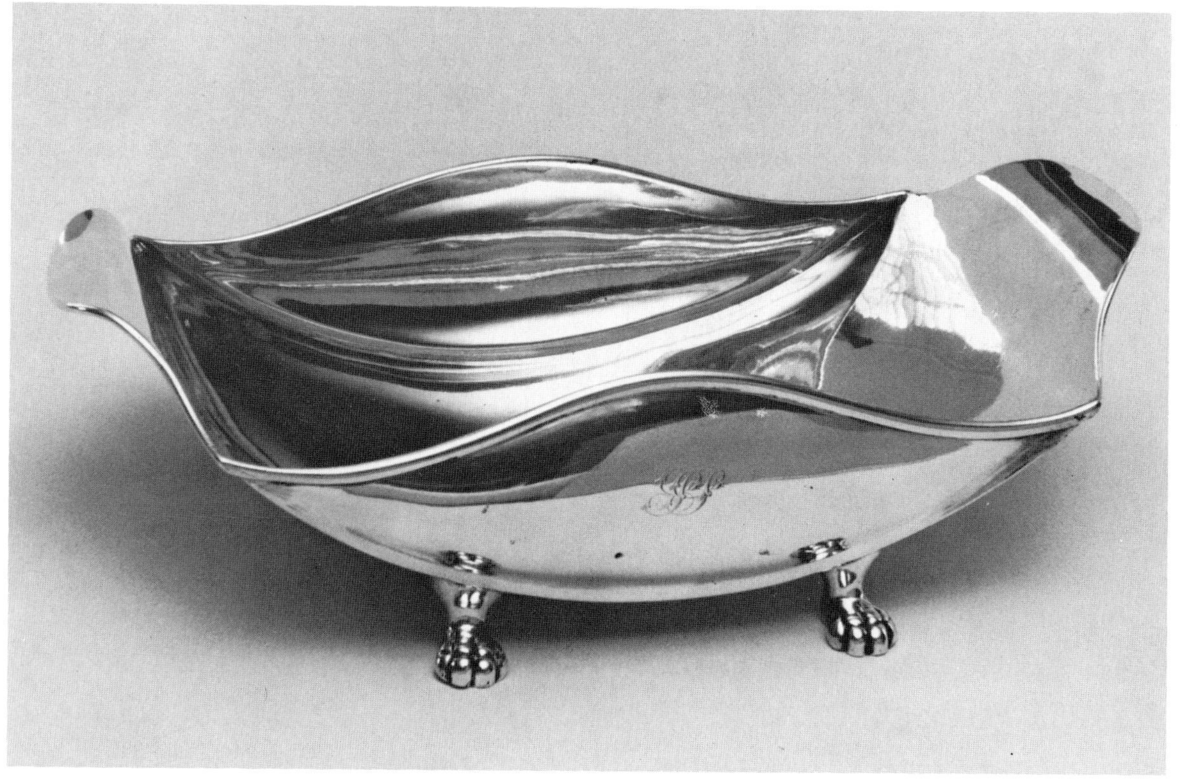

The French, when eating fruit, considered cheese a good accompaniment, and their spokesman, Brillat-Savarin, rhapsodized over the combination, comparing fruit without cheese to a woman with only one eye. Adulated as Brillat-Savarin was by every Briton and American who read his *Physiology of Taste*, cheese and fruit should have been inseparable on English and American tables from that time on. But the British did not allow the two to meet. They made a special course of cheese, serving it after the meat and vegetables. With it they offered such foods as anchovies or baked, pickled, or potted fish of some kind, together with cucumbers, salad, biscuits, and butter. During this course the cheese took the place of honor at the top or bottom of the table, while the butter took the center. Americans, scorning fish with cheese, offered salad with the cheese and put it in the center of the table. They often added matching dishes of radishes and placed them at two opposite corners. On occasion instead of a cheese they offered some such cheese dish as cheese omelet, cheese ramekin, or macaroni and cheese.[18]

In the 1860s Mrs. Beeton introduced cheese in various guises along with sweets and small meats. She scattered "fondue," "macaroni with Parmesan cheese," or just "cheese" sparingly among her 256 menus, by no means including them with every dinner. She put cheese with apple tart and custard, with plum or jam puddings, or all alone at the end of family dinners; or included it with jellies, puddings, and game birds just before fruit. She often added "cheese cakes," but because cheesecakes up to and including her lifetime were little puff pastries of apples, almonds, or nutmeg custard, and only occasionally of cheese curd, they cannot always be counted as cheese. Cheesecakes persist to this century in some families as chess cakes or chess pies, having nothing whatever to do with cheese as the product of the cow but everything to do with the word *cheese* as *fromage*, meaning a mixture of ingredients as in *fromage glacé*, the frozen flavored and sweetened cream we call ice cream.[19]

Both the British and the Americans at the end of the nineteenth century cut a partially eaten cheese into medium-sized wedges for a neat appearance and had them passed in oval or rectangular glass or ceramic covered plates. Called cheese dishes, the plates had deep covers similar to those of butter dishes. Some hosts took it upon themselves to cut a large cheese into small pieces at the table. The German author of the 1851 *Illustrated Guide to London* described the process: "The cheese at dessert time is passed about, i.e. the master of the house places a number of little pieces on a plate and has them passed around. It is not good manners to take more than a little piece of cheese because it is not a course but a post-meal aid to digestion."[20]

Beverages

To round out the story of the table and its dessert all that remains are the liquid refreshments. At the beginning of a meal their place, as we have seen, was on the serving table or sideboard until asked for by diners. There they waited in an assortment of such vessels as flagons, pitchers, jugs, and bottles; tankards, mugs, cans, beakers, tumblers, and footed glasses; beer bowls, beer glasses, ale flutes, cider pots, cider flutes, cider glasses with covers, rummers, and silver sack bowls (Fig. 6:13).

The beverages that diners of high and low degree asked for to accompany the first course were beer and cider, those potions with firm reputations as health-givers. Cider Poor Richard called a "wholesome and cheerful liquor . . . which suits both constitution and pocket much better than West-India spirits." To make cider was easier than to brew beer, consequently more of it was produced. Lieutenant Klinkowström, visiting in New York, assumed that it was the Americans' only every-meal drink, used as his countrymen used light beer. Its good name endured into this century. If we looked in on a supper eaten in 1912 we would still see effervescent and mildly alcoholic cider supplied to old and young.[21]

FIG. 6:13. Drinking vessels, England and America, 1700–1850. (Winterthur Museum.)

Wine

As the eighteenth-century meal progressed past the meats and vegetables, diners asked for wine. It would be brought to them in vessels as varied as the Venetian glasses Cotton Mather owned in 1687 and the quart wine tankard Jonathan Dickinson owned in 1722. The wines largely came from Spain and Portugal. Thomas and Abigail Kelland of Boston kept a supply typical of the wine supplies of their well-to-do contemporaries. Stored in their "little entry" in 1683 were one hogshead, five butts, and thirteen pipes of malaga, sherry, canary, port, madeira, and fayal. Madeira, canary, and fayal came from the Portugese islands of those names; malaga, or white mountain wine, from Spain's southeastern seaport of Malaga. Sherry largely came from Andalusia in the area around Jerez de la Frontera, a Spanish city north of Cadiz, a few miles above Gibraltar; port, from around Oporto and other northern Portuguese towns of the Douro River valley. Of all these wines madeira gained the distinction of being the favorite of Americans (Pl. 6:14). It was a fortified wine that Peter Kalm thought harsh and fiery and Lieutenant Klinkowström considered "hot," but in spite of, or because of, this ungentle quality, travelers met it on every table and seldom failed to comment on it. Ambassador Bagot found that Americans drank "scarcely any other wine than madeira" and that they offered it to him in a quality much better than he could hope to give them. He told his successor Stratford Canning: "They all import their own wine and keep it with great care, consequently it is hardly ever to be bought."[22]

Madeira

Lisbon, Claret, and Sack

Eighteenth-century descendants of the Kellands as well as their contemporaries drank wines not only like those that sat in the Kellands' entry but also such wines as lisbon, claret, and sack. Lisbon was a white wine from the area near Portugal's capital of that name. Margareta Schuyler bought it often in quart and in gallon bottles from her grandson. Claret and sack were any of a number of red and white wines that came from France, Spain, and Portugal. The word *claret*, from the Latin *clarus*, "clear," signified light rose-colored wines in the seventeenth century and true red wines later (Fig. 6:15). The word *sack*, possibly from the Spanish *saco*, which has such varied meanings as "bag" or "sack," "extraction," and "exportation," refers to strong golden table wine that came from various places in southern Spain. The wines were lightly fortified with brandy to improve their traveling ability and were often used in syllabubs, caudles, and possets.[23]

Stores of Wines

Like the Kellands' seventeenth-century household, many eighteenth-century households kept large stores of wines. They also kept large stores of other liquids. It was a gentlemanly necessity to have a great cellar in an age when sack posset for breakfast, rum punch before dinner, and beer, cider, and wine for both dinner and supper were usual, and in a century when brandy, rum, and gin drinking were on the increase. The cellar of Edward Lloyd was typical. In it, to be inventoried at the end of Lloyd's life in 1796, lay 1,220 bottles of porter, ale, beer, port, whiskey, brandy, and gin; uncounted bottles of pale ale, English beer, cider, and stout; 3 demijohns, equal to about 15 gallons, of twenty-one-year-old apple brandy; 1 pipe, equal to some 125 gallons, of old French

FIG. 6:15. Claret bottle, England, dated 1640. Delft; H. 13 cm. (Winterthur Museum, 64.691.)

brandy; 1 hogshead, equal to about 63 gallons, of New England rum; 6 demijohns of cherry bounce; 677 bottles of madeira; 1,822 bottles of sweet wine; and some 66 assorted bottles of sherry, lisbon, claret, champagne, burgundy, and rhenish wines.[24]

Sources of Wines

French and German wines like those in Lloyd's store of beverages came to England and her colonies throughout the seventeenth and eighteenth centuries, They came in small quantities, however, because of the wars between England and France. In spite of the difficulties of wartime transport a man could, if he had the money and know-how, round out his cellar with rhine wines, champagne, burgundy, and old French brandy.

Champagne

Champagne that came from France's northeastern vineyards sparkled on many American tables between dinner and dessert as it did on the Virginian Hill Carters'. Pale red in color, it was drunk from tall champagne flutes not only at dinner but with blancmanges and ices at evening parties. After observing Washington society Bagot warned Canning: "You will be judged of by your champagne of which the Americans prefer the sweet and sparkling. I think a dinner or supper is prized and talked of exactly in proportion to the quantity of champagne given and the noise it makes in uncorking!"[25]

Homemade Beverages

Whereas wealthy men like Edward Lloyd imported their own wines and spirits from abroad, ordinary householders bought theirs from the grocer or made them at home. Madam Schuyler, for one, acquired from Cuyler several times a week various bottles of madeira, brandy, porter, and geneva (vulgarly known as gin), on which she paid a deposit of sixpence per bottle. If she wished to buy empty bottles for homemade brandy or cordials, she paid four to sixpence apiece for them and four shillings the gross for corks.[26]

Making drinks at home took much housewifely attention. Under the direction of the mistress, all of the members of a household gathered fruits and berries to make the wine, brandies, cordials, and waters, or "simples," that were an essential part of entertaining. To supplement the imported beverages of the wine cellar the mistress and servants turned peaches, apples, strawberries, and cherries into brandy, and pears into ciderlike perry. They made acceptable wines out of dandelions, elderberries, currants, persimmons, blackberries, and such grapes as the muscadine scuppernong, named after a North Carolina river. With the help of small stills like Captain William Alden's pewter alembic, which he kept stored in a room with three barrels of cider and fifteen gallons of New England rum, housewives could distill fruits and herbs to make cordials beneficial to the heart, the organ that gave the drink its name. They put fresh-picked mint, bergamot, lemon rind, or new roses into the still so that steam and time could extract their fragrant oils. They hung aniseed, caraway, peppermint, cinammon, or pennyroyal over the alembic to distill the seeds' and herbs' health-giving properties, then added lemon juice, peach jam, or almond paste, and always brandy and sugar, to make "aromatic spiritous liquors." They left out the brandy in making simple waters, which, containing no spirits, lost every contest for popularity but when sipped by ladies from cordial cups and saucers or from cordial glasses in between bites of seedcakes, queen cakes, or wafers warmed the cockles well enough.[27]

Ratafia

Certainly ratafia (pronounced ratta-fee-a) could bring a glow to the cheek. John Nott's 1724 recipe for it required brandy, French wine, orange-flower water, apricot stones, sugar, and twice daily stirring for a month and a half. Other ratafia recipes called for a combination of mashed cherries, gooseberries, raspberries, almonds, brandy, and a half dozen spices. The Ridgelys of Delaware made their ratafia out of quince juice. It made a "fine red colour" and was properly drunk from tall slender ratafia glasses. Governor Burnet kept his supply near his jars of sweetmeats in a case of bottles holding "ratafie &c." The et cetera in the governor's bottle case probably included noyau, a popular apricot-brandy-orange-flower liqueur similar to ratafia. It probably also included orgeat, another drink for convivial occasions. Originally made in France of *orge* ("barley"), orgeat was composed of almonds pounded to a paste in sugar and orange-flower water thinned with cold spring water. The *Family Receipt Book* considered it, before thinning, "one of the finest and most lubricating liquids for all public speakers, readers, singers &c.," and Mrs. David Randolph of Virginia pronounced it "a necessary refreshment at all parties." To her orgeat Mary Randolph added cold or lukewarm milk, cinnamon, and rosewater and served it in glasses with handles.[28]

Orgeat

Cherry Bounce

Cherry bounce, of which Edward Lloyd had six demijohns in his cellar, involved both sweet and sour cherries in equal parts plus whiskey and sugar. The young daughters of Eleuthère Irénée du Pont helped to make a supply for their household on the Brandywine River by stuffing cherries into a jug and shouting "Pound! Pound!"[29]

Negus

Still another party refresher, negus, a descendant of the ancient spicy hippocras, combined port or sherry with nutmeg, lemon, sugar or honey, and hot water. A popular seventeenth-century way of taking wine, it acquired its name from a Colonel Francis Negus who was particularly fond of it—so much so that following his death in 1732 he was credited with inventing it. A century later, when Stratford Canning planned his journey to Washington, Sir Charles Bagot advised him to order a certain number of ice, negus, and lemonade glasses. "These" he said, "with tea cups, coffee cups, and wine glasses (for they hand Madeira round at all parties) furnish all the matériel for your conversaziones." By Mrs. Beeton's time, however, negus had become a drink only for children's parties.[30]

Shrub

Drinks based on a fruit shrub were universally popular. The words *shrub* and *sherbet* were synonyms for a basic fruit and sugar syrup to which water, wine, or brandy could be added. A typical recipe for homemade shrub merely called for squeezing fruit and bottling the strained and sugared juice. But some men like Charles Carroll supplemented the homemade kind. In 1768 Carroll ordered from London six bottles of orange shrub, well corked, together with the recipe. In 1768 it probably would have been easier to mix the shrub at home than to write an order in longhand, make a copy for the letter book, write a second order to insure the original against loss at sea, and send a draft for payment as well as additional drafts for the costs of handling, cartage, wharfage, taxes, and all the other incidental shipping expenses that were customarily incurred on both sides of the Atlantic.[31]

Fruit Vinegar

Lightly alcoholic or nonalcoholic fruit drinks also provided refreshment for moderate revelers at an eighteenth-century party. Fruit vinegar was one such drink. It consisted simply of wine vinegar and fruit juice that had been allowed to stand in the sun for six weeks to produce an acid considered pleasant and refreshing. Lemonade, too, was a favorite. Although usually made with spirits, this still very popular drink in the late eighteenth century was sometimes only a sherbet of lemon juice, lemon rind, sugar syrup, and *capillaire*, or syrup of fern, diluted with water. *The Italian Confectioner* contended that these ingredients, if allowed to stand before straining through a flannel bag, made a most pleasant and wholesome iced drink for parties, balls, and routs. In fact, the author believed that no drinks were as elegant or could be so safely recommended as lemonade or orangeade. Lady Temple in 1809 kept ten lemonade glasses and a dozen green glasses for these refreshing drinks.[32]

Lemonade

Punch

Much of the whiskey, brandy, and rum that formed about a fourth of Lloyd's cellar and other cellars went into punch, that salubrious concoction loved by the British and their colonials (Fig. 6:16). To the scorn of Europeans who drank wine and spirits straight, punch lovers mixed rum or brandy with sugar, lime or lemon juice, and the zest, or essence, of the rind, diluting this shrub with hot or cold water according to the season and the capacity of the drinkers. It is said by some that the term *punch* was Hindi, learned in India as early as 1632 by the British who were trading and colonizing there. They believe that it signified "five" for five ingredients. Others argue for different derivations. One argument holds that whereas the word *punch* in Hindi was pronounced "punch," in seventeenth-century English it was "poonsh," as it still is in northern England today; it could not, therefore, derive from the Hindi word. "Poonsh" is so documented in Dr. Johnson's "Who's for Poonsh?" and in the seventeenth-century Dutch *palepunts*, German *palepunz*, and French *bolleponge*, which copied more or less phonetically the English "bowl o' poonsh." A second argument holds that punch ingredients are seldom five but vary from three to six and are most often four. A scholar offering this argument suggests the word *puncheon* as the origin, reminding us that punch in early references is frequently a sailor's drink of lime juice, sugar, and water mixed with a ration of rum doled out from a puncheon. In any case and however pronounced, the word sounded sweet to the ears of merchants, sailors, and planters, each one of whom prided himself on his ability to mix the world's best libation. All punch makers drank each others' brews directly from bowls small enough for one or two people, or from wineglasses filled by the ladleful from punch bowls large enough to serve from three to thirty people (Pl. 6:17). They drank to the launching of a ship, welcoming home a venture, and sealing a bargain. Or they drank simply to wet the whistle. It was a sure sign of hospitality when the punch bowl was brought out.

FIG. 6:16. George Roupel, *Peter Manigault and His Friends.* Charleston, S.C., 1768. Ink and wash; H. 27.4 cm., W. 30.9 cm. (Winterthur Museum, 63.73.)

The Boston Merchant Harrison Gray Otis used to have a ten-gallon blue and white bowl filled and placed on his stair landing every afternoon so that his visitors would not go dry. Other gentlemen hosts would seldom fail to fill a bowl before dinner and lead their masculine guests away from the ladies for a glass or two.[33]

Cocktails

About 1800, Americans grew creative. Building on the old English fancy for sweetening wine, brandy, and spirits and on the many varieties of punch, they invented bracers and gave them bracing names. *Cocktail* was one of their inventions. No one knows where or why it was born, but it appeared in print in 1806. *Sherry cobbler* was another. Washington Irving in 1809 gave Marylanders credit for putting this drink together. Whether or not they chose the word *cobbler* from *cob*, a "lump" or "piece," because of the lump of sugar that was in the drink, he did not reveal. In the late 1840s impressive names like *stone-fence* or *stone-wall* for a union of hard cider and rum, and *timber-doodle* and *hold-fast* for other awe-inspiring mergers entered masculine vocabularies. The new drinks were kept to masculine haunts on through the century and never disgraced private homes.[34]

Drinking Paraphernalia

All of the early morning, late-night, and in-between drinking of the two centuries required considerably more matériel than Bagot told Canning to bring with him to the United States. Hours alone at the dinner table when servants had gone back to the kitchen to stay and ladies had withdrawn to the withdrawing room, and hours without servants at gentlemen's suppers, oyster parties, and punch parties, made do-it-yourself devices a necessity.

Bottle Coasters

Casters, or stands with or without wheels, and "neat pierced and polished silver coasters or bottle stands" such as Edmond Milne of Philadelphia advertised in 1764 held bottles or decanters and made it easy for gentlemen to pass the madeira. They could shove the canary or mountain down the table on mahogany sliders like those Thomas Duncan of New York owned in 1757 along with a silver punch strainer and crane, or on round leather sliders like the six Solomon Ingraham owned in 1805 in Norwich, Connecticut.

Wineglass Rinsers

Small glass or ceramic bowls or glass cylinders with two lips, variously called glass wash basins, washing cups and saucers, and glass coolers, made it possible for the drinkers to rinse their wineglasses between wines (Figs. 6:18, 6:19). When George Washington in 1759 ordered from Robert Carey and Company of London a "fashionable set of dessert glasses and stands for sweetmeats, jelly, etc. together with wash glasses and a proper stand for these also," he was supplying his dessert table not only with dessert dishes and their plates but with wineglass washers and their plates.[35]

Finger Bowls

Other small glass bowls and cylinders with or without plates brought the convenience of after-meal finger rinsing and lip rinsing to the dessert table. These were the "finger glasses and stands" that Philip Ludwell, as a good Virginian host, provided his guests in 1767. They were also the "lip-glasses for the company to wash their mouth in" that Cosnett wrote of in 1826. Such bowls had been used in the seventeenth century regularly for mouth-rinsing pur-

FIG. 6:18. Detail of a fruit dessert with wash glass and doily. From W. H. Simmons, *The Vice*. London, 1841. Mezzotint after A. Crowquill. (The Old Print Shop, New York City.)

poses, and in certain circles this use had persisted into the eighteenth century. Tobias Smollett wrote in 1766 that he knew of "no custom more beastly than that of using water glasses in which polite company spit, and squirt, and spew the filthy scourings of their gums." By the end of the eighteenth century it was probable that most polite company used wash glasses only for finger and lip rinsing, having adopted the alternative terms *wash-hand glass*, *finger cup*, *lip glass*, and *finger bowl*. People could buy "elegant blue finger cups in fine cut glass" from Richard Capes who offered them in the *New York Daily Advertiser* in 1797. Robert Roberts put "finger glasses" to the right side of diners as he removed the second course plates. Lady Temple kept at least twenty-eight "finger cups" in her china closet. It was finger cups that the Reverend John Trusler described in his *Honours of the Table* as "water-glasses used after dinner to wash the fingers." Although John Quincy Adams when dining at the Mansion House with the lord mayor of London in 1816 dipped his fingers in the rosewater dish that his fellow diners wet corners of their napkins in for wiping their mouths and fingers before dessert, and although in 1828 Mrs. William Parkes, cookbook author, advocated the use of a common glass rosewater bowl, the communal dish lost out to individual bowls.[36]

FIG. 6:19. Wash glass, Europe, 1790–1820. One of ten remaining from a set of a dozen. Lead glass, lavender threading; H. 7.6 cm., D. 12.7 cm. (Winterthur Museum, 64.133.1–10.)

FIG. 6:20. Wine cistern, southern United States, probably Charleston, S.C., ca. 1790. Mahogany and lead with copper lining; H. 70.8 cm., W. 67.3 cm., D. 54 cm. (Winterthur Museum, 57.698.)

Cisterns and Monteiths

For the cooling of wine bottles and the cooling and rinsing of wineglasses men used a half dozen different vessels. The oldest kind was a cistern of pewter, brass, silver, copper, bell metal, earthenware, porcelain, or wood bound with brass hoops, which sat on the floor near the sideboard (Fig. 6:20). Holding bottles in cold water, it kept the wine at least as cold as it had been in the cellar. Thomas Kelland owned one of pewter in 1683, and Captain Ingraham one of wood and brass in 1805. A scallop-edged metal or ceramic cistern, called a monteith, held both bottles and glasses (Fig. 6:21). James Geddy of Williamsburg used a pewter monteith in 1744, and Elias Hasket Derby of Salem in the

FIG. 6:21a. Monteith, England, 1725–75. Pewter; H. 22.5 cm., W. 39.5 cm. (Winterthur Museum, 59.4.2, ex. coll. Joseph Downs.)

FIG. 6:21b. Wine bottles in a monteith. (Bowers Parlor, 1760, Winterthur Museum.)

1780s used a pair made of Sheffield plate. Small ceramic versions of monteiths, known as glass coolers, glass trays, *verrières*, or *rafraîchissoirs*, sat on the table convenient to the drinker (Figs. 6:22, 6:23). Joseph Barrell of Boston owned a silver-plated set, which he termed "coolers for the table,—two for glasses and four for decanters."[37] The coolers for decanters were probably the urns that became stylish in the second half of the eighteenth century for holding individual bottles (Pl. 6:24, Fig. 6:25). Such urns went usually by the name of wine cooler (Figs. 6:26, 6:27), although the Leeds pottery used the term *ice pail*. Elias Hasket Derby's Sheffield pair of urns for cooling wine, whether "wine coolers" or "ice pails," dignified his dining table when it was in full dessert regalia.[38]

FIG. 6:22. Ice pail and liner, wine cooler, and glass tray, or verrière, with cake plate. From a dessert service, Sèvres, 1753–65. Porcelain; H. (glass tray) 19 cm., W. 26.4 cm. (Winterthur Museum, 65.2919.4.)

FIG. 6:23. Detail of a dessert with verrière, wine cooler, and cistern. From Pierre-Antoine Fraichot (1690–1763), *Table de cuisine*, from Act 2, Scene 1, *La Femme qui a raison*, Besançon, ca. 1750. Engraving. (Winterthur Museum Library.)

FIG. 6:25. A pair of wine coolers, China, 1790–1810. Export porcelain; H. 20 cm., D. 29.9 cm. (Winterthur Museum, 66.607.1, 2.)

FIG. 6:26. Embossed antique wine cooler. From a manuscript potter's manual, attributed to the Spode factory, England, ca. 1815–21, p. 57. (Winterthur Museum Library, DMMC.)

FIG. 6:27. Gadroon wine cooler. From a manuscript potter's manual, attributed to the Spode, factory, England, ca. 1815–21, p. 143. (Winterthur Museum Library, DMMC.)

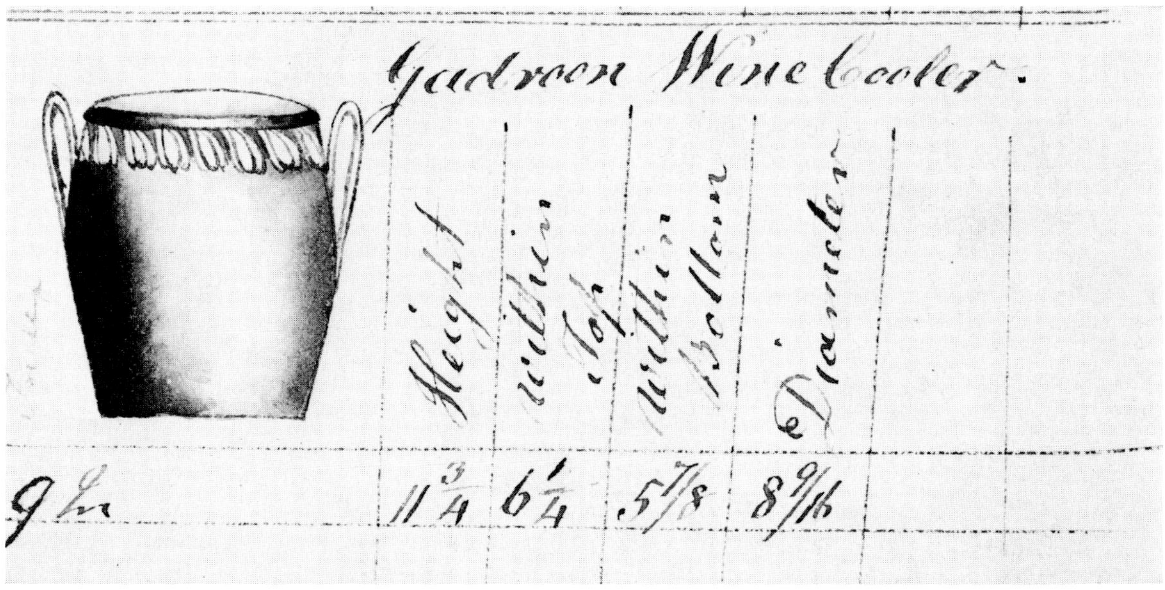

Water

Although beer, cider, and wine predominated as drinks on the eighteenth-century table, plain water began to win popularity as well. For people who diluted champagne and burgundy for the sake of sobriety there were special wine-and-water glasses to be had. As early as 1763 if there were no water on the table, drinkers among the guests visiting Dr. Edward Shippen of Philadelphia could ask for a mixture from the sideboard and drink it from the fourteen wine-and-water glasses he had ordered from London. By the early years of the nineteenth century plain water was served regularly on tables in the best houses. Thomas Cosnett in 1826 reminded butlers to set the sideboard at dinner time with carafes of water and to put two filled water decanters on the supper and dessert tables. Robert Roberts of Boston about the same time specifically directed his fellow servants to put a tumbler for water at the right side of each dinner plate with the foot of a wineglass just touching it in front. Even at mid-century the timidity of some people, dubious about water for drinking, moved Catharine Beecher to pronounce the liquid safe and acceptable at table "provided that it was drunk to satisfy natural thirst only."[39]

By the time Mrs. Beecher had given her blessings to water taken in moderation, both Americans and Englishmen of high degree were thoroughly familiar with it at the table. Americans, however, were more accustomed to ice water than the English were, and when British visitors came to this country they did not hesitate to express themselves on the subject. Henry Tudor was one who delighted in being served "iced water and iced wine," which, he said in 1831, "our American friends possess in greater perfection than any other nation I have ever visited, and which, with the thermometer at 90°, I found most grateful to the palate." He was charmed by the ice, finding it "pellucid and beautiful as the clearest crystal." He envied this country the cold of its northern winters because it allowed ice to be collected "*ad libitum* in huge and solid masses" without anyone's having, "like the inhabitants of the 'mother country,' to send for it to the North Pole."[40]

Tea, Coffee, and Chocolate

Hot tea, coffee, and chocolate, at the time Mr. Tudor was singing the praises of iced drinks, had for almost two hundred years been everyday European solaces. They had been welcomed as novelties and bearers of beneficial properties when the East India trading companies in the early seventeenth century brought them from China, the Near East, and South America. At first only the rich could afford such exotic liquids, but early in the eighteenth century nearly everyone managed to have chocolate, if not coffee and tea, for breakfast. By mid century, tea became the general breakfast drink even for the poor, and for people with social pretensions it came to be a necessity not only at breakfast but in the late afternoon with buttered bread and cakes to fill the void between noon dinner and nine o'clock supper (Fig. 6:28).

Afternoon tea at the end of the century moved into the evening. It happened that, as the noon dinner hour was put later and later, dinner ran into afternoon tea, so that when ladies left the dinner table and withdrew to the withdrawing room they almost immediately found themselves drinking tea or coffee and

FIG. 6:28. Johann Eckstein, *The Samuels Family*. Philadelphia, 1788. Oil on canvas; H. 64.7 cm., W. 76.2 cm. (Museum of Fine Arts, Boston, Ellery Kelleran Gardner Fund.)

nibbling at bread and butter and cakes. When the gentlemen joined the ladies they also confronted tea and coffee. Ann Warder experienced after-dinner tea and coffee in transition when she dined at the house of John Clifford in Philadelphia in 1786. She and a dozen guests had been invited for three o'clock. After an hour's conversational wait upstairs in the drawing room they dined and enjoyed dessert during a leisurely three hours. The ladies then left the men alone to enjoy their pipes, which they did until tea was served an hour later at eight o'clock. The ceremony of after-dinner coffee, followed about an hour later by tea, was practiced by American families for another hundred years. A British butler named Samuel Adams described the ceremonies in such houses as Christopher Gore's:

> When the ladies have retired from the dining-room and the drawing-room bell rings for coffee, the footman enters with the tray . . . of coffee . . . bread and butter, cakes, toast, &c., the under butler or some other servant following to take away the empty cups and saucers on a waiter or tray. At tea time, the butler carries up the tea tray, and the footman the toast, muffins, &c. . . . Tea is announced to the gentlemen by the footman, and the gentlemen having joined the ladies, the tea and coffee is handed round by the butler, and bread and butter, toast, &c. by the footman, the under butler following to take away the cups and saucers.[41]

To people who think of American tea in terms of hoecake and the kitchen table, such service may seem impossibly upper class and British. They may rest assured that, although eighteenth-century European travelers found American servants notoriously ill-trained and independent, wealthy households in the eighteenth and nineteenth centuries were staffed with servants who adhered to English serving procedures. Edward Lloyd, whose postillions wore caps with gold bands and tassels and whose house servants had blue, yellow, and olive lace-edged livery, ran a ménage that could well accomplish the Adams's ceremony. So, too, did David Parish, American representative in Philadelphia for Baring Brothers of London and Hope and Company of Amsterdam, who kept servants in full livery with epaulets and who owned silver service extensive enough "not for a single course, or for a few persons, but through at least three courses for twenty."[42]

Evening Tea Parties, Routs, or Drums

Evening tea, whether attended by three menservants or one maid-of-all-work, became a favorite occasion to share with friends. With all of the refreshments of the dessert table added, tea was elevated to a convivial and amusing "tea party." The party could be small and informal of the kind Brissot de Warville attended in Boston, New York, and Philadelphia in 1791 and concluded was "one of the principal pleasures of the inhabitants who in their whole manner of living resemble the English, . . . their principal expense, especially after dinner, being for the tea they drank in quantity." Or it could be large, crowded, and noisy, in fact—to use British slang—a rout, also called a drum "for the noise and emptiness of the entertainment," or so Smollett quipped. At a late nineteenth-century drum a white-linened table was set with fruit, salads, cold entrées, ice and ice cream, cake, punch, eggnog, tea, coffee, wine, and claret cup or champagne, but "always," Miss Corson said in *Practical American Cookery*, "with the intent to escape vulgar profusion." At afternoon teas, called kettledrums with a punning reference to the teakettle, refreshments consisted of delicate sandwiches, relishes, tea, cake, coffee, and oysters or salads, with the table never overloaded in "ostentatious display." Mrs. Henry Adams went to a kettledrum in 1882 at General Sherman's in Washington, D.C., which, she said, was "not exhilarating."[43]

Tea, or Supper

Tea, as it left its eighteenth-century late-afternoon position, assumed another character around 1800 for many country and working people who still dined at noon. With dried or "hung" beef, ham, sausage, or other meats added to the usual bread, butter, and cakes, tea became six o'clock supper, or high tea, and late supper was forgotten. At Mrs. Fiske's evening meal, which she called tea, cold meat, tongue, cheese, fish, butter, and toast or bread were the staples.[44]

Afternoon Tea Revived

About 1840, afternoon tea was revived (Fig. 6:29). First in England, then in the United States, ladies once more met around four o'clock over the cups. In 1876, when the United States was celebrating its hundredth birthday, the afternoon gathering was looked upon as a patriotic revival of the "old-fashioned tea-party such as Mrs. Washington used to give." Ladies went to each other's houses in afternoon dress, "their bonnets and cloaks laid aside," to gather for a couple of hours' tea and gossip until their husbands, on the way home from the office, stopped in to join them around a table to eat chicken, oysters, compote, and cake.[45]

For all of the occasions when tea was drunk—breakfast, afternoon tea, after-dinner tea or coffee, and evening tea—the paraphernalia was the same: a large tray holding teapots and/or coffeepots, hot-water pots, tea and/or coffee cups and saucers, teaspoons, sugar bowl and tongs, cream pitcher, and waste bowl, with additions in some households of a strainer or strainer spoon, tea caddy, caddy spoon, and spoon tray. For afternoon tea and after-dinner tea the tray sat on a drawing room tea table. For evening tea parties it sat on a dining room sideboard, side table, or serving table, or on a small table in a room that took the place of the dining room. For breakfast and for supper, or high tea, it dominated one end of the dining table or other sizable table.

Away from the footlights, on a sideboard or side table, tea and the other liquids we have talked about played a minor role at evening parties whereas the sweetmeats and fruit that have starred in the preceding chapters shone on a big table in the spotlight. To end this account of dinner tables, dessert tables, and tea tables, here is a big bright table set with ingenuity by Emily Swift of Amenia, New York, for a postwedding celebration in 1829 as she described it to her brother in New Haven:

> Wednesday I had a party of about thirty to tea. Cake dressed with frosting and toys; preserves and other good things for a tea table. Cake in the

> middle of the table in the form of a pyramid; three other kinds about the table arranged with all the taste I possess. Tea and coffee. After tea the Malaga, tenerife, and brandy went freely around, after which almonds, filberts, beech nuts, walnuts, and apples were served. Our west room after tea was filled with chairs along the sides, the ladies seated. Dancing commenced with music [of a] violin and two flutes. This lasted until twelve in the evening.[46]

With its sweetmeats, cakes, pyramid and sugar images, its fruits, nuts, wines, tea, and coffee, Mrs. Swift's party is the very model of the evening tea parties that were held in this country for a century and a half. Through Mrs. Swift's report of the occasion we see American hostesses throughout two hundred years giving thought to table setting and enjoying themselves in the practicing of a minor art.

FIG. 6:29. Tea and cakes. Tucker porcelain. (Empire Parlor, ca. 1839, Winterthur Museum.)

Recipes

Here are recipes for the desserts mentioned in the preceding chapters. They are included because they do not often appear in cookbooks today. Here also are translations of the recipes in today's terms. The orange-flower water and rosewater that is used in them can be bought from a wholesale druggist, if not from the specialty grocer.

CAKES

Big dark cakes filled to bursting with citron, lemon peel, raisins, currants, and spices stand out as the favorite cakes of the seventeenth and eighteenth centuries. Seedcakes take second place. Seldom if ever made in layers in the eighteenth century, and often uniced, cakes of all kinds nearly always contained yeast in the form of barm, the leftover from beer making, which gave them a coffeecake kind of texture. Big cakes were baked in a metal hoop on a tin sheet pan covered with as many as twelve layers of paper to prevent burning. Smaller cakes, particularly in the nineteenth century, were baked in ceramic or metal molds, most often of a turk's-cap shape. A newly iced cake was always placed in a warm oven for drying and hardening. The smart cook scored the icing while it was still soft in order to make cake cutting easy. When an icing recipe said "beat for three hours" it was understood that the beating would be done in and around other kitchen chores. Cakes were served whole. Even a half or a quarter cake appeared on the table and was cut only when someone asked for a piece. The recipes that follow represent the three grades of cake that many cookbooks and copybooks labeled Common Cake, A Very Good Cake, and An Excellent or Very Rich Cake.

Cider Cake

A cup of butter; 2 of sugar; 4 of flour; one or 2 cups of choped raisins or curants; 4 or 5 eggs; cup of cider; tea spoonful of sallaratus; a nutmeg; a t spoonful of cinamon.

bake slow until a nitting needle can be run through it & come out clean.

Recipe book of L. Fiske, Beverly, Mass. (?), ca. 1860

Cider Cake

Cream
- 1 cup butter
- 2 cups sugar

Add
- 4 eggs well beaten

Stir in
- 3¼ cups flour sifted with
- 1 teaspoon baking powder
- ½ teaspoon nutmeg
- ½ teaspoon cinnamon

Alternately with
- 1 cup cider

Fold in
- 1 cup raisins or dried currants dredged with
- ½ cup flour

Bake in mold at 350° F. about 40 minutes.

Election Cake

Pint milk; 1 lb. raisins; pint shortning; 1 yeast cake; ½ lb. brown sugar will do; Pint mollasses; clove nutmeg cinemon; teaspoon soda.

Stir flour about like bread / eggs are better but I do not use them usually / bake same as Bread.

Recipe book of L. Fiske, Beverly, Mass. (?), ca. 1860

Election Cake

Work, using the hand
- ½ cup butter into
- 1 cup bread dough (can be bought frozen)
- 1 egg well beaten
- 1 cup brown sugar

Add
- 1¼ cups flour sifted with
- 1 teaspoon cinnamon
- ¼ teaspoon cloves
- ¼ teaspoon mace
- ¼ teaspoon nutmeg
- 1 teaspoon salt

Alternately with
- ½ cup sour milk
- ½ teaspoon soda
- ½ cup molasses

Mix and add
- 2 tablespoons flour
- 1 cup seeded raisins or ⅔ cup raisins and 8 finely chopped figs

Put into a well-buttered bread pan, cover, and let rise 1¼ hours. Bake 1 hour in slow oven (300° F.). Cover with Milk Frosting.

Milk Frosting

Melt
- 1 teaspoon butter

Add and heat to boiling point while stirring
- 1½ cups sugar
- ½ cup milk

Boil without stirring until mixture forms a soft ball when tried in cold water (234° F.). Cool and beat until mixture is of the right consistency to spread. If too stiff, place over hot water. Add 1 teaspoon vanilla and pour over cake, spreading evenly with the back of a spoon. Crease as soon as firm. (Adapted from Fanny Farmer, *The Boston Cooking School Cook Book* [Boston: Little, Brown & Co., 1936].)

A Plumb Cake

Take five Pounds of fine Flour, and put to it half a Pound of Sugar; and of Nutmegs, Cloves, and Mace finely beaten, of each half an Ounce, and a little Salt, mix these well together; then take a Quart of Cream, let it boil, and take it off, and cut into it three Pounds of fresh Butter, let it stand till 'tis melted, and when 'tis blood warm mix with it a Quart of Ale-yeast, and a Pint of Sack, and twenty Eggs, ten Whites well beaten; put six Pounds of Currants to your

Flour, and make a Hole in the Middle, and pour in the Milk and other Things, and make up your Cake, mixing it well with your Hands; cover it warm, and set it before the Fire to rise for half an Hour; then put it in the Hoop; if the Oven be hot, two Hours will bake it; the Oven must be quick; you may perfume it with Ambergrease, or put Sweetmeats in it, if you please. Ice it when cold, and paper it up.

E. Smith, *The Compleat Housewife*,
Williamsburg, 1742

Plum Cake

Cream together thoroughly
- ⅓ cup butter
- ½ cup sugar

Add
- 2 eggs well beaten with
- ½ cup sugar

Combine mixtures well.
Sift
- ¾ cup flour
- ½ teaspoon salt
- ¼ teaspoon cloves
- ¼ teaspoon mace
- ½ teaspoon fresh nutmeg grated
- 2 teaspoons baking powder

Add alternately with
- ½ cup milk and ½ cup sherry

Beat thoroughly and add
- ½ teaspoon vanilla

Dredge and fold in
- 1 cup currants
- 1 tablespoon flour

Bake in high round pan or mold for 20 to 30 minutes at 375° F.

Twelfth Cake

Alexandria, Va., January 7. Last night I went to the Ball . . . a large rich cake is provided and cut into small pieces and handed round to the company who at the same time draw a ticket out of a Hat with something merry wrote on it. He that draws the King has the Honor of treating the company with a Ball the next year, which generally costs him six or seven pounds. The lady that draws the Queen has the trouble of making the cake.

The Journal of Nicholas Cresswell,
1774–1777, New York, 1942

A Very Rich Twelfth Cake

Put into seven pounds of fine flour, two pounds and a half of fresh butter, and seven pounds of nicely picked and cleansed currants; with two large nutmegs, half an ounce of mace, a quarter of an ounce of cloves, and a pound of loaf sugar, all finely beaten and grated; sixteen eggs, leaving out four whites; and a pint and a half of the best yeast. Warm as much cream as will wet this mass, and pour mountain wine to make it as thick as batter; beat, grossly, a pound of almonds, mountain and orange-flower water, and put in a pound and a half of candied orange, lemon, and citron peel. Mix the whole well together; and put the cake into a hoop with paste under it, to save the bottom while it is baking.

Family Receipt-Book, London, ca. 1811

Twelfth Night Cake

Cream until light
    1 lb. butter
    1 cup light brown sugar
Beat until thick and lemon colored and add
    9 egg yolks
Beat until stiff but not dry
    9 egg whites
Fold in a second cup of light brown sugar and add to first mixture.
Sift
    3¼ cups flour
    2 teaspoons mace
    2 teaspoons cinnamon
    1 teaspoon soda
Stir into flour mixture
    3 lbs. currants
    2 lbs. seeded raisins cut into small pieces
    ¾ cup almonds blanched and chopped or cut into strips
Add to first mixture.

Line deep pans with waxed paper buttered on both sides. Fill each ⅔ full, adding as you go layers of 1 cup citron and candied peel cut into thin strips. Cover loosely with buttered paper and tie firmly in place. Steam 3 hours and bake 1½ hours in a slow oven (300° F.). Or bake 4 hours at 275° F. without steaming. Rich fruitcake is always more satisfactory if part of the cooking is accomplished by steaming.

Press surface with finger; if cake feels firm and does not retain imprint of finger, it is done. A wire cake tester, inserted in center of cake, will come out clean and dry if cake is done. Run knife around inside of pans and remove cake when nearly cool. Slice with very sharp knife. (Adapted from Fanny Farmer, *The Boston Cooking School Cook Book*, Boston, 1936.)

To Ice a Very Large Cake

Beat the whites of twenty fresh eggs, then by degrees beat a pound of double refined sugar sifted through a lawn sieve; mix these well in a deep earthen pan; add orange-flower water, and a piece of fresh lemon-peel; of the former enough to flavour, and no more. Whisk it for three hours till the mixture is thick and white; then with a thin broad bit of board spread it all over the top and sides and set it in a cool oven, and an hour will harden it.

[The Duane family of New York used 8 ounces of sugar, 4 spoonfuls of rose-water, and the whites of 2 eggs "for a large cake." (Duane recipe books, 1760–90, New-York Historical Society.)]

Maria Eliza Rundell, *The American Domestic Cookery* (New York: Evert Duykinck, 1823)

White Icing

Beat for 3 minutes
- 3 egg whites
- 2 tablespoons 4X sugar

Repeat additions of sugar until you have used up
- 1½ cups 4X sugar

Add
- 1 teaspoon lemon peel grated
- 2 tablespoons orange-flower water

Beat until the icing is stiff enough to stay parted when a knife cuts through it. Smooth it onto the top and sides of a cake. Let it dry and harden in a 200° F. oven for 1 hour. (Adapted from Fanny Farmer, *The Boston Cooking School Cook Book*, Boston, 1936.)

COOKIES

The word *cake* in the eighteenth century meant a large round loaf cake; the word *cakes* meant little cakes. Little cakes included macaroons, meringues, a variety of little flat cakes or drop cakes, and cakes baked in teacups. The Scots called little flat cakes cookies for a reason that remains obscure. Today they use the term for a plain bun. Americans also called flat sweet cakes cookies from the Dutch *koekjes*. The British called them, on occasion, biskets from the French *bisquit* for twice cooked, which referred to moderately hard, flat, crisp, plain or sweet "cakes" of flour and water.

Like loaf cakes, little flat cakes more often than not contained seeds, sometimes whole, sometimes ground in a mortar with a pestle. Orange-flower water or rosewater flavored them as vanilla does today's cakes. Sugar almost invariably was sprinkled over them before baking; nonpareils sometimes covered them.

Among many similar little cakes were jumbals, shrewsbury cakes, and seed-cakes. All were rolled thin and cut out with the top of a canister, a cup, a glass, or a tin cake cutter. The cutters made animal, bird, or geometric shapes. To bake the thin little cakes an oven's heat had to be "quick" but not too quick for fear of burning. As with large cakes, several sheets of paper underlay the cut-out dough.

Common Seed Cakes

A large spoonful of lard / rub it in a little flour / rool a cup of sugar / add it with a cup of sour milk half a tea spoonful of bread soda a tea spoonful of cinamon a tea spoonful of seeds / flour the moulding board after needing it sufficient & rool out / cut in rounds / bake in a moderate oven 5 or 10 minutes / rool out thin as pie crust.

Recipe book of L. Fiske, Beverly, Mass. (?), ca. 1860

Seedcakes, or Cardamom Cookies

Cream together

- ½ cup butter
- 1 cup sugar

Add alternately

- 1 cup sour milk and 1 teaspoon soda
- 2 cups flour sifted with
- 1 teaspoon cinnamon
- 1 teaspoon salt
- 1 teaspoon ground cardamom seeds

Roll out thin on floured board. Cut in rounds and place on greased cookie sheet. Sift sugar over them and bake at 350° F. for 5 minutes or until medium brown on bottom.

Ratafia Cakes

A Quarter of a pound of bitter almonds, a quarter of a pound of sweet almonds, half a pound of loaf-sugar, and the whites of three eggs: a quarter of an hour will bake them.

Charlotte Mason, *The Lady's Assistant*,
London, 1801

Ratafia cakes, like macaroons, were made of almond paste, but instead of being oval and flat like macaroons, they were round and slightly mounded. Both were drop cookies. Ratafia cakes were made to be eaten with the drink ratafia at parties. The drink was almond flavored, but it was often made of peach or apricot kernels instead of almond kernels.

Ratafia Cakes

Mix thoroughly

- 1 cup or 1 package (7 ounces) almond paste
- ⅞ cup sugar
- 2 egg whites
- 1 teaspoon almond extract

Form mixture into one-inch footballs. Place on paper laid on a cookie sheet. Bake about 15 minutes at 325° F.

or

Beat

- 3 egg whites

Add

- 1 cup sugar
- 2 tablespoons rosewater
- 1 cup almond paste
- ½ teaspoon almond extract

Fold in

- 2 cups flour

Drop from teaspoon onto well-greased cookie sheet. Bake at 325° F. 10 minutes or less.

To Make Wafers

To a pint of cream put the yolks of two eggs well beat; mix it with flour well dried (as thick as a pudding) sugar and orange-flower water to the taste; put in warm water enough to make it as thin as fine pancakes; mix them very smooth, and bake them over a stove; butter the irons when they stick.

Charlotte Mason, *The Lady's Assistant*,
London, 1801

Wafers

Beat
    1 egg yolk
    ½ cup sugar
Add
    1 cup flour
    ½ cup sugar
Alternately with
    1 cup cream
    2 tablespoons orange-flower water

Batter should be as thin as cold syrup. Butter a wafer iron and heat it until very hot. Put 2 tablespoons of batter on it and hold it over a fire for 1 minute each side. Remove wafer with a knife, and while still warm roll it around the handle of a wooden spoon.

To Make Wigs

Take a quarter of a pound of flour, and a pound of butter, rub half in the flour, the other half in the milk, four eggs one ounce of carraway-seed, and some yeast; make it up stiff, let it stand by the fire to rise, work one pound of sugar in the paste; butter the tins, and lay them on.

Charlotte Mason, *The Lady's Assistant*,
London, 1801

Whigs, or *wigs*, were rather plain buns formed into diamonds or triangles. Narrow on the ends and high in the middle described some whigs. The Duane family of New York ate whigs in the early 1800s.

Whigs

Rub
    ½ lb. butter into
    3 cups flour
Add
    ½ cup warm milk
    1 package yeast dissolved in
    ¼ cup warm water

Mix and put in a warm place to rise until double in bulk.

Punch down and add
    3 beaten eggs
    1 cup sugar
    2 tablespoons caraway seeds

Roll out on floured board into a large, round cake. Cut into eighths or twelfths. Allow wedges to rise. Place on greased baking sheets. Bake at 375° F. for 20 minutes.

To Make Jumbals

Take the Whites of three Eggs, beat them well, and take off the Froth; then take a little Milk, and a little Flour, near a Pound, as much Sugar sifted, and a few Carraway-seeds beaten very fine; work all these in a very stiff Paste, and make them into what Form you please. Bake them on white Paper.

E. Smith, *The Compleat Housewife, Williamsburg, 1742*

Jumbals were plain seedcakes, or, without seeds, plain cookies that today we call sugar cookies. They could be cut into any shape but most often appeared in rings or bowknots. Elizabeth Putnam in *Mrs. Putnam's Receipt Book* (Boston, 1849) suggested cutting them with a tumbler and a wineglass to form a ring.

Jumbals

Cream
- ½ cup butter
- 1 cup sugar

Add
- 3 egg whites well beaten
- 2 tablespoons milk or cream
- ½ teaspoon vanilla or 2 teaspoons grated lemon rind and juice, and/or almond extract
- 2 cups flour sifted with
- 2 teaspoons baking powder

Stir in
- 1½ tablespoons caraway seeds crushed in a mortar

Chill, roll ¼ inch thick, and cut into disks or rings. Or cut into narrow strips 3 inches long and tie each into a single knot. Place on greased cookie sheet and bake at 375° F. about 8 minutes.

Shrewsbury Cakes

Sift one pound of sugar, some pounded cinnamon, and a nutmeg grated, into three pounds of flour, the finest sort; add a little rosewater to three eggs, well beaten, and mix these with the flour, &c. then pour into it as much butter, melted, as will make it a good thickness to roll out.

Mould it well, and roll thin, and cut into such shapes as you like.

Maria Eliza Rundell, *A New System of Domestic Cookery*, Philadelphia, 1810

Shrewsbury cakes were short, crisp, plain cookies cut into disks, diamonds, stars, crescents, flowerets, animals, etc. Lucy Emerson in *The New England Cookery* (Boston, 1802) rolled her shrewsbury cakes into "plain small cakes."

Shrewsbury Cakes

Beat well
- 1 egg
- 2 tablespoons rosewater

Sift and add
- 1 cup sugar
- ½ teaspoon cinnamon
- ½ teaspoon nutmeg
- 2½ cups flour

Stir in approximately
- ½ lb. butter melted

Roll out thin on a floured board and cut into such shapes as diamonds and crescents. Place on greased cookie sheet and bake at 350° F. about 10 minutes.

To Make Naples Biskett

Take a pound & ½ of Loaf Sugar sifted very fine take 16 Eggs take 4 whites, beat ye Eggs and Sugar 3 quarter of an hour then put in a Gill of Sack ½ a Gill of brandy 1 lb. & ½ of fine flower dryed by ye fire & Shake it in, butter your pan & flower, fill them not too full a Quarter of an hour will bake.

Recipe book of Elizabeth Coultas,
England and Philadelphia (?), 1749/50

Naples Biscuits

Beat until light
- 4 whole eggs
- 1 egg white

Add a little at a time
- ⅔ cup sugar

Stir in
- 2 tablespoons sherry
- 2 tablespoons brandy
- 1½ cups flour

Put in buttered naples biscuit pans and bake at 325° F. about 15 minutes. Makes about 16 2″ × 3″ biscuits. If naples biscuit pans are not available, make 2″ × 3″ pans of cardboard or heavy paper. A 4″ × 6″ index card cut across the short way makes a good small pan. Fold up the sides and ends ½ inch and pinch the corners "like little dripping pans," as the *Ladies Delight* (London, 1759) prescribed. Many Americans, among them George Washington and an early John Dickinson, owned naples biscuit pans that were flat rectangular tins divided into many small rectangles.

Rout Drop Cakes

Mix two pounds of flour, one ditto butter, one ditto sugar, one ditto currants clean and dry; then wet into a stiff paste, with two eggs, a large spoon of orange-flower water, ditto rose water, ditto sweet wine, ditto brandy, drop on a tin plate floured; a very short time bakes them.

Maria Eliza Rundell, *The American Domestic Cookery*, New York, 1823

Rout Drop Cakes

Cream
- ½ lb. butter
- 1 cup sugar

Add
- 2 eggs well beaten
- 2 tablespoons orange-flower water
- 2 tablespoons rosewater
- 2 tablespoons sweet wine
- 2 tablespoons brandy

Beat in a little at a time
- 3 cups flour sifted with
- 1 teaspoon salt

Add
- 1 cup currants

Drop by teaspoonsful onto buttered and floured cookie sheet. Bake at 350° F. for 5 minutes or until just tan on the bottom.

Fine Savoy Biscuits

Break twelve eggs and put the yolks in a bason, then put in twelve ounces of powdered sugar with the yolks, then rasp the rind of four lemons, and mix and stir the rind up with the yolks and sugar, and beat them with a wooden spoon ten minutes, then whisk the whites in a copper pan, but do not leave whisking them till they are almost strong enough to bear an egg, or they will go to water and be spoiled, and when you think you have whisked them enough, then mix the yolks with them, with a wooden spoon as light as possible, when it is mixed well, take ten ounces of fine flour as dry as possible, and stir it up with the eggs and sugar, but not too much only till it mixes with the eggs; then take a small tea-spoon and take out a spoonful of the batter and pull it along the paper, and as you pull the spoon along the paper push the batter down with your finger, so as to make the biscuit about three inches long, and about half an inch wide; then sift some sugar over them before you put them in the oven, which must be very hot, but be careful they are not burnt, for they soon scorch if you do not watch them; and when they are done cut them off the paper whilst they are hot.

Frederic Nutt, *The Complete Confectioner*,
New York, 1807

Savoy Cakes

Beat
    6 egg whites until stiff
Add gradually while beating
    ⅔ cup 4X sugar
Beat until thick and lemon colored and fold in
    6 egg yolks
    1 teaspoon vanilla
Sift together and fold in
    ⅔ cup flour
    ¼ teaspoon salt

Bake in lady finger tins or shape 1½″ × 4″ on cookie sheets lined with paper, using a cookie press with a plain hole. Sprinkle with sugar and bake 12 minutes at 350° F. Remove from paper with a knife. (Adapted from Fanny Farmer, *The Boston Cooking School Cook Book*, Boston, 1936.)

CREAMS

Rennet-set junkets, gelatined desserts like our Spanish Cream, flavored whipped cream, and soft custards belonged to the family of creams in the eighteenth century. Either jelled in molds or in small glasses, or served in bowls large or small, creams made a decorative addition to a party table, especially if they were studded with fresh flowers and comfits or other sweetmeats.

Steeple Cream

Take two ounces of ivory and five ounces of hartshorn, and put them into a stone bottle. Fill it up to the neck with water and put in a small quantity of gum arabic and gum tragacanth. Then tie up the Bottle very close, and set it into a pot of water, with hay at the bottom of it. Let it stand six hours then take it out, and let it stand an hour before you open it, lest it fly in your face. Then strain it and it will be a strong jelly. Take a pound of blanched almonds beat very fine, and mix it with a pint of thick cream. Let it stand a little then strain it out and mix it with a pound of jelly. Set it over the fire till it be scalding hot, and sweeten it to your taste with double refined sugar. Then take it out, put in a little amber and pour it into high gallipots like a sugar loaf at the top. When they be cold, turn them out, and lay cold whipt cream about them in heaps. Take care that it be not suffered to boil after the cream be put into it.

John Farley, *The London Art of Cookery,*
London, 1792

Steeple Cream

Dissolve over a slow fire

- 2 tablespoons gelatin
- ½ cup water

Add

- 1 teaspoon almond extract
- 1½ cups cream
- ½ cup sugar
- 4 drops yellow coloring

Stir until sugar dissolves. Pour into small tapering glasses and refrigerate. To unmold dip glass into hot water and turn over on a platter. Surround with mounds of sweetened whipped cream. Scatter chopped almonds over all.

Everlasting or Solid Syllabubs

Mix a quart of thick raw cream, one pound of refined sugar, a pint of white, and half a pint of sweet wine in a deep pan; put to it the grated peel and the juice of three lemons. Beat, or whisk it one way half an hour, then pour it into glasses. It will keep good, in a cool place, ten days.

Maria Eliza Rundell, *A New System of Domestic Cookery*, Philadelphia, 1810

Everlasting Syllabub

Beat until moderately stiff
    2 cups whipping cream
Add
    ½ cup 4X sugar
    ¼ cup sherry, rum, brandy, or white wine
    1 teaspoon lemon juice
    1 teaspoon grated lemon rind
Spoon into wineglasses or sherbet glasses. Keep covered in refrigerator 8 hours before serving. Eat with a spoon.

Orange Fool

Mix the juice of three Seville oranges, three eggs well beaten, a pint of cream, a little nutmeg and cinnamon, and sweeten to your taste. Set the whole over a slow fire, and stir till it becomes as thick as good melted butter, but it must not be boiled; then pour it into a dish for eating cold.

The Experienced American Housekeeper, by a Lady (New York: N. L. Nafis; Philadelphia: John B. Ferry, 1838)

Orange Fool

Beat well
    3 eggs
Add and stir in well
    1 cup orange juice
    ¼ cup lemon juice
    1 cup sugar
Stir in
    2 cups cream
Place in double boiler over hot water and cook, stirring, until mixture coats the spoon. Serve cold in pudding bowl.

Lemon Cream

Take five large lemons, pare them as thin as possible, steep them all night in twenty spoonfuls of spring water, with the juice of the lemons, then strain it through a jelly-bag into a silver sauce-pan, if you have one, the whites of six eggs beat well, ten ounces of double refined sugar, set over a very slow charcoal fire, stir it all the time one way, skim it, and when it is hot as you can bear your fingers in, pour it into glasses.

Hannah Glasse, *The Art of Cookery*,
Alexandria, 1805

Lemon Cream

Soak overnight in a slow oven or crockpot
- the juice and rind cut thin of 5 lemons
- 1 cup water

Strain, and add
- 6 egg whites beaten with
- 1¼ cups sugar

Cook slowly until hot but not boiling. Pour into parfait glasses, wineglasses, or sauce dishes. Eat warm.

A Floating Island

Mix three half pints of thin cream with a quarter of a pint of raisin wine, a little lemon juice, orange flower water, and sugar; put into a dish for the middle of the table, and put on the cream a froth like the [following], which may be made of raspberry or currantjelly.

A Froth to Set on Cream, Custard, or Trifle, Which Looks and Eats Well

Sweeten half a pound of the pulp of damsons, or any other sort of scalded fruit; put to it the whites of four eggs beaten, and beat the pulp with them, until it will stand as high as you choose; and being put on the cream, &c. with a spoon, it will take any form. It should be rough to imitate a rock.

Floating Island Another Way

Scald a codlin before it be ripe, or any sharp apple, and pulp it through a sieve. Beat the whites of two eggs with sugar, and a spoonful of orange flower water; mix in by degrees the pulp, and beat altogether until you have a large quantity of froth. Serve it on a raspberry cream; or you may colour the froth with beetroot, raspberry, or currantjelly, and set it on a white cream, having given it the flavour of lemon, sugar, and wine as above; or, put the froth on a custard.

Maria Eliza Rundell, *A New System of Domestic Cookery*, Philadelphia, 1810

Floating Island

Mix

3 cups cream
½ cup white wine
1 cup raspberry or strawberry purée
½ cup sugar

Pour into a shallow bowl. Spoon onto it in a large mound or several small mounds a froth made in the following way:

Beat until stiff

2 egg whites
½ cup sugar
1 teaspoon orange-flower water or ½ cup tart applesauce

Flummery

Boil one ounce of isinglass in a little water till melted; pour to it a pint of cream, a bit of lemon peel, a little brandy, and sugar to the taste; boil and strain it; put it into a mould; turn it out.

Charlotte Mason, *The Lady's Assistant*, London, 1801

Flummery

Dissolve over a slow fire

2 tablespoons gelatin in
½ cup water

Add

2 cups cream
½ cup sugar

Simmer until dissolved—about 3 minutes. Remove from heat.

Add

1 tablespoon grated lemon peel
1 tablespoon brandy

Pour into a mold and place in refrigerator until set.

DRINKS

People drank not only for exhilaration but for nourishment and warmth. The following selection includes recipes to serve both purposes. All save the syllabubs, possets, and caudles were served at large gatherings. Two centuries ago several different kinds of syllabubs were in favor, from clotted cream and curdled varieties, to liquid kinds heaped with whipped cream, to solid whipped creams. All were made with milk or cream, wine or cider, lemon, and sugar. In the seventeenth and early eighteenth centuries syllabub was made in a bowl, a large two-handled cup, or a syllabub pot. Later, when whips were in style, it was made in a bowl and served in syllabub glasses. Or it was laid over a trifle.

To Make a Fine Syllabub from the Cow

Make your syllabub of either cider or wine, sweeten it pretty sweet, and grate nutmeg in, then milk the milk into the liquor; when this is done, pour over the top half a pint or a pint of cream, according to the quantity of syllabub you make.

You may make this syllabub at home, only have new milk; make it as hot as milk from the cow, and out of a tea-pot, or any such thing, pour it in holding your hand very high.

Hannah Glasse, *The Art of Cookery*,
London, 1760

To Make Whipt Syllabubs

Take a quart of Cream, not to thick, and a Pint of Sack, and the Juice of two Lemons; sweeten it to your Palate, and put it into a broad earthen Pan, and with a Whisk whip it, and as the Froth rises, take it off with a Spoon, and lay it in your Syllabub glasses; but first you must sweeten some Claret, or Sack, or White wine, and strain it, and put seven or eight Spoonfuls of the Wine into your Glasses, and then gently lay in your Froth. Set them by. Do not make them long before you use them.

E. Smith, *The Compleat Housewife*,
Williamsburg, 1742

Whipped Syllabub

Stir well
½ cup granulated sugar
1½ cups red or white wine or sherry
2 cups half-and-half
grated rind and juice of 1 lemon

Pour into wineglasses.

Whip
½ pint heavy cream
½ cup 4X sugar
¼ cup red or white wine or sherry
grated rind and juice of 1 lemon

Pile as high as possible on the glasses of cream mixture. Drink with the help of a spoon.

(*Note:* Red wine and cream produce a blue pink rather unappealing to the twentieth-century eye.)

A Fine Caudle

Take a Pint of Milk, turn it with Sack; then strain it, and when 'tis cold, put it in a Skillet, with Mace, Nutmeg, and some white Bread sliced; let all these boil, and then beat the Yolks of four or five Eggs, the Whites of two, and thicken your Caudle, stirring it all one way for fear it curdle; let it warm together, then take it off, and sweeten it to your Taste.

E. Smith, *The Compleat Housewife*,
Williamsburg, 1742

As with syllabub there were many different ways to make *caudle* and *posset*. Here are recipes that use eggs, bread, or naples biscuit as the invariable thickener.

Caudle

Heat
2 cups rich milk or half-and-half
½ cup white wine or sherry

Add and stir
¼ teaspoon mace
¼ teaspoon nutmeg
4 slices white bread crumbled, omitting crusts
½ cup sugar

Beat
4 eggs
2 egg whites

Add a little of the warm milk to the eggs while stirring, then add the eggs to the milk mixture. Heat slowly until slightly thickened. Serve warm in mugs with nutmeg grated on top.

A Sack Posset Without Eggs

Take a Quart of Cream or new Milk, and grate three Naples-biskets in it, and let them boil in the Cream; grate some Nutmeg in it, and sweeten it to your Taste; let it stand a little to cool, and then put half a Pint of Sack, a little warm in your Bason, and pour your Cream to it, holding it up high in the pouring; let it stand a little, and serve it.

E. Smith, *The Compleat Housewife*,
Williamsburg, 1742

Posset

Heat

1 cup crushed naples biscuit or other plain cookie, or the equivalent in stale cake
4 cups rich milk or cream slightly warm
½ teaspoon freshly grated nutmeg
½ cup sugar

Put in a punch bowl

1 cup white wine or sherry slightly warmed

Pour the cream mixture into the punch bowl from a height to raise a froth. Serve warm or cold in large, two-handled bowls, or in demitasses, punch cups, or Old Fashioned glasses.

Excellent Shrub as Made in the West Indies

Having first made a good syrup with twelve lbs. of best moist sugar, they add 3 quarts of lime juice, and 9 quarts of rum; mixing them well together, and fining the liquid in the same manner as wine. A few pints of brandy, with proportionably less rum, is considered an improvement.

Family Receipt-Book, London, ca. 1811

Maryland Raspberry Shrub

One quart of raspberry juice, half a pound of loaf sugar, dissolved, a pint of Jamaica rum, or part rum and part brandy. Mix thoroughly. Bottle for use.

Raspberry Shrub

5 quarts red raspberries
1 quart mild vinegar

Let stand 24 hours, then strain. Add ½ pound sugar to each quart of juice. Let come to a boil, cool and bottle. One dozen cloves put in add to the flavor.

Fanny Farmer, *The Boston Cooking School Cook Book*, Boston, 1936

Shrub

In the eighteenth century *shrub* usually meant simply a mixture of liquor, fruit, and sugar to which water could be added to make a drink. In the nineteenth century shrub came to be the name of a drink.

Ratafia

Blanch two ounces each of peach and apricot kernels, bruise and put them into a bottle, and fill nearly up with brandy. Dissolve half a pound of white sugarcandy in a cup of cold water, and add to the brandy after it has stood a month on the kernels, and they are strained off; then filter through paper, and bottle for use. [*Other ratafia recipes contained crushed almonds.*]

Maria Eliza Rundell, *A New System of Domestic Cookery*, Philadelphia, 1810

Ratafia

Mix

- 1 bottle Amaretto liqueur
- 1 bottle light rum
- ½ bottle brandy

or

Mix

- 2 cups raspberry or strawberry liqueur
- 2 cups rum
- 1 cup brandy

Serve in liqueur glasses or in small, stemmed cocktail glasses to approach in appearance the tall, narrow small-bowled ratafia glasses of the eighteenth century.

Orgeat

Boil a quart of new milk with a stick of cinnamon, sweeten to your taste, and let it grow cold; then pour it by degrees to three ounces of almonds, and twenty bitter that have been blanched and beaten to a paste, with a little water to prevent oiling; boil all together, and stir till cold, then add half a glass of brandy.

The Experienced American Housekeeper, New York, 1838

Orgeat

Heat and stir for 5 minutes

- 1 cup milk
- ¾ cup sugar
- 1 stick cinnamon

Let stand until cool.
Remove cinnamon.
Add

- 3½ ounces (½ package) almond paste
- 1 cup cream
- 2 cups milk
- ½ cup brandy
- 2 teaspoons almond extract

Serve hot or cold with a dash of cinnamon in Old Fashioned glasses or punch cups.

Genuine French Noyau, as Made at Paris

In nine pints of white brandy, to which must be added a pint of orange-flower water with six ounces of sugar in another pint of brandy, infuse for six weeks . . . fresh apricot kernels.

Family Receipt-Book, London, ca. 1811

Noyau

Mix

2 bottles brandy
⅔ cup sugar
1 cup orange-flower water
1 cup apricot kernels bruised, or 4 teaspoons almond extract

Let stand for six weeks. Strain. Serve in narrow, stemmed glasses.

To Make Negus

Negus

To every pint of port wine allow 1 quart of boiling water, ¼ lb. of sugar, 1 lemon, grated nutmeg to taste. . . . Allow 1 pint of wine, with the other ingredients in proportion, for a party of 9 or 10 children.

Isabella Beeton, *The Book of Household Management*, London, 1861

Roman Punch

3 coffee cups of lemonade (strong and sweet), 1 glass champagne, 1 glass rum, 2 oranges juice only, 2 eggs—whites only—well whipped, ½ lb. powdered sugar, beaten into the stiffened whites. You must ice abundantly or, if you prefer, freeze.

Marion Harland, *Common Sense in the Household* (New York: C. Scribner & Son, 1871)

Roman Punch

Mix

2 cups strong sweet lemonade
½ cup champagne or other sparkling wine
½ cup rum
juice of 2 oranges
whites of 2 eggs well beaten with
1 cup 4X sugar

Refrigerate until very cold and serve in punch cups. Or put into freezing tray until partially frozen. Stir until smooth, then allow to freeze throughout. Stir well again and serve in sherbet glasses or punch cups at dinner.

Genuine British Punch

A fine large bowl of this liquor, which will be found to please most palates, may be made in the following manner—Procure half a dozen ripe, sound, and fresh lemons, or a proportionate number of limes, and a couple of Seville oranges. Rub off the yellow rinds of three or four of the lemons, with lumps of fine loaf sugar; putting each lump into the bowl, as soon as it is sufficiently saturated or clogged with the essence of grated rind. Then thinly pare the other lemons and Seville orange, and put these rinds also in the bowl; to which, adding plenty of sugar, pour a very small quantity of boiling water, and immediately squeeze the juice of nearly all the fruit, followed by a little more hot water. Incorporate the whole well together with the punch ladle; and, putting a little of the sherbet thus composed into a glass, try its richness and flavour by the palate. . . . If straining should be found necessary, this is the period for using a lawn sieve . . . ; a few parings of the orange and lemon rind are generally considered as having an agreeable appearance flouting in the bowl. . . . Spirit should be added in the proportion of a bottle of the best Jamaica rum to every pint of the finest Cogniac brandy; the entire strength or weakness may be suited to the general inclination of the company for which it is prepared. The above quantity of fruit, with about a pound and a half of sugar, will make sufficient sherbet for a two gallon bowl.

Family Receipt-Book, London, ca. 1811

British Punch

Rub
    ½ lb. sugar lumps on
    the rind of 4 lemons and 1 orange to extract the oil
Place lumps in a 2-gallon bowl.
Pare thin and add the parings of
    2 lemons and 1 orange
Add
    2 cups sugar dissolved in
    1 cup boiling water
    juice of above fruit
    1/5 gallon Jamaica rum
    1 pint brandy

Cover and allow this shrub, or sherbet, to blend for several days to improve the flavor. To serve, add as much water as conscience dictates—hot water in winter, cold in summer. Serve in wineglasses.

FIGURES FOR DECORATION

Little edible figures could be made either of almond paste, gum and sugar, or sugar and water boiled to the crack stage and could be formed by various methods. Almond paste and gum sugar paste could be formed by hand or pressed into molds. Sugar syrup could be run around the inside of an alabaster mold to form hollow figures. The gum sugar figures made pretty ornaments on top of iced cakes, according to John Farley (*The London Art of Cookery*, London, 1792). They were to be "stuck on twelfth cakes or introduced in desserts," as the *Family Receipt-Book* (London, ca. 1811) directed. Or they were "to garnish marchpanes withal," as Mrs. Custis's recipe book, "A Booke of Sweetmeats" (England, 1550–1625), said. Gum tragacanth (gum dragon) and gum arabic are increasingly hard to find. Gelatin has been substituted with questionable results.

Gum Paste Figures

Steep one ounce of gum dragon, in a tea cupful of cold water all night; the next morning have a pound of double refined sugar pounded and sifted through a silk sieve, run the gum through a hair sieve with a spoon, then mix the gum and sugar together with a strong hand, and by working it will become as white as snow, then take a little fine flour and make it into a stiff paste, roll it out, and cut it into what form you please, to put over several fruits, &c. or work it into moulds, first rubbing them with a feather dipped in sweet oil, turn it out, and put in on Savoy cakes, or anything that you want to ornament with it, and dry it in a cool oven, or before a fire.

Richard Briggs, *The New Art of Cookery*,
Philadelphia, 1792

To Make All Kind of Birds and Beasts Which Must Be Cast in Moulds

Shake well your double moulds being Layd in water 2 hours. Dry them well with a cloth, then put your hot sugar / and gum dragon / into them & let them stand until they are cold, then take them out and gild them.

"A Booke of Sweetmeats," England, 1550–1625

Sugar Paste Figures

Heat
    1 tablespoon gelatin in
    ¼ cup water over a low fire until dissolved
Add a little at a time to
    2 cups 4X sugar
Add to make a mixture that can be molded or modeled
    ½ cup or so flour
Roll out on a board dusted with 4X sugar. Cut into shapes, mold with wet fingers, or press into wet molds. Allow to dry and paint with vegetable colors. When making strawberries or raspberries, roll in red sugar before drying. If you wish to work with colored paste, divide gelatin and water into several parts and color each part differently before adding to sugar.

Almond Paste

With this paste you may imitate any fruit you have a mould for, engraved on wood and colour the paste according to the fruit you imitate. . . . You may with this paste make anything you please besides fruit, as flowers, animals, and even temples, pyramids, or ornaments of any kind; it is in this respect, like gum paste, and may be candied.

G. A. Jarrin, *The Italian Confectioner*,
London, 1820

Almond Paste Figures

Mix
    1 7-ounce package almond paste
    1 egg white
    ½ cup 4X sugar
Add to make mixture plastic
    ½ cup or so 4X sugar
Press into molds dusted with 4X sugar to prevent sticking. Leave in molds until edges are almost dry, then remove.

JELLIES

Ivory dust jelled the desserts of our ancestors well into the eighteenth century. Deer horn shavings and isinglass took its place in the eighteenth century and on into the nineteenth. As with calves' feet the ivory powder and horn had to be stewed in water for several hours until they were dissolved. Strained, they were added to milk, cream, or fruit juice in order to jellify them into flummeries, fools, and jellies. People liked jellies of many colors. They invented ribbon jelly, which they made by solidifying layers of various colors one on top of the other, allowing each layer to harden before adding the next. Jellies molded with fruits or figures of different colors showing through delighted them.

Hartshorn Jelly

Simmer eight ounces of hartshorn shavings with two quarts of water to one; strain it, and boil it with the rinds of four China oranges and two lemons pared thin; when cool, add the juice of both, half a pound of sugar, and the whites of six eggs beaten to a froth; let the jelly have three or four boils without stirring, and strain it through a jelly bag.

Maria Eliza Rundell, *The American Domestic Cookery*, New York, 1823

Wine Jelly

Mix

- 3 tablespoons gelatin
- ½ cup water

Add

- 1½ cups boiling water and stir until dissolved

Stir in

- 1 cup sherry or madeira, or
- 1 cup sherry, 2 tablespoons brandy, and 6 tablespoons kirsch
- ¼ cup orange juice
- ¼ cup lemon juice
- 1 teaspoon grated orange rind
- 3 drops red vegetable coloring

Pour into quart mold and chill. Turn out and decorate with whipped cream. Or add ¼ cup more water or fruit juice and pour into large wineglasses to jell.

PIES

Many dishes that today we would call pies and tarts, two hundred years ago were called florentines, puddings, cheesecakes, tarts, and pies. The common denominator was pastry crust, or a "coffin." We use the word *tart* for a small pie; our ancestors used the word *tartlet*. Tart to them meant a large, shallow pie. Other small pastries we call patty shells and turnovers; two hundred years ago they were called patties, puffs, and pasties.

A Very Fine Crust for Orange Cheese-cakes or Sweetmeats, When to Be Particularly Nice

Dry a pound of the finest flour, and mix with it three ounces of refined sugar; then work half a pound of butter with your hand until it comes to a froth. Put the flour into it by degrees; and work into it, well beaten, and strained, the yelks of three and the whites of two eggs. If too limber, put some flour and sugar to make it fit to roll. Line your pattypans and fill. A little above fifteen minutes will bake them. Against they come out, have ready some refined sugar, beat up with the white of an egg as thick as you can: ice them all over: set them in the oven to harden, and serve cold. Use fresh butter.

Salt butter will make a very fine flaky crust; but if for mince-pies, or any sweet thing, should be washed.

Maria Eliza Rundell, *A New System of Domestic Cookery*, Philadelphia, 1810

Tarts

Sift

- 2 cups flour with
- ½ cup sugar
- ½ teaspoon salt

Work in gradually with your hand

- ½ lb. soft butter
- 2 beaten eggs
- 1 beaten yolk

Add enough sugar and flour to make a dough that can be rolled ¼ inch thin. Line a pie pan or several small tart pans. Bake at 400° F. for 10 minutes. Fill with preserved fruit, jam, or a *fromage* for a "cheesecake."

Filling for a Chess Cake, or Chess Pie

Mix well

1 cup sugar
½ cup almond paste
2 tablespoons orange-flower water
the puréed rind of 3 lemons that have been boiled until tender
2 egg whites
juice of 3 lemons
½ cup melted butter

Add

4 egg yolks well beaten

Pour into a baked shell of fine crust and bake for 15 minutes at 325° F. Do not overbake. Ice with 1 egg white beaten with 1 cup sugar.

To Make Orange or Lemon Tarts

Take six large Lemons, and rub them very well with Salt, and put them in Water for two Days, with a Handful of Salt in it; then change them into fresh Water without Salt, every other Day for a Fortnight; then boil them for two or three Hours 'til they are tender; then cut them in half Quarters, and then cut them thus ◁ as thin as you can; then take Pippins pared, cored and quartered, and a Pint of fair Water, let them boil 'til the Pippins break; put the Liquor to your Orange or Lemon, and half the Pippins well broken, and a Pound of Sugar, boil these together a quarter of an Hour; then put it in a Gallipot, and squeeze an Orange in it, if it be Lemon; or a Lemon, if it is Orange; 2 Spoonfuls is enough for a Tart; Your Pippins must be small and shallow; put fine Puff-paste, and very thin; a little while will bake it. Just as your Tarts are going into the Oven, with a Feather do them over with melted Butter, and then Sift double refined Sugar on them, and this is a pretty Icing on them.

E. Smith, *The Compleat Housewife*,
Williamsburg, 1742

Orange or Lemon Tarts

Slice thin

4 thin-skinned oranges
1 lemon

Measure sliced fruit and add

twice as much water

Let stand for 24 hours. Cook slowly in the same water for 2 hours. Remove slices from water and cut into quarters.

Add

4 apples pared, cored, quartered, and sliced thin that have been cooked covered until soft in
½ cup water
1 cup sugar

Boil all of the fruit together 10 minutes and place in an 8″ pie tin lined with baked crust. Add the juice of a lemon if you are making orange tarts, of an orange if you are making lemon tarts. Brush with melted butter, and sift over with sugar. Bake at 350° F. for 15 minutes. The tarts will be shallow like jam tarts.

A Tansey Pudding

Beat seven eggs, yolks and whites separately; add a pint of cream, near the same of spinach-juice, and a little tansy-juice gained by pounding in a stone mortar, a quarter of a pound of Naples biscuit, sugar to taste, a glass of white wine, and some nutmeg. Set all in a saucepan, just to thicken over the fire; then put it into a dish, lined with paste, to turn out, and bake it.

Maria Eliza Rundell, *The American Domestic Cookery*, New York, 1823

Tansy Pudding

Soak for 20 minutes
 1 cup crumbled naples biscuit or other plain cookie
 2 cups cream

Strain and add
 2 drops green vegetable coloring
 2 large tansy leaves (no stems) puréed in blender with
 2 tablespoons water
 ¾ cup sugar
 ¾ cup white wine
 ½ teaspoon nutmeg

Pour onto
 6 egg yolks well beaten

Cook over boiling water until mixture coats spoon.

Fold in
 6 egg whites beaten until stiff

Pour into 9″ pie pan lined with pastry that has been pricked and baked at 400° F. for 10 minutes. Bake at 325° F. for about 15 minutes. Do not overbake.

PUDDINGS

Puddings that were baked in pie crust have been included in the pie section above. Following are recipes for pudding stirred over a fire, boiled in a cloth, boiled in a bowl and cloth, or baked in the oven.

Flummery

Put three large handfuls of very small white oatmeal to steep a day and night in cold water; then pour it off clear, and add as much more water, and let it stand the same time. Strain it through a fine hair sieve, and boil it till it be as thick as hasty pudding; stirring it well all the time. When first strained, put to it one large spoonful of white sugar and two of orange-flower water. Pour it into shallow dishes, and serve to eat with wine, cider, milk or cream, or sugar. It is very good.

The Experienced American Housekeeper,
New York, 1838

Flummery

Boil 20 minutes
 1 cup oatmeal
 2 cups water
Press through a fine sieve or purée fine in a blender.
Add
 2 tablespoons sugar
 2 tablespoons orange-flower water or 1 tablespoon orange extract
Mixture should be as thick as thick applesauce. Serve in sauce dishes with cream and sugar or with sweet wine or cider.

Sunderland Pudding

1 qt milk
3 eggs
4 large spoonfull of flour
salt
Bake
Sweet sauce

spoonful of molasses d° of flour beat together / 3 or 4 of sugar. Pour boiling water on / stir and (sit on the fire a little) some butter / half a nutmeg or essence of lemon. Cold sause white of one egg / half nutmeg / white sugar and butter / beat together well / set to cool / form pineapple.

Recipe book of L. Fiske, Beverly, Mass.(?), ca. 1860

Sunderland Pudding

Beat

3 eggs

Add

1 quart milk
8 tablespoons flour
1 teaspoon salt
½ cup sugar
1 teaspoon vanilla

Bake in casserole at 325° F. for 1 hour in pan of hot water. Serve hot with Sweet Sauce or Cold Sauce.

Sweet Sauce

Mix

1 tablespoon molasses
1 tablespoon flour
4 tablespoons sugar

Add

1 cup boiling water

Stir over the fire until hot.

Add

1 tablespoon butter
½ teaspoon nutmeg or lemon extract

Cold Sauce

Mix

1 egg white
1 teaspoon nutmeg
2 to 2½ cups 4X sugar
½ cup butter

Form into the shape of a pineapple, score, and add a green topknot. Refrigerate.

A Fine Biscuit Pudding

Grate three Naples biscuit, and pour a pint of cream or milk over them hot. Cover it close till cold, then add a little grated nutmeg, the yolks of four eggs and two white beat in a little orange flower or rose-water, two ounces of powdered sugar, and half a spoonful of flour. Mix these well, and boil them in a China bason, tied in a cloth, for an hour. Turn it out of the bason, and serve it up in a dish with melted butter, and some fine sugar sprinkled over it.

Lucy Emerson, *New England Cookery*,
Montpelier, Vt., 1808

Biscuit Pudding

Pour
- 2 cups hot cream or rich milk over
- 2 cups crumbled naples biscuit or other plain cookie

Cool and add
- ¼ cup sugar
- 2 tablespoons flour
- 1 teaspoon nutmeg

Alternately with
- 4 egg yolks and 2 egg whites well beaten
- 2 tablespoons orange-flour water

Put into a china bowl tied in a cloth and boil in a deep kettle of water for 1 hour. Or put into a mold with a tight lid and boil for an hour with boiling water halfway up the side of the mold. Dip into cold water, turn out, sift sugar over, and serve with melted butter.

Old Fashion Indian Pudding

One scant cup of sifted Indian meal too one qt. of milk / scald part of the milk / turn on the meal and stir it well / add half cup of mollasses salt (cinomon or orange peel) stir it well then turn on the cold milk, stir it once or twice in baking 3 to 6 hours.

cream or milk for sauce.

Recipe book of L. Fiske,
Beverly, Mass. (?), ca. 1860

Indian Pudding

Scald
- 1 pint milk

Add
- 1 cup sifted cornmeal gradually while stirring
- ½ cup molasses
- 1 teaspoon cinnamon, ginger, or grated orange peel

Stir well.

Add

1 pint cold milk

Pour into a deep buttered casserole or baking dish. Bake 2 to 3 hours, stirring once or twice. Serve with cream or ice cream.

Whortleberry Pudding

Whortleberries are good both in flour and Indian puddings. A pint of milk, with a little salt a little molasses, stirred quite stiff with Indian meal, and a quart of berries stirred in gradually with a spoon, makes a good-sized pudding. Leave room for it to swell; and let it boil three hours.

When you put them into flour, make your pudding just like batter-puddings; but considerably thicker, or the berries will sink. Two hours is plenty long enough to boil. No pudding should be put in till the water boils. Leave room to swell.

Lydia Child, *The Frugal Housewife*,
Boston, 1829

Blueberry Bag Pudding

Stir

1 cup white cornmeal into
2 cups hot milk
½ cup molasses

Boil gently, stirring until thickened.
Add

1 quart blueberries

Pour into a 2-quart deep bowl. Gather a cloth around the bowl, tying it tightly but with room for the pudding to swell and lower the encased bowl into boiling water. Let the pudding simmer rapidly for 3 hours. Remove the cloth-covered bowl, dip it into cold water, and turn the pudding out. Serve at the beginning of a meal.

A Christmas Pudding That Will Keep Two Months

1½ lb. of flour 1½ beef sewet chopped very fine 1½ lb. of sugar 1½ currants / the same of stoned raisins 1 gill of brandy 1 gill of wine 10 eggs 1 nutmeg a very little ground clove 1 oz. citron mix the dry before / wet the cloth then flour it well / boil it 6 hours / it is best boil them in very small buddings / about a pint of this / or they can be baked in small pans. a cold sauce

Recipe book of L. Fiske, Beverly, Mass.(?),
ca. 1860

Christmas Pudding

Beat well
- 10 eggs

Stir in and beat
- 3 cups sugar

Add
- ½ cup brandy
- ½ cup white wine

Alternately with
- 5 cups flour sifted with
- 2 teaspoons grated nutmeg
- ½ teaspoon ground cloves

Dredge in 1 cup flour and fold in
- 3 cups chopped beef suet
- 3 cups currants
- 3 cups seedless or seeded raisins
- 2 tablespoons chopped citron

Wet a strong cloth 36″ square with boiling water. Place in a pan of 1 gallon capacity. Add pudding and tie the cloth tightly leaving enough space for pudding to swell. Put pudding in a large preserving kettle in fast-boiling water to cover and boil it steadily for 6 hours, adding more boiling water as necessary to keep the pudding covered. When ready to serve, dip cloth-covered pudding in cold water to make the pudding come out easily. Stick pudding with citron and blanched almonds and serve with Hard Sauce or Wine Sauce.

Hard Sauce

Cream
- 1 cup butter
- 3 cups 4X sugar

Add
- ½ cup brandy

Beat well. Refrigerate.

Wine Sauce

Melt
- 1 lb. butter gently

When butter simmers skim it. Let it stand 5 minutes then pour it clear of the sediment.

Stir in until smooth
- 2 cups 4X sugar

Add
- ½ cup very good wine
- the juice and grated rind of 1 lemon

DRY SWEETMEATS

Dry sweetmeats included all of the sugared fruit, flowers, nuts, and seeds that could be eaten without getting overly sticky: sugar-plate of gum paste, comfits of sugar-coated seeds; faggots, chips, and prawlongs of sugared fruit peel; wafers, cakes, biscuits, drops, and pastilles of sugar and fruit juice; paste, leather, and cheese of fruit cooked long with sugar. A few descendants of these dry delights can be found in shops today in glacéed apricots, peaches, pineapple, and prunes; candied orange and lemon peel; Turkish delight and Aplets; gum drops, jujubes, lemon drops, chewy penny candy figures, and creamy peppermint drops. They can be found also in burnt almonds, Jordan almonds, sugar-covered hazelnuts that resemble moth balls, marzipan fruits and vegetables, and little chocolate pastilles covered with white nonpareils.

To Make Sugar Plates

Take an ounce of gum tragacanth, add rose-water and sugar til stiff. roule it out & print it in y^r moulds, dry it or use ut otherwise as you pleas.

"A Booke of Sweetmeats,"
England, 1550–1625

Sugar-plate

Simmer until dissolved
  3 tablespoons gelatin in
  ½ cup water
Add
  1 cup sugar and simmer until dissolved
Stir in
  2 tablespoons rosewater
  the grated rind and juice of 2 lemons
  2 drops vegetable coloring
Pour into a flat pan and refrigerate. When set, cut into squares or interesting shapes. Dust with 4X sugar. Or, instead of refrigerating, allow it to jell partially and put it into molds.

Raspberry Cakes

Pick out any bad raspberries that are among the fruit, weigh and boil what quantity you please, and when mashed, and the liquor is waste, put to it sugar the weight of the fruit you first put into the pan, mix it well off the fire until perfectly dissolved, then put it on China plates, and dry it in the sun. As soon as the top part dries, cut with the cover of a cannister into small cakes, turn them on fresh plates, and when dry, put them in boxes with layers of paper.

Maria Eliza Rundell, *The American Domestic Cookery*, New York, 1823

Chewy Raspberry Paste

Cook long and carefully in a heavy pot until cooked down to a thick sauce, stirring often

1 lb. raspberries
1 lb. sugar

Add and stir well

2 packages powdered pectin

Boil for 1 minute. Spread about ¼ inch thick on cookie sheets covered with plastic wrap. Put in oven at 200° F. overnight or until dry on top. Cut with round or shaped cookie cutters. Turn them over on clean wrap-covered pans. Cover with waxed paper and let dry for several days. Store with plastic wrap between layers.

To Candy Rose Leaves to Look Fresh

Take of the fayrest rose leavs red or damask and sprinkle them with rose water & lay them one by one, on white paper on a hot sunshiney day then beat some double refind sugar very small & sift it thinly on the roses, thorough fine laune sive & they will candy as they ly in the hot sun then turne the leaves & strow some rose water on the other side, & sift some sugar in like manner on them, turne then often sometimes strowing on water, & sometimes sifting on sugar till they be enough, then lay them in boxes betwixt clean papers & soe keep them all the year.

"A Booke of Sweetmeats,"
England, 1550–1625

To Candy Fruit, Nuts, and Flowers

Make a syrup of

2 cups sugar
1 cup water
⅔ cup light corn syrup

Boil without stirring to the hard crack stage (300° F.). Remove from the fire and put the pan into a large pan of boiling water to keep the syrup from hardening. Drop into it pieces of pineapples, peaches, oranges, or other fruit. Spread on cookie sheets covered with plastic wrap until nearly dry. Sift over with sugar.

Rosepetals, pinks, marigolds, mint leaves, and nuts may be treated this way. Violets, pansies, nasturtiums, and other tender blossoms do better under the treatment described in "A Booke of Sweetmeats."

To Candy Orange Chips

Pare your Orange and soak the Peelings in Water two Days, and shift the water twice; but if you love them bitter soak them not: Tie your Peels up in a Cloth, and when you Water boils, put them in, and let them boil till they are tender; then take what double refin'd Sugar will do, and break it small and wet it with a little Water, and let it boil till 'tis near candy-high, then cut your Peels of what Length you please, and put 'em into the Syrup; set 'em on the Fire and let 'em heat well thro', then let them stand a while, heat them twice a Day, but not boil: Let them be so done till they begin to candy, then take them out and put them on Plates to dry, and when they are dry, keep them near the Fire.

E. Smith, *The Compleat Housewife*,
Williamsburg, 1742

Candied Orange Peel

Soak

4 cups of orange peel in
2 cups of water for 24 hours

Pour off the water. Soak again for 24 hours. Tie up in a cheesecloth and boil until tender. Drain. Cut into small rounds or short strips. Dry well. Boil until candy thermometer reads 300° F.

2 cups sugar
1 cup water

Add the orange pieces and allow them to stand 24 hours in the syrup. Heat again. Do not boil. Let them stand 24 hours. Do it again if necessary to candy them to a stage of translucence. Spread them out to dry.

To Make Pastils

Take double-refin'd Sugar beaten and sifted as fine as Flour; perfume it with Musk and Ambergrease; then have ready steeped some Gum arabick in Orange-flower Water, and with that make the Sugar into a stiff Paste; drop into some of it 3 or 4 Drops of Oil of Mint, or Oil of Cloves, or Oil of Cinamon, or of what Oil you like, and let some only have the Perfume; then roll them up in your Hand like little Pellets, and squeeze them flat with a Seal. Dry them in the Sun.

E. Smith, *The Compleat Housewife*,
Williamsburg, 1742

Pastilles

Simmer until dissolved

1 tablespoon gelatin
¼ cup water

Add to

1 cup 4X sugar or more
4 drops peppermint or spearmint oil, oil of cloves or cinnamon, lemon or orange oil, or almond extract
4 drops appropriate vegetable coloring

Roll into balls and flatten with a seal or fork to make pastilles.

Peppermint Drops

Squeeze 3 or 4 lemons into a bason, and mix some powedered sugar with the juice, the sugar must be sifted through a lawn sieve; make it of proper thickness, and put some oil of peppermint in with it, as much as you think proper to your palate; make it of a proper thickness with sugar, put it in a saucepan and dry it over the fire, stirring it with a wooden spoon for 5 minutes, then drop them off a knife on your writing paper, the same size as the last receipt mentions ["about the size of a silver twopence"] and let them stand till they are cold, and they will come off easily, then put them in your papered box.

Frederic Nutt, *The Complete Confectioner*,
New York, 1807

Peppermint Drops

Beat until blended
1 egg white
1 tablespoon lemon juice
5 drops peppermint oil
Add gradually and beat until stiff but not dry
2 cups 4X sugar
Stir over low fire until almost dry. Drop from teaspoon onto writing paper. (Adapted from Fanny Farmer, *The Boston Cooking School Cook Book*, Boston, 1936.)

To Make Royal March-panes

Blanch and pound your Almonds, moistening them with Orange-flower water, and the White of an Egg, draw out your Paste, and dry it in a Bason with powder'd Sugar 'till it is become a pliable Paste; roll it out the thickness of a Finger, then cut it into Lengths fit to make Rings or Wreaths about your Finger, turn it round your Finger, and make Wreaths of it, then close the two Ends so that they may be separated again; mix a Spoonful of Marmalade of Apricocks with the White of an Egg, dip the Rings into it, roll them in powder'd Sugar; and if they take up too much Sugar, blow it off. Lay them on white Paper, and bake them in a Campaign Oven with Fire at top and bottom; because they are ic'd on both sides at the same Instant. Then there will rise in the middle a sort of Puff in the form of a Coronet, to adorn while you are dressing them, put upon the void spaces of these Rings a small round Pellet of some Paste, or a small Grain of some Fruit, such as Rasberry, Cherry, or the like.

John Nott, *The Cooks and Confectioners Dictionary*, London, 1724

John Nott in a similar recipe for plain marchpane tells the reader to make it "into what Forms you please, either round, long, oval, or jagged in the shape of an Heart." To make Marchpane Gilded and Garnished he directed the reader to "make Impressions round it with a Marking Iron us'd in Pastry, then take off your Paper,; then beat up the Whites of Eggs in Rose-water and Sugar and ice it over, bake it, and when it is drawn, garnish it with Comfits; then take Leaves of Gold, cut them into divers Forms, wash your March-pane over with Gum-water and lay on your Leaf-gold."

"A Booke of Sweetmeats" says simply: "To make Marchpane Conceits take a pound of almond paste made for marchpan & dry it in a dish, on a chafing-dish of coles till it wax white, then print some with moulds & some wth hands or what fashion you pleas, then gild them and store them."

Marchpane

Grind fine in a blender
  3 cups blanched almonds
  2 tablespoons orange-flower water
Or substitute 1 package (7 ounces) almond paste.
Mix with
  1 egg white beaten slightly
Add
  1 cup 4X sugar or more to make a stiff paste
  ½ teaspoon almond extract

Allow mixture to stand covered several hours then mold it by hand into the shapes of fruits, or press it into molds. Brush some of the conceits over with egg white and cover with gold leaf. Or roll some of the paste into 4 inch lengths, curl them into rings, dip them into egg white mixed with apricot jam, and cover with 4X sugar. Bake on a cake rack at 300° F. for 15 minutes or until light brown. Center with a strawberry, raspberry, or cherry or with a small ball of almond paste or an almond paste fruit to imitate a coronet.

WET SWEETMEATS

The term *sweetmeats* before the middle of the eighteenth century referred to everything wet or dry that had been treated with sugar for a banquet, or dessert. Late in the eighteenth century it came largely to mean preserved fruit, stewed fruit, and brandied fruit. The stylish term *comport*, or *compote*, of fruit replaced "sweetmeats" as the old century closed, and continued throughout the new century.

Comport Red Pears

Let your pears be large and sound; pare and cut them in quarters; prepare them as [*in*] *the former receipt* [*put them in a pan of water, and over the fire which must be slow; let them simmer three quarters of an hour very slowly; then put lemon peel in a pan of thin syrup; drain all the water from them; when your syrup boils, put them in and give them five or six boils; then put them in an earthen flat pan, and the next day boil them again, till you think the syrup is got well into them*], *only put cochineal in to colour them while they are simmering over the fire; put in by degrees, till you see it becomes a fine red.*

Frederic Nutt, *The Complete Confectioner*,
New York, 1807

Pear Compote

Pare, cut into quarters, and arrange in shallow baking dish
- 6 almost ripe pears

Simmer for 5 minutes
- ½ cup water
- ¾ cup sugar
- peel of 1 lemon

Add
- juice of 1 lemon
- 4 drops red vegetable coloring

Pour over pears and bake covered at 350° F. until tender but still firm. Pour off syrup and cook it until of the consistency of honey. Add to the pears. Serve hot or cold in a compotier. (Adapted from Fanny Farmer, *The Boston Cooking School Cook Book*, Boston, 1936.) This recipe can be used with apples, apricots, plums, figs, oranges, peaches, and nectarines. Strawberries and raspberries require a heavier syrup of ½ cup water to 1 cup sugar.

Notes

PREFACE

1. Helen McKearin, "Sweetmeats in Splendor: Eighteenth-Century Desserts and Their Dressing Out," *Antiques* 65, no. 3 (March 1955): 216–25.

2. [Eleanor] Parkinson, *The Complete Confectioner, Pastry Cook, and Baker*, p. 3; Isabella Beeton, *The Book of Household Management* (1861), p. 759.

CHAPTER 1

1. Marion Tinling, ed., "Cawson's, Virginia, in 1759–1796: Excerpts from the Diary Kept by Mrs. Martha Blodget at Cawson's, Prince George County, Va. in the Years 1795 and 1796," *William and Mary Quarterly*, 3d ser., 3, no. 2 (April 1946): 283.

2. Mrs. Benjamin Stoddert, Philadelphia, to her sister, November 17, 1798, quoted in Robert C. Alberts, *The Golden Voyage*, pp. 358–59.

3. Mrs. Benjamin Stoddert to her sister, 1798, quoted in Alberts, *The Golden Voyage*, pp. 358–59.

4. M. Halsey Thomas, ed., *The Diary of Samuel Sewall, 1674–1729*, 1:460.

5. George Corwin inventory, Salem, Mass., 1684/85, quoted in George Francis Dow, *Every Day Life in the Massachusetts Bay Colony*, pp. 278–80; Samuel Mavericke inventory, Boston, March 28, 1663/64, Suffolk County Probate Court Records (hereafter Suff. Prob.) 4:257, Joseph Downs Manuscript and Microfilm Collection, Winterthur Museum Library (hereafter DMMC).

6. Ann Uttinge will, Dedham, Mass., 1642, Suff. Prob. 1:13, DMMC; Captain Joseph Weld inventory, Roxbury, Mass., February 4, 1646/47, quoted in Dow, *Massachusetts Bay Colony*, pp. 242–43; Hezekiah Usher inventory, Boston, July 30, 1697, Suff. Prob. 11:343, DMMC; Captain William Holberton inventory, Boston, September 26, 1716, Suff. Prob. 20:416, DMMC.

7. Joseph Gillam inventory, Boston, April 26, 1681, Suff. Prob. 9:193, DMMC; John Baker inventory, Boston, July 3, 1666, Suff. Prob. 4:277, DMMC; Antipas Boyce inventory, Boston, August 4, 1669, Suff. Prob. 5:182, DMMC; Jonathan Rainsford inventory, Boston, May 16, 1671, Suff. Prob. 7:128, DMMC.

8. B. D. Bargar, ed., "Governor Tryon's House in Fort George," *New York History* 35, no. 3 (July 1954): 300; Thomas Duncan inventory, New York, January 3, 1757, appraisement book of Christopher Bancker, Brandt Schuyler, and Joris Brinkerhoff, New York, 1750–62 (hereafter Bancker appraisements), p. 75, DMMC.

9. *Boston News-Letter*, March 21/28, 1723; *Boston News-Letter*, June 8/15, 1719, quoted in George Francis Dow, *The Arts and Crafts in New England, 1704–1775*, p. 154; Joseph Marshall, *Travels Through Holland, Flanders, Germany . . . in the Years 1768, 1769, and 1770*, 4 vols. (London: J. Almon, 1772–76), 1:232; John Horner, *The Linen Trade of Europe During the Spinning Wheel Period*, p. 355; John Banister day-

book, Middletown, R.I., September 27, 1751, p. 155, John Banister Papers, Newport Historical Society (hereafter NHS); John Moore inventory, New York, October 27, 1757, Bancker appraisements, p. 43, DMMC.

10. The Reverend John Williams inventory, Deerfield, Mass., September 19, 1729, Pocumtuck Valley Memorial Association Library; Moore inventory, Bancker appraisements, p. 46, DMMC.

11. F. A. Vethake advertisement, *New York Morning Chronicle*, July 12, 1804, quoted in Rita Susswein Gottesman, *The Arts and Crafts in New York, 1800–1804: Advertisements and News Items from New York City Newspapers* (New York: The New-York Historical Society, 1965), p. 348; Bours, MacGregor, & Co., New York, bill to Mr. Codman, Boston, January 2, 1804, Elias Hasket Derby Papers, Essex Institute; Catharine Esther Beecher, *Miss Beecher's Domestic Recipt Book*, 3d ed., p. 243; Juliet Corson, *Practical American Cookery and Household Management*, p. 105.

12. Bargar, "Governor Tryon's House," p. 304; Carroll, Annapolis, Md., to Messrs. William and James Anderson, London, November 19, 1768, in "Letters of Charles Carroll, Barrister," *Maryland Historical Magazine* 38, no. 4 (December 1943): 363; John Gardner inventory, Newport, R.I., November 28, 1749, Rhode Island Historical Society (hereafter RIHS); Joseph Gerrish inventory, Newport, R.I., March 30, 1750, RIHS.

13. Bargar," Governor Tryon's House," p. 304.

14. Anthony and Cornelia Rutgers inventory, New York, May 12, 1760, Bancker appraisements, p. 70, DMMC; Duncan inventory, Bancker appraisements, p. 75, DMMC; Joseph Stansbury advertisement, *Pennsylvania Evening Post* (Philadelphia), July 11, 1776; N. Thomas advertisement, *Relf's Philadelphia Gazette and Daily Advertiser*, May 21, 1811; Isaac Macaulay advertisement, *Paxton's Philadelphia Directory and Register*, n.p.; Lydia Maria Child, *The Frugal Housewife Dedicated to Those Who Are Not Ashamed of Economy*, n.p.; Catharine Esther Beecher, *Letters to Persons Who Are Engaged in Domestic Service*, p. 214.

15. *Oxford English Dictionary* (1933) (hereafter *OED*), s.v. "Doily"; Eliza Ware Farrar, *The Young Lady's Friend*, p. 348; John B. Lyon inventory, Newport, R.I., February 4, 1837, Newport Wills and Inventories, p. 19, Newport City Hall; Bernard C. Steiner, ed., "The South Atlantic States in 1833 as Seen by a New Englander: Being a Narrative of a Tour Taken by Henry Barnard," *Maryland Historical Magazine* 13, no. 4 (December 1918): 319.

16. Steiner, "Henry Barnard," pp. 317, 318.

17. Amelia Simmons, *American Cookery* (Hartford: Hudson & Goodwin, 1796); John Farley, *The London Art of Cookery and Housekeeper's Complete Assistant* (1783; London: J. Scatcherd, J. Whitaker, G. & T. Wilkie, 1792).

18. Thomas Cosnett, *The Footman's Directory and Butler's Remembrancer*, frontispiece; Robert Roberts, *The House Servant's Directory*, 2d ed. (Boston: Munroe & Francis, 1828); see also Eleanor Lowenstein, *Bibliography of American Cookery Books, 1742–1860*, p. 23; Robert Roberts, *The House Servant's Directory*, with a foreword by Charles A. Hammond (Waltham, Mass.: The Gore Place Society, 1977). Facsimile of the 1827 ed.

19. Roberts, *The House Servant's Directory* (1827), pp. 46–53.

20. E. G. Storke, ed., *The Family and Householder's Guide* (Auburn, N.Y.: Auburn Publishing Co., 1859); L. Fiske recipe book, Beverly, Mass. (?), ca. 1860, DMMC.

21. Harriet J. Willard, *Familiar Lessons for Little Girls on Kitchen and Dining-Room Work*, p. 15.

22. Cosnett, *Footman's Directory*, p. 118.

23. See William Bentley ledger, Otsego Co., N.Y., February 23, 1814, p. 79, DMMC; Richard Henry Lee to Thomas Lee Shippen, New York, October 14, 1785, quoted in Edmund Jennings Lee, ed., *Lee of Virginia*, p. 197; Elizabeth, Lady Temple, inventory,

Boston, December 4, 1809, Bowdouin and Temple Papers, Widener Library, Harvard University.

24. See Roberts, *The House Servant's Directory* (1827), p. 59; Balfour & Barraud advertisement, *Virginia Gazette* (Williamsburg), July 25, 1766.

25. *The Workwoman's Guide, Containing Instructions to the Inexperienced . . . by a Lady*, 2d ed., rev. and corr., p. 275; Beecher, *A Treatise on Domestic Economy* (1848), p. 307.

26. Mrs. William Parkes, *Domestic Duties*, p. 63; Una Pope-Hennessy, ed., *The Aristocratic Journey* (hereafter *Mrs. Hall in America, 1827–1828*), p. 19; Jonathan Ashley inventory, Deerfield, Mass., May 30, 1787, Pocumtuck Valley Memorial Association Library; Elias Hasket Derby inventory, Salem, Mass., March 4, 1805, Essex County Probate Court Records.

27. Thomas Walker, *The Art of Dining*, pp. 56, 57; Catherine M. Sedgwick, *Letters from Abroad*, quoted in Helen McKearin, "Sweetmeats in Splendor: Eighteenth-Century Desserts and Their Dressing Out," *Antiques* 67, no. 3 (March 1955): 225.

28. Georgiana Reynolds Smith, *Table Decoration Yesterday, Today, and Tomorrow*, p. 31.

29. Allan Nevins, ed., *The Diary of Philip Hone, 1828–1850*, 2:462; Storke, *The Family and Householder's Guide*, p. 29.

30. Steiner, "Henry Barnard," p. 319.

31. Steiner, "Henry Barnard," p. 319.

32. Walter L. Arnstein, trans. and ed., "A German View of Society," *Victorian Studies* 16, no. 2 (December 1972): 196.

33. *Cassell's Household Guide*, 1:371; Mary F. Henderson, *Practical Cooking and Dinner Giving*, p. 351.

34. Harriet S. Blaine Beale, ed., *Letters of Mrs. James G. Blaine*, 1:81; see also Ward Thoron, ed., *The Letters of Mrs. Henry Adams, 1865–1883*, p. 386.

35. Beeton, *The Book of Household Management* (1861), p. 905.

36. Beeton, *The Book of Household Management* (1861; facsimile ed., New York: Farrar, Straus & Giroux, 1977).

37. Beeton, *The Book of Household Management* (1861), p. 15; *The Home Cook Book*, pp. 26, 27.

38. Beeton, *The Book of Household Management* (1861), pp. 13, 14; *The Home Cook Book*, p. 29.

39. Henderson, *Practical Cooking*, pp. 13ff.; Corson, *Practical American Cookery*, p. 105.

40. Fiske, recipe book, DMMC; Corson, *Practical American Cookery*, p. 97; Storke, *The Family and Householder's Guide*, p. 34; Katie Stewart, *The Joy of Eating*, p. 120.

41. Willard, *Lessons on Dining-Room Work*, p. 17.

42. *The Home Cook Book*, p. 370; Willard, *Lessons on Dining-Room Work*, p. 17.

CHAPTER 2

1. Joseph Barrell, Boston, to John Hoskins, England, December 21, 1795, letter book of Joseph Barrell, p. 226, Massachusetts Historical Society.

2. Thomas Jones, Williamsburg, Va., to Mrs. Jones, England, September 30, 1728, "Jones Papers: From the Originals in the Library of Congress," *Virginia Magazine of History and Biography* 26, no. 2 (April 1918): 173; Mary Norton inventory, January 22, 1677, Suff. Prob. 12:197, DMMC; Governor Burnet inventory, October 13, 1729, Suff. Prob. 28:339, DMMC.

3. Randle Holme, *The Academy of Armoury*, vol. 2, bk. 3, ch. 14, fig. 2, p. 1; fig. 19, p. 5.

4. Thomas Blount, *Glossographia*, 2d ed., s.v. "Salver"; Carroll to Messrs. Anderson, September 24, 1768, in "Letters of Charles Carroll, Barrister," *Maryland Historical Magazine* 38, no. 4 (December 1943): 363.

5. Joseph Richardson, Jr., account book, May 5, 1796, "William Crammond: To repairing a plated Table Cross & Candlestick 3 / ," Richardson Family Papers, Historical Society of Pennsylvania (hereafter HSP); Edward Lloyd IV inventory, Wye, Md., November 14, 1796, Talbot County Inventories, Maryland Hall of Records; Washington, Princeton, N.J., to Lafayette, October 30, 1783, quoted in John C. Fitzpatrick, ed., *Writings of Washington from the Original Manuscript Sources, 1745–1799*, 27:217; Edmond Milne advertisement, *Pennsylvania Gazette*, December 15, 1763, no. 1825.

6. John Nott, *The Cooks and Confectioners Dictionary*, 2d ed., with additions, rev., "The Manner of Setting Out a Desert of Fruits and Sweetmeats" (following the dictionary), n.p.; Elizabeth Pitts inventory, Boston, July 11, 1726, Suff. Prob. 25:5, DMMC.

7. François Massialot, *Nouvelle instruction pour les confitures, les liqueurs et les fruits . . . avec la manière de bien ordonner un dessert*, 2d ed., p. 350; Nott, *The Cooks and Confectioners Dictionary*, n.p., follows Z; Charles Carter, *The Compleat Practical Cook*, p. 189; Catharine Esther Beecher, *Miss Beecher's Domestic Receipt Book*, 3d ed., p. 182.

8. Henry Busk, *The Dessert: A Poem* (London: Printed for Baldwin, Cradock & Joy, 1819).

9. Hannah Glasse, *The Complete Confectioner*, p. 263.

10. Rebecca Abbot advertisement, January 24, 1731 / 32, *New England Journal* (Boston), quoted in George Francis Dow, *The Arts and Crafts in New England, 1704–1775*, p. 97; Samuel Gray advertisement, December 31, 1772, *Boston News-Letter*, quoted in Dow, *Arts and Crafts*, p. 102; Henry William Stiegel advertisement, June 4, 1772, *Pennsylvania Gazette*, quoted in Alfred Coxe Prime, *The Arts and Crafts in Philadelphia, Maryland, and South Carolina*, p. 148; Mansell, Corbett & Co. advertisement, *South Carolina Gazette* (Charleston), October 13–20, 1766, p. 5; Andrew Oliver inventory, April 15, 1774, in Alice Hanson Jones, *American Colonial Wealth*, 2:966.

11. Ebenezer Bridgham advertisement, *Boston News-Letter*, December 31, 1772, quoted in Dow, *Arts and Crafts*, p. 95; manual of sketches and dimensions used in making pottery vessels at a British pottery, attributed to the Spode factory, ca. 1815–21 (hereafter Potter's Manual), DMMC.

12. James Brooks inventory, New York, November 16, 1835, p. 2, DMMC.

13. Lloyd inventory, p. 129, Maryland Hall of Records; Bingham furniture at auction, November 18, 1805, in *Claypoole's American Daily Advertiser* (Philadelphia), November 1805, Photostat in N. Luporini, "Landsdowne: A Cultural Document of Its Time" (M.A. thesis, University of Delaware, 1967); H. A. Washington, ed., *The Writings of Thomas Jefferson*, 4:99.

14. Barrell, Boston, to Hoskins, England, April 15, 1795, letter book of Joseph Barrell, p. 189, Massachusetts Historical Society; Benson J. Lossing, *Mount Vernon and Its Associations Historical, Biographical, and Pictorial*, p. 284.

15. Marie Kimball, *The Martha Washington Cook Book*, pp. 28, 29.

16. William Greene, Washington, D.C., to his daughter, Kate Roelker, Cincinnati, Ohio, March 9, 1841, Greene-Roelker Papers, Cincinnati Historical Society.

17. Plateaux of painted wood in the Lever Gallery, Port Sunlight, Derbyshire; Charles, Lord Colchester, ed., *Diary and Correspondence of Charles Abbot, Lord Colchester*, 1:34, in *OED*, s.v. "Plateau."

18. François Massialot, *Nouvelle instruction pour les confitures, les liqueurs et les fruits . . .*, new ed., p. 516; *OED*, s.v. "Epergne."

19. Stephen Deblois advertisement, *Boston Gazette*, October 16 / 17, 1757, quoted in Dow, *Arts and Crafts*, p. 116; list of the plate at Westover, will of William Byrd III,

August 10, 1769, "Will of William Byrd of Westover, Virginia," *Virginia Magazine of History and Biography* 9, no. 1 (July 1901): 82.

20. Epergne marked W. P. bearing hallmarks of London 1785 / 6 and initials *MAS* for Mary Ann Sawyer, second wife of Philip Schuyler, Museum of the City of New York; Jane Cayford, "The Sullivan Dorr House in Providence, Rhode Island" (M.A. thesis, University of Delaware, 1961), pl. 16, following p. 162; James Williams, *The Footman's Guide*, pl. II, frontispiece.

21. Edouard R. Massey, trans. and ed., "Rhode Island in 1780 by Louis L. J. B. S. Robertnier," *RIHS Collections* 16, no. 3 (July 1923): 69.

22. John Farley, *The London Art of Cookery and Housekeeper's Complete Assistant*, 7th ed., p. 373. The 1785 edition appears in the Library Company of Philadelphia's list of its holdings, 1835.

23. Joseph Gilliers, *Le Cannameliste français* (1768), pl. 5, facing p. 116.

24. John Wilkes Miller advertisement, *Pennsylvania Journal*, June 6–October 14, 1765, s.v. "Confectioners," in Prime File: The names and advertisements transcribed from seventy American newspapers, 1723–1823, filed by craft, Decorative Arts Photographic Collection, Winterthur Museum Library (hereafter DAPC).

25. Frederick Kreitner advertisement, *South Carolina Gazette* (Charleston), December 14, 1777.

26. G. A. Jarrin, *The Italian Confectioner*, pp. 206, 219, 236.

27. Louis Eustache Ude, *The French Cook*, p. 419; Kimball, *Martha Washington Cook Book*, p. 151; "A Booke of Sweetmeats," a recipe book written in England between 1550 and 1625 and owned by Frances Parke Custis of Queens Creek, Va., ca. 1700–47, HSP. Many recipes from the manuscript appear in Kimball, *Martha Washington Cook Book*. The manuscript, annotated by Karen Hess, was published by Columbia University Press in 1981.

28. Francis Buckley, *A History of Old English Glass*, p. 143; Chelsea pottery catalogue, printed as an appendix to George Savage, *Eighteenth-Century English Porcelain*, pp. 352–412.

29. Stephen Deblois advertisement, *Boston Gazette*, October 17, 1757, quoted in Dow, *Arts and Crafts*, p. 116; Elizabeth Hutchinson inventory, Boston, August 2, 1765, Suff. Prob. 64:586, DMMC; Balfour & Barraud advertisement, *Virginia Gazette* (Williamsburg), July 25, 1766; Phyllis Kihn, "Captain Solomon Ingraham Died at Madras, India, August 15, 1805," *Connecticut Historical Society Bulletin* 29, no. 1 (January 1964): 27; Francis Child, Jr., advertisement, *New York Commercial Advertiser*, July 9, 1822; Governor William Tryon inventory of the furniture destroyed by fire, Fort George, New York, December 29, 1773, Dartmouth MSS, New York State Historical Association; Kimball, *Martha Washington Cook Book*, pp. 29, 30.

30. Farley, *The London Art of Cookery*, p. 375; *Family Receipt-Book* [ca. 1811], p. 292; S. W. M'Getrick, *The New Whole Art of Confectionary, Sugar Boiling, Iceing, Candying, Jelly and Wine Making &c &c &c . . .*, p. 30; Sarah Harrison, *The House-Keeper's Pocket-Book, and Compleat Family Cook* (1733), pp. 138, 156; Richard Briggs, *The New Art of Cookery According to the Present Practice*, pp. 406, 407.

31. John Welch advertisement, *Boston News-Letter*, April 20, 1758, quoted in Dow, *Arts and Crafts*, p. 117; Nicholas Bayard, New York, 1765, owned "1 flower pot of silver," Bayard Papers, Rutgers University Library; Holme, *Armoury*, vol. 2, bk. 3, ch. 14, fig. 5, p. 2.

32. Michael Wright, *An Account of . . . Castlemaine's Embassy . . . to . . . Innocent XI* (London: Thomas Snowden, 1688), quoted in Georgiana Reynolds Smith, *Table Decoration Yesterday, Today, and Tomorrow*, p. 31; Massialot, *Nouvelle instruction* (new ed.) facing p. 516; Potter's Manual, DMMC.

33. Hannah Firth Jones, Philadelphia, to Samuel Tonkin Jones, London, June 19, 1826, typescript, owned by Mrs. Robert Metz, a descendant.

34. Thomas Walker, *The Art of Dining*, p. 22; Catherine M. Sedgwick, *Letters from Abroad*, quoted in Helen McKearin, "Sweetmeats in Splendor: Eighteenth-Century Desserts and Their Dressing Out," *Antiques* 67, no. 3 (March 1955): 225.

35. Nicholas B. Wainwright, ed., *A Philadelphia Perspective*, p. 272. Dr. Rush was the seventh of Dr. Benjamin Rush's thirteen children.

36. Isabella Beeton, *The Book of Household Management* (1861), p. 801.

37. Isabella Beeton, *The Book of Household Management* ([1880]), pp. 1289, 1290.

38. Winslow Ames, *Prince Albert and Victorian Taste*, p. 50; Beeton, *The Book of Household Management* ([1880]), p. 1289.

CHAPTER 3

1. William Howard Gardiner to William H. Prescott, Boston, July 1, 1817, quoted in Samuel Eliot Morison, *Life and Letters of Harrison Gray Otis, 1765–1848*, 2:208.

2. J. Hall Pleasants, ed., "The Letters of Molly and Hetty Tilghman," *Maryland Historical Society Magazine* 21, no. 2 (June 1926): 145; Stewart Mitchell, ed., *New Letters of Abigail Adams, 1788–1801*, p. 77.

3. Morison, *Harrison Gray Otis*, 2:212, 213.

4. Mrs. William Parkes, *Domestic Duties*, pp. 82, 83, 86.

5. Una Pope-Hennessy, ed., *Mrs. Hall in America, 1827–1828*, pp. 62, 63.

6. Parkes, *Domestic Duties*, p. 86; Pope-Hennessy, ed., *Mrs. Hall in America, 1827–1828*, p. 127.

7. Harold Donaldson Eberlein and Cortlandt Van Dyke Hubbard, *Portrait of a Colonial City, Philadelphia 1670–1838*, p. 373; Pope-Hennessy, *Mrs. Hall in America, 1827–1828*, p. 127.

8. John Josselyn, *Two Voyages to New-England Made During the Years 1638, 1663*, p. 146.

9. John Franklin Jamison, ed., *Johnson's Wonder-Working Providence of Sion's Saviour in New England, 1628–1651*, pp. 69, 71, 210–11.

10. The Reverend Samuel Skelton's Accompte, Salem, Mass., 1629, George Francis Dow, *Every Day Life in the Massachusetts Bay Colony*, Appendix 3, pp. 239, 240; Alexander Hamilton inventory, Boston, November 17, 1680, Suff. Prob. 9:12, transcript of 1892, DMMC.

11. William Harrison, *Description of England*, 2d ed. (1587), quoted in John Dover Wilson, comp., *Life in Shakespeare's England*, p. 275; George F. Williams, *Saints and Strangers*, p. 15.

12. G. Bernard Hughes, "The Old English Banquet," *Country Life* 117, no. 3031 (February 17, 1955): 473–75; *OED*, s.v. "Banquet," "Voidee," "Voider," "Dessert."

13. S. L. Erath, ed., *The Plimouth Colony Cook Book*, p. 85; Gervase Markham, *The English House-wife* (London: Printed by B. Alsop for John Harison, 1649); *The Compleat Cook, Expertly Prescribing the Most Ready Wayes, Whether Italian, Spanish, or French, For Dressing of Flesh and Fish, Ordering of Sauces, or Making of Pastry* (London: N. Brook, 1655); W. M., transcriber, *The Queen's Closet Opened* (London: Nathaniel Brook, 1655); Robert May, *The Accomplisht Cook*, p. i.

14. Elizabeth Meade recipe book, England, before 1697, Wilson Papers, Cincinnati Historical Society.

15. Gulielma Penn recipe book, England, 1702, Penn Papers, HSP. Many of the recipes are to be found in *Penn Family Recipes: Cooking Recipes of William Penn's Wife, Gulielma* (York, Pa.: George Shumway, 1966), made readable by its editor, Evelyn Abraham Benson. Benson painstakingly transcribed the crabbed hand of Edward Blackfans, the scribe who had written at Madam Penn's direction.

16. Thomas Swift inventory, Dorchester, Mass., June 18, 1675, in Abbott Lowell Cummings, *Rural Household Inventories*, p. 7.

17. Ethel Armes, ed., *Nancy Shippen*, 2:204.

18. Sarah Harrison, *House-Keeper's Pocket-Book, and Compleat Family Cook* (1733), p. 3; Skelton's Accompte, in Dow, *Massachusetts Bay Colony*, p. 240; Henry Lloyd account books, Lloyds' Neck, N.Y., 1706[1704]–11, p. 62, Long Island Historical Society (hereafter LIHS); Margareta Schuyler account of supplies ordered September 1765 to November 1770 from Peter Cuyler, estate papers, 1765–82, Albany, N.Y., Albany Institute of History and Art (hereafter AIHA); Edouard R. Massey, trans. and ed., "Rhode Island in 1780 by Louis L. J. B. S. Robertnier," *RIHS Collections* 16, no. 3 (July 1923): 69.

19. See Frederic Nutt, *The Complete Confectioner*, p. 47; Isabella Beeton, *The Book of Household Management* ([1880]), p. 21.

20. "Letters of Charles Carroll, Barrister," *Maryland Historical Magazine* 37, no. 1 (June 1943): 189; Thomas Balston, ed., *The Housekeeping Book of Susanna Whatman, 1776–1800*, p. 37.

21. E. Smith, *The Compleat Housewife*, p. 118; Amelia Simmons, *American Cookery* (1796), p. 39.

22. Bills and receipts for purchases by Sarah Ann Bailey before and after her marriage to Henry Latimer, Wilmington, Del., 1821–22, Latimer Family Papers, DMMC; James Brooks inventory, New York, November 16, 1835, DMMC.

23. B. Case, *Accomplish'd Female Instructor*, pp. 72, 73; Mary Johnson, *Madam Johnson's Present*, p. 154; *The Young Woman's Companion*, p. 20; Isabella Beeton, *The Book of Household Management* (1861), pp. 775, 798; Beeton, *Book of Household Management* [1880], pp. 1202, 1203; L. Fiske recipe book, Beverly, Mass. (?), ca. 1860, DMMC.

24. Lloyd account books, pp. 120ff.; waste book, 2d page, LIHS. Governor Burnet inventory, Boston, October 13, 1729, Suff. Prob. 27:347, DMMC; Mitchell, *Abigail Adams, 1788–1801*, p. 9.

25. G. Bernard Hughes, *English, Scottish, and Irish Table Glass*, p. 28; Victor du Pont book of personal and family expense, begun May 1, 1802, Winterthur MSS, Eleutherian Mills Historical Library (hereafter EMHL); Phyllis Kihn, "Captain Solomon Ingraham Died at Madras, India, August 15, 1805," *Connecticut Historical Society Bulletin* 29, no. 1 (January 1964): 29.

26. James and Helena Claypoole inventory, Philadelphia, "on or about the Midle of the Seventh Month," 1688, Office of the Register of Wills, County Building; Jonathan Dickinson inventory, Philadelphia, 20th of Fifth Month, 1722, in Harrold E. Gillingham, "The Estate of Jonathan Dickinson (1663–1722)," *Pennsylvania Magazine of History and Biography* 59, no. 4 (October 1935): 424 (hereafter *PMHB*); John Marshall Phillips, *American Silver*, p. 28; C. Louise Avery, *Early American Silver*, p. 179; for women holding forks see, among other paintings, *Bohnenfest* and *Das Fest des Bohnenkönigs* by Jacob Jordaens (1593–1678) (Print Collection, Chicago Public Library); Peter Erondelle, *The French Garden* (1605), "Set at every trencher plate a Knife, a spoone, and a silver forke," quoted in Carl Bridenbaugh, *Vexed and Troubled Englishmen, 1590–1642*, p. 194.

27. John Paul Grimke, jeweller, advertisement, *South Carolina Gazette* (Charleston), September 26, 1743, no. 496.

28. Burnet inventory, Suff. Prob. 28:338, DMMC; John Cadwalader account with Henry Shepherd, London, June 3, 1769, in Nicholas B. Wainwright, *Colonial Grandeur in Philadelphia*, p. 81 (hereafter *Cadwalader*); William Dawson advertisement, *Pennsylvania Packet*, April 26, 1793, quoted in Alfred Coxe Prime, *Arts and Crafts in Philadelphia, Maryland, and South Carolina*, p. 112; Stephen Richard bill to Victor

du Pont, 1801, Winterther MSS, EMHL; Elizabeth, Lady Temple, inventory, Boston, December 4, 1809, Bowdouin and Temple Papers, Widener Library, Harvard University; Abigail Robinson will, Newport, R.I., April 8, 1835, Newport Wills and Inventories, p. 176, Newport City Hall.

29. Benson, *Penn Family Recipes*, p. 107; Elizabeth Hutchinson inventory, Boston, August 2, 1765, Suff. Prob. 64:590, DMMC; *The Lady's Book* (*Godey's Lady's Book*) (Philadelphia), 1 (October 1830): 124.

30. "A Booke of Sweetmeats," recipe book, England, 1550–1625, HSP; E. Smith, *Compleat Housewife*, p. 120.

31. Smith, *Compleat Housewife*, pp. 105, 106.

32. John Nott, *The Cooks and Confectioners Dictionary*, A, no. 23.

33. Antipas Boyce inventory, Boston, August 4, 1669, Suff. Prob. 5:180, DMMC; Francis Bacon, *Sylva Sylvarum*, p. 502; Case, *Accomplish'd Female Instructor*, p. 103; Hedewick Sorgen advertisement, *South Carolina Gazette; and Country Journal*, November 30, 1773, no. 418.

34. Nathan Bailey, *Dictionarium Domesticum*, s.v. "Comfits."

35. Hezekiah Usher II account book, Boston and Newport, August 21, 1751, NHS.

36. Helen Sprackling, "Fruit Trenchers of the Sixteenth and Seventeenth Centuries," *Antiques* 78, no. 1 (July 1960): 48–51; Rates on Imports and Exports Established by the House of Parliament, June 24, 1660, as listed in Dow, *Massachusetts Bay Colony*, p. 254.

37. Celia Woodward, "Pickle Leaves," *Antiquarian* 15, no. 3 (September 1930): 45; Joseph Stansbury advertisement, *Pennsylvania Evening Post* (Philadelphia), July 11, 1776, quoted in Prime, *Arts and Crafts in Philadelphia*, p. 129; Lewis C. Rubenstein, "Johnson Hall" (M.A. thesis, University of Delaware, 1958), p. 277; Wainwright, *Cadwalader*, p. 54.

38. *Designs of Earthenware at Leeds Pottery*, [1814], p. 8, facsimile in Donald Towner, *The Leeds Pottery*, following p. 58; Wainwright, *Cadwalader*, p. 55; Invoice from F. F. Wessels of Wessels & Primavesi, Amsterdam, to T. H. Backer, Baltimore, April 12, 1806, Maryland Historical Society (hereafter MHS); Nott, *The Cooks and Confectioners Dictionary*, text following first page of index.

CHAPTER 4

1. Una Pope-Hennessy, ed., *Mrs. Hall in America, 1827–1828*, p. 209.

2. William Kitchiner, *The Cook's Oracle*, p. 33.

3. Louis B. Wright and Marion Tinling, eds., *The Secret Diary of William Byrd of Westover, 1709–12*, p. 25; Edward Oliver Fitch, ed., *The Diaries of Benjamin Lynde and Benjamin Lynde, Jr.*, p. 29.

4. Governor Tryon inventory, Fort George, N.Y., December 29, 1773, in B. D. Barger, ed., "Governor Tryon's House in Fort George," *New York History* 35, no. 3 (July 1954): 305; Carroll, Annapolis, Md., to William Anderson, merchant, London, February 2, 1767, in "Letters of Charles Carroll, Barrister," *Maryland Historical Magazine* 37, no. 1 (March 1942): 60.

5. Arthur H. Bullen, ed., *Sir Giles Goosecappe [1582]: A Collection of Old English Plays*, 4 vols. (London: Wyman & Sons, 1882–85), 3:40, in *OED*, s.v. "Posset"; E. Smith, *The Compleat Housewife*, pp. 91, 96.

6. John Freack inventory, Boston, July 24, 1675, Suff. Prob. 5:295, DMMC; Governor Burnet inventory, Boston, October 13, 1729, Suff. Prob. 27:338, DMMC; Tryon inventory, in Barger, "Governor Tryon's House," p. 305; Potter's Manual, ca. 1815–21, pp. 49, 50, 102, DMMC.

7. Balfour & Barraud advertisement, *Virginia Gazette* (Williamsburg), July 25, 1766,

p. 2; Margaretta Tarleton party notebooks, 1740–61, Tarleton Papers, Liverpool Record Office.

8. *Family Receipt-Book* [ca. 1811], p. 180.

9. Thomas Wright, ed., *Dictionary of Obsolete and Provincial English*, 2 vols. (London: Henry G. Bohn, 1851), p. 981; *Family Receipt-Book Containing 800 Valuable Receipts in Various Branches of Domestic Economy*, p. 180; James and Arthur Jarvis advertisement, *New York Gazette*, December 6, 1771, quoted in Rita Susswein Gottesman, *The Arts and Crafts in New York, 1726–1776*, p. 98; Elizabeth Raffald, *The Experienced English Housekeeper, for the Use and Ease of Ladies, Housekeepers, Cooks, &c.* . . . , p. 214.

10. Mary Eubbs recipe book, New York, 1824–ca.1841, Museum of the City of New York; Hannah Glasse, *The Art of Cookery Made Plain and Easy*, p. 290. American editions, 1805, 1812; Sarah Cadbury, "Extracts from the Diary of Mrs. Ann Warder [1786–88]," *PMHB* 17, no. 4 (1893): 460; Eliza Leslie, *Miss Leslie's New Cookery Book;* Elizabeth Hutchinson inventory, Boston, August 2, 1765, Suff. Prob 64:587, DMMC; B. Case, *Accomplish'd Female Instructor*, pp. 49, 101; Marie Kimball, *Thomas Jefferson's Cook Book*, p. 107.

11. Mary (Mrs. David Meade) Randolph, *The Virginia House-wife*, p. 150; John Austin, "Williamsburg: The Ceramics," *Antiques* 95, no. 1 (January 1969): 119.

12. *Family Receipt-Book* [ca. 1811], p. 397.

13. Robina (Mrs. Alexander) Napier, ed., *A Noble Boke off Cookry ffor a Prynce Houssolde or Any Other Estately Houssolde;* Norborne Berkeley, Baron de Botetourt, inventory, Williamsburg, Va., October 24, 1770, Botetourt Papers, O. A. Hawkins Collection of Virginians, Virginia State Library; R. Alonzo Brock, ed., "Journal of William Black [1744]," *PMBH* 1, no. 2 (1877): 126; Kimball, *Thomas Jefferson's Cook Book*, p. 2; Stewart Mitchell, ed., *New Letters of Abigail Adams, 1788–1801*, p. 19; Henry Wansey, *An Excursion to the United States of North America, in the Summer of 1794*, p. 213.

14. Randolph, *The Virginia House-wife*, p. 146; Pope-Hennessy, *Mrs. Hall in America, 1827–1828*, p. 89; Potter's Manual, pp. 68, 69, 78, 80, DMMC; *Designs of Earthenware at Leeds Pottery* [1814], plate nos. 90, 93, 94, facsimile in Donald Towner, *The Leeds Pottery;* Joseph Stansbury advertisement, *Pennsylvania Evening Post* (Philadelphia), July 11, 1776.

15. Edward Lloyd IV inventory, Wye, Md., November 14, 1796, p. 63, Talbot County Inventories, Maryland Hall of Records; Emy, *L'Art de bien faire les glaces d'office*, p. 98; Theodorick Bland, Cawson, Va., to St. George Tucker, New York, August 14, 1786, Tucker-Coleman Collection, Swem Library, College of William and Mary; Pope-Hennessy, *Mrs. Hall in America, 1827–1828*, p. 66; Mary F. Henderson, *Practical Cooking and Dinner Giving*, p. 306.

16. Raffald, *The Experienced English Housekeeper*, p. 209; Randolph, *The Virginia House-wife*, p. 146; *O'Brien's Philadelphia Wholesale Business Directory*, pp. 74, 75; *Peterson's Manufactory & Wareroom Catalogue*, n.p.

17. Emy, *Les Glaces*, pp. iv, 3; Jane Janvier recipe book, Philadelphia, 1817–37, HSP.

18. N. Luporini, "Lansdowne: A Cultural Document of Its Time" (M.A. thesis, University of Delaware, 1967); Victor du Pont account book, p. 12, Winterthur MSS, EMHL; Franklin D. Scott, trans. and ed., *Baron Klinkowström's America, 1818–1820*, p. 158; P. C. F. Smith, *Crystal Blocks of Yankee Coldness*, p. 14; see also Jennie G. Everson, *Tidewater Ice of the Kennebec River*.

19. Abraham Rees, *The Cyclopaedia*, 1st Am. ed., rev., corr., enl., s.v. "Vanilla"; Kimball, *Thomas Jefferson's Cook Book*, p. 2; Eliza Leslie, *Seventy-five Receipts for Pastry, Cakes, and Sweetmeats* (1828), p. 45; Eliza Leslie, *New Receipts for Cooking*, p. 107.

20. Scott, *Baron Klinkowström's America*, p. 115.

21. Eubbs recipe book, Museum of the City of New York; Balfour & Barraud advertisement, *Virginia Gazette* (Williamsburg), July 25, 1766; Samuel and Sarah Adams, *The Complete Servant*, p. 221.

22. Bill to T. & T. Powell, Baltimore, from Stevens Glass Concern, Bristol, England, July 10, 1797, MHS.

23. Sarah Harrison, *The House-Keeper's Pocket-Book, and Compleat Family Cook* (1748), p. 162; Richard Briggs, *The New Art of Cookery According to the Present Practice*, pp. 402, 405, 412; Raffald, *The Experienced English Housekeeper*, pp. 170, 171; S. W. M'Getrick, *The New Whole Art of Confectionary, Sugar Boiling, Iceing, Candying, Jelly and Wine Making &c. &c. &c. . . .*, p. 29; Isabella Beeton, *The Book of Household Management* ([1880]), p. 728.

24. Maria Eliza Rundell, *A New System of Domestic Cookery* (1810), p. 181; Maria Eliza Rundell, *American Domestic Cookery*, p. 221.

25. Lloyd inventory, p. 128, Maryland Hall of Records.

26. Smith, *The Compleat Housewife*, pp. 90, 91; Elizabeth Coultas recipe book, England and Philadelphia (?), dated 1749 / 50, DMMC.

27. Wyndham Beawes, *Lex Mercatoria Rediviva*, pp. 611, 612; *OED*, s.v. "Isinglass"; Frances Norton Mason, ed., *John Norton and Sons*, p. 329; Lloyd inventory, p. 72, Maryland Hall of Records; Janvier recipe book, HSP; Catherine Flint recipe book, Boston, 1830–60, American Antiquarian Society.

28. *Family Receipt-Book* [ca. 1811], pp. 194, 195; Coultas recipe book, DMMC.

29. Zabdiel Boylston advertisement, *Boston News-Letter*, May 5 / 12, 1710 / 11, quoted in George Francis Dow, *The Arts and Crafts in New England, 1704–1775*, p. 237; Peter Lorent advertisement, *Boston News-Letter*, July 13, 1769, quoted in Dow, *Arts and Crafts*, p. 296; Henry Lloyd account books, Lloyds' Neck, N.Y., 1706 [1704]–11, p. 81, LIHS; Beawes, *Lex Mercatoria Rediviva;* Savary des Bruslons, *Dictionnaire Universel de Commerce*, 1760, 2:33, 165.

30. Benjamin Betterton advertisement, *Pennsylvania Journal and Weekly Advertiser*, no. 274, February 16, 1747 / 48, s.v. "Bakers," in Prime File, DAPC; Joseph Calvert advertisement, *South Carolina Gazette* (Charleston), September 9, 1745; Jane Magg advertisement, *Maryland Journal and Baltimore Universal Daily Advertiser*, May 7 and 14, 1793, s.v. "Bakers," in Prime File, DAPC; Henry Ridgely, Baltimore, to Ann Ridgely, Dover, Del., April 28, 1833, in *A Calendar of Ridgely Papers*, ed., Leon de Valinger, 1:297; Alexis Soyer, *The Modern Housewife, or Ménagère* (1849), p. 394.

31. Joseph Greswold advertisement, *New York Weekly Journal*, July 6, 1747, quoted in Gottesman, *Arts and Crafts*, p. 299; Carroll, Baltimore, to Messrs. Lux and Potts, Barbados, March 17, 1769, "Letters of Charles Carroll," 38, no. 4 (December 1943): 367.

32. Joseph Corré advertisement, *Dunlap and Claypoole's American Daily Advertiser* (Philadelphia), June 11, 27, 30, 1795; Bossé advertisement, *The Aurora Daily Advertiser* (Philadelphia), July 19, 1800, s.v. "Confectioners," in Prime File, DAPC; Collott (Collet) advertisement, *Pennsylvania Packet*, May 13, 1795; Kenneth Roberts, trans. and ed., *Moreau de St. Méry's American Journey, 1793–1798*, p. 323; Victor du Pont, book of personal and family expense, begun May 1, 1802, Winterthur MSS, EMHL; Eleuthère Irénée du Pont, bills and receipts, July 31 to December 12, 1801, February 10 and May 21, 1802, Winterthur MSS, EMHL; Eliza Southgate Boune, *A Girl's Life Eighty Years Ago* (1797–1809), p. 154.

33. Frederick Kreitner advertisement, *South Carolina Gazette* (Charleston), November 23, 1773, s.v. "Confectioners," in Prime File, DAPC; Joseph Delacroix advertisement, *Pennsylvania Packet*, January 8, 1791, s.v. "Confectioners," in Prime File, DAPC; *The Cincinnati Directory* (Cincinnati: Oliver Farnsworth, 1819).

34. Erastus Corning Papers, 1810–18, AIHA.

CHAPTER 5

1. Elizabeth Wentworth inventory, Portsmouth, N.H., December 11, 1802, Jane Giffin, ed., "The Estate of Madam Elizabeth Wentworth of Portsmouth," *Historical New Hampshire* 23, no. 1 (Spring 1968): 31–49.

2. Anne Grant, *Memoirs of an American Lady*, p. 74.

3. Invoice of goods carried from Boston to Newport, R.I., and Queen's Village on Lloyds' Neck, L.I., 1711, Henry Lloyd account books, Lloyds' Neck, N.Y., 1706 [1704]–11, p. 32, LIHS; Captain Francis Browne account book for the sloop *Speedwell*, 1706–16, Yale University Library; *Dunlap and Claypoole's American Daily Advertiser* (Philadelphia), February 5, 1795.

4. Supplies ordered by Margareta Schuyler, September 1765 to November 1770, from Philip Cuyler, estate papers, Albany, N.Y., 1765–82, AIHA.

5. Nathaniel Dominy ledger, Easthampton, N.Y., March 26, 1807, p. 62, DMMC; Robert Scadin daybook, Cooperstown, N.Y., May 10, 1831, New York State Historical Association (hereafter NYSHA).

6. Cornelis Steenwyck (d. 1686), New Amsterdam, N.Y., in Esther Singleton, *The Furniture of Our Forefathers*, 1:247; Jane Janvier recipe book, Philadelphia, 1817–37, HSP.

7. John Morison Duncan, *Travels Through Part of the United States and Canada in 1818 and 1819*, 2:286; Benjamin Miles ledger, 1821–28, Cooperstown, N.Y., March 5, 1821, p. 6, NYSHA.

8. Elizabeth Raffald, *The Experienced English Housekeeper, for the Use and Ease of Ladies, Housekeepers, Cooks, &c. . . .*, p. 232.

9. Harold E. Gillingham, "The Estate of Jonathan Dickinson (1663–1722)" *PMHB* 59, no. 4 (October 1935): 427; *Inventory of the Contents of Mount Vernon, 1810*, p. 41.

10. G. A. Jarrin, *The Italian Confectioner*, p. 161.

11. The undated and unsigned recipe for icing, written on a single sheet of paper in mid-nineteenth-century script, was found in a copy of Esther Allen Howland, *The New England Economical Housekeeper, and Family Receipt Book* (New London, Conn.: Bolles & Williams, 1848). It is preserved in the Pocumtuck Valley Memorial Association Library, Deerfield, Mass.

12. Donald Pilcher, *The Regency Style*, fig. 7, p. 4; Hezekiah Usher II inventory, Boston, August 21, 1751, account book, Boston and Newport, NHS; account by Mrs. Louis Albert Cazenove of wedding of Anne Eliza Gardner to C. F. Lee, Alexandria, Va., April 15, 1846, in G. Lee Cazenove, Jr., accounts and letters, DMMC.

13. See *The Journal of Nicholas Cresswell, 1774–1777*, pp. 52, 53.

14. Charles Francis Adams, ed., *Letters of Mrs. Adams, the Wife of John Adams*, 2:79, 80; Jack P. Greene, ed., *The Diary of Colonel Landon Carter of Sabine Hall, 1752–78*, 1:344; J. Hall Pleasants, ed., "The Letters of Molly and Hetty Tilghman," *Maryland Historical Society Magazine* 21, no. 3 (September 1926): 234.

15. Lamson family recipe book, inscribed "8 April 1768, Parish of Wolsingham, County of Durham," Chicago Historical Society.

16. Theodore F. Garrett, ed., *The Encyclopaedia of Practical Cookery*, 2:381; Alexis Soyer, *The Modern Housewife, or Ménagère* (1849), facing p. 404; advertisement from *Connecticut Courant*, September 17, 1822, for "Portey's Patent Cooking Stove . . . manufactured in New York . . . also . . . Philadelphia Baking Stoves . . . Miles Beach & Sons, Sept. 17 [1822]," in *Food, Drink, and Recipes of Early New England*, ed. Catherine Fennelly, p. 21; Samuel Ward inventory, Newport, R.I., 1840, p. 21, Newport Wills and Inventories, Newport City Hall; Hannah Widdefield, *Widdefield's New Cook Book*, p. 246; *Peterson's Manufactory & Wareroom Catalogue*, p. 29.

17. William Kitchiner, *The Cook's Oracle*, p. 68; D. Meredith Reese, *An Encyclopedia of Domestic Economy*, p. 859; Sara Josepha Hale, *The Ladies' New Book of Cook-*

ery (1852), pp. xvl, 6. Mrs. Hale was editor of the periodical *Godey's Lady's Book;* see also Mary Hooker Cornelius, *The Young Housekeeper's Friend*, p. 48; Isabella Beeton, *The Book of Household Management* (1861), p. 40; *The Home Cook Book*, p. 50.

18. Edward Lloyd IV inventory, Wye, Md., November 14, 1796, p. 131, Talbot County Inventories, Maryland Hall of Records; Scadin daybook, October 4, 1830, NYSHA; Elizabeth E. Lea, *Domestic Cookery, Useful Receipts, and Hints to Young Housekeepers*, p. 85.

19. John P. Kennedy, *Memoirs of the Life of William Wirt, Attorney General of the United States*, 2:143.

20. Garrett, *The Encyclopaedia of Practical Cookery*, 2:337; Leon de Valinger, ed., *A Calendar of Ridgely Papers*, 1:340.

21. Stewart Mitchell, ed., *New Letters of Abigail Adams, 1788–1801*, p. 98.

22. Sara Josepha Hale, *The Good Housekeeper*, p. 96.

23. Howard C. Rice, Jr., trans. and ed., *Travels in North America in the Years 1780, 1781, and 1782 by the Marquis de Chastellux*, 2:132; Una Pope-Hennessy, ed., *Mrs. Hall in America*, 1827–1828, p. 28.

24. Eliza Leslie, *Seventy-five Receipts for Pastry, Cakes, and Sweetmeats* (1845), frontispiece; E. Lloyd inventory, pp. 64, 131, Maryland Hall of Records.

25. Frances Trollope, *Domestic Manners of the Americans*, 2:104.

26. Martha Gazley advertisement, *New York Gazette* (December 21, 1731), quoted in Rita Susswein Gottesman, *The Arts and Crafts in New York, 1726–1776*, p. 275; Peter Pekin advertisement, *South Carolina Gazette* (Charleston), December 29, 1746, s.v. "Confectioners," in Prime File, DAPC; L. Fiske recipe book, Beverly, Mass. (?), ca. 1860, DMMC.

27. Amelia Simmons, *American Cookery* (1958), p. 29; Edward Oliver Fitch, ed., *The Diaries of Benjamin Lynde and Benjamin Lynde, Jr.* (1690–1780), p. 33.

28. William Wright inventory, New York, March 21, 1757; John Loddle inventory, New York, January 24, 1754; Edward Graham inventory, New York, February 13, 1757; Bancker appraisements, pp. 26, 41, 49, DMMC; Eleuthère Irénée du Pont bill from John Ranger, July 2, 1802, Winterthur MSS bills and receipts, EMHL.

29. Joseph Dowding inventory, Boston, September 17, 1716/17, Suff. Prob. 19:185, 186, DMMC; Samuel Allen inventory, Deerfield, Mass., 1749, Pocumtuck Valley Inventories, Pocumtuck Valley Memorial Association Library.

30. Francis Thurman inventory, New York, September 20, 1758; Thomas Duncan inventory, New York, January 3, 1757, Bancker appraisements, pp. 60, 75, DMMC; Elizabeth Hutchinson inventory, Boston, October 25, 1765, Suff. Prob. 64:587, DMMC; Tryon inventory in B. D. Barger, ed., "Governor Tryon's House in Fort George," *New York History* 35, no. 3 (July 1954): 297; John Adams, advertisement, *Boston Gazette*, June 7, 1773; account with Philip Cuyler, April 20, 1765, Schuyler estate papers, AIHA.

31. *New American Cookery*, pp. 14, 42, 43; *The Domestic's Companion*, p. 32.

32. Eliza Leslie, *Seventy-five Receipts for Pastry, Cakes, and Sweetmeats* (1828), p. 8; Mary Johnson, *Madam Johnson's Present*, p. 144.

33. Richard Briggs, *The New Art of Cookery According to the Present Practice*, p. 339; Randle Holme, *The Academy of Armoury*, vol. 2, bk. 3, ch. 22, fig. 40, p. 274.

34. "China tart moulds" are listed in the Joseph Prentis inventory, Williamsburg, Va., July 24, 1809, Swem Library, College of William and Mary.

35. Briggs, *The New Art of Cookery*, p. 338; Leslie, *Seventy-five Receipts* (1828), p. 18.

36. *Stettinisches Koch-buch für Jünge Frauen und Köchinnen*, p. 133; *Columbian Magazine* (Philadelphia) 1 (1787): 596.

37. Henry Bradshaw Fearon, *Sketches of America*, p. 110.

38. Benjamin Franklin, "Distresses of a Modest Man," *Father Abraham's Almanac*,

n.p.; *The Home Cook Book*, p. 318; Mrs. B. C. Howard, *Fifty Years in a Maryland Kitchen*, p. 151.

39. Elizabeth Coultas recipe book, England and Philadelphia (?), dated 1749/50, DMMC.

40. Simmons, *American Cookery* (1796), pp. 26, 27; Leslie, *Seventy-five Receipts* (1828), p. 35.

41. Eliza Leslie, *Miss Leslie's New Cookery Book*, p. 474.

42. Anthony and Cornelia Rutgers inventory, New York, May 12, 1760, Bancker appraisements, p. 70, DMMC; John Reed personal accounts, Philadelphia, 1799–1811, p. 50, DMMC; Lucy Emerson, *New England Cookery*, pp. 45, 51.

43. Nicholas B. Wainwright, *Cadwalader* (d. 1786), p. 53; first bill for silver pudding dish and silver pudding knife from Shepherd and Boyd to Mrs. Pierre van Cortlandt II (Anne Stevenson), dated March 25, 1814; later bill dated November 14, 1814 (van Cortlandt Papers, Museum of the City of New York); separate bills for each item issued July 22, 1815 (for the dish) and July 31, 1815 (for the knife) (collection of Mrs. Robert P. Browne); Thomas F. Field, 87 Water Street, New York City, bill to George W. Merrill, Chicago, April 17, 1839, Merrill account book, Chicago Historical Society; John Ridgway bill headed "Porcelain and Earthenware Manufacturer, Cauldron Place in the Staffordshire Potteries," July 7, 1835, to Robinson Tyndale, pottery dealer, Philadelphia, DMMC.

CHAPTER 6

1. Reminiscences of Charles N. Buck, Esq., Consul General of Hamburg to the United States of America, 1791–1840, p. 54, HSP.

2. Sara Josepha Hale, *The Good Housekeeper*, p. 87; Carl Bridenbaugh, ed., *Gentleman's Progress*, p. 173; Sarah Cadbury, ed., "Extracts from the Diary of Mrs. Ann Warder [1786–88]," *PMBH* 17, no. 4 (1893): 448, 459; Una Pope-Hennessy, ed., *Mrs. Hall in America, 1827–1828*, p. 293; John P. Kennedy, *Memoirs of the Life of William Wirt, Attorney General of the United States*, 2:101.

3. Peter Kalm, *Travels into North America*, 1:288; *Columbian Magazine* (Philadelphia) 1 (November 1787): 758.

4. "Letter Written by a Gentleman to a Lady in the Country . . . July 16, 1782," *Columbian Magazine* (Philadelphia) 1 (February 1787): 262.

5. G. Bernard Hughes, "The Old English Banquet," *Country Life* 117, no. 3031 (February 17, 1955): 474; *Henry IV, Part 2*, act 5, sc. 3.

6. "Description of Virginia by Captain John Smith," in *Narratives of Early Virginia, 1606–1625*, ed. Lyon Gardiner Tyler, p. 90; Kalm, *Travels into North America*, 1:100.

7. Joan Parry Dutton, *The Flower World of Williamsburg*, p. 115; Van Doren, Mark, ed., *Samuel Sewall's Diary* (b. 1652, d. 1730), p. 22; "Diary of Samuel Sewall [1714–30]," in *Collections of the Massachusetts Historical Society*, 5th ser., 7:364.

8. E. Merton Coulter, ed., *Journal of William Stephens, 1741–43*, p. 35.

9. Cadbury, "Diary of Ann Warder," p. 488; Henry Tudor, *Narrative of a Tour in North America . . . [1831–32]*, 1:356; Heather Miller, "The Pineapple, King of Fruits," *Horticulture* 57, no. 12 (December 1979): 39.

10. Edward Oliver Fitch, ed., *The Diaries of Benjamin Lynde and Benjamin Lynde, Jr.*, p. 53; Henry Wansey, *An Excursion to the United States of North America, in the Summer of 1794*, p. 54.

11. Miller, "The Pineapple," p. 44; Maureen Stafford and Dora Ware, *An Illustrated Dictionary of Ornament*, p. 168.

12. Thomas Swift inventory, Dorchester, Mass., June 18, 1675, in Abbott Lowell Cummings, *Rural Household Inventories*, p. 7; James and Helena Claypoole inventory,

Philadelphia, "on or about the Midle of the Seventh Month," 1688, p. 2, Office of the Register of Wills, County Building; Governor Burnet inventory, Boston, October 13, 1729, Suff. Prob. 27:337–48, DMMC; Nicholas B. Wainwright, *Cadwalader* (d. 1786, Philadelphia), p. 55; pair of pierced blue and gold fruit baskets on stand marked J. B., initials of John Brown, RIHS Collection; sixty-four pieces of President James Monroe's service are in the Winterthur Museum's collections (58.1606); Robert Oliver inventory, Baltimore County, July 10, 1835, Maryland Register of Wills.

13. Bill of John E. White to Eleuthère Irénée du Pont, April 21, 1806, Longwood MSS, EMHL; John F. Mifflin inventory, Philadelphia, 1813, in *Furnishing Plan for the Bishop White House*, 2:Appendix K, p. 4.

14. François Massialot, *Nouvelle instruction pour les confitures, les liqueurs, et les fruits* . . . (1740), pp. 512, 513; John Baker inventory, Boston, July 3, 1666, Suff. Prob. 4:227, DMMC; Antipas Boyce inventory, Boston, August 4, 1669, Suff. Prob. 5:179, DMMC.

15. Charlotte Mason, *The Lady's Assistant for Regulating and Supplying the Table*, pp. 46–49; Elizabeth, Lady Temple, inventory, Boston, December 4, 1809, Bowdouin and Temple Papers, Widener Library, Harvard University; Pope-Hennessy, *Mrs. Hall in America, 1827–1828*, p. 89.

16. Isabella Beeton, *The Book of Household Management* (1861), pp. 804, 805.

17. Jane Austen, *Mansfield Park*, p. 108.

18. Brillat-Savarin, *The Physiology of Taste*, p. 4; Alexander Murray, *The Domestic Oracle*, pp. 500, 502, 533; Robert Roberts, *The House Servant's Directory* (1827), pp. 51, 59.

19. Beeton, *The Book of Household Management* (1861), pp. 940–60.

20. Walter Arnstein, trans. and ed., "A German View of Society," *Victorian Studies* 16, no. 2 (December 1972): 196.

21. *Poor Richard Revived Being the Farmer's Diary*, n.p.; Franklin D. Scott, ed., *Baron Klinkowström's America, 1818–1820*, p. 16; *The Expert Waitress*, p. 52.

22. "Diary of Samuel Sewall [1674–1729]," 5:183; Harrold E. Gillingham, "The Estate of Jonathan Dickinson (1663–1722)," *PMBH* 59, no. 4 (October 1935): 424; Thomas and Abigail Kelland inventory, Boston, December 21, 1683, Suff. Prob. 9:156, DMMC; Samuel Eliot Morison, "Charles Bagot's Notes on Housekeeping and Entertaining at Washington, 1819," *Publications of the Colonial Society of Massachusetts: Transactions 1924–1926* (Boston: Published by the Society, 1927), 26:438–46.

23. Schuyler account with Philip Cuyler, April 20, 1768, Schuyler estate papers, Albany, N.Y., 1765–82, AIHA.

24. Edward Lloyd IV inventory, Wye, Md., November 14, 1796, pp. 103–105, Talbot County Inventories, Maryland Hall of Records.

25. Morison, "Bagot's Notes," p. 442.

26. Schuyler account with Cuyler, December 7, 1765, AIHA.

27. William Alden inventory, Boston, June 26, 1732, Suff. Prob. 31:28, DMMC.

28. John Nott, *The Cooks and Confectioners Dictionary*, RA, no. 32; Leon de Valinger, ed., *A Calendar of Ridgely Papers*, 1:120; Burnet inventory, Suff. Prob. 27:346, DMMC; *Family Receipt-Book* [ca. 1811], p. 105; Mary Randolph, *The Virginia Housewife*, p. 175.

29. See the Eleuthera du Pont watercolor, ca. 1827, Winterthur MSS, EMHL.

30. *OED*, s.v. "Negus"; Morison, "Bagot's Notes," p. 441.

31. Carroll, Annapolis, Md., to Messrs. Williams, London, July 21, 1768, "Letters of Charles Carroll, Barrister," *Maryland Historical Magazine* 38, no. 2 (June 1943): 190; 38, no. 4 (December 1943): 363.

32. G. A. Jarrin, *The Italian Confectioner*, pp. 156, 157; Temple inventory, Widener Library.

33. *OED*, s.v. "Punch"; Samuel Eliot Morison, *Life and Letters of Harrison Gray Otis, 1765–1848*, 1:232.

34. H. L. Mencken, *The American Language, Supplement I*, p. 261; Washington Irving (Diedrich Knickerbocker), *A History of New York*, p. 410; Alex Rivington, *Reminiscences of America in 1869 by Two Englishmen*, 2d ed., rev. (London: S. Law, Son and Marston, 1870), p. 68.

35. Edmond Milne advertisement, *Pennsylvania Journal*, November 8, 1764; Thomas Duncan inventory, New York, January 3, 1757, Bancker appraisements, p. 75, DMMC; Phyllis Kihn, "Captain Solomon Ingraham Died at Madras, India, August 15, 1805," *Connecticut Historical Society Bulletin* 29, no. 1 (January 1964): 27; invoice from Robert Carey & Co., London, to George Washington, New York, n.d., 1759, in Paul Wilstach, *Mount Vernon, Washington's Home and the Nation's Shrine*, p. 69.

36. "Appraisment of the Estate of Philip Ludwell, Esq. Dec'd," *Virginia Magazine of History and Biography* 21 (1913): 409 (Ludwell died on September 1767 in London); Thomas Cosnett, *The Footman's Directory and Butler's Remembrancer*, pp. 99, 113; Tobias Smollett, *Travels* (1766), 1:5, in E. M. Elville, *Paper Weights and Other Glass Curiosities*, p. 104; Richard Capes advertisement, *Daily Advertiser* (New York), January 5, 1797; Roberts, *The House Servant's Directory* (1827), p. 59; Temple inventory, Widener Library; John Trusler, *Honours of the Table*, p. 15; Allan Nevins, ed., *The Diary of John Quincy Adams, 1794–1845*, p. 174; Mrs. William Parkes, *Domestic Duties*, p. 63.

37. Kelland inventory, Suff. Prob. 9:156, DMMC; Kihn, "Ingraham, 1805," p. 29; James Geddy inventory, Williamsburg, Va., November 19, 1744, pp. 321–22, York County Wills and Inventories, State House, Richmond, Va.; pair of Elias Hasket Derby sheffield monteiths, Collection of the Museum of Fine Arts, Boston; the monteiths appear in his inventory of March 4, 1805, Salem, Mass., Essex County Probate Court Records; Joseph Barrell letter book, Boston, 1792–97, p. 238, Massachusetts Historical Society.

38. *Designs of Earthenware at Leeds Pottery* [ca. 1814], p. 6, and nos. 93, 94, facsimile in Donald Towner, *The Leeds Pottery*, following p. 58; Derby sheffield wine coolers, Collection of the Museum of Fine Arts, Boston.

39. Order from Edward Shippen, Philadelphia, to Messrs. Francis and Relfe, London, January 19, 1763, DMMC; Cosnett, *The Footman's Directory*, p. 75; Roberts, *The House Servant's Directory* (1827), pp. 47–49; Catharine Esther Beecher, *A Treatise on Domestic Economy for the Use of Young Ladies at Home and at School*, pp. 111, 310.

40. Tudor, *Tour in North America* [*1831–32*], 1:18.

41. Cadbury, "Diary of Ann Warder," p. 460; Samuel and Sarah Adams, *The Complete Servant*, pp. 382–83; see also Juliet Corson, *Practical American Cookery and Household Management*, p. 127.

42. George Ticknor to his parents, January 6, 1815, in *Life, Letters, and Journal of George Ticknor*, ed. George S. Hillard, 1:27.

43. Jean Pierre Brissot de Warville, *Nouveau voyage dans les États Unis de l' Amérique septentrionale* (1788), in Oscar Handlin, *This was America*, p. 70; *OED*, s.v. "Drum"; Corson, *Practical American Cookery*, p. 154; Ward Thoron, ed., *The Letters of Mrs. Henry Adams, 1865–1883*, p. 386.

44. L. Fiske recipe book, Beverly, Mass. (?), ca. 1860, DMMC.

45. *The Home Cook Book*, pp. 35, 36.

46. Emily G. Swift, Amenia, N.Y., to William Grant, New Haven, Conn., February 13, 1829, DMMC.

Glossary

Many of the following definitions have been adapted from the *Oxford English Dictionary* (1933). To suggest a range of the usage of terms, the earliest and latest dates the dictionary gives have been included. A few other sources, to be found in the bibliography, have similarly been cited with the date of their publication.

Alembic An apparatus of glass or metal formerly used in distillation. From the Greek *ambix*, "cup." Now superseded by the retort or worm still. *OED* ca. 1374, 1851.

Alkanet A plant of the Anchusa family whose roots yield a red dye. Also called bugloss. *OED* 1326, 1876.

Ambergris A waxlike substance of marbled ashy color found floating in tropical seas, and as a morbid secretion in the intestine of the sperm whale. It is odoriferous and used in perfumery; formerly in cookery. *OED* 1481, 1874.

Angelica An aromatic umbrella-shaped plant with compound leaves and white-to-greenish flower clusters. Its stem and leaf ribs are often candied. *OED* 1578, 1874.

Baize, or bay A coarse open woolen stuff having a long nap. Its name derives from bay, or chestnut, color which was the fabric's original hue. *OED* 1576, 1882. Often green or red in the eighteenth century.

Banket-letter A cookie in the shape of a letter made in Holland at Christmastime.

Banquet Formerly a repast of sweetmeats, fruit, and wine served between meals. *OED* 1509, 1703. Also a feast or sumptuous entertainment of food and drink, as it is now. *OED* 1483, 1885. From the Italian *banchetto*, "little bench," the diminutive of *banco*, "table."

Barrel A container made of wooden staves, with flat bottom and top, containing varying amounts of liquids and solids. Usually thirty-one and a half gallons of liquid or thirty-one gallons of fermented liquid. The sixteenth-century English barrel of wine was thirty-six gallons, and of ale thirty-two gallons.

Basin An open, rounded vessel formerly used for holding either liquids or solids, today largely for holding liquids. In seventeenth-century England the term implied a shallow dish, whereas there today it means a deep bowl. In America the term has always meant either a deep dish or a shallow dish.

Benné An African term for seasame seeds, which are small oval flat seeds of the *Sesamum indicum*, an annual East Indian herb used as a flavoring agent. Benné cakes or cookies.

Bergamot 1. A tree (*Citrus bergamia*) with a pear-shaped fruit whose rind yields an essential oil much used in perfumery. *OED* 1706, 1850. 2. Any of several mints whose oil resembles essence of bergamot. *OED* 1858, 1866. 3. A fine kind of pear. *OED* 1616, 1868.

Bigarrade A bitter orange called the Seville (pronounced "sevvle") orange (q.v.). From the French *bigarré*, "variegated."

Bird's-eye A fabric woven with a pattern of small diamonds each having a dot in the center. *OED* 1665, 1841.

Blancmange A flavored and sweetened milk pudding. *OED* 1377, 1862. In fourteenth-century England the term meant the new French "white food" of chicken, fish, rice, almonds, cream, eggs, etc., that had none of the color of the usual English roasts.

Bocking A coarse woolen baize (q.v.) dyed black, brown, or green, much of it made in Bocking, Essex. *OED* 1759. Used to cover floors or to protect carpets. *OED* 1848, 1860.

Brandywine An early term for brandy. The word was derived from the Dutch *brandt*, "burnt," for burnt, or distilled, wine. *OED* 1622, 1719.

Broadcloth Any number of double-width materials. A double width was two yards between selvages. The green broadcloth used on tables and under tables was most often wool baize but was sometimes cotton or linen. *OED* 1420, 1833.

Burnt China Porcelain. Called burnt in the seventeenth and eighteenth centuries because of the high firing needed to produce it.

Butt A cask of varying capacity. In England in 1443 a butt of Rhenish wine held 36 British gallons; in 1510 a butt of malmsey, 100–105 gallons; at the end of the fifteenth century, 126 gallons by statute, as it does in the United States today.

Cake A pleasant food, or thin flat loaf, sometimes made of plain flour and water and sometimes with very rich ingredients mixed with eggs, fruit, etc. Dyche and Pardon, 1765.

Capillary, or Capillaire A syrup of maidenhair fern, water, and sugar used with added cold water to make a refreshing drink. Willich, 1802. *OED* 1754, 1851.

Carafe A glass bottle for serving wine or water at table; a decanter. From the Arabic *gharafa*, "to dip." *OED* 1786, 1868.

Caraway Aromatic seed of the *Carum carui*, used in cakes, sweetmeats, etc., and yielding a volatile oil. *OED* 1440, 1861.

Cardamom A spice consisting of the seed capsules of various species of *Amomum* and *Elettaria*, natives of Ceylon, the East Indies, and China, used in medicine as a stomachic and also for flavoring sauces and curry. *OED* 1398, 1883. The seeds were often individually coated with sugar as comfits.

Carminative Cleansing by expelling gas from the stomach and intestines. Peppermint water is a carminative. *OED* 1655, 1875.

Caster A small glass, ceramic, or metal bottle with a perforated top for sprinkling pepper, sugar, dry mustard, etc. Extended to other vessels used to contain condiments at the table, as in "a set of casters." *OED* 1676, 1861. A sugar caster was used to cast sugar on pies and tarts before baking.

Caudle A warm drink consisting of bread, eggs, or thin gruel mixed with wine or ale, sweetened and spiced. Given chiefly to sick people, especially women in childbed; also given to their visitors. *OED* 1297, 1855.

Cauldron See **Kettle.**

Charlotte In England a dish made of apple marmalade covered with toasted crumbs. In the United States a dessert of whipped cream in a casing of cake slices or lady fingers. *OED* 1855, 1860.

Charlotte Russe A dessert of Bavarian cream or of custard set in a mold lined with lady fingers or sponge cake.

Cheesecake A cake or tart originally containing cheese, currants, almonds, eggs, butter, and spices. *OED* 1440, 1853.

Chelsea Cake, or Chelsea Bun A sweetened yeast dough rolled as for a jelly roll, brushed with butter, and sprinkled with currants and sugar, then sliced and baked.

Cherry Bounce A colloquial term for cherry brandy. Made (often at home) of cherry juice and rum or whiskey. *OED* 1693, 1844.

Chess Cake, or Chess Pie A colloquial term for an old form of cheesecake, usually made without cheese but with eggs, cream, sugar, and spices in pastry.

Chip 1. A thick, irregular slice of fruit or fruit peel preserved in sugar. *OED* 1769, 1796. Also found as a thin piece or strip. 2. Formerly also a paste of fine flour and gum tragacanth rolled thin, cut in pieces, and "speck[ed] with divers colours." Holme, 1701.

Chocolate Mill A wooden stick with enlarged end used to beat or whip chocolate to a froth. Other similar mills were used to beat cream, eggs, etc. *OED*, 1897.

Cistern A large vessel to hold bottles in cold water. Usually placed on the floor near the sideboard of a dining room. Also a vessel to hold a large supply of punch or other liquor. *OED* 1667, 1859.

Citron A juicy fruit of the tree *Citrus medica* having a pale yellow rind; it is larger than a lemon, less acid, and has a thicker rind. The term formerly included the lemon and perhaps the lime. The rind is used in confectionery. *OED* 1530, 1870. Preserved melon rind was often called American citron.

Claret Before 1660 any of a number of yellowish or light red wines distinguished from red and white wines. From Latin *clarus*, "clear." *OED* 1400, 1860. Now red wines from Bordeaux.

Clouted Said of thick or clotted cream obtained by scalding or heating milk. *OED* 1542, 1807.

Cochineal A brilliant red dye obtained from the dried bodies of the insect *Coccus cacti*, which feeds on certain cacti. *OED* 1586, 1870.

Cochlearia, or Cochlearin A crystal-like substance obtained from winter cress or scurvy grass. *OED* 1863–72. Fresh green scurvy grass was considered a stimulant and diuretic. *The Americana*, 1903–08.

Codiniac Quince marmalade, quidanny. *OED* 1539, 1668.

Codlin, Codling, Quodling A variety of apple; a hard, half-grown apple. *OED* ca. 1440, 1755.

Collared Rolled up and tied with a string, as a piece of meat from which the bones have been removed; the meat of the head and other parts of the pig, ox, etc., cut into small pieces and pressed into the shape of a roll. *OED* 1681, 1873. Immersed in pickle in a stoneware crock.

Comfit, or Confect Candy, confection, sweetmeat, or sugarplum generally solid, in the shape of a small sphere or egg. Hall, 1829. Sugar-coated caraway seed, almond, etc. *OED* 1334, 1852. From the Latin *confectus*, past participle of *conficere*, "to make with." *London Encyclopedia*, 1829.

Compote Fruit stewed in syrup. *OED* 1693, 1883. Incorrectly used to mean compotier, the footed dish used to hold a compote of fruit.

Compotier Pedestaled or footed dish used to hold a compote of stewed fruit, or fresh fruit, nuts, and candies. *OED* 1885.

Cordial Liquor with properties stimulating to the heart. From the Latin *cor, cordis*, "heart." *OED* ca. 1386, 1847.

Cosset See **Motto.**

Cracknel A light, crisp biscuit of a curved or hollowed shape. *OED* ca. 1440, 1884.

Cream Dessert made of sweetened flavored cream variously colored, jelled, frozen, or plain. *OED* 1430, 1836.

Crewel Loosely twisted wool yarn used for tapestry and embroidery and for making fringes, hosiery, etc. *OED* 1494, 1880.

Curd The coagulated substance formed from milk by the action of acids. In the seventeenth century, curds were often sweetened and eaten with cream. *OED* 1362, 1856.

Damask A rich patterned fabric of wool, cotton, silk, or linen; a twilled linen fabric, woven with a design in satin weave that shows up by opposing reflections of light from the surface. *OED* 1542, 1877.

Darmick, Darnix, Darnock, or Dornick A silk or worsted fabric used for hangings, carpets, vestments, etc. *OED* 1489, 1851. Originally from the Flemish city Doornik, now Tournai, Belgium.

Demijohn A glass or stoneware bottle covered with wickerwork holding from one to ten gallons, usually about five gallons. From the French, *Dame Jeanne*.

Delft Like majolica and faience a tin-glazed earthenware. Made in England and Holland. *OED* 1714, 1884.

Dessert Such fruits and sweetmeats as are served up at the conclusion of a feast. Rolt, 1761. From the French *dessert*, "removal of the dishes." *OED* 1539.

Diaper A fabric of cotton or linen with a pattern of small duplicative diamond-shaped figures. From Medieval Greek, *diaspros: dia*, "thoroughly," and *aspros*, "white," "shining," "new."

Dish Cross A metal cross with four feet, used to raise and support a dish on the table. The same fitted with an oil lamp for raising the dish and maintaining the warmth of the food it holds.

Doily Originally doily-napkin, a small ornamental napkin used at the dessert of fruit and wine. *OED* 1711, 1855. A small ornamental napkin of lace, linen, or other material used to adorn and protect a table.

Dormant A dish that remains on the table throughout a repast; a frame, middleboard, plateau, epergne, surtout (q.v.), or other centerpiece that remains on the table. *OED* ca. 1725, 1845.

Dowlas A coarse kind of linen much used in the sixteenth and seventeenth centuries. *OED* 1493, 1882. Women's shifts, napkins, etc., were made of it.

Dragon See **Gum Dragon.**

Drudger, Dredger, or Drudging Box "The box out of which flour is thrown on roast meat." Sheridan, 1790. "A small, portable box commonly made of brass or tin with small holes bored or punched in the top or cover to let the flour contained in the box come out in a shower upon the meat that is roasting at the fire . . . to dry up the moisture that is upon it, in order to baste it with butter to make it look beautiful to the eye." Dyche and Pardon, 1765.

Entrée 1. Originally a dish served immediately before the main dishes of a meal in the centuries when dishes were brought in to a wealthy man's table in a procession and arranged before him. 2. Now in England a made dish served between the fish and the joint. 3. In the United States the main dish of an ordinary meal or a small dish served between the main courses of a formal dinner.

Entremets Originally a spectacular entertainment between the main courses of a feast. Now side dishes such as vegetables and desserts served in addition to the main courses.

Epergne A center dish or center ornament for the dinner table. *OED* 1761, 1813. Usually holding bottles and/or baskets for condiments, pickles, fruits, and sweetmeats. Perhaps a corruption of the French *épargne*, "saving," "economy." A *surtout de table* (q.v.).

Eryngo, or Eringo Candied aromatic sea holly root, formerly regarded as an aphrodisiac. *OED* 1598, 1848.

Faggot A bundle of sticks, twigs, or small branches bound together. Orange peel cut to resemble twigs and preserved in sugar in small bunches.

Fairing A present given at or brought from a fair. Cakes or sweets sold at fairs, especially little hard ginger cookies called gingerbread nuts. *OED* 1574, 1888.

Fayal An island in the center of the Portuguese-owned Azores in the north Atlantic. A white wine from grapes grown there.

Florentine, or Florendine A kind of pie or tart, especially of meat, baked in a dish with a cover of paste. *OED* 1567, 1870.

Flummery Before the eighteenth century a jelly of fermented, boiled oatmeal. In the eighteenth century any of several soft or jellied desserts such as blancmange or custard. *OED* 1623, 1877.

Fool Before the eighteenth century a kind of clotted cream or custard, spiced and served on bread with sugar and comfits. Now a dessert made of crushed stewed fruit mixed with cream or custard, served cold. *OED* 1598, 1845.

Frame See **Middleboard.**

Fromage The French word for cheese, a mixture, often used in English cookbooks. From the Latin *formare*, "to give form to." Refers to the form obtained after milk is coagulated; pork is ground for sausage; cream, sugar, and eggs are mixed for custard or ice cream (*fromage glacé*, "iced cheese"); etc.

Gamboge A gum resin from trees of the *Garcinia* family, which grow in parts of Southeast Asia (including Cambodia, hence the name). Largely used as a pigment, it gives a bright orange-yellow color.

Gingerbread A plain hard cake or cookie of ginger, molasses, and flour cut into shapes of men, animals, and letters, formerly often covered with gold leaf. Also a plain soft flat ginger and molasses cake. The word is a corruption of the Old French *ginginbras*, "preserved ginger."

Glacier, Glacière, Ice Pail, or Sorbétière A three-part ceramic covered cylinder containing crushed ice and a smaller cylinder to hold fruit ice, sherbet, or ice cream, the cover a shallow cylinder to hold more crushed ice. Used in pairs or quartets on a dessert table.

Granite Ware Late nineteenth-century ironware with a speckled coloring.

Grog A drink consisting of spirits (originally rum) and water. The word is said to be short for grogram, a stiff fabric of mohair and wool, and to have been applied to Admiral Edward Vernon who wore a grogram cloak. It afterward was applied to the mixture the admiral ordered in 1740 to be served to British sailors instead of neat spirits. *OED* 1770, 1883.

Gum Arabic A gum exuded by certain species of acacia tree. Used in confectionery work in powdered form. *OED* 1500, 1866.

Gum Tragacanth, or Gum Dragon A gum exuded by several species of *Astralagus*, a thorny plant found in certain Asiatic and East European regions. Used in powdered form in medicine and confectionery.

Hartshorn A substance obtained by rasping or slicing and calcining the horn or antler of the hart, or male deer. In the eighteenth century used in the form of shavings to be stewed in order to jell blancmanges, flummeries, jellies, etc. *OED* 1796. Formerly the chief source of ammonia and smelling salts (salt of hartshorn) *OED* 1685, 1875.

Hasty Pudding A pudding made of flour, oatmeal, barley meal, or rye meal stirred into boiling milk or water to the consistency of a thick batter. In the United States it is made of cornmeal, formerly called Indian meal, and water. *OED* 1599, 1820.

Hedgehog Pudding Any of several boiled or baked puddings whose upper surface has been stuck about with slivered almonds before serving.

Hippocras A cordial drink of wine and spices, especially pepper, favored largely before the eighteenth century. *OED* ca. 1386, 1843.

Hogshead A large cask to hold 62.5 to 146 gallons of liquids, etc. From the early fifteenth century its capacity was 63 wine gallons, 54 beer gallons, 48 ale gallons, 60 cider gallons. In the late nineteenth century its capacity was 46 claret, 57 port, 54 sherry, 46 madeira. *OED* 1483, 1897.

Holland A linen fabric originally called holland cloth from the Netherland province of Holland. When unbleached, called brown holland. *OED* 1427, 1884. White holland was considered whiter than other white linens, and the term *holland* was extended to other very white linens.

Huckabuck A stout linen fabric with the weft threads thrown alternately up so as to form a rough surface. *OED* 1690, 1876.

Ice A frozen confection. Fruit ice, cream ice, or ice cream. *OED* 1716, 1850.

Iced Cheese See **Fromage.**

Ice Pail See **Glacier,** also **Wine Pail.**

Ironstone A hard kind of white pottery made in the nineteenth century. *OED* 1825, 1897.

Isinglass A firm whitish semitransparent substance obtained from the air bladders of some fresh-water fish, especially the sturgeon, whose name in Old Dutch was *huisenblas*. Used in cookery in making jellies and clarifying liquors. The term is also extended to similar substances made from hides, hooves, etc. and to mica because of its resemblance. *OED* 1527, 1879.

Jelly A food consisting chiefly of gelatine. Sweetened and jelled fruit juice was a dessert jelly eaten with or without whipped cream.

Jelly Glass A footed trumpet-shaped glass used during dessert to hold sweetened jelled fruit juice. At the beginning of the eighteenth century sometimes with two handles. Throughout the rest of the century sometimes with one handle or none.

Johnnycake A flat cake said to be of Negro origin. Made of cornmeal (in the southern United States) and baked before a fire, or of rice (South Carolina) and usually fried in a pan. Origin of the name uncertain but referred to in 1775 as "journey-cake," which may be the original form. *OED* 1775, 1892.

Jumble Small thin sugar cookie usually shaped in a ring, sometimes in the form of a knot. *OED* 1615, 1816.

Junket A dessert of sweetened and flavored milk set with rennet. In England a cream cheese or curds sweetened and flavored and served with scalded cream on the top. Formerly also any sweetmeat, cake, or confection; a delicacy, a kickshaw (q.v.). *OED* ca. 1460, 1881.

Kettle, or Cauldron A broad open vessel used to boil liquors, foods, etc. Dyche and Pardon, 1765. The term *pot* is given to the boiler that grows narrower at the top and the term *kettle* to that which grows wider. Johnson, 1755. *OED* before 700.

Kettledrum An afternoon tea party on a large scale. *OED* 1861, 1888.

Kickshaw A fancy dish in cookery. Sometimes dainty, elegant, and unsubstantial; a trifle, gewgaw. From the French *quelque chose*, "something." *OED* 1598, 1878.

Laced Ornamented or trimmed with lace, with edgings or trimmings of lace, with braids or cords of gold or silver lace. *OED* 1668, 1873.

Lear A sauce of flour, verjuice (q.v.) or vinegar, and spice for adding flavor and digestibility to gravies, meat pies, etc. *OED* ca. 1390, 1837.

Level See **Plateau.**

Linsey Woolsey A textile with wool warp and linen weft woven usually at home in simple under-and-over weave. *OED* 1483, 1855.

Loaf In the seventeenth and eighteenth centuries a loaf of bread was a low rounded cylinder, not rectangular as at present.

Macaroon A small sweet cake consisting chiefly of ground almonds, egg white, and sugar. *OED* 1611, 1898.

Made Dish A dish compounded or made of several sorts of meat minced or cut in pieces, stewed or baked in paste, being liquored with wine, butter, and sugar, as opposed to a plain roast. Holme, 1701.

Majolica A fine kind of Italian pottery coated with an opaque white tin oxide enamel and ornamented with metallic colors; similar to faience, or faienza, and delft. From Majorca (called Majolica in the fourteenth century), where the best ware was made. *OED* 1555, 1673.

Malmsey A strong sweet wine originally the product of Monemvasia (the area around Naples) but now obtained from Spain, the Azores, Madeira, and the Canaries as well as from Greece. *OED* ca. 1475, 1902.

Manchet 1. The finest kind of wheaten bread. *OED* 1420, 1791. 2. A small round and flattish loaf or roll, thicker in the middle than at the ends, made of fine wheaten bread.

Marchpane A paste of sugar and almonds or other nuts made into flat cakes or cookies or molded into ornamental forms. Before the nineteenth century the cookies were often pressed with a decorative mold and covered with gold leaf. *OED* 1494, 1901. Now most often referred to by the German term *marzipan*.

Marlborough Pudding A custard baked with applesauce, jam, or stewed apples in a pastry crust.

Marmolet, or Marmalade A preserve or confection made by boiling fruits (originally quinces) in sugar to form a mass. *OED* 1524, 1862. The consistency of the mass was sometimes like that of jam, sometimes as stiff as fruit paste.

Maser, or Mazer A bowl or footless cup originally made of hardwood, most often maple. *OED* 1311, 1851.

Mass Cake A small sweet wafer, which, although not necessarily made for religious purposes, doubtless has a religious origin.

Medlar A small brown fruit with leathery skin much cultivated in Europe, not unlike a crabapple. When decayed to a pulpy state used as a base for jams and jellies. *OED* 1366, 1873.

Middleboard, or Frame In the seventeenth century a raised hexagonal or star-shaped traylike structure of wood and wicker designed to display and serve pyramided fruit and sweetmeats in the center of a dessert table.

Mold To mix, blend, or knead dough. *OED* 1430, 1841. To shape in or as in a mold. *OED* 1573, 1879.

Monteith A scalloped basin in which to cool glasses. *OED* 1683, 1901. On occasion, used to cool wine bottles or to serve punch. According to a seventeenth-century definition, the term derived from "Monteigh" (pronounced by the Scots monteeth), the name of a "fantastical Scot" who, around 1683, wore a notched coat. *OED* 1683, 1901.

Motto, or Cosset The poetical lines contained in a motto-kiss or sweetmeat wrapped in fancy paper.

Muscadine Old term for a sweet dessert wine made from the muscat, or musky, grape of the southern United States. Also in the seventeenth century a sweetmeat perfumed with musk; sometimes called rising comfits (to be taken on rising?), or kissing comfits. *OED* 1665, 1706.

Muscovado Raw or unrefined sugar obtained from the juice of the sugar cane by evaporation and draining off the molasses without claying. *OED* 1642, 1903.

Naples Biscuit Large (eight inches by three) thick (one inch) sponge cakes or cookies used mainly as a base for nourishing drinks and trifles. In the nineteenth century, small and thin.

Nappy An earthenware or glass dish with sloping sides. *OED* 1873. The term was used by dealers for small sauce dishes in the nineteenth century as it is today.

Neat's Tongue, Neat's Hoof Tongue or hoof of a cow, bullock, ox, or other variety of cattle. *OED* ca. 825, 1895.

Negus A drink named about 1732 for Colonel Francis Negus, who was especially fond of it. Made of wine (most often port or sherry) and hot water sweetened with honey and flavored with lemon and nutmeg. *OED* 1743, 1843.

Nog, or Nogg A strong beer or ale especially brewed in East Anglia. *OED* 1693, 1893.

Nonpareil Minute colored comfit, called also harlequin seed. *OED* 1697, 1862.

Noyau, or Noyeau A liqueur made of whiskey or brandy and milk flavored with crushed almonds and lemons or the kernels of peaches or apricots. *OED* 1797, 1882.

Orgeat A syrup or cooling drink made originally from barley (French *orge*), later from almonds and orange-flower water. Pronounced "orjah." *OED* 1754, 1864.

Paste 1. A sort of thick marmalade made by boiling fruit to the point of its being able to retain all sorts of forms; after the paste has been put in molds it is dried in the oven. Diderot, 1751–65. 2. Flour moistened with water or milk and kneaded; dough; also such dough with the addition of butter, lard, suet, or the like used in making pastry. *OED* 1377, 1888. 3. Various sweet confections of doughy consistency made of sugar, spices, and gum tragacanth. *OED* 1389, 1858.

Pastry The collective term for articles of food made of flour paste. *OED* 1539, 1844.

Pasty Something made of or with flour paste. A pie, usually of meat, enclosed in a crust of pastry and baked without a dish; a meat pie. *OED* 1300, 1880.

Patty A little pie or pastry. From the Old French *pasté* and modern French *pâté*, "pasty." *OED* 1710, 1870.

Pennyroyal A small-leaved European mint that grows low to the ground. Also several western American oil-producing herbs formerly used in medicine. *OED* 1530, 1858.

Persimmon Small pink-orange fruit of trees of the genus *Diospyros* edible only when ripe. The name of Algonquin Indian origin having to do with dried fruit.

Pièce Montée A large table decoration popular in the nineteenth century. Made of cast, or molded, sugar and gum tragacanth and pieces of pastry sculpted and put together with sugar mortar in the forms of temples, cottages, windmills, etc. A set piece made up of joined parts as opposed to being cast in one piece.

Pipe A large cask used especially for wine or oil equal to half a tun, two hogsheads, or four barrels (q.v.). It holds 138 modern United States gallons or 105 British imperial gallons; in the fifteenth century it held 126 wine gallons. Sometimes identified with butt (q.v.). *OED* 1376, 1842.

Pipkin A small metal or earthenware straight-handled pot or pan used chiefly in cookery. *OED* 1565, 1854.

Pippin The name of numerous varieties of apple raised from seed. *OED* 1432, 1866. A green, roundish apple, sometimes reddish on the side. Holme, 1701.

Plat de Ménage A large platter or plateau holding, as some epergnes do, casters, bottles, and baskets for the necessities of the table.

Plate Such domestic silver or gold hollowware as dishes, bowls, platters, flagons, cups. *OED* ca. 1400, 1885.

Plateau, or Level A three-part mirrored tray with gallery holding figures and candlesticks used as a table centerpiece in the late eighteenth and early nineteenth century. *OED* 1791, 1861.

Plum Pudding A boiled bag pudding filled with raisins and/or currants. The word *plum* probably a carryover from the day dried plums, or prunes, were used in the pudding. *OED* 1660, 1884.

Pomecitron Large citron (q.v.). *OED* 1555, 1709.

Porringer A round one- or two-handled ceramic or metal bowl out of which food was eaten. In America and some areas of England a porringer was a shallow bowl. In other parts of England it was deep. *OED* 1522, 1871.

Porter A kind of beer of a dark brown color and bitter taste brewed from malt partly charred or browned by drying at a high temperature. The name probably was applied because the beer originally was made for or chiefly drunk by porters and the lower class of laborer. *OED* 1727, 1846.

Posnet A metal pot or skillet with three feet and a long straight handle. *OED* 1327, 1863.

Posset A drink composed of hot milk curdled with ale, wine, or other liquid, sugared, thickened with naples biscuit, eggs, or porridge, and spiced. *OED* ca. 1440, 1876.

Pot 1. Ceramic or metal cylindrical drinking vessel. 2. A metal vessel used in cooking. A "flesh pott," according to Holme, 1701, was a sloping cylinder with three feet and two short side handles. Dyche and Pardon, 1765, said that a pot was hung over the fire by an iron bail or handle.

Potash Potassium carbonate, white transparent granular powder isolated by Sir Humphry Davy (1778–1829) from wood ashes leached in a pot, the lye evaporated, and the residue calcined. An ingredient of soft soap. When purified called pearlash. In the eighteenth century sometimes used as a leaven in baking.

Pudding 1. A mixture of meat, suet, oatmeal, and seasoning boiled in the stomach or one of the entrails of a pig, sheep, or other animal. *OED* ca. 1305, 1801. 2. A mixture of flour, bread, gruel, sugar, fruit, and spices boiled or steamed in such a container, in a cloth, or in a bowl covered with a cloth. 3. A mixture of flour, fruit, eggs, and flavorings baked in a crust-lined dish. 4. Such a mixture baked in a dish without a crust. *OED* 1544, 1883.

Pyramid Any conelike or triangular figure, object, or formation suggestive of a pyramid. A pyramid of fruit, a pyramid of sweetmeats, a pyramid of salvers of graduated sizes.

Queen Cake A round white loaf cake usually iced with hard white icing, very popular in the eighteenth century.

Queen's Cake, or Queen's Biscuit A small currant cake either diamond- or heart-shaped, sometimes iced.

Queensware A light-bodied earthenware with lead glaze introduced by Josiah Wedgwood in Staffordshire in 1750 and named in honor of Queen Charlotte, wife of George III.

Quodling See **Codlin.**

Ramekin A small vessel. The term originally meant a mixture of cheese, bread crumbs, and eggs baked in a small pan or in a pie pan. *OED* 1706, 1894.

Ratafia A cordial or liqueur flavored with certain fruits and their kernels, usually peach, cherry, or apricot, and almonds. *OED* 1699, 1852.

Ratafia Drop A cookie having the flavor of ratafia or made with almond paste to be eaten along with the drink. *OED* 1845, ca. 1870.

Remove The act of taking away a dish or dishes at a meal in order to put others in their place; a dish thus removed or brought on in place of one removed. *OED* 1773, 1852.

Roman Punch A drink made of lemons, spirits, and water. *OED* 1757, 1828. Such a drink with frozen sherbet added, or the frozen drink itself, much used between courses of Victorian dinners to clear the palate.

Rosewater Water distilled from roses or impregnated with essence of roses and used as a perfume or in confectionery. *OED* 1398, 1898.

Roundel A circular wooden trencher (q.v.). In England most often of beechwood. In Elizabethan times provided for a spice banquet in sets of twelve, often painted or otherwise decorated, and often containing verses.

Rout 1. A company, assembly, band, or troop of persons, cattle, or things. 2. A disorderly or disreputable crowd of persons. 3. A fashionable gathering or assembly; a large evening party or reception much in vogue in the eighteenth and early nineteenth centuries. *OED* 1742, 1898.

Sack A class of white wines formerly imported from Spain and the Canaries. *OED* 1536, 1771.

Saleratus A name applied by Americans in the early nineteenth century to sodium bicarbonate, or baking soda. *Sal aeratus*, "aerated salt."

Savoy Cake, or Sponge Cake A large sponge cake baked in a mold. *OED* 1764, 1892.

Savoy Cake, or Savoy Drop An oval or finger-shaped sponge cookie sifted over with sugar. From the mid-nineteenth century called lady fingers.

Seville Orange The bitter orange (*Citrus bigaradia*) grown best near Seville in Spain. *OED* 1593, 1892.

Shaddock The fruit of *Citrus decumana*, also called pompelmoose, resembling an orange but very much larger. In stricter use applied to the large pear-shaped varieties, the smaller and rounder being called grapefruit. Named after a Captain Shaddock who, it is said, took the fruit to Barbados. *OED* 1696, 1884.

Shrewsbury Cake A flat, round, crisp, sugar cookie flavored with cinnamon, nutmeg, or cardamom, and caraway seeds. *OED* 1728, 1849.

Shrub 1. A drink made with the juice of oranges or lemons or other acid fruit and with sugar, rum, or other spirit. *OED* 1747, 1863. 2. In the United States in the nineteenth century a cordial or syrup made from the juice of the raspberry with vinegar and sugar. *OED* 1860, 1884. 3. A syrup made of spirits, fruit juice, fruit rind, and sugar aged in crockery, glass, or wood to be diluted with water and drunk. E. Smith, 1742. Like the words *Sherbet* and *Sorbet*, from the Arabic *Sharbah* and *Sharab*, "drink," "beverage."

Side One of the dishes that in the eighteenth century were ranged down the side of a table. Side dish, entrée (q.v.). *OED* 1848.

Snow A light, white dessert of sweetened whipped cream and/or beaten egg whites with flavoring. Apple Snow. *OED* 1597, 1887.

Sorbet, or Sherbet 1. A drink. *OED* 1585, 1844. 2. An ice. *OED* 1864, 1885. See also **Shrub.**

Sorbétière See **Glacier.**

Spice, or Spicery Throughout England between the fourteenth and sixteenth centuries and in certain locations thereafter a term for raisins, dried plums, figs, and currants, also sweetmeats and gingerbread. *OED* 1300, 1855.

Spirits Any of various liquids produced by distillation such as brandy and usquebaugh, or whiskey. *OED* 1610, 1884.

Standing Dish A dish that appears on the table each day or at every meal. Standing as in *standing offer*. *OED* n.d.

Standing Pie A meat pie of hard cylindrical crust that maintains an upright position without support.

Steeple Cream A cream fashioned into a form pointed at the top. *OED* 1747, 1769.

Stove A set of shelves made of wire to hold sweetmeats

that are to be dried. *OED* 1706, 1769. A press cupboard with a dish of charcoal in the bottom. De Lasteyrie, 1820.

Subtlety A highly ornamented device wholly or chiefly made of sugar and gum, sometimes eaten, sometimes used merely as a table decoration. The term little used after the sixteenth century. *OED* ca. 1390, 1552.

Sucket, Succade, or Succate Fruit, fruit rind, and nuts preserved in sugar, either candied or in syrup. Sweetmeats of candied fruit. The term little used after the eighteenth century. *OED* 1463, 1836.

Sugar-Bread Sugared bread. Harrison, 1577, in Wilson, 1968.

Sugar-Plate A confection or sweetmeat made in a flat cake, sometimes formed with a decorative flat wooden mold. The term not much used after the seventeenth century. *OED* 1355, 1688.

Sugarplum A small round or oval sweetmeat made of boiled sugar and various flavors, sometimes colored. See **Comfit.** *OED* 1608, 1883.

Sunderland Pudding A light, spongy custard flavored with nutmeg and eaten with a sauce of sugar and wine.

Surtout, or *Surtout de Table* A decorative and useful object, usually of silver or of silver and glass holding oil bottles, sugar shakers, fruit and/or pickles and sweetmeats that remains in the center of a table during an entire meal. Gilliers, 1768. An epergne. *The New Cassell's French Dictionary*, 1965. Also applied to various fancy dishes such as pistachios in surtout, pigeons dressed in surtout, a surtout of soles. *OED* 1706, 1743.

Sweetmeat 1. Dry sucket of glacéed or glazed fruit, fruit peel, nuts, flowers; comfits of aromatic seeds covered with sugar; cake, cakes, cookies. 2. Wet sucket of fruit in heavy syrup; stewed, preserved, or brandied fruit (the usual meaning in the nineteenth century); jellies and creams (in the eighteenth century).

Sweetmeat Glass A broad bell-shaped bowl with tall stem and foot. For holding dry sweetmeats on a dessert table or on the summit of a pyramid of salvers. Before ca. 1715 short stemmed and not used on pyramids. Some before 1760 with open basketwork of looped glass, some from ca. 1740 of cut glass.

Sweetmeat Pole The eighteenth-century term for a glass epergne consisting of a center pole with horizontal arms holding baskets for dry sweetmeats and/or pickles.

Syllabub, or Sillabub 1. A drink or dish made of milk (frequently as drawn from the cow) or cream curdled by the admixture of wine, cider, or other acid and often sweetened and flavored. Largely eaten in curdled form before the eighteenth century. Origin of the term obscure. *OED* ca. 1537, 1861. 2. A drink or dish made of cream whipped with wine, lemon, and sugar.

Syllabub Glass A footed lily-shaped glass of the eighteenth century with top third spreading to hold froth. Somewhat larger than the jelly glass. Also used to hold creams.

Tamarind, or Tamarine The fruit of the tree *Tamarindus indica*, a brown pod containing one to twelve seeds embedded in soft brown or reddish black acid pulp, valued for its medicinal qualities and also used in cookery as a relish. *OED* 1533, 1872. In the eighteenth century the pulp of the pod was freed from its stringy fibers and preserved in syrup in casks and glass.

Tansy An erect herbaceous plant, *Tanacetum vulgare*, growing about two feet high with deeply cut and divided leaves and yellow, buttonlike flowers. All parts of the plant have a strong aromatic scent and bitter taste. Formerly used in medicine as a stomachic and for flavoring desserts. Also used like parsley for garnishing dishes. *OED* ca. 1265, 1885.

Tart The term used for various dishes consisting of a crust of baked pastry enclosing different ingredients; formerly with meat, fish, cheese, fruit, etc., the same or nearly the same as a pie. In current use restricted to (1) a flat, usually small piece of pastry with no crust on the top (so distinguished from a pie) filled with fruit or jam; (2) a covered fruit pie, formerly dialectical or local, now in polite or fashionable use. *OED* 1400, 1899. In the United States recently a small open, closed, or latticed baked crust filled with fruit or jam or other sweet mixture.

Tazza A shallow ornamental bowl or vase, properly one supported on a foot. From the Italian *tazza*, "cup." *OED* 1841, 1895. Sometimes in the early twentieth century incorrectly applied to a footed salver.

Toy A small article of little intrinsic value but prized as an ornament or curiosity; a knickknack, trinket, gewgaw. *OED* 1596, 1888. The term used in this way among others in the eighteenth century to refer to the ceramic figurines that decorated mantels and dessert tables.

Tragacanth See **Gum Tragacanth.**

Trencher 1. Before the sixteenth century a slice of bread used as a plate or platter. *OED* ca. 1380, 1490. 2. A flat piece of wood, square or circular, on which meat was served and cut up; a plate or platter of wood, metal, or earthenware. From the French *trancher*, "to cut," and *tranche*, "slice" (as of bread).

Trifle 1. A dish composed of cream boiled with various spices. A kind of clouted cream. *OED* 1598, 1736. 2. A light confection of sponge cake or naples biscuit drenched with wine or spirit and served with custard and whipped cream or whipped syllabub. From the Italian *truffa*, "trickery," "deception." *OED* 1781, 1860.

Tun A large cask or barrel, usually for liquids, especially wine, ale, or beer but also for other provisions. Equal to two pipes and four hogsheads containing 252 old wine gallons. *OED* ca. 725, 1909. Equals 302½ modern American gallons.

Verjuice The acid juice of green or unripe grapes, crabapples, or other sour fruit, formerly used in cooking as a condiment or for medicinal purposes. *OED* 1302, 1881. Since the mid nineteenth century supplanted by vinegar. Also in the nineteenth century used as a rub for sprains.

Void, or Voyd 1. An abbreviation of voide, voidee, voydee (q.v.), a small repast. *OED* 1461, 1616. 2. To clean a table of dishes, the remains of food, etc., after a meal. *OED* 1400, 1657.

Voide, Voidee, or Voydee Sometimes void, or voyd. A collation consisting of wine accompanied by spices, comfits, or the like partaken of before retiring to rest or the departure of guests; a repast of this nature following upon a feast. A parting dish. *OED* ca. 1374, 1650.

Voider, or Voyder 1. A tray, basket, or other vessel in which dirty dishes or utensils, fragments of broken food, etc., are placed in clearing the table or during a meal. *OED* 1466. 2. A tray, basket, or large plate, especially one of ornamental pattern or design, for holding, carrying, or handing around sweetmeats. *OED* 1676, 1706.

Whig, or Wig A kind of bun or small cake made of fine flour, yeast, currants, etc. Usually square or triangular in shape. *OED* 1376, 1888.

Whortleberry A sweet, edible European blackberry (*Vaccinium ovatum*) that is purplish black with a glaucous bloom. Has come to mean huckleberry (*Gaylussia*) or blueberry (*Vaccinium*), although a huckleberry is smaller and more acid than a blueberry.

Wine Pail An urn-shaped or cylindrical vessel designed to sit on a table and hold a wine bottle cold in water or ice. Made in pairs or in sets of four or more.

A Selected Bibliography

BOOKS AND ARTICLES

Adams, Charles Francis, ed. *Letters of Mrs. Adams, the Wife of John Adams*. 2 vols. 2d ed. Boston: Charles C. Little & James Brown, 1840.

Adams, Samuel, and Sarah. *The Complete Servant: Being a Practical Guide to the Peculiar Duties and Business of All Descriptions of Servants*. . . . London: Knight & Lacey, 1825.

Alberts, Robert C. *The Golden Voyage: The Life and Times of William Bingham, 1752–1804*. Boston: Houghton Mifflin & Co., 1969.

The Americana: A Universal Reference Library. New York: Scientific American, 1903–08.

Ames, Winslow. *Prince Albert and Victorian Taste*. London: Chapman & Hall, 1968.

Armes, Ethel, ed. *Nancy Shippen: Her Journal Book*. 2 vols. Philadelphia: J. Lippincott Co., 1935.

Arnstein, Walter L., trans. and ed. "A German View of Society." *Victorian Studies* 16, no. 2 (December 1972): 183–203.

Austen, Jane. *Mansfield Park*. 1814. New ed. New York: Pantheon Books, 1949.

Austin, John. "Williamsburg: The Ceramics." *Antiques* 95, no. 1 (January 1969): 112–20.

Avery, C. Louise. *Early American Silver*. New York and London: Century Co., 1930.

Bacon, Francis. *Sylva Sylvarum; or, A Naturall Historie*. 2d ed. London: Printed by J. H. for William Lee, 1628.

Bailer, J. L., rev. *Neues Orbis Pictus für die Jügend . . . nach der Früdern Aulage des Comenius* . . . . Reutlingen: J. C. Maecken, 1838.

Bailey, Nathan. *Dictionarium Domesticum: Being a New and Compleat Household Dictionary*. London: C. Hitch et al., 1736.

Balston, Thomas, ed. *The Housekeeping Book of Susanna Whatman, 1776–1800*. London: Geoffrey Bles, 1956.

Barger, B. D., ed. "Governor Tryon's House in Fort George." *New York History: The Quarterly Journal of the New York Historical Association* 35, no. 3 (July 1954): 297–309.

Beale, Harriet S. Blaine, ed. *Letters of Mrs. James G. Blaine*. 2 vols. New York: Duffield & Co., 1908.

Beawes, Wyndham. *Lex Mercatoria Rediviva; or, The Merchants' Dictionary: Being a Compleat Guide to All Men in Business* . . . . London: J. Moore, 1752.

Beecher, Catharine Esther. *Letters to Persons Who Are Engaged in Domestic Service*. New York: Leavitt & Trow, 1842.

———. *Miss Beecher's Domestic Receipt Book: Designed as a Supplement to Her Treatise on Domestic Economy*. 1846. 3d ed. New York: Harper & Bros., 1848.

———. *A Treastise on Domestic Economy for the Use of Young Ladies at Home and at School*. Rev. ed. New York: Harper & Bros., 1848.

Beeton, Isabella. *The Book of Household Management*. London: S. O. Beeton, 1861.

———. *The Book of Household Management*. New ed., rev. and corr. London: Ward, Lock & Co., [1880].

Benson, Evelyn Abraham, ed. *Penn Family Recipes: Cooking Recipes of William Penn's Wife, Gulielma*. York, Pa.: George Shumway, 1966.

Bitting, Katherine Golden. *Gastronomic Bibliography*. San Francisco: A. W. Bitting, 1939.

Blount, Thomas. *Glossographia; A Dictionary, Interpreting all . . . words . . . now used in our Refined English Tongue* . . . . 2d ed. London: Printed by Thomas Newcomb for George Sawbridge, 1661.

Boune, Eliza Southgate. *A Girl's Life Eighty Years Ago*. New York: Charles Scribner's Sons, 1887.

Bridenbaugh, Carl. *Vexed and Troubled Englishmen, 1590–1642*. New York: Oxford University Press, 1967.

———, ed., *Gentleman's Progress: The Itinerarium of Dr. Alexander Hamilton, 1744*. Williamsburg, Va.: Institute of Early American History and Culture, 1948.

Briggs, Richard. *The New Art of Cookery According to the Present Practice*. 1788. Philadelphia: W. Spottswood, R. Campbell & E. Johnson, 1792.

Brillat-Savarin, Jean Anthelme. *The Physiology of Taste; or, Meditations on Transcendental Gastronomy*. 1825.

1st Am. trans., 1854. Reprint. New York: Dover Publications, 1960.

Brock, R. Alonzo, ed. "Journal of William Black, 1744." *Pennsylvania Magazine of History and Biography* 1, no. 2 (1877): 117–32, 233–49, 404–19.

Buckley, Francis. *A History of Old English Glass*. London: Ernest Benn, 1925.

Busk, Henry. *The Dessert: A Poem*. London: Printed for Baldwin, Cradock & Joy, 1819.

Le Cabinet du Roi [Paris]: n.p., n.d. Volume titled on spine *Festes à Versailles*. [1727].

Cadbury, Sarah. "Extracts from the Diary of Mrs. Ann Warder, [1786–88]." *Pennsylvania Magazine of History and Biography* 17, no. 4 (1893): 444–61.

Caraman, Pierre de. "Les Bonheurs et les dangers du Comte de Caraman, ou la vie d'un gentilhomme au XVIIIe Siècle Illustrée par lui-meme." *L'Illustration*, no. 4787 (December 1, 1934): n.p.

Carter, Charles. *The Compleat Practical Cook, or, A New System of the Whole Art and Mystery of Cookery*. London: W. Meadows et al., 1730.

Case, B. *Accomplish'd Female Instructor*. London: J. Knapton, 1704.

Cassell's Household Guide: Being a Complete Encyclopedia of Domestic and Social Economy . . . . 4 vols. London, Paris, and New York: Cassell, Petter, & Galpin, [187–].

Cayford, Jane. "The Sullivan Dorr House in Providence, Rhode Island." Master's thesis, University of Delaware, 1961.

Child, Lydia Maria. *The Frugal Housewife Dedicated to Those Who Are Not Ashamed of Economy*. Boston: Marsh & Capen, and Carter & Hendee, 1829.

Colchester, Charles, Lord, ed. *Diary and Correspondence of Charles Abbot, Lord Colchester*. 3 vols. London: J. Murray, 1861.

The Compleat Cook, Expertly Prescribing the Most Ready Wayes, Whether Italian, Spanish, or French, for Dressing of Flesh and Fish, Ordering of Sauces, or Making of Pastry. 1655. London: Printed by T. C. for Nathaniel Brook, 1662.

Cornelius, Mary Hooker. *The Young Housekeeper's Friend; or, A Guide to Domestic Economy and Comfort*. Boston: Tappan, Whittemore & Mason, 1850.

Corson, Juliet. *Practical American Cookery and Household Management*. New York: Dodd Mead & Co., 1886.

Cosnett, Thomas. *The Footman's Directory and Butler's Remembrancer*. London: Simpkin & Marshall, Henry Holburn, et al., 1825 (date on cover, 1826).

Coulter, E. Merton, ed. *Journal of William Stephens, 1741–43*. Athens, Ga.: University of Georgia Press, 1958.

Cummings, Abbott Lowell. *Rural Household Inventories: Establishing the Names, Uses and Furnishings of Rooms in the Colonial New England Home, 1675–1775*. Boston: The Society for the Preservation of New England Antiquities, 1964.

De Lasteyrie, Le Conte. *Collection de machines, d'instrumens, etc.* 2 vols. Paris, 1820.

de Valinger, Leon, ed. *A Calendar of Ridgley Papers: Letters, 1742–1899*. 3 vols. Dover, Del.: Published privately, 1948.

Diderot, Denis, ed. *Encyclopédie, ou dictionnaire raisonné des sciences, des arts, et des métiers*. Paris: Briasson, 1751–65. 17 vols. *Recueil des planches sur les sciences, les arts libéraux et les arts méchaniques*. 11 vols. Paris: Briasson, 1762–72.

The Domestic's Companion: Comprising the Most Perfect, Easy, and Expeditious Methods of Getting Through Their Work . . . . New York: Edward W. Martin, 1834. Bound with M'Getrick, *The Housewife's Guide*.

Dow, George Francis. *The Arts and Crafts in New England, 1704–1775*. Topsfield, Mass.: Wayside Press, 1927.

———. *Every Day Life in the Massachusetts Bay Colony*. Boston: The Society for the Preservation of New England Antiquities, 1935.

———, ed. *The Probate Records of Essex County, Masachusetts, 1635–*. Salem, Mass.: The Essex Institute, 1916–.

Duncan, John Morison. *Travels Through Part of the United States and Canada in 1818 and 1819*. 2 vols. New York: W. B. Gilley, 1823.

Dutton, Joan Parry. *The Flower World of Williamsburg*. Williamsburg, Va.: Colonial Williamsburg, 1962.

Dyche, Thomas. *A New General English Dictionary*. 12th ed. London: C. & R. Ware, 1765. Begun by Dyche, finished by William Pardon.

Eberlein, Harold Donaldson, and Cortlandt Van Dyke Hubbard. *Portrait of a Colonial City: Philadelphia, 1670–1838*. New York and Philadelphia: J. B. Lippincott, 1939.

Elville, E. M. *Paper Weights and Other Glass Curiosities*. London: Country Life, 1957.

Emerson, Lucy. *New England Cookery; or, The Art of Dressing All Kinds of Flesh, Fish, and Vegetables and the Best Modes of Making Pastes, Puffs, Pies, Tarts, Puddings, Custards, and Preserves, and All Kinds of Cakes, from the Imperial Plumb to Plain Cake. Particularly Adapted to This Part of Our Country*. Montpelier, Vt.: Josiah Parks, 1808.

Emy. *L'Art de bien faire les glaces d'office, ou les vrais principes pour congeler tous les rafraîchissements*. Paris: Chez Le Clerc, 1768.

Erath, S. L., ed. *The Plimouth Colony Cook Book.* 2d ed. Plymouth, Mass.: Plymouth Antiquarian Society, 1964.

Everson, Jennie G. *Tidewater Ice of the Kennebec River.* Freeport, Me.: Maine State Museum, 1970.

The Expert Waitress: A Manual for the Pantry and Dining Room. New York: Harper & Bros., 1912.

The Family and Householder's Guide; or, How to Keep House . . . . Auburn, N.Y.: Auburn Publishing Co., 1859.

Family Receipt-Book; or, Universal Repository of Useful Knowledge and Experience in all the Various Branches of Domestic Economy . . . . London: Oddy & Co., W. Oddy, [ca. 1811].

Family Receipt-Book Containing 800 Valuable Receipts in Various Branches of Domestic Economy. . . . 2d Am. ed. Pittsburgh: Randolph Barnes, 1819.

Farley, John. *The London Art of Cookery and Housekeeper's Complete Assistant.* 1783. 7th ed. London: J. Scatcherd, J. Whitaker, G. & T. Wilkie, 1792.

[Farrar, Eliza Ware]. *The Young Lady's Friend.* By a Lady. Boston: American Stationers' Co., John B. Russell, 1836.

Fearon, Henry Bradshaw. *Sketches of America: A Narrative of a Journey of Five Thousand Miles Through the Eastern and Western States of America . . . .* 2d ed. London: Longman, Hurst, Rees, Orme, & Brown, 1818.

Fennelly, Catherine, ed. *Food, Drink, and Recipes of Early New England.* Old Sturbridge Village, Mass., 1964.

Fitch, Edward Oliver, ed., *The Diaries of Benjamin Lynde and Benjamin Lynde, Jr.* Boston: Privately printed, Cambridge, Riverside Press, 1880.

Fitzpatrick, John C., ed. *Writings of Washington from the Original Manuscript Sources, 1745–1799.* 39 vols. Washington, D.C.: U.S. Government Printing Agency, 1938.

Franklin, Benjamin. "Distresses of a Modest Man." In *Father Abraham's Almanac.* Philadelphia: H. P. Rice, 1802.

Furnishing Plan for the Bishop White House. 2 vols. Philadelphia: Independence National Historical Park, 1961.

Garrett, Theodore F., ed. *The Encyclopaedia of Practical Cookery: A Complete Dictionary of All Pertaining to the Art of Cookery and Table Service.* 8 vols. Philadelphia: Hudson Importing Co., 1890.

Giffen, Jane [Cayford], ed. "The Estate of Madam Elizabeth Wentworth of Portsmouth [1802]." *Historical New Hampshire* 23, no. 1 (Spring 1968): 31–49.

Gillespie, Charles C., ed. *A Diderot Pictorial Encyclopedia of Trades and Industry.* 2 vols. New York: Dover Publications, 1959.

Gilliers, Joseph. *Le Cannameliste français ou nouvelle instruction pour ceux qui désirent d'apprendre l'office.* Nancy: Nancy: Jean-Baptiste-Hiacinthe Leclerc, 1768.

Gillingham, Harrold E. "The Estate of Jonathan Dickinson (1663–1722)." *Pennsylvania Magazine of History and Biography* 59, no. 4 (October 1935): 420–29.

Glasse, Hannah. *The Art of Cookery Made Plain and Easy.* 1747. 7th ed. London: A. Miller, R. Tomson, et al., 1760.

———. *The Art of Cookery Made Plain and Easy.* 1747. New ed. Alexandria, Va.: Cottom & Stewart, 1805.

———. *The Complete Confectioner.* 1760. Reprint. New York: R. Scott, 1807.

Gloag, John. *A Short Dictionary of Furniture.* Rev. and enl. London: George Allen & Unwin, 1969.

Gottesman, Rita Susswein. *The Arts and Crafts in New York, 1726–1776: Advertisements and News Items from New York Newspapers.* New York: The New-York Historical Society, 1938.

Grant, Anne [MacVicar]. *Memoirs of an American Lady: With Sketches of Manners and Scenes in America, as They Existed Previous to the Revolution.* 1808. Reprint. Albany: Joel Munsell, 1876.

Greene, Jack P., ed. *The Diary of Colonel Landon Carter of Sabine Hall, 1752–78.* 2 vols. Charlottesville, Va.: Virginia Historical Society, University Press of Virginia, 1965.

Hagger, Conrad. *Neues Saltzburgisches Koch-buch.* Augsburg, 1719.

Hale, Sara Josepha. *The Good Housekeeper: or, The Way to Live Well and to be Well While We Live.* 2d ed. Boston: Weeks, Jordan & Co., 1839.

———. *The Ladies' New Book of Cookery: A Practical System for Private Families in Town and Country.* 5th ed. New York: H. Long & Bro., 1852.

Handlin, Oscar. *This Was America.* Cambridge: Harvard University Press, 1949.

Harrison, Sarah. *The House-Keeper's Pocket-Book, and Compleat Family Cook.* London: T. Worrall, 1733.

———. *The House-Keeper's Pocket-Book, and Compleat Family Cook.* 1733. 4th ed. London: R. Ware, 1748.

Henderson, Mary F. *Practical Cooking and Dinner Giving.* New York: Harper & Bros., 1880.

Hillard, George S., ed. *Life, Letters, and Journal of George Ticknor.* 2 vols. Boston: J. R. Osgood & Co., 1876.

Holme, Randle. *The Academy of Armoury; or, A Display of Heraldry.* Vol. 1 (Books 1, 2, 3 [first 13 chapters]). 1688. London and Westminster, 1701. Vol. 2. M. I. H. Jeayes, ed. London: Roxburghe Club of London Publications, 1905.

The Home Cook Book: Compiled from Recipes Contributed by Ladies of Chicago . . . . Chicago: J. Fred Waggoner, 1876.

Horner, John. *The Linen Trade of Europe During the Spinning Wheel Period.* Belfast: M'Caw, Stevenson & Orr, 1920.

Howard, Mrs. B. C. *Fifty Years in a Maryland Kitchen.* 3d ed. Baltimore: Turnbull Bros., 1877.

Howland, Esther Allen. *The American Economical Housekeeper and Family Receipt Book.* Worcester, Mass.: William Allen, 1845.

———. *The New England Economical Housekeeper, and Family Receipt Book.* Worcester, Mass.: S. Howland, 1847.

Hughes, G. Bernard. *English, Scottish, and Irish Table Glass.* New York: Bramhall House, 1956.

———. "The Old English Banquet." *Country Life* 117, no. 3031 (February 17, 1955): 473–75.

Inventory of the Contents of Mount Vernon, 1810. Portland, Oreg.: Kilham Stationery & Printing Co., 1909.

Irving, Washington [Diedrich Knickerbocker]. *A History of New York.* 1809. Author's rev. ed. New York: G. P. Putnam, 1861.

Irvington, Alex. *Reminiscences of America in 1869 by Two Englishmen.* 2d ed., rev. London: Stow & Son and Marston, 1870.

Jamison, John Franklin, ed. *Johnson's Wonder-Working Providence of Sion's Saviour in New England, 1628–1651.* Reprint. New York: Barnes & Noble, 1946.

Jarrin, G. A. *The Italian Confectioner; or, Complete Economy of Desserts.* London: J. Harding and the Author, 1820.

Johnson, Mary. *Madam Johnson's Present; or, The Best Instructions for Young Women in Useful and Universal Knowledge . . . .* 1753. 2d ed. London: H. Owen, 1759.

Johnson, Samuel. *A Dictionary of the English Language.* 6th ed. 2 vols. London: C. Rivington, L. Davis, T. Payne & Son, et al., 1785.

Jones, Alice Hanson. *American Colonial Wealth: Documents and Methods.* 2 vols. New York: Arno Press, 1977.

"Jones Papers: From the Originals in the Library of Congress." *Virginia Magazine of History and Biography* 26, no. 2 (April 1918): 162–81.

Josselyn, John. *Two Voyages to New-England Made During the Years 1638, 1663.* 1674. Reprint. Boston: William Veazie, 1865.

Kalm, Peter. *Travels into North America: Containing Its Natural History, and a Circumstantial Account of Its Plantations and Agriculture in General . . . .* 1754. 2d ed. 2 vols. Translated by John Reinhold Forster. London: T. Lowndes, 1772.

Kennedy, John P. *Memoirs of the Life of William Wirt, Attorney General of the United States.* 2 vols. Philadelphia: Lea & Blanchard, 1849–50.

Kimball, Marie. *The Martha Washington Cook Book.* New York: Coward-McCann, 1940.

———. *Thomas Jefferson's Cook Book.* Richmond, Va.: Garrett & Massie, 1938.

Kihn, Phyllis. "Captain Solomon Ingraham Died at Madras, India, August 15, 1805." *Connecticut Historical Society Bulletin* 29, no. 1 (January 1964): 17–32.

Kitchiner, William. *The Cook's Oracle: Containing Receipts for Plain Cookery on the Most Economical Plan for Private Families . . . .* Boston: Munroe & Francis, 1822.

Ladies' Delight or Cook-Maids' Best Instructor. London: Henry Woodgate & Samuel Brooks, 1759.

Lea, Elizabeth E. *Domestic Cookery, Useful Receipts, and Hints to Young Housekeepers.* Baltimore: H. Colburn, 1845.

Lee, Edmund Jennings, ed. *Lee of Virginia.* Philadelphia: Edward Jennings Lee [Franklin Printing Co.], 1895.

Leslie, Eliza. *Miss Leslie's New Cookery Book.* Philadelphia: T. B. Peterson & Bros., 1859.

———. *New Receipts for Cooking: Containing All the New and Approved Methods . . . .* Philadelphia: T. B. Peterson, 1854.

———. *Seventy-five Receipts for Pastry, Cakes, and Sweetmeats.* 1827. Boston: Munroe & Francis, 1828.

———. *Seventy-five Receipts for Pastry, Cakes, and Sweetmeats.* 1827. Boston: Munroe & Francis, 1845.

"Letter Written by a Gentleman to a Lady in the Country . . . July 16, 1782." *Columbian Magazine* (Philadelphia) 1 (February 1787): 260.

"Letters of Charles Carroll, Barrister." *Maryland Historical Magazine* 37, no. 1 (March 1942): 57–68; 38, no. 2 (June 1943): 181–91; 38, no. 4 (December 1943): 362–69.

"Letters of William Byrd 2d of Westover, Virginia." *Virginia Magazine of History and Biography* 9, no. 2 (October 1901): 113–30; 9, no. 3 (January 1902): 225–51.

A Little Pretty Pocket-Book. Worcester, Mass.: Isaiah Thomas, 1787.

The London Encyclopedia or Universal Dictionary. 22 vols. London: Thomas Tegg, 1829.

Lossing, Benson J. *The Home of Washington.* Hartford: A. S. Hale & Co., 1870.

———. *Mount Vernon and Its Associations Historical, Biographical, and Pictorial.* New York: W. A. Townsend & Co., 1859.

Loveridge, Henry, & Co. *Catalogue [of Tinware].* Wolverhampton, England, 1864.

Lowenstein, Eleanor. *Bibliography of American Cookery Books, 1742–1860.* Worcester, Mass.: American Antiquarian Society; New York: Corner Book Shop, 1972.

M'Getrick, M., ed. *The Housewife's Guide; or, A Complete System of Modern Cookery . . . .* rev. and corr. New York: G. F. Bunce, 1834. Bound with *The Domestic's Companion.*

M'Getrick, S. W. *The New Whole Art of Confectionary, Sugar Boiling, Iceing, Candying, Jelly and Wine Making &c &c &c . . . .* 1st Am., from the 11th London, ed. New York: William Mitchell, 1834.

McKearin, Helen. "Sweetmeats in Splendor: Eighteenth-Century Desserts and Their Dressing Out." *Antiques* 67, no. 3 (March 1955): 216–25.

Markham, Gervase. *The English House-wife: Containing the Inward and Outward Vertues Which Ought to Be in a Compleat Woman . . . .* 1615. London: Printed by B. Alsop for John Harison, 1649.

Mason, Charlotte. *The Lady's Assistant for Regulating and Supply the Table.* 1773. 8th ed. London: J. Walter, Vernor & Hood, J. Scatcherd, etc., 1801.

Mason, Frances Norton, ed. *John Norton and Sons: Merchants of London and Virginia, Being the Papers from Their Counting House for the Years 1750 to 1795.* Richmond, Va.: Dietz Press, 1937.

Massey, Edouard R., trans. and ed. "Rhode Island in 1780 by Louis L. J. B. S. Robertnier." *Rhode Island Historical Society Collections* 16, no. 3 (July 1923): 65–78.

Massialot, François. *Le Cuisinier roial et bourgeois.* Paris: C. de Sercy, 1698.

———. *Nouvelle instruction pour les confitures, les-liqueurs, et les fruits . . . avec la manière de bien ordonner un dessert.* 1692. 2d ed. Paris: Charles de Sercy, 1698.

———. *Nouvelle instruction pour les confitures, les liqueurs, et les fruits . . . .* New ed. Paris: Saugrain, Fils, 1740.

May, Robert. *The Accomplisht Cook.* London: Obadiah Blagrave, 1660.

Mencken, H. L. *The American Language, Supplement I.* New York: Alfred A. Knopf, 1966.

Miller, Heather. "The Pineapple, King of Fruits." *Horticulture* 57, no. 12 (December 1979): 39–43.

Mitchell, Stewart, ed. *New Letters of Abigail Adams, 1788–1801.* Boston: Houghton Mifflin Co., 1947.

Morison, Samuel Eliot. "Charles Bagot's Notes on Housekeeping and Entertaining at Washington, 1819." In *Publications of the Colonial Society of Massachusetts: Transactions 1924–1926.* Vol. 26, pp. 438–46. Boston: Published by the society, 1927.

———. *Life and Letters of Harrison Gray Otis, 1765–1848.* 2 vols. Boston and New York: Houghton Mifflin & Co., 1913.

Murray, Alexander. *The Domestic Oracle; or, A Complete System of Modern Cookery and Family Economy . . . .* London: H. Fisher Son & Co., [1834].

Murray, James A. H., et al., eds. *The Oxford English Dictonary.* 13 vols. Oxford: Clarendon Press, 1933.

Napier, Robina [Mrs. Alexander], ed. *A Noble Boke off Cookry ffor a Prynce Houssolde or Any Other Estately Houssolde.* 1500. Reprinted verbatim from a Holkham manuscript. London: Elliott Stock, 1882.

Nevins, Allan, ed. *The Diary of John Quincy Adams, 1794–1845.* New York: Charles Scribner's Sons, 1951.

———. *The Diary of Philip Hone, 1828–1850.* 2 vols. New York: Dodd Mead & Co., 1927.

New American Cookery; or, Female Companion Containing Full and Ample Direction for Roasting . . . . By an American Lady. New York: D. D. Smith, 1805.

Nott, John. *The Cooks and Confectioners Dictionary; or, The Accomplished Housewives Companion.* 1723. 2d ed. with additions, rev. London: C. Rivington, 1724.

Nutt, Frederic. *The Complete Confectioner; or, The Whole Art of Confectionary Made Easy . . . .* 1789. 4th ed. Reprint. New York: Richard Scott, 1807.

O'Brien's Philadelphia Wholesale Business Directory. Philadelphia: J. G. O'Brien, 1845.

Parkes, Frances Byerly [Mrs. William]. *Domestic Duties; or, Instructions to Young Married Ladies, on the Management of Their Households . . . .* 1st Am., from the 3d London, ed. New York: J. & J. Harper, 1828.

Parkinson, [Eleanor]. *The Complete Confectioner, Pastry Cook, and Baker.* Bound with J. M. Sanderson, *The Complete Cook.* Philadelphia: Leary & Getz, [1849].

Paxton's Philadelphia Directory and Register. Philadelphia: Edward and Richard Parker, 1818.

Peterson's Manufactory & Wareroom, 144 Bowery, N.Y.: Catalogue of House Furnishing Goods, Stoves, etc., etc. for Sale. New York: Miller & Holman, 1857.

Phillips, John Marshall. *American Silver.* New York: Chanticleer Press, 1949.

Pilcher, Donald. *The Regency Style.* London: B. T. Batsford, 1947.

Pleasants, J. Hall, ed. "The Letters of Molly and Hetty Tilghman." *Maryland Historical Society Magazine* 21, no. 2 (June 1926): 123–49; 21, no. 3 (September 1926): 219–40.

Poor Richard Revived Being the Farmer's Diary; or, Barber and Southwick's Albany Almanac for the Year of Our Lord 1796. By Old Father Richard, Mathemat. Albany: Printed and sold by Barber & Southwick, 1796.

Pope-Hennessy, Una, ed. *The Aristocratic Journey: Being the Outspoken Letters of Mrs. Basil Hall Written During a Fourteen Months' Sojourn in America, 1827–1828.* New York: G. P. Putnam's Sons, 1931.

Prime, Alfred Coxe. *The Arts and Crafts in Philadelphia, Maryland, and South Carolina . . . Gleanings from Newspapers. 2 vols.* [Topsfield, Mass.]: The Walpole Society, 1929–32.

Prime, Phoebe Phillips, comp. *The Alfred Coxe Prime Directory of Craftsmen from Philadelphia City Directories, 1785–1800.* Listed by subject and alphabetically by name. Microfilmed and reproduced by xerography, February 1960.

Putnam, Mrs. Elizabeth H. *Mrs. Putnam's Receipt Book; and Young Housekeeper's Assistant.* Boston: Ticknor, Reed, & Fields, 1849.

The Queen's Closet Opened. Incomparable secrets in physick, chirurgery, preserving, candying, and cookery; as they were presented to the queen by the most experienced persons of our times . . . . Transcribed from the true copies of Her Majesties own receipt-books, by W. M. one of her late servants . . . . London: Nathaniel Brook [etc.], 1655.

Raffald, Elizabeth. *The Experienced English Housekeeper, for the Use and Ease of Ladies, Housekeepers, Cooks, &c. . . . .* 1769. New ed. Philadelphia: James Webster, 1818.

Randolph, Mary [Mrs. David Meade]. *The Virginia House-wife; or, Methodical Cook.* 1824. 4th ed. Washington, D.C.: P. Thompson, 1830.

Rees, Abraham. *The Cyclopaedia; or, Universal Dictionary of Arts, Sciences, and Literature.* 1st Am. ed., rev., corr., enl. 41 vols. Philadelphia: S. F. Bradford, 1810–24.

Reese, D. Meredith. *An Encyclopedia of Domestic Economy.* 5th ed. New York: Harper & Bros., 1845.

Rice, Howard C., Jr., trans. and ed. *Travels in North America in the Years 1780, 1781, and 1782 by the Marquis de Chastellux.* Rev. 2 vols. Chapel Hill, N.C.: Institute of Early American History and Culture, 1963.

Roberts, Kenneth, trans. and ed. *Moreau de St. Méry's American Journey, 1793–1798.* Garden City, N.Y.: Doubleday & Co., 1947.

Roberts, Robert. *The House Servant's Directory.* Boston: Munroe & Francis, 1827.

———. *The House Servant's Directory.* Facsimile of the 1827, Boston ed. Foreword by Charles A. Hammond. Waltham, Mass.: The Gore Place Society, 1977.

Rolt, Richard. *A New Dictionary of Trade and Commerce.* 2d ed. London: Printed for G. Keith, 1761.

Rundell, Maria Eliza. *American Domestic Cookery: Formed on Principles of Economy, for the Use of Private Families.* Baltimore: Fielding Lucas, 1819.

[———]. *A New System of Domestic Cookery: Formed upon Principles of Economy, and Adapted to the Use of Private Familes.* By a Lady. Boston: William Andrews, 1807.

[———]. *A New System of Domestic Cookery: Formed upon Principles of Economy and Adapted to the Use of Private Families.* By a Lady. 3d Phil. ed. Philadelphia: Benjamin C. Busby, 1810.

Savage, George. *Eighteenth-Century English Porcelain.* London: Rockliff, [1952].

Savary des Bruslons, Jacques. *Dictionnaire universel de commerce, d'histoire naturelle et des arts et metiers.* 5 vols. Copenhagen: C. & L. Philibert, 1760.

Scott, Franklin D., trans. and ed. *Baron Klinkowström's America, 1818–1820.* Evanston, Ill.: Northwestern University Press, 1952.

Sedgwick, Catherine M. *Letters from Abroad to Kindred at Home . . . .* New York: Harper & Bros., 1841.

Sewall, Samuel. *Diary of Samuel Sewall.* Vols. 1–3, 1674–1729. *Collections of the Massachusetts Historical Society,* Series 5, vols. 5–7. Boston: Massachusetts Historical Society, 1878–82.

Sheridan, Thomas. *A Complete Dictionary of the English Language.* 3d ed., rev., corr., and enl. 2 vols. London: Charles Dilly, 1790.

Simmons, Amelia. *American Cookery.* Hartford: Hudson & Goodwin, 1796.

———. *American Cookery.* Facsimile of the 1st ed., 1796. New York: Oxford University Press, 1958.

Singleton, Esther. *The Furniture of Our Forefathers.* 2 vols. New York: Doubleday, Page & Co., 1906.

Smith, E. *The Compleat Housewife; or, Accomplish'd Gentlewoman's Companion . . . .* Collected from the 5th London ed. Williamsburg, Va.: William Parks, 1742.

Smith, Georgiana Reynolds. *Table Decoration Yesterday, Today, and Tomorrow.* Rutland, Vt., and Tokyo: Charles F. Tuttle Co., 1968.

Smith, P. C. F. *Crystal Blocks of Yankee Coldness.* Wenham, Mass.: Wenham Historical Association and Museum reprint from Essex Institute Historical Collections, 1961.

Soyer, Alexis. *The Modern Housewife, or Ménagère.* London: Simpkin, Marshall, & Co., 1849.

———. *The Modern Housewife, or Ménagère.* Edited by an American Housekeeper. New York: D. Appleton & Co., 1850.

Sprackling, Helen. "Fruit Trenchers of the Sixteenth and Seventeenth Centuries." *Antiques* 78, no. 1 (July 1960): 48–51.

Stafford, Maureen, and Dora Ware. *An Illustrated Dictionary of Ornament.* London: George Allen & Unwin, 1974.

Steiner, Bernard C., ed. "The South Atlantic States in 1833 as Seen by a New Englander: Being a Narrative of a Tour Taken by Henry Barnard," *Maryland Historical Magazine* 13, no. 4 (December 1918): 295–386.

Stettinisches Koch-buch für Jünge Frauen und Köchinen. Stettin, 1797.

Stewart, Katie. *The Joy of Eating*. Owings Mills, Md.: Stemmer House Publishers, 1977.

Storke, E. G., ed. *The Family and Householder's Guide; or, How to Keep House . . . .* Auburn, N.Y.: Auburn Publishing Co., 1859.

Thomas, M. Halsey, ed. *The Diary of Samuel Sewall, 1674–1729*. 2 vols. New York: Farrar, Straus and Giroux, 1973.

Thoron, Ward, ed. *The Letters of Mrs. Henry Adams, 1865–1883*. Boston: Little, Brown & Co., 1936.

Tinling, Marion, ed. "Cawson's, Virginia in 1795–1796: Excerpts from the Diary Kept by Mrs. Martha Blodget at Cawson's, Prince George County, Va. in the Years 1795 and 1796." *William and Mary Quarterly*, 3d ser., 3, no. 2 (April 1946): 281–91.

To The Trifler. *Columbian Magazine* (Philadelphia) 1, no. 15 (November 1787): 758–60.

Towner, Donald. *The Leeds Pottery*. New York: Taplinger Publishing Co., 1965.

Trollope, Frances [Milton]. *Domestic Manners of the Americans*. 2 vols. London: Whittaker, Treacher & Co., 1832.

Trusler, John. *Honours of the Table; or, Rules of Behaviour During Meals*. 1788. 2d ed. London: The Author, 1791.

Tudor, Henry. *Narrative of a Tour in North America . . .* [*1831–32*]. 2 vols. London: James Duncan, 1834.

Tyler, Lyon Gardiner, ed. "Description of Virginia by Captain John Smith." In *Narratives of Early Virginia, 1606–1625*. New York: Charles Scribner's Sons, 1907.

Ude, Louis Eustache. *The French Cook; or, The Art of Cookery Developed in All Its Various Branches*. 1813. Philadelphia: Carey, Lea & Carey, 1828.

van de Aanhaugzel. *Volmaakte Hollandsche Keuken-Meid*. Amsterdam, 1750.

Van Doren, Mark, ed. *Samuel Sewall's Diary*. New York: Macy-Masius Publishers, 1927.

Vicaire, Georges. *Bibliographie Gastronomique: A Bibliography of Books Appertaining to Food and Drink and Related Subjects, from the Beginning of Printing to 1890*. 2d ed. London: Derek Verschoyle, 1954.

Volz, Gustav Berthold. "Ein Geschent Friedrichs des Grossen an Katharina II." *Hohenzollern Jahrbuch; Forschungen und Abbildungen zur Geschichte der Hohenzollern in Brandenburg Preussen* (Berlin, Leipsig), October 22, 1908, pp. 49–61.

Wainwright, Nicholas B. *Colonial Grandeur in Philadelphia: The House and Furniture of General John Cadwalader*. Philadelphia: Historical Society of Pennsylvania, 1964.

———, ed. *A Philadelphia Perspective: The Diary of Sydney George Fisher Covering the Years 1834–1871*. Philadelphia: Historical Society of Pennsylvania, 1967.

Walker, Thomas. *The Art of Dining; and the Art of Attaining High Health, with a few hints on suppers*. Philadelphia: E. L. Carey & A. Hart, 1837.

Wansey, Henry. *An Excursion to the United States of North America, in the Summer of 1794*. 2d ed., with additions. Salisbury: J. Easton [etc.], 1798.

Washington, H. A., ed. *The Writings of Thomas Jefferson: Being His Autobiography, Correspondence, Reports, Messages, Addresses, and Other Writings, Official and Private*. 9 vols. New York: John C. Riker; Washington, D.C.: Taylor & Maury, 1853–54.

Widdifield, Hannah. *Widdifield's New Cook Book; or, Practical Receipts for the Housewife*. Philadelphia: T. B. Peterson, [1856].

"Will of William Byrd of Westover, Virginia." *Virginia Magazine of History and Biography* 9, no. 1 (July 1901): 80–88.

Willard, Harriet J. *Familiar Lessons for Little Girls on Kitchen and Dining-Room Work*. Chicago: George Sherwood & Co., 1880.

Williams, George F. *Saints and Strangers*. New York: Reynal & Hitchcock, 1945.

Williams, James. *The Footman's Guide: Containing Plain Instructions for the Footman and Butler . . . in Large or Small Families. Embellished with appropriate plates, and bills of fare*. 4th ed. London: Thomas Dean & Co., [1847].

Willich, A. F. M., *The Domestic Encyclopaedia; or, A Dictionary of Facts, and Useful Knowledge . . . .* 4 vols. London: Murray & Highley, 1802.

Wilson, John Dover, comp. *Life in Shakespeare's England: A Book of Elizabethan Prose*. Baltimore: Penguin Books, 1968.

Wilstach, Paul. *Mount Vernon, Washington's Home and the Nation's Shrine*. Garden City, N.Y.: Doubleday, Page & Co., 1927.

Woodward, Celia. "Pickle Leaves." *Antiquarian* 15, no. 3 (September 1930): 44–45.

The Works of James Gillray. Bronx, N.Y.: Benjamin Blom, 1968.

The Workwoman's Guide, Containing Instructions to the Inexperienced . . . . By a Lady. 2d ed., rev. and corr. London: Simpkin, Marshall & Co., 1840.

Wright, Louis B., and Marion Tinling, eds. *The Secret*

Diary of William Byrd of Westover, 1709–1712. Richmond, Va.: Dietz Press, 1941.

The Young Tradesman; or, The Book of English Trades: Being a Library of the Useful Arts, for Commercial Education . . . . New ed., enl. London: Whittaker & Co., 1839.

The Young Woman's Companion; or, Frugal Housewife. Manchester: Russell & Allen, 1811.

MANUSCRIPTS

Note: DMMC indicates source also available in the Joseph Downs Manuscript and Microfilm Collection, Winterthur Museum Library.

Backer, T. H. Baltimore. Invoice from F. F. Wessels, Amsterdam, April 12, 1806. Maryland Historical Society.

Baltimore County Inventories. County Courthouse.

Bancker, Christopher, and Brandt Schuyler. Appraisement book, New York, 1750–52. Bound with Bancker, Schuyler, and Joris Brinkerhoff appraisement book, New York, 1750–62. Joseph Downs Manuscript and Microfilm Collection, Winterthur Museum Library.

Banister, John. Papers, Newport, R.I., 1695–1771. Newport Historical Society. DMMC.

Barrell, Joseph. Letter book, Boston, 1792–97. Massachusetts Historical Society. DMMC.

Bayard, Nicholas. Papers, New York, 1710–48. Rutgers University Library.

Bentley, William. Ledger, Otsego County, N.Y., 1812–27. Joseph Downs Manuscript and Microfilm Collection, Winterthur Museum Library.

"A Booke of Sweatmeats." Recipe book, England, 1550–1625. Historical Society of Pennsylvania.

Botetourt, Norborne Berkeley, Baron de. Inventory, Williamsburg, Va., October 24, 1770. Botetourt Papers. O. A. Hawkins Collection of Virginians, Virginia State Library.

Brooks, James. Inventory, New York, November 16, 1835. Joseph Downs Manuscript and Microfilm Collection, Winterthur Museum Library.

Browne, Francis. Account book, sloop *Speedwell*, 1706–16. Yale University Library. DMMC.

Buck, Charles. Reminiscences, 1791–1840. Historical Society of Pennsylvania, gift of John F. Lewis.

Claypoole, James and Helena. Inventory, Philadelphia, "on or about the Midle of the Seventh Month," 1688. Office of the Register of Wills, County Building. DMMC.

Corning, Erastus. Papers, Albany, N.Y., 1810–72. Albany Institute of History and Art.

Coultas, Elizabeth. Recipe book, England and Philadelphia (?), dated 1749/50. Joseph Downs Manuscript and Microfilm Collection, Winterthur Museum Library.

Derby, Elias Hasket. Inventory, Salem, Mass., March 4, 1805. Essex County Probate Court Records. DMMC.

———. Papers, Salem, Mass., 1795–99. Essex Institute.

Dominy, Nathaniel. Ledger, Easthampton, N.Y., 1807. Joseph Downs Manuscript and Microfilm Collection, Winterthur Museum Library.

du Pont, Eleuthère Irénée. Longwood MSS. Eleutherian Mills Historical Library.

———. Winterthur MSS, bills and receipts. Eleutherian Mills Historical Library.

du Pont, Victor. Book of personal and family expense, begun May 1, 1802. Winterthur MSS. Eleutherian Mills Historical Library.

Eubbs, Mary. Recipe book, New York, 1824–ca. 1841. Museum of the City of New York.

Fiske, L. Recipe book, Beverly, Mass. (?), ca. 1860. Joseph Downs Manuscript and Microfilm Collection, Winterthur Museum Library.

Flint, Catherine. Recipe book, Boston, 1830–60. American Antiquarian Society.

Geddy, James. Inventory, Williamsburg, Va., November 19, 1744. York County Wills and Inventories, State House, Richmond, Va.

Greene-Roelker Papers. Cincinnati Historical Society.

Janvier, Jane. Recipe book, Philadelphia, 1817–37. Historical Society of Pennsylvania.

Jones, Hannah Firth. H. Jones, Philadelphia, 1826, to Samuel Jones, London. Typescript owned by Mrs. Robert Metz, a descendant.

Joslin Family. Household book, Ireland, 1747. Joseph Downs Manuscript and Microfilm Collection, Winterthur Museum Library.

Lamson Family. Recipe book, Durham County, begun April 8, 1768. Chicago Historical Society.

Latimer Family. Papers, Wilmington, Del., 1821–22. Joseph Downs Manuscript and Microfilm Collection, Winterthur Museum Library.

Lloyd, Edward, IV. Inventory, Wye, Md., November 14, 1796. Talbot County Inventories, Maryland Hall of Records. DMMC.

Lloyd, Henry. Account books, Lloyds' Neck, N.Y., 1706 [1704]–11. Long Island Historical Society.

Meade, Elizabeth. Recipe book, England, written before 1697. Wilson Papers. Cincinnati Historical Society.

Merrill, George W. Account book, Chicago, 1839. Chicago Historical Society.

Miles, Benjamin. Ledger, Cooperstown, N.Y., 1821–28. New York State Historical Association. DMMC.

Newport [R.I.] Wills and Inventories. Newport City Hall. DMMC.

Penn, Gulielma. Recipe book, England, 1702. Penn Papers. Historical Society of Pennsylvania.

Philadelphia Wills and Inventories. Office of the Register of Wills, County Building.

Pocumtuck Valley Inventories. Pocumtuck Valley Memorial Association Library, Deerfield, Mass.

Potter's Manual. Attributed to the Spode factory, ca. 1815–21. Joseph Downs Manuscript and Microfilm Collection, Winterthur Museum Library.

Powell, T. & T. Account, Baltimore, with Stevens Glass Concern, Bristol, England, July 10, 1797. Maryland Historical Society. DMMC.

Prentis, Joseph. Inventory, Williamsburg, Va., July 24, 1809. Swem Library, College of William and Mary.

Prime File. The names and advertisements transcribed from seventy American newspapers, 1723–1823, filed by craft. Decorative Arts Photographic Collection, Winterthur Museum Library.

Reed, John. Personal accounts, Philadelphia, 1799–1811. Joseph Downs Manuscript and Microfilm Collection, Winterthur Museum Library.

Rhode Island Inventories. Rhode Island Historical Society.

Richardson Family. Papers, Philadelphia, 1734–1801. Historical Society of Pennsylvania. DMMC.

Richardson, Joseph. Ledger, Philadelphia, 1734–40. Joseph Downs Manuscript and Microfilm Collection, Winterthur Museum Library.

Richardson, Joseph, Jr. Daybook and ledger, Philadelphia, 1796–1802. Historical Society of Pennsylvania. DMMC.

Ridgway, John. Staffordshire, England, bill to Robinson Tyndale, Philadelphia, July 7, 1835. Joseph Downs Manuscript and Microfilm Collection, Winterthur Museum Library.

Scadin, Robert. Daybook, Cooperstown, N.Y., 1829–31. New York State Historical Association. DMMC.

Schuyler, Margareta. Estate papers, Albany, N.Y., 1765–82. Albany Institute of History and Art.

Shippen, Edward. Order, Philadelphia, to Messrs. Francis & Relfe, London, January 19, 1763. Joseph Downs Manuscript and Microfilm Collection, Winterthur Museum Library.

Stansbury, Joseph. Inventory, New York, February 8, 1810. Joseph Downs Manuscript and Microfilm Collection, Winterthur Museum Library.

Stevenson, Anne (Mrs. Pierre van Cortlandt II). Bills from Shepherd and Boyd, March 25, 1814, and November 14, 1814, van Cortlandt Papers. Museum of the City of New York.

Suffolk County [Mass.] Probate Court Records. Joseph Downs Manuscript and Microfilm Collection, Winterthur Museum Library.

Swift, Emily G. Letter, Amenia, N.Y., to William Grant, New Haven, Conn., February 13, 1829. Joseph Downs Manuscript and Microfilm Collection, Winterthur Museum Library.

Tarleton, Margaretta. Party notebooks, England, 1740–61. Tarleton Papers. Liverpool Record Office. DMMC.

Temple, Elizabeth, Lady. Bowdouin and Temple Papers, Boston, 1809. Widener Library, Harvard University. DMMC.

Tryon, William. Inventory of furniture destroyed by fire, Fort George, N.Y., December 29, 1773. Dartmouth MSS. New York State Historical Association.

Usher, Hezekiah, II. Account book, Boston and Newport. Newport Historical Society.

Williams, John, Reverend. Inventory, Deerfield, Mass., September 19, 1729. Pocumtuck Valley Memorial Association Library.

Wilson Family. Papers. Cincinnati Historical Society.

Index

(Page numbers in *italics* refer to illustrations.)

A

Accomplish'd Female Instructor, The, 108, 124, 141
Accomplisht Cook, The (May), 97
Adams, Abigail, 63, 91, 108, 141, 146, 186, 190, 207
Adams, John (merchant), 200
Adams, John (president), 93–95, 141, 207
Adams, John Quincy, 241
Adams, Samuel, 250
Alden, John, 125
Alden, William, 235
ale, *see* beer
Alexander the Great, 152
Allen, Samuel, 197
almond paste, 76, *76*, 98, 100, 101, 186, 279
American Agriculturalist, 34
American Cookery (Simmons), 19, 107, 195
American Domestic Cookery, The (Rundell), 160, 260, 265, 280, 283, 290
Ames, Winslow, 90
Art de bien faire les glaces d'office, L' (Emy), 150
Art of Cookery, The (Glasse), 270, 272
Art of Dining, The (Walker), 33
Ashley, Mr. and Mrs. Jonathan, 33
Austen, Jane, 230

B

Bacon, Sir Francis, 124, 152
Bagot, Charles, 91–92, 233, 235, 236
bag puddings, 208, 287
Bailey, Nathan, 124
Bailey, Sarah Ann, 108
Baker, John, 10, 228
bakers, 144, *212*, 213
baking soda (saleratus), 183
Ball Supper (Watson), *223*
ball suppers, 4–5, 91–92, 156–58, 220, *223*
banquet letters, 174
banquet pavilions, 96
banquets (dessert), 96, 97, 221
Barlow, Joel, 208
Barnard, Henry, 17–19, 34–35
Barrell, Joseph, 63, 222, 245

baskets:
  cake, 71, 169
  comfit, 134
  table-clearing, 30, *31*, 134
Bayard, Nicholas, 81
Beale, William, 186
Beecher, Catharine, 14, 15, 33, 53, 248
beer, 17, 232
Beeton, Isabella, 37–38, 85–88, *88*, *89*, 104, 108, 228, 231, 236, 276
Beeton Home Books, The, 37
Betterton, Benjamin, 167
beverages, 17, 34, 38, 135, 195, 231–53
  homemade, 235–39
  recipes for, 272–77
Bingham, Mr. and Mrs. William, 4–5, 48, 63, 154, 186
biscuit pudding, 286
biscuits, 101, *176*, 182
biskets, 261
Black, William, 145
Bladen, Thomas, 145
Blaine, Mr. and Mrs. James G., 36–37
Blanck, Jurian Jeurisen, Jr., *136*
blancmange, 5, 161, 235
blancmange molds, *151*, *156*, 157, *157*, 158
Bland, Theodorick, 150
Blodget, Martha, 3
blueberry bag pudding, 287
bonbonnières, 134
"Booke of Sweetmeats, A," 278, 289, 290, 293
Book of Household Management (Beeton), 37–38, *88*, *89*, 104, 276
border cutters, *206*
Bosse, M., 167–68
Boston Cooking School Cook Book, The (Farmer), 274
Boston Gazette, 67, 79
Boston News-Letter, 13, 55
Botetourt, Lord, 145, 154
bottle coasters, 239
Boune, Eliza, 168
Bours, MacGregor, & Co., 13–14
bowpot centers, 83
Boyce, Antipas, 10, 124, 228
Boylston, Zabdiel, 165
Bradbury, Theophilus, 63–64
braziers, 101, *102*
Brewster, William, 96
Brian, Joseph, 168
Bridgham, Ebenezar, 59
Briggs, Richard, 158, 204, 207, 213, 278
Brissot de Warville, 250
British punch, 277
Brooks, James, 108
Brown, Mr. and Mrs. John, 224
Buck, Charles, 219
Burnet, William, 41, 108, 115, 138, 224, 236
Busk, Henry, 55
butter, butter plates, 39
Byrd, William, 135
Byrd, William, III, 67

C

Cadwalader, Mr. and Mrs., 48, 115, 218, 224
cake baskets, 71, 169
cake boxes, 189
cake cutters, 173, 178, *178*, *179*
cake molds, 173–74, *173*, *174*
cake pans, *175*, *176*, 177, *177*, 182, 189
cake plates, dishes, 59, 169
cakepots, *188*
cakes, 85, 120, 168–90, *170*, *171*, *175*, *183*, *184*, 248, 250, 251
  almond, 101
  confectioners', 167–68
  decoration of, 184, 186, 189
  icing for, 183, 188, 257, 260
  imported ingredients for, 172
  leavening of, 182–83
  making of, 186–88, *187*
  measurements and, 186–88
  nineteenth-century inventions for, 186
  recipes for, 255–60
  seed, 101, 255
Calvert, Joseph, 167
calves' feet, 164
candied fruit peels (chips), 120, 122, 291
candied orange peel, 122, 291
candying, 101, 122, 290–93
Cannameliste français, Le (Gilliers), *72*, 73, *73*, *225*
Capes, Richard, 241
carafes, 85
cardamom cookies, 261
carpets:
  floor, *12*, 13
  table, 6–7, *6*, *7*, 9–10, *11*, *Pl. 6:5*
Carroll, Charles, 14, 106, 136, 167, 236
Carter, Charles, 52, 53
Carter, Mr. and Mrs. Hill, 17–19, 34–35, 235
Carter, Mr. and Mrs. Landon, 186
carving, 19–21, 33–34
carving knives and forks, *118*
Cassell's Household Guide, 36
Castelmaine, Lord, 82
casters, 66, 71, *71*, 72
Catherine II, empress of Russia, 77, *77*
caudle cups, 138, *138*
caudles, 96, 137–38, 233, 273
centers, 33, 41–90, *62*, 189
  baskets and casters as, 71, *71*
  bowpot, 83
  compotiers as, 59–60

centers (*continued*)
  flowers in, 33, 73, 79–90, *80*, *81*, *82*
  fruit pyramids as, *49*, *50*, 51, *51*, *78*
  glass and ceramic figures for, *76*, 77–79, *77*, *78*
  homemade pastry and sugar scenes as, 72–73, *72*, *73*
  late nineteenth-century, 85–90, *88*, *89*
  middleboards for, 49–55, *49*
  plateaux as, 63–66, *64*, 73
  professional sugarwork as, 74, 85, *86*, 168, 184
  raising of middle dishes in, 41–49, *43*, *44*, *45*, *46*, *47*, 182
  roasts or vegetables as, 19, 41, *43*
  salver pyramids as, 41, 55, *Pl. 2:41*
  salvers as, *46*
  step pyramids as, 59
  sugar scenes as, 3, 72–76, *72*, *73*, *75*
  surtouts (epergnes) as, *65*, 66–69, *66*, *67*, *68*, *69*, *70*, 82
  sweetmeat poles as, *58*, 59
  sweetmeat pyramids as, 51–55, *52*, *53*, *54*
  tall, 90
  tazzas as, 85–90, *87*, *88*
  trees as, 4, 189
  Victorian, *84*, 85, 90
chafing dishes, 101, *102*
Chair, The (Simmons), 16
champagne, 17, 235, 248, 251
Charles II, king of England, 96, 222
Chastellux, Marquis de, 190
cheese, 228–31
cheesecakes, 101, 231, 281
cheese cradles, 230, *230*
cheese scoops, 230
cherry bounce, 235, 236
chess cakes or pies, 231, 282
chewy raspberry paste, 290
Child, Francis, Jr., 79
Child, Lydia, 15, 287
Christmas pudding, 287–88
cider, 232
  see also beverages
cider cake, 256
claret, 233, *234*, 251
Claypoole, James, 115, 222
Clifford, John, 141, 250
Clinton, Mr. and Mrs. De Witt, 34, 92–93, 150
coasters, 239
cochineal, 160
cocktails, 239
coffee, 85, 248–51
colanders, 100, *100*
cold sauce, 285
Columbian Magazine, 207, 220,
comfit dishes, 56, 125–30, *128*, *129*, *130*, *131*, 134
comfits, 96, 120, *123*, 124–34, *126*, 140, 158, *162*, 168
  gum flowers and fruits, 25, 124, *126*, *127*
  nuts as, 124
  of sugared seeds, 124–25, *126*, *127*
Common Sense in the Household (Harland), 276
Compleat Cook, The, 97
Compleat Housewife, The (Smith), 107, 120, 257–58, 264, 272, 273, 274, 282, 291
Compleat Practical Cook, The (Carter), 52, 53
Complete Confectioner, The (Nutt), 266–67, 292, 294
compote, 59–60, 251, 294
compotiers, 59–60, *59*
confectionery baskets, *133*
confectionery shops, 165–68, *164*, *165*, *166*
confectioners, 73–74, *162*, *163*, *164*, 164–68
confectioner's stove, 101
confects, *see* comfits
conserves, 97
cookbooks, 97, 107
cookies, 71, 166, 178
  recipes for, 261–67
cooking utensils, 98–101
Cooks and Confectioners Dictionary (Nott), 49, 124, 292
Cook's Oracle (Kitchiner), 135, 187
cordials, 235–36
Cornell, Samuel and Susannah, 41
corner dishes, 19, 157–58, 165
Corning, Erastus, 168
Corson, Juliet, 38, 251
Corwin, George, 6
Cosnett, Thomas, 24, 25, 30, 239, 248
cossets, 184
Coultas, Elizabeth, 161, 164, 208, *209*, *210*, 213, 265
Country Club, The (Bunbury), *23*
cream bowls, 142, *142*, *143*
cream buckets, 142
cream cups, 142, *144*, *146*
cream glasses, *159*, *162*
cream pots and cups, *77*, 142
creams, dessert, 4, 60, 98, 100, 101, 135–54, 157
  recipes for, 141, 268–71
creams, molded, 144
Creswell, John, 36
cribbage cards, 158
Cripps, William, *67*
Cromwell, Oliver, 222
Cuisinier royal et bourgeois, Le (Massialot), *51*
cupboard, court, 10
cupboard cloth, 10
cups, two-handled, 136, *136*
curds, 136

custard cups, *138*, 144, *144*
custards, 3, 21, 98, 101, 135, 144, 180, 184, 208, 213
Custis, Frances Parke, 76
Custis, Mrs. John, 120, 124
Cuyler, Philip, 172
Cyclopaedia (Rees), 154

D

David, John, *71*
Dawson, William, 115
Deblois, Stephen, 67, 79
deep pies, 193–95
Delacroix, Joseph, 168
delicate cake, 188
Derby, Mr. and Mrs. Elias Hasket, 33, 243–45
Description of England (Harrison), 96–97
Dessert, The (Busk), 55
dessert displays, 3–4, *50*, *52*, *53*, 95, 157, 168, 189
dessert forks, 115–120, *116*, *117*, *118*, *119*
dessert knives, 115–120, *117*, *118*
Dessert of Wafers (Baugin), *181*
dessert pails, 146, *147*
dessert plates, 125–30, *129*, *226*
desserts, 3, 17, 19, 21, 34–35, *77*, 96–97
  cheese as, 228–31
  confectioners', 168
  middleboards for, 49–55, *49*
dessert services, 60, 224, *226*, 228, *245*
dessert spoons, 115– 20, *117*
dessert tables, 3–4, 70, 85, *175*
Dickerson, Mahlon, *143*
Dickinson, John, 265
Dickinson, Jonathan, 115, 182, 233
Dictionarium Domesticum (Bailey), 124
Diderot, Denis, 125, *126*, *127*
dining rooms:
  floor coverings for, 13
  seventeenth-century, 5–6
  eighteenth-century, 10
Dinner of Kings (Bosse), *47*
Dinner Party, The (Sargent), *12*, 13
dinners, dinner parties, 4, 5, 17, 35–37, 93–96
  everyday, 17, 19, *29*, 34, *43*
  half hour before, 37–38
  late nineteenth-century procedure for, 36–40
  old service holdovers for, 34–35
  service *à la russe* for, 33–37, 38
  table arrangements for, 19, *20*, *21*, *22*, *23*, *24*, *27*, *28*, 33
dinner tables, 4–5
  afternoon, 5, 93, 95
  carpets for, 6–7
  clearing of, 30–31
  crowded, 5, 27, 33–34
  procedure for, 17–40
  eighteenth-century coverings for, 10, *11*, 13
  nineteenth-century coverings for, 10–14, 24
  late nineteenth-century, 38–40
dish covers, 33
dish crosses, 48–49, *48*, 59
dish rings, 41, *44*
doilies, *16*, 17, *18*, 39, *240*
Domestic Cookery (Lea), 189
Dominy, Nathaniel, 174
Dorr, Sullivan, 69, *69*
Dowding, Joseph and Anne, 197
drinking vessels, 17, 231–32, *232*
drinks, *see* beverages
drums, 250–51
Dumourier Dining in State at St. James (Gillray), *15*
Duncan, John Morrison, 178
Duncan, Thomas, 14, 200, 239
du Pont, Eleuthère, 168, 196, 228, 236
du Pont, Victor, 110, 115, 154, 168

E

earthenware, 100
eggnog, 251
eggs and bacon (jelly), 158
election cake, 256–57
Elizabeth I, queen of England, 96, 125
Elizabethan fruit banquets, 220
Embarras de choix, L' (Gatine), *166*
Emerson, Lucy, 214, 265, 286
Emy, M., 150, 152
Encyclopedia (Diderot), 125, *126*, *127*
Encyclopedia of Domestic Economy, 187
Engelbrecht, Martin, 222–24, *224*
English Housewife, The (Markham), 97
Englishman's Domestic Magazine, 37
epergnes, 63, 65, 66–71, *66*, *67*, *68*, *69*, *70*
Eubb, Mary, 140–41, 158
evergreens, 4
Experienced American Housekeeper, The, 269, 275, 284

F

Family and Householder's Guide, 27, 28, 34
Family Receipt-Book, 140, 236, 259, 274, 276, 277
Farley, John, 19, *20*, 72, 268

Farmer, Fanny, 274
Farrar, Straus & Giroux, 37
Fearon, Henry Bradshaw, 207
feather cake, 188
figures, 5, 63–64, *72–79*, *73*, *75*, *76*, *77*, *78*, *81*, 85, 125, *126*, *127*, 135, 184, *184*, 189, 251
finger biscuits, 182
finger bowls, 39, 239–41
first course, serving of, 19–21
fish, as first-course serving, 19
Fisher, Sydney George, 85
Fiske, Mrs. L., 27, *29*, 34, 71, 108, 193–95, 213, 251, 256, 261, 285, 286, 287
flatware baskets, 30, *31*
flavoring, 154, 186, 188, 189
Flint, Catherine, 161
floating island, 79, 140–41, 270–71
flower bottles, *56*
flowerpots, 81–83
flowers, artificial, 55, 79
flowers, fresh, 55–56, *57*, *77*, 79–90, *80*, *81*, *82*, *84*, 140, 144, 158, 160
flowers, gum, 124, *126*, 184
flowers, sugared, 101, 124, 290
flummeries, 157, 158, 160, 161, 165, 271, 284
flummery molds, 144, *156*
food for the gods, *145*
fools, 141, 269
footed dishes, 59–60, *59*, *60*, *61*, *62*, 85, 228
Footman's Directory and Butler's Remembrancer (Cosnett), 24, *25*, 30
Footman's Guide, The (Williams), *18*, 69, *70*
Forbes, John W., 63
forks, 115
frames, 49–55, *49*, 59
Franklin, Benjamin, 142
Freack, John, 138
Frederick the Great, king of Prussia, *77*, *77*
French Cook, The, 76
fromage, 152, 231
fromage glacé, 231
froth, 270
Frugal Housewife, The, 287
fruit, 219–28, *240*, *Pl. 6:5*
  on boards and trays, 168, 228
  colonists and, 221–22
  mixing of, 228, *Pl. 6:11*
  at parties, 220
fruit banquets, Elizabethan, 220
fruit baskets, 224, *225*, *226*, *227*, 228
fruit cakes, 120
fruitcakes (heavy plum cakes), 188
fruit dishes or bowls, 59, *61*, 101, *206*, 222–24, *224*, *225*, 228, *Pl. 6:5*, *Pl. 6:11*
fruit drops, 120
fruit in glasses, 73
fruit pastes, 98, 120
fruit peels, 120, 122
fruit pyramids, *49*, *50*, 51, *51*, *78*, *165*, 228, *229*
fruits, gum, sugar, 76, 124
fruit vinegar, 237

G

Gardiner, William Howard, 91
Gazley, Martha, 193
Geddy, James, 243
gelatine, 99
"Geschent Friedrich des Grossen an Katharina II, Ein" (Volz), *77*
Gillam, Joseph, 10
Gilliers, Joseph, *72*, 73, *73*, *225*
Gillray, James, *15*, *22*, *162*
ginger, 96
gingerbread, 96, 99, 100, 167, 169, 173–74, *174*
gingerbread boards, 173–74, *173*, *174*
glacier (glacière), 146, *147*, *223*
glass-baskets, 30
glass coolers (trays), 245, *245*, *246*
Glasse, Hannah, 55, 141, 270, 272
glassware, 101, 239
Godey's Lady's Book, 120
Gore, Christopher, 24, 250
grand trifle, 140
Grant, Anne, 169–72, 180
Green, Ward, and Green, 69
Greene, William, 64
green melon in jelly, 158
Greswold, Joseph, 167
Grosses Schauessen (Flegel), *121*
gum flowers and fruits, 124, *126*, *127*
gum sugar figures, 125, *126*, *127*, 278

H

Habit de Paticier, *175*
Hale, Sara Josepha, 187–88, 190, 219
Hall, Mrs. Basil, 33, 92–93, 95, 135, 146–48, 150, 190–93, 219, 228
Halsted, Benjamin, 63
Hamilton, Alexander (barber), 96
Hamilton, Dr. Alexander, 219
hard sauce, 288
Harland, Marion, 276
Harrison, Sarah, 158
Harrison, William, 96–97
hartshorn, 100, 161, 164
hartshorn jelly, 280
Harvey, Ashton, 222
hasty pudding, 208

Henderson, Mary, 36, 38, 152
Henry VIII, king of England, 110
hens and chickens (jelly), 158
Heroes Recruiting at Kelsey's; or, Guard-Day at St. James (Gillray), *162*
Holberton, William, 9
hollands, 13
Holme, Randle, 45, 81, 204
Hone, Philip, 34
Honours of the Table (Trusler), 241
hot chocolate, 248
House-Keeper's Pocket-Book (Harrison), 158
House Servant's Directory (Roberts), 24
Hudson Bay Company, 161
Hutchinson, Elizabeth, 79, 120, 141, 200
Hyver, L' (Bosse), *8*

I

ice, 154, 248
ice (sherbet), 93, 193, 235, 251
ice cellars, 148
ice cream, 145–54, 190, 231, 251
  confectioners', 167–68
  flavors of, 154
  making of, *145*, 152–54, *153*
ice-cream cups, *145*, *146*, *153*
ice-cream molds, 146, *148*, 150–52, *151*
icehouses, 154
ice pails, 146–48, *149*, *150*, *153*, 245, *245*
icings, 101, 183, 188
  recipes for, 183, 257, 260
Illustrated Guide to London, The, 35, 231
Indian pudding, 207–8, 286–87
Indische Familie (Wigmana), 110
Ingraham, Solomon, 79, 110, 239, 243
Irving, Washington, 239
Isaac Royall and Family (Feke), *6*
isinglass, 161, 164
Italian Confectioner, The (Jarrin), 74, 182, 237, 279
ivory, 161

J

Jane Magg's Pastry Business, 167
Janvier, Jane, 152–54, 161, 177, 213
Jarrin, G. A., 74, 182, 237, 279
Jefferson, Thomas, 63, 141, 154, 186
jellies, 3–5, 21, 60, 79, 96, 98, 102, 120, 140, 153–54, *155*, 158, 165, 167, 180, 184, 280
  arrangements of, 140, 157–58
  clear, 160–61
  coloring of, 160
  decorations for, 158–60
  hartshorn, 100
  jelling agents for, 161–64
  recipes for, 120, 161, 164, 280
jelly glasses, 55–57, *56*, *57*, 158, *159*
jelly molds, *151*, 152, *156*, *157*
John Norton and Sons, 161
Johnson, Edward, 95
Johnson, Sir William, 130
Jones, Mr. and Mrs. Thomas, 41
Josselyn, John, 95
Journal of Nicholas Cresswell, The, 258
jumbals, 169, 264

K

Kalm, Peter, 220, 233
Kelland, Thomas and Abigail, 233, 243
kettledrums, 251
kettles, 99
Kitchiner, William, 135
Klinkowström, Baron Axel Leonhard, 154–57, 232, 233
knife rests (knife racks), 32, *32*
knife trays, baskets, 30, *30*
knives, 39, 118, *185*, 205, *216*
koekjes, 178, 261
Kreitner, Frederick, 74, 168

L

Ladies Delight, 265
ladles, 101, 208, 232, 237
lady fingers, 182
Lady's Assistant (Mason), 228, 262, 263, 271
Lamson, Mrs., 186
Lansdowne estate, 4–5
Latimer, Henry, 108
Lauzun, Chevalier de, 220
Lawrence, Augustus, 156–57
Lea, Elizabeth, 189
leaf decorations, 88–90
lemonade, 168, 190, 237
lemon cream, 270
lemon tarts, 282
le Pautre, Jean, 53
Leslie, Eliza, 141, 154, 207, 208, 213
Letters from Abroad (Sedgwick), 33
limonier, 66
Lisbon wine, 233
Lloyd, Mr. and Mrs. Edward, 48, 63, 150, 158, 160, 161, 189, 193, 233–35, 236, 250
Lloyd, Henry, 104, 108, 166
loaf cakes, round, 182–83, *183*, *184*

London Art of Cookery (Farley), 19, *20*, *72*, 268
Lorent, Peter, 165–66
Louis XV, king of France, 82, *82*
Loveridge, Henry, & Co., *31*, *203*
Ludwell, Philip, 239
Lynde, Benjamin, 135, 195, 222
Lyon, John B., 17

M

McCafferty and Holmes, 168
macaroons, 100, 166
Macaulay, Isaac, 15
Maclay, William, 79
Madam Johnson's Present, 108
madeira wine, 233, 239
Mansell, Corbett & Company, 56
Mansfield Park (Austen), 230
marchpane, 76, 96, 100, 174, 177, 292–93
Markham, Gervase, 97
marmalade, 96, 97, 98
Maryland raspberry shrub, 274
marzipan, 76, 96, 100, 174, 177, 292–93
maser, 101
Mason, Charlotte, 228, 262, 263, 271
mass cakes, 100, 101
massepain, 100, 174, 177, 292–93
Massialot, François, 49, 51, *51*, 66, *66*, 82, 228
Mather, Cotton, 233
mats, table, dish, cup, 14–15, *15*, *22*, 39, 134
Mavericke, Samuel, 7
May, Robert, 97
Maydwell and Windle's Cut-Glass Warehouse, 57
Meade, Elizabeth, 97
measurements, cooking, 187–88
meringues, 99, 168, 169
Merrymakers, The (Steen), 7
middleboards, 49–55, *49*, 63
Mifflin, Governor, 228
Miles, Benjamin, 178
milk frosting, 257
Milne, Edmond, 49, 239
Minzies, James, 161
molds, dessert, 60, 124, 144, 146, *148*, 150–52, *151*, 158, *164*
  for cake, 173, *173*, *174*, 182, *182*
  for figures, 74–76, *75*
  for fruit and flowers, 124
  for pies, 204
Monroe, James, 64, 224
monteiths, 243–45, *243*, *244*
Moore, John, 13
Moreau de Saint Méry, 167–68
Morris, Thomas, 156–57
mortars, 101
mottoes, 168, 184, *184*
Mrs. Beeton's All About Cookery, 37
Mrs. Putnam's Receipt Book, 264
Myers, Myer, 41, *44*, 48, *48*

N

napkin presses, 9, *9*
napkin rings, 33
napkins, table:
  seventeenth-century, 9–10, *Pl. 6:15*
  eighteenth-century, 13, 14, 17, *246*
  nineteenth-century, 14, 39
  late nineteenth-century, 38–39
Naples biscuits, *175*, 182, 265
negus, 236, 276
Negus, Francis, 236
New Art of Cookery, The (Briggs), 158, 204, 207
New Cookery Book (Leslie), 213, 278
New England Cookery (Emerson), 214, 265, 286
New England Economical Housekeeper, The (Howland), *192*
New England Journal, 55
New Receipts for Cooking (Leslie), 154
New System of Domestic Cookery, A (Rundell), 160, 264, 269, 271, 275, 281
New York Gazette, 193
Norton, Mary, 41
Nott, John, 49, 53, 124, 134, 236, 292–93
Nouvelle instruction pour les confitures (Massialot), 49, 66, *66*, 82, 228
noyau, 236, 276
nuts, 205, 253
  sugared, 124, 168
Nutt, Frederick, 266–67, 292, 294
Nys, Johannes, 115

O

Oliver, Andrew, 56
Oliver, Robert, 224
orange cheese-cakes, 281
orange chips, 122
orange fool, 269
orange glasses, 55
orange tarts, 282
orchards, 221
orgeat, 236, 275
"oriental" carpets, 6–7
Otis, Harrison Gray, 92, 239
Oudry, Jean-Baptiste, 214, *215*

P

pans, 99, 104, *175*, *176*, *191*, 195, 196, *196*
Parish, David, 250
Parkes, Mrs. William, 92, 241
pasties, 97
pastilles, 291
pastries, 97, 169, *176*, 190–207
  making, 193–95, *191*, *192*
  puddings in, 213
  see also pies
pastry cutters, 204–7, *206*
pastry plates, 200
pastry scenes, 72–73
pastry wheels, *176*, *187*, *205*
pasty plates, 200
patriotic cakes, 190
patties, patty pans, 97, 169, *176*, 178–79, *198*, *199*, 200–202, *200*, *201*
Payne, Mr. and Mrs. Isaac, 174
Peale, Raphaelle, *183*, *227*
pear compote, 294
Pekin, Peter, 193
Penn, Gulielma, 98–101, 120, 124, 161
Pennsylvania Evening Post, 130
Pennsylvania Gazette, 56
peppermint drops, 292
Peter Manigault and His Friends (Roupel), *238*
Peterson's Manufactory and Wareroom, 152
pewter, 100
Physiology of Taste (Brillat-Savarin), 231
pickle dishes, 130, *131*
pickles, 100, 130
pièces montées, 85, *86*
pie pans, dishes, plates, 99, 196, 197, *197*, 202, 209, *Pl. 5:22*
pies, 95, 98, *176*, 190–207, *194*
  decorations for, 204–7, *204*, *205*, 213
  deep, 193–95, 204
  recipes for, 281–83
  schools for making of, 193
pineapple designs, 222
pineapples, 93, 150, *162*, 219, 221–22, 228
pineapple stands, 222, *223*, *Pl. 6:1*
pipkins, 100
Pitts, Elizabeth, 49
Pitts, William, 69
place settings:
  old styles in, 27
  eighteenth-century, 21, *22*, *23*
  nineteenth-century, 24, *25*
  late nineteenth-century, 39
  nineteenth-century middle-class, 27–30, *28*, *29*
plateaux, 63–66, *64*, 73, 168
plate baskets, 30, *31*
platters, 53, 101
plumb cake, 257–58
plum cake, 188, 258
Polk, James K., 64
Poor Richard, 232
Porcelain Maker (Engelbrecht), 222–24, *224*
porringer, 100, 101
porter, *see* beer
posnets, 99, 101
posset pots, 137, *137*
possets, 137, 182, 233, 274
pots, 99, 100
pots à crème, 142
Potwine, John, 102, *102*
pound cakes, 183
Powell, Messrs. T. & T., 158
Practical American Cookery (Corson), 38, 251
Practical Cooking and Dinner Giving (Henderson), 38
preserves, 98, 100, 102, *103*, 144, 167
pudding basins, *217*, 218
pudding dishes, 169, *202*, 214–18, *214*, *215*, *216*, *217*
pudding knives, *216*, 218
puddings, 98, 182, 207–18
  bag, *176*, 208, 287
  baked, 99, *187*, 208–13, *210*, *212*
  baking vessels for, *212*, 213
  boiled, 207, 208, 214, *217*
  hasty, 98, 208
  Indian, 207–8
  in pastry, 213
  meat, 98, 100
  recipes for, *210*, 283–88
  serving dishes for, *202*, 214–18, *214*, *215*, *216*, *217*
puff pans, *195*, *196*
puff pastries, 101, 195, 231
puffs, 99, 168, 169, 195
punch, 34, 37, *81*, 136, 219, 233, 237–39, *238*, 251, 276–77, *Pl. 6:17*
punch bowls, 237–39
Putnam, Elizabeth, 264
pyramids, 13, 51–59, *55*, *79*, 85, 93, 124, 140, 150, *163*, *165*, 168, 189, 219, 228, *229*, 253, *Pl. 2:9*, *2:12*, *2:20*, *2:41*, *2:47*

Q

"Quatrieme Journée, 1676, La" (le Pautre), *53*
queen cake pans, *176*, 177, *177*
queen cakes, 169, 177, 189, 236, *Pl. 6:14*
queen's biscuit, 71
Queen's Closet Opened, The, 97
Quincy, Josiah, *146*

R

Raffald, Elizabeth, 140, 152, 158, 180
rafraîchissoirs, 245
Rainbow Tavern, The (Rowlandson), *22*
Rainsford, Jonathan, 10
Randolph, Mary, 142, 146, 152, 236
Ranger, John, 196
raspberry cakes, 290
raspberry shrub, 274
ratafia, 236, 275
ratafia cakes, 168, 262
Rea, John, 221
reception, 85
recipe books, 97, 107
Reed, John, 214
Rees, Abraham, 154
removes, 19
Richard, Stephen, 115
Ridgely, Henry, 167, 236
Ridgely, Wilhelmina, 189, 236
Ridgway, Phoebe Ann, 85
roasts, 19–21
Roberts, Mr. and Mrs. Robert, 24, 241, 248
Robinson, Abigail, 120
Roman punch, 276
Rose, John, 222
roundels, 125, *128*
Rouse, William, 115
rout drop cookies, 266
routs, 91, 93, 237, 250–51
royal march-panes, 292
Rundell, Maria Eliza, 160, 260, 264, 266, 269, 271, 275, 280, 281, 283, 290
Rush, Dr. Benjamin, 220
Rush, Dr. and Mrs. James, 85
Rutgers, Anthony and Cornelia, 14, 214

S

sack posset, 274
sack wine, 96, 233
saleratus (baking soda), 183, 186
salts, *see* standing salts
salvers, 3, 46, 55, 56, 57, *162*, *165*, 180, 182
Samuels Family, The (Eckstein), *249*
Sargent, Henry, *12*, 13, *94*
Satterlee, E. R., 168
sauceboats, 4, 208, *211*
sauces, 71, 208
savoy cakes, 182–83, 266–67
Scadin, Robert, 174, 189
Schuyler, Margareta, 104, 169–73, 200, 233, 235
Schuyler, Philip, 69
second course, serving of, 21
Sedgwick, Catherine, 33, 85
seedcakes, 101, 178, *187*, 261
seeds, sugared, 124–25, *126*, *127*
service à la russe, 33–37, 38
serving dishes, 19, *20*
serving tables, setting of, *26*, 27
set pieces, 85, *86*
Seventy-five Receipts for Pastry, Cakes, and Sweetmeats (Leslie), 154
Sewall, Samuel, 5, 221
Shaw, Samuel, 144, *146*
Shepherd, Henry, 115
Shepherd and Boyd, 218
sherbet, 236–37
  see also ice (sherbet)
sherry cobbler, 239
Shippen, Dr. Edward, 248
Shippen, Nancy, 102
Shirley plantation, 17
shrewsbury cakes, 264–65
shrub, 236–37, 274
sideboards, setting of, 24, *26*, 231, 248
side tables, 27
sieves, 101, 104, 186
silverware, 39, 101
Simmons, Amelia, 19, 107, 195, 208
Simmons, W. H., *16*, *240*
skillets, 98, *98*, 101
Smith, E., 107, 160–61, 257–58, 264, 272, 273, 274, 282, 291
Smith, John, 221
Smollet, Tobias, 241, 250
Solomon's Temple in Flummery, 158
sorbet, 152
sorbétière, 152, *153*
Sorgen, Hedewick, 124
soup, as first-course serving, 19
soup plates, 202, *202*, *203*
South Carolina Gazette, 115, 193
Soyer, Alexis, 167
spice banquets, 96, 220
spice plates, 125
spicery, 49, 96, 97, 125, 220
spices, 95, 172–73, 183, 186, *201*
sponge cakes, 182–83
standing pies, *194*, 195
standing salts, *8*, 45, *45*, *46*, *47*, *234*, *Pl. 6:5*
stands, 130
Stansbury, Joseph, 14
Steenwyck, Cornelius, 177
steeple cream, 158, 268
Stephens, William, 221
step pyramids, 59
Stevens Glass Concern, 158
Stevenson, Anne, 218
Stiegel, Henry William, 56

Still Life (Treck), *46*
Still Life (Zurbaran), *171*
Still Life with Candy (vander Hamen), *122*
Still Life with Peaches (Peale), *227*
Still Life with Raisin Cake (Peale), *183*
Stoddert, Mrs. Benjamin, 4–5
subtleties, 73
sucket (succade), 95–98, 102
sucket forks, *114*, 115
sugar, 95–96, 104, 172, 183
 breaking of, 106, 186
 refining of, 97, 101, 102, 104, *105*
sugar cakes, 178
sugar cones, 104, *105*, 106
sugar figures, 5, 63–64, 72–76, 125, *126*, *127*, 184, 279
sugar hammers, 106, *106*
sugar loaves, 104, *105*, 106
sugar molds, 74–76, *75*
sugar nippers, 106, *107*
sugar plate, 97, 120, 289
sugarplums, *see* comfits
sugar scenes, 72–76, *72*, *73*, *123*, 168
Sunderland pudding, 284–85
supper, 251
surtout de table, 63, 65, 66–69, *66*, *67*, *68*, *69*, *70*, 82, *123*
sweetmeat banquets, 96–97
sweetmeat baskets, *132*, *133*, 134
sweetmeat cream, 141
sweetmeat dishes, 110, *110*, *111*, *112*, *113*, 122, 130, *130*, *131*
sweetmeat forks, *114*, 115
sweetmeat jars, 102, 108, *109*, 236
 sealing of, 108
sweetmeat poles, 58, 59
sweetmeat pyramids, 3, 51–55, *52*, *53*, *54*, 122
sweetmeats, 91–134, 166–67, *166*, 193, 281
 cooking vessels for, 98–101
 dry, 95, 97, 101, *102*, 120, 124, 168, 289–93
 imported, 108, 166–67
 presentation of, 91–95, *94*
 production of, 102–7, *103*
 recipes for, 97–98, 124, 289–93
 wet, 95, 97, 99, 102, *103*, 107, 108, 110, 115, 193, 294
sweet sauce, 285
Swift, Emily, 251–53
Swift, Thomas, 101, 222
syllabub cups, 136
syllabub glasses, 3, 55–57, *56*, *57*, *136*, 139, *139*, 158
syllabubs, 135–37, 139–40, 233, 272
 making of, 136
 solid (everlasting), 140, 269
 whipped, 139–40, 272–73
Sylva Sylvarum; or, A Naturall Historie (Bacon), 124
syrups, 99
 confectioners', 166–68

T

table, serving, 27
table bells, 32
table brushes, 32
table carpets, 6–7, 9–10, *11*
tablecloths:
 clearing of, 21, 30
 presses for, 9, 9, 13
 for sideboards, tea tables, and breakfast tables, 14
 seventeenth-century, 7, 8, 9
 eighteenth-century, 10, *11*, 13
 nineteenth-century, 10–14, 34
 late nineteenth-century, 39, 85
table forks, *116*, *118*
table knives, *22*, *23*, 27, *118*
table mats, 14–15, *15*, 39
table plates, 203
table setting, 19–40, *20*, *24*, *28*, *42*, *43*
Table Still Life, A (Claesz), 205
tansy pudding, 283
tart pans, 99, 200
tarts, 95, 98, 99, *176*, 195, 281–82
tazzas, 85–88, *87*, 228, *Pl. 2:50*
tea, 248–51, *249*
 as supper, 251
tea parties, 92–93, *94*, 248–53, *249*, 252
 afternoon, 248–51, *249*, 252
 evening, 92–93, *94*, 250–53
 paraphernalia for, 251
Tea Party, The (Sargent), *94*
tea party tables, 4
Tellende, Henry, 222
Temperance Enjoying a Frugal Meal (Gillray), 22
Temple, Lady, 115–20, 158, 228, 237, 241
Thomas, N., 14–15
Thomas, Roger and Elizabeth, *68*
Thurman, Francis, 200
Ticknor, Professor and Mrs., 146–48
Tilghman, Billy, 91
trade cards, *163*
trenchers, 125
trifle dish, 140, *141*
trifles, 135, 140
Trionfi, 73
Trollope, Frances, 193
Trusler, John, 241
Tryon, William, 14, 79, 136, 138, 200
Tudor, Henry, 221, 248

tureens, 4, 208, *211*
Turkey carpets, 6–7, 10
turk's cap cake mold, *182*
turk's cap cakes, 182–83
turnovers, 168, 195
Twelfth Night (Cruikshank), 184
Twelfth Night cakes, 184–86, *184*, *185*, 258–59, 294
Twelfth Night parties, 184–86

U

Universal Dictionary, 167
Usher, Hezekiah, 9
Usher, Hezekiah, II, 125, 184
Uttinge, Ann, 7

V

van Cortlandt, Pierre, II, 218
van der Paas, Crispin, the Elder, 125, *128*
vanilla, 154
vases, 82–90, *82*, *84*
Verplanck, Mr. and Mrs. Daniel Crommelin, 63
verrières, 245, *245*, *246*
  see also glass coolers (trays)
Vethake, F. A., 13
Vice, The (Simmons), *240*
View of the Inside of Guildhall as It Appear'd on Lord Mayor's Day, 1760, A (Read), *42*
vinegar, fruit, 237
vineyards, 221
Virginia Gazette, 79, 158
voide drink, 96
voiders, 49, 96
Volmaakte Hollandsche Keuken-Meid (van de Aanhaugzel), *191*

W

wafer irons, *176*, 180, *180*
wafers, 99, 180, *181*, 236, 262–63
Walker, Thomas, 33, 85
Wansey, Henry, 222
Ward, Locke & Company, 37
Ward, Samuel, 186
Warder, Ann, 141, 219, 221, 250
Warren, Mr. and Mrs. Julius, 174
wash glasses, 239–41, *240*, *241*
Washington, George, 49, 63–64, 145–46, 182, 190, 239, 265
Washington, Martha, 63–64, 79, 145–46, 190
water, 248
waters, confectioners', 167
Watson, C., *223*
weddings, wedding cakes, 74, 96, 138, 168, 189, 221, 251
Welch, John, 81
Weld, Joseph, 9
Wentworth, Elizabeth, 169
Wessels, F. F., 134
Whatman, Susanna, 106
Whieldon, Thomas, *42*
whigs (wigs), 263
White Duck, The (Oudry), 214, *215*
white icing, 260
whortleberry pudding, 287
"Who's for Poonsh?" (Johnson), 237
Williams, James, *18*, 69, *70*, *71*
Williams, John, 13
Williams & Co., 152
wine, 17, 21, 95–96, 168, 233–47, 253
  homemade, 221, 235
  sources of, 233, 235
  vessels, *232*, 233
wine cisterns, *223*, *242*, 243–45, *246*
wine coolers, 148, 243–45, *245*, *246*, *247*, *Pl. 6:24*
wineglass rinsers, 239, *240*, *241*
wine jelly, 280
wine sauce, 288
Winslow, Edward, 125
Wirt, William, 189, 219
Wishart, Hugh, *119*
Wonder-Working Providence of Sion's Saviour in New England (Johnson), 95
woodenware, 101, 180
Workwoman's Guide, The, 33
Wright, William, 196

Y

yeast, ale, 182–83
Young Lady's Friend, The, 17
Young Woman's Companion, The, 108